Esha Patel is a contemporary romance author. When she isn't writing, you can usually find her studying or baking therapeutic apple spice cake. She is an avid fan of both the Ferrari F1 team and Real Madrid. She is a college student based out of the US, Iowa two-thirds of the year (Illinois the other third), but you can always get in touch by visiting her website at eshapatelauthor.com or follow Esha on Instagram @eshapatelauthor.

ESHA
PATEL

Offtrack

avon.

Published by AVON
A division of HarperCollins*Publishers* Ltd
1 London Bridge Street
London SE1 9GF

www.harpercollins.co.uk

HarperCollins*Publishers*
Macken House,
39/40 Mayor Street Upper,
Dublin 1
D01 C9W8
Ireland

This paperback edition 2024
24 25 26 27 28 LBC 6 5 4 3 2
First published in 2023 as *Offtrack*

A catalogue record for this book is available from the British Library.

ISBN: 978-0-00-869393-0

This novel is entirely a work of fiction.
The names, characters and incidents portrayed in it are
the work of the author's imagination. Any resemblance to
actual persons, living or dead, events or localities is
entirely coincidental.

Typeset in Birka by Palimpsest Book Production Limited, Falkirk, Stirlingshire

Printed and bound in the United States

To any girl who has ever been told no.
Only you decide what you are and are not capable of.
Go turn the world on its head.

2022 Driver Line-up

TEAM	DRIVER 1	DRIVER 2
Scuderia Revello	Miguel de la Fuente (DLF 88, Spain)	Andrea Russo (RUS 12, Italy)
Heidelberg Hybridge F1 Team	Peter Albrecht (ALB 09, Australia)	Darien Cardoso-Magalhães (CAR 67, Brazil)
Jolt Archambeau Racing	TBD	Kasper Ramsey (RAM 17, UK)
Kramer F1 Team	Ansel Hermann (HER 57, Netherlands)	Craig Grant (GRA 37, USA)
Griffith	Nicolò Necci (NEC 21, Italy)	Alexander Romilly (ALR 11, France)
Burgess F1 Team	Jules Beaumont (BEA 04, Monaco)	Benjamin Kittington (KIT 52, UK)
Misaki	Banyu Setiawan (SET 49, Indonesia)	Jonas Hauser (HAU 36, Germany)
Wilson Nitro	Thomas Zhang (ZHE 79, China)	Michael Cade (CAD 15, Australia)
Laurens	Erhan Solak (SOL 38, Turkey)	León Villena (VIL 57, Mexico)
Vittore Monterey	Christian Clay (CLA 03, Denmark)	Byron Hargreaves (HAR 18, Canada)

2022 Formula One Grands Prix Schedule

1. Saudi Arabian Grand Prix
2. Emilia-Romagna Grand Prix (Imola)
3. Miami Grand Prix
4. Australian Grand Prix
5. Spanish Grand Prix (Barcelona)
6. Monaco Grand Prix
7. Azerbaijan Grand Prix
8. Austrian Grand Prix
9. French Grand Prix
10. Hungarian Grand Prix
11. Canadian Grand Prix
12. British Grand Prix (Silverstone)
13. Jaipur Grand Prix
14. United States Grand Prix (Austin)
15. Belgian Grand Prix (Spa)
16. Italian Grand Prix (Monza)
17. Dutch Grand Prix
18. Singapore Grand Prix
19. Japanese Grand Prix
20. Mexican Grand Prix
21. Brazilian Grand Prix
22. Abu Dhabi Grand Prix

2021 Season

'It's not often we get the chance to do something like this. We race like we will not live to see tomorrow.'

Eduardo 'Eddie' Palomas
#21, Jolt Archambeau Racing

Chapter One

Miguel

'Mig, this is not looking good.' Paula paced back and forth across the floor of my personal backroom. I couldn't think of a race where she didn't start to do her terrifying stalking. It was her most effective coping method for when I pissed her off, shit hit the fan, or both. This time, it was both.

'What's our strategy?' I asked, desperately hoping she'd have an answer. If anyone knew how to revive our race, it would be Paula. 'You want me to overtake my way to the top?'

'That will have to do. You're all the way at the back of the grid because of the damned chassis mess from yesterday.' Paula chewed on the inside of her cheek. 'Pressure on the turns. That is what you do best.'

I nodded. 'Okay. Pressure, I can do that.'

'You know' – Paula shot me a look – 'we wouldn't be in this position if you hadn't been overzealous in the qualifier.'

And here she goes again. I let out a laugh. 'Jesus, Pauli, these things happen. Accidents happen.'

'Accidents in which our team has to break their backs on last-minute repairs?' Paula lowered her voice. 'We all know you are number one, Mig, easily over Russo, but remember you race for a *team*.'

I couldn't help but roll my eyes, recalling the million times prior that my big sister had given me this same talk. Well, she wasn't my big sister out here. She was my race engineer.

Paula was exceptional at her job and, in the pit, she immediately morphed into the devil in a windbreaker. As one of the team managers and my race engineer, Paula de la Fuente was the only person allowed to speak to me once I was in the vehicle. She was in charge of the ultimate race outcome and, with that prestigious a job, she was responsible for the failures as well as the successes – say, a broken chassis from pushing too hard in qualifiers.

Paula smacked my arm. Evidently, my eye roll had not gone undetected. '*Ya*, Miguel! We cannot lose this title lead because *you* decided to be a cowboy.'

'That term is in my job description.' I tapped the logo of the red and green crown and shield on my white racing suit. 'Cowboy.'

I shot Paula a grin as I left the garage and made my way to our car with the crew, ignoring her exasperated expression. I could already smell the blistering tyres, and like it did every race, the scent took over my senses, bringing me back to the beginning.

My childhood reeked of gas and rubber. I grew up in go-karts, same as my father, and his father before him. Addiction to racing was in my blood: sparks that flew when the back of your car scraped the asphalt, vicious chicane curves, neck-jarring crashes and hazy smoke clouds. It wasn't something that the de la Fuentes chose. It was simply destiny, through which my late grandfather brought the family into the lucrative racing circuit known to the world as Formula 1.

The de la Fuentes are assholes of the highest degree. We hail from Barcelona. We hate staying still. We worship the Barça football club. We love money, and we waste it on aged wine cellars. We have raced in Formula 1 for three generations now; from the moment my grandfather sat down in a race car, we have had only one goal: to place podium in the Drivers' Championship title, maybe even win the Championship, which so far nobody had accomplished. It was my promise to the de la Fuente family that I would try my very best to bring the title home before the end of my career.

Paula, though she was as much a cutthroat competitive de la Fuente as the rest of us, once suggested this pompous attitude was an attribute of too much toxic masculinity. Our father just chuckled at that. 'Paulita, delicate female necks are not built to withstand six Gs.'

Everyone may have cracked up at that but, as unfortunate as it was for Paula, Papá was right. At its core, racing is a uniform sport. It is fuelled by a community that discourages change, unless that change makes the cars go faster and names jump up the leaderboards.

So over time, my sister, like the rest of us, reluctantly fell into step with the rest of the Formula 1 world. She unhappily resigned herself to accept F1's machismo when her attempts to recruit more female engineers failed. The reason? The female engineers in question were reluctant to deal with the drivers' diva-like behaviour.

Just beyond the garage doorway, the crowd roared. I decided to skirt round my car and step out of the pit just for a moment, waving as I went. The screams only got louder as my cheering section – armed with posters, flags, signs and banners – went wild. Someone blasted the song with which the Scuderia's followers had knighted me: 'Whatta Man' by Salt-N-Pepa. I felt the confidence flood my chest as I raised both arms and nodded as if to give them a 'HELL YEAH!' of approval.

Over my time in Formula 1, I had gained fans from all over the globe, mostly in Spain – my birthplace, as well as the country for which I raced – and Canada, where I had been brought up for a time. They were diehard, that much was for sure. I'd had some pretty interesting items thrown at me during victory laps on account of them. At first, it took me aback, though I came to get used to them as races flew by. That didn't mean they were any less to me – my fans made each and every grand prix one to remember.

I returned to the garage and donned my radio system and helmet before sliding into the cockpit of the car as our team worked around me.

'Check, Mig,' Paula's voice said into my earpiece. 'Can you hear me?'

I could tell she wasn't exactly pleased from the way her Spanish accent thickened, the normally buttery syllables growing a dangerous edge. Paula, having been born and raised in Barcelona for most of her childhood, maintained the accent even when we moved to Canada, and it came back in full force when we returned to Spain. My accent tended to live within the vaguely Canadian range, rarely what anyone would call Spanish.

'Yep,' I said to pacify her.

'You had better.'

The announcer came on over loudspeaker, something I could barely hear because of my earplugs, helmet, and the omnipresent buzz in my ears since yesterday's crash. In the meantime, my team parted to form a wide berth for my car.

'Let's cruise on down,' said Paula unhappily. 'You are at the back of the grid. Andrea is on pole. But at the very least, the odds of a Revello win today are good. Just do your best.'

The cars pulled out for the line-up, moving from the pits to take their places for the formation lap behind the safety car. I trailed behind, eighteenth position on the grid. Way up at the front was my Revello teammate: Andrea Russo, racing in the first position.

There was no doubt commentators were living it up over this. A *Revello* car out in Q1, leaving one pole and one the caboose. The thought angered me so much that I unconsciously tapped the gas and made the car growl greedily on my way past the cheerleaders.

Yes, it was true. There were cheerleaders here. I was no rookie to racing, but I had yet to race at a grand prix more strangely dramatic than the United States. Here in Austin, at the Circuit of the Americas, or COTA, as we called it, the Americans went ballistic. Cheerleaders on the sidelines, extravagant celebrations both before and after, rodeo shows, cowboy hats incorporated into everyone's arrival outfits, it was really something. I would have enjoyed how over-the-top it all was if I had not been planning my attack from eighteenth place.

'Screw me,' I grumbled, pulling into the grid. At least I wasn't dead last. I was just ahead of Vittore and Laurens. Third to last. Fun.

'I heard that,' Paula's voice chided.

I gritted my teeth and focused on the track at hand. The formation lap began, a slow go-around that required me to steer in and out, weaving my tyres to get heat into the compound. It wasn't hard. Texas was baking, about thirty-five degrees Celsius in the air and no doubt over forty on the track. By the time the formation lap ended, and we returned to the start to pull into grid positions, sweat had already soaked my forehead beneath my balaclava, and was starting to trickle down my face. My hair wasn't helping matters. At its current length, it only exacerbated the feeling of overheating. Paula was right when she said I needed to get a haircut. I wanted to shave it all off in the moment, I was struggling so hard not to collapse of heat exhaustion. I pressed the button on my steering wheel with a gloved finger as we waited, allowing the electrolyte solution stocked in the car for my convenience to shoot up through a straw around my helmet and into my mouth. Respite at last.

Soon enough, the green flag was up. The countdown lights turned on above our heads. With vengeful intent, I shook off my drowsiness and goaded on my engine till it roared.

'Top six, Mig,' Paula warned me. 'Get to the top six.'

The red lights flashed on one by one, illuminating all five. And finally, with a beep, they all went out.

Engines screamed. The cars in front of me took off on the

first of fifty-six laps. It was open season. I caught the slipstream of the other Laurens in front of me, setting up for an overtake, and slid cleanly around the car.

'P17, Miguel,' said Paula.

We soared across Turn One, and already I heard a screeching behind me as I passed both Wilson Nitros easily. 'Who was that?'

'Vittore of Clay had a skid, but he's back on,' Paula replied. 'Keep going, you are P15 now.'

I yanked the car around and upped pressure at the back of the Burgess in front of me: another simple overtake. It took some jumping and swerving to get to the top, a method I rarely had to use but was well versed in. By about Lap Twenty, Paula told me what I both knew and wanted to hear.

'You are holding steady at P4, Mig. I need you to push a little harder on the straights. You have fuel.'

'Who's in front?'

'P3, Palomas for Jolt, P2, Albrecht for Heidelberg, P1, Russo.'

'Cool. Let's run this.'

At this point in the game, my odds were low, but I think going from P18 to P4 was good on its own. I had a long way to go till first.

'Listen, Mig, we box this lap. Box, box,' Paula commanded two laps later.

I pulled into the pit, and around me hydraulics whirred as Revello's top-tier crew changed my tyres at lightning speed. Just over two seconds and I was pulling out, fresh from a stop that would give me significant leverage over Jolt Archambeau's third-place car.

I popped out of the pit lane in P6 and picked my way back

to P4. 'Yes, we're on his ass,' I hooted. I could practically see Paula shaking her head in disapproval. Potty talk, as Paula liked to call it, was not something my sister tolerated.

We hit Lap Forty, and finally, I pressed the Jolt on to overtake Eduardo Palomas.

'P3!'

'Yes, keep going, we have next the Heidelberg.'

The race was running smoothly for one so aggressive, with such fierce competition. Then, rather abruptly, as I was exiting Turn Eleven, a loud thud from behind me shook the track.

I cursed. 'Pauli, what was that?'

'Well, Mig,' she said, 'yellow flag is up. Slow down. Something has happened with Palomas.'

'I just passed him, right?'

'Yes. Something happened. He overcut on Turn Eleven, and it looks like he has spun into the wall. There is damage.'

'What damage?'

'Focus!' chided Paula, voice shaky.

'Is there fire?'

'No, just . . . *Oh my God!*'

Her shout coincided directly with a huge boom. The red flags came out with urgency as a safety car zoomed onto the track to control the cars still running. 'What the *hell* is happening?'

'Mig, the car – the fuel blew, they're taking Eddie out now. It's okay. Red flag in the meantime. Just stay behind the safety car, *tío*.'

At the finish, we were met immediately by a slew of blockades and traffic coordinators. The race would temporarily end here, it seemed, from their presence stretching all the way across the width of the track. Around me, confused drivers parked and climbed out of their cars, looking around for something that might constitute an answer.

I did the same. I ripped off my helmet just in time to hear an announcement.

'The United States Grand Prix will resume upon the FIA's instruction. We apologize for the inconvenience. Racers, please make your way out of your cars. Avoid any unnecessary contact with your vehicle once you have left it.'

I was P3. For a guy who started at the back, this was huge. This was a top-tier performance, and there was no doubt Revello would commend me for it later on. I'd done what I needed to – top six – and then some. But my gut told me it wasn't the time to gloat as all of us, the ones who'd gotten out and stood on the sidelines included, watched the smoke rise in the sky far down on the track.

'Is he good?' I yelled as I abandoned my car and ran directly to Paula, who looked about as bewildered as I felt.

'It's bad,' she told me unsteadily. 'The fuel tank had ruptured in the crash and . . .'

I glared at the thick cloud of smoke, heard the wailing of the race ambulance and safety teams. This was one of the last races of the season. It was far too late for Jolt to sustain any blows at the top of their game. But forget about that. I'd made my way from karting into Formula watching Eduardo Palomas drive. He was one of my biggest role models, and no matter how dirty the races got, I'd always retained the greatest degree of respect for him. I couldn't believe it was Eddie who'd got into this kind of an accident, but I had to believe he'd come out of it able to drive again.

The flag eventually did end, and the race resumed. But whatever was left of it was half-hearted and on edge. I finished it P3. It didn't even matter to me any more. Eddie had to be okay. He just had to.

Chapter Two

Miguel

As cold as ice, pride ran through the veins of the de la Fuentes in excess. But if there was one thing that humbled the holier-than-thou perspectives of my family, it was tragedy on the racetrack.

It was an inevitability in this sport, no matter what safety procedures were brought in. Our father's cousin Cruz succumbed to injuries from a brutal accident on-track many years ago, which urged Papá to take every safety precaution he could with our cars. Through his board seat on Revello, he even provided a hand in the development of the lifesaving halo device. Of course, he was not the only one to think this way. Formula 1 had become significantly safer since Tío Cruz's crash due to the kinds of measures the FIA had introduced. However, a risk was still run. And in the accident today, it seemed the inevitable consequences had fallen on Eduardo Palomas's shoulders.

Post-race, I had to drag myself through the obligatory podium celebration and hastily answered press enquiries. 'I'd like to go to the hospital,' I said bluntly to my sister. 'Paula, it's not right to stay here and pretend it's not Eddie of all people over there in trouble. I *have* to go. Andrea can stay and bask in his own glory.'

And so we sped to the nearest hospital, where Palomas had been taken, waiting on an update from doctors.

Dutifully, Paula sat with me in the crammed hospital waiting room. I knew we looked ridiculously out of place, me in my racing jumpsuit and third-place cap, her in the team windbreaker, getting odd looks every now and then. I must've clearly been tense, though; I guess this scared away the onlookers.

About half an hour after we got there, a physician emerged from the urgent care. 'Eduardo will be all right,' he announced. 'Mild concussion, some scrapes and bruises.'

The press in there with us immediately got to bombarding the poor doctor with questions. I let out a long-held breath. 'Thank God.'

We were able to go inside and speak with him. Paula gave me a look like she figured this would be good for me as we walked through the halls. Like most drivers, I found a sort of kinship in the Formula 1 circuit. As competitive as the sport got, all the guys came together in the end. Ever since I'd started driving, Eddie and I were no different.

Eduardo Palomas sat on the side of his hospital bed, legs hanging over casually, completely unlike someone who'd just gone into the wall in an open-cockpit car. He didn't look too bad at all, given some of the horror stories of crashes I had heard – and seen – in the past. He still wore his jumpsuit, pulled down to his waist so you could see the Nomex long sleeve he had on underneath. While this layer was somewhat scorched, black marks marring the white fabric like a dusting of soot, it had probably saved him from life-threatening burns. There were a few scratches across his face, one hand wrapped in gauze, a couple of still-red bruises, some burns on his neck, but he was otherwise unscathed, at least to the observer.

'Aw, man, Eddie,' I groaned. I pulled my friend into a back-smacking hug. 'What happened?'

Eddie sighed. 'I don't even know. One minute I was fine, and the next, I overshot. I was spinning, and that's all I remember. They told me I blacked out.'

'Jeez. They clear you?'

'Yeah. Yeah, they did clear me, I can be back next race. But . . .'

There was stark reluctance in Eddie's eyes. I wasn't sure if I saw it correctly. It almost looked as if he didn't *want* to race. And if I was being honest, that was far worse than any injury.

'What's up?' I asked tentatively. I could tell from the anxiety in his voice that he noticed it, too.

'Miguel, man, I love this sport.' He looked up at us both. 'But these kinds of things take a toll on me. And that pressure, it's nothing compared to what Belén and Angelica have to go through.'

I exhaled hard as I thought. Belén, Eddie's wife, was a sweet woman, angel of the paddocks, areas that were normally filled with snappy, resentful girlfriends. Their daughter, Angelica, was just two years old. I know Paula felt her heart jump every time my Revello shot off at the beginning of a race. She'd told me in tears many times before. I couldn't imagine the emotions Eddie's family dealt with.

'Hey. You're a legendary driver,' I assured Eddie. 'These accidents, they happen to everyone. Doesn't mean we have to spiral. You've trained harder than anybody else. It's nothing you need to worry about, dude.'

'That's the thing, Miguel.' Eddie smiled sadly. 'These accidents happen to everyone. They can happen at any time. My family wasn't prepared for it today, and no matter what, they will not be prepared if it happens again.'

I tried my best to shake off the unsettling conversation with Eduardo Palomas. No one ever talked about the risks we took as drivers, and when they did, it hit you like a train: anything was possible in this sport.

It was no surprise, then, that something seemed to grab hold of me, so that – immediately after we exited Eddie's room – I insisted we return to Spain to rendezvous with Jatziry Fernanda at her all-girls' college in Barcelona. Even for me, this was off, because Paula liked to say I could not care less about Jatziry Fernanda Calderón Blanco, despite our marriage essentially being guaranteed.

We reached Barcelona in the middle of the night, so we stopped at a local hotel. Recognition was immediate: the owner refused to let us pay. When it was time to get up next morning, I slipped five hundred-euro notes under the pillows in both our rooms.

Paula stifled a yawn as we got into the car we'd rented out, a Revello Catanzaro, true to the spirit of our team. There wasn't a day where Team Revello didn't insist on having us rep the brand (except the one time they'd let Paula have a Mercedes to get from Madrid to Barcelona, and even then, you could tell they weren't loving it). I yanked open the door for her, and she raised a slightly scrutinizing eyebrow my way.

'What, you don't want me to be nice and open your door?' I prodded.

'I think you're rattled,' was all she said before hopping into the passenger seat.

I shook my head, trying to figure out what the hell my cryptic sister was on to now. I rounded the car and buckled into the driver's seat. 'You think I'm *rattled*?'

'Well,' she said pointedly, raising her voice over the thrum of the engine. 'You know what drivers do after something like Eddie's incident happens, don't you?'

I sighed as I backed the car out of the lot. She was right, as usual. Racing incidents, as I said, never lost their punch. After the fireball we'd witnessed on-track, I knew it wasn't just me. The whole grid had to be busying themselves visiting all their family members out of a warped sense of guilt right now. Except that was my problem, and it always had been. I felt awful, because I had Jatziry, but at the same time, it was like I didn't.

El Universidad Católica Santa Teresa de Avila was situated just outside of the larger city, where its female population remained sequestered from civilization under an order of straitlaced nuns. That Paula and I were allowed inside was a boon on account of the headmistress, Sister Alejandra, being a massive closeted DLF fan.

I barely had a foot through the doors of the school when

said headmistress appeared seemingly out of thin air with a huge grin plastered to her face. 'Señor de la Fuente!'

My sister and I exchanged a lightning-fast sibling look before returning to the old nun with gracious smiles.

'Beautiful as always, Sister Alejandra,' I replied smoothly, adding a smirk for a little extra oomph. 'We were hoping to meet Jatziry Fernanda Calderón Blanco, *porfa*.'

Happily, Sister led us to the dining hall. 'You sound like *un gringo*,' Paula taunted me. '*Bobo*.'

'*Bruja*,' I whispered back.

The dining hall of Santa Teresa soon loomed before us, with its high, churchlike ceilings and excessive stained-glass windows. Paula shuddered, and I was pretty sure she was fighting back flashbacks from her own days in Catholic college, almost seven years prior. My big sister was now twenty-eight, and controversial within the family because of her refusal to marry. I was twenty-four, coming off the bachelor's in health administration I'd finished just a year back while racing. My family might have had their heads in the race, but my sister was the one whose voice echoed in the back of my head with her knowing insistence that education had to come first. Sport consumed a truckload of my time, but I finished high school and college – I remember tacking flashcards to the top of the lifting rack so I could study while my trainer put me through mandatory workouts. Ultimately, however, I sprang into Formula 1 with everything I had rather than a traditional career.

I quickly spotted Jatziry with her friends, loud and boisterous as she was until we came within ten feet of her. We darted between tables, weaving among groups of starstruck girls till we reached Jatziry, at which point she suddenly went silent.

Her friends' jaws dropped, eyes wide, as they realized we were standing before them.

'Excuse me, may I have a word with Jatziry Fernanda?' I said, my tone as even and polite as I could muster. 'I'll just steal her for a moment.'

One of the friends swooned. Another turned to Jatziry. 'You *know* Miguel de la Fuente?'

A smile played at Jatziry's lips as she stood, smoothing down the creases in her uniform skirt. '*Un momento*, guys.'

Jatziry was the kind of beautiful that was subtle yet insistent. She had on the default uniform, the plaid skirt and blazer with the university crest. Her hair was thrown into a ponytail of dark waves that tumbled down her back. Her face was young, hazel eyes and a pensive expression with no wrinkles at rest, still unmarred from the stress of Formula 1. Above all, Jatziry maintained a great deal of poise, something I certainly didn't have, which my mom crooned would serve her well when she became the wife who would have to deal with all the forces of motorsport and press thrown at her on account of yours truly.

'Hey, uh, Pauli.' I nudged Paula, clearing my throat awkwardly. 'Let me and Jatziry talk a little, alone.'

She sucked in a breath. 'But, Mig, Sister—'

'Will leave us be,' I finished. 'Not long. I promise.'

'Ay . . .' My sister sighed. 'Okay. Five minutes. Be back soon.'

Jatziry Fernanda and I sat together on a bench outside the dining hall, the closest I had ever been to her since the implicit, and then explicit, announcement of our betrothal so many years ago.

We were both Spanish, obviously, but we had little else in

common. We were from different worlds, as clichéd as that sounded. Paula had once told me that my English rolled off my tongue like river water off heather-clad hills. She then added that Jatziry's English was a drive through the Sahara Desert without your seatbelt on. We didn't really talk, Jatziry and I. I guess I figured she didn't care much for me, which was why it perplexed me that we were sharing such a moment, even though it was my fault that we were here in the first place.

I removed my Revello cap, and immediately felt a little too vulnerable sitting there with her. Just in jeans and a T-shirt and trainers. When I put on the race suit, that was a wall – that was armour. This felt like a level of honesty I didn't think I'd previously reached with Jatziry . . . ever. She looked so innocent, but I knew she wasn't naïve to the weight of this conversation. I wouldn't have come all this way to see her just because I felt like it.

'How are you, Jatziry?' I asked dumbly. 'How's college?'

'I'm keeping well,' she replied. 'I graduate early, in December.'

It was funny how mature she sounded for a girl only two years younger than me.

'Is it hard?' That was a stupid question. It's *college*.

'School is difficult,' she admitted, her eyes still lowered to avoid mine, 'but that may just be the nuns always up my ass.'

And suddenly she clapped a hand over her mouth, eyes wide, as if in complete shock over the fact that she'd expressed a semblance of personality to me.

I couldn't help it. I snorted. And then I laughed – actually laughed. It was different, a change from the fabricated media chuckles we were trained to give them in interviews. With the weight of the incident with Eddie, I'd needed a laugh.

'You know,' I said with a smile once I'd got a grip on myself, 'you can be yourself around me. It's fine.'

'Is it, though?' Jatziry said. She realized too late that she was still speaking through her hand and dropped it abruptly. 'You didn't ask for me. You don't even know what you signed up for. I just . . . I know you the same way the public does. Nothing more.' Her confession was like an anvil pressing against my chest; it might have been a weight off her shoulders, but I could feel it crushing mine. 'Through your races and your GPs and your ads. I don't know how to act around you, Miguel.'

'That's . . . why I'm here.' Awkwardly, I shifted on the bench before finally turning to her and met her eyes, almost willing them to level with mine. 'Last night, there was an accident. I don't know if you heard, but it was bad. It was a driver I really looked up to, with a wife and kid, and he was okay, but I just thought about everyone I was taking for granted. The regrets I'd have if that were me. I came here because, honestly, Jatziry, I really want to get to know you.'

'I had heard,' she said quietly.

I ran a hand through my hair nervously. She adjusted her skirt, eyes trained on her shoes. What if I'd said something wrong? I couldn't mess this up. So much was riding on this – on us.

'I like you better without the hat.'

I tilted my head. My *hat*? 'Come again?'

'That is one thing about me.' She shrugged. 'I am not a huge racing fan. So I like you the way you are, Miguel, without Revello and the sponsorships. I like natural things.'

I exhaled out of relief. And then exactly what she'd said hit me, and I inhaled again. 'Oh. I see.'

And maybe this *was* guilt, like Paula had said. But in this moment, everything, to me, was temporary. Safety was temporary, the people you cared about were temporary. I could lose everything with the blink of an eye. If I didn't hold on to this relationship, we'd lose this, too.

So I tossed my cap behind the bench. It felt unnatural, being without that part of me. I always raced like I would never race again; the sport was everything to me. I could have said this was nothing but a hat, an accessory that meant little to nothing. Instead, it felt like losing a limb.

I knew Jatziry meant well in saying she wanted more of me and less of the façade. I knew my adherence to racing was a necessary sacrifice to give Jatziry the respect she deserved. I convinced myself I knew that much.

'*Mig!*' A woman's voice broke the tension between the two of us.

I chuckled awkwardly, hoping she couldn't tell I was quite glad to have my sister pull me from my thoughts. 'Paula.'

We both stood. I didn't really care about my hat itself, even though Jatziry's eyes flitted towards it curiously once or twice, so I didn't move to pick it back up. As we moved from the bench, I leaned in and did something unusual for a Canadian: the Spanish cheek kisses, one each side. I never did that – at least, not usually – because it just wasn't the way I'd been brought up. It was a custom that Paula adhered to more than I did, yet here, I guess it would become second nature. Jatziry was going to be my wife. My *wife*.

I prayed I wasn't going red as I walked her back into the school.

'No more hats,' I whispered just before we reached Jatziry's table. I wasn't sure if I was convincing her or myself. 'Just me. I promise.'

When we left, I could feel it in the air. Something had definitely changed – whether that was my promise or my understanding of this responsibility. I wondered if Jatziry felt the same way when I thought of the cap in the bushes, if she truly realized the extent to which racing gripped me. Formula 1 was a precarious little dance I followed day by day, a well-choreographed routine, and I'd just broken off from it.

I had to break off from it. Even with the knot that was beginning to tie itself up in my chest, telling me this wasn't as easy as a switch I could flip . . . this had to work. I had to make it.

Chapter Three

Miguel

Champagne soared through the air and splattered my jumpsuit as I whooped, raising my trophy high. Fans roared from the stands, ecstatic at the culmination of this rocky season.

For the first time, I had made the podium. I was second place in the Formula 1 Drivers' Championship for 2021, and as the cameras flashed and the crowd cheered at the end of the Abu Dhabi Grand Prix that had claimed part of my car's front left wing, I felt on top of the world. Of course, I wanted to win first place next season but, for the moment, I couldn't have been happier with what I had.

Above me on P1 stood Heidelberg Hybridge's Peter Albrecht, and in third, Andrea, same top three as COTA and the Championship standings. As far as Eddie Palomas was concerned, Jolt had confirmed that he was relatively uninjured. He had finished off the season, but something had been missing. He'd underperformed and lost steam, falling down the ranks. If it hadn't been for the accident, I thought, he'd be on the podium instead of Andrea. This was a dream come true for me, something I'd wanted since I was in karts, but it also felt incomplete without a legend like Eddie sharing in the glory.

Later, we partied the night away in the Rosa Dorada Lounge, the official travelling Formula 1 club for exclusive post-race bashes, and the sole remnant of the team my late grandfather once drove for. Our staff, family, friends and sponsors filled the lounge as drinks flowed and talk of next season already abounded. The first to bring anything up to me, naturally, was Andrea Russo.

'Hey, Miguel.' He occupied the barstool beside me in what I guess he thought was a smooth manner. 'You heard anything about Eddie's contract?'

I tried to conceal an excessive eye roll. 'No, Andrea, as I am not a member of team Jolt, I would not know.'

'Really?' He raised an eyebrow, chugging back the rest of his drink. 'Because I heard something, my man. Something I know *you* wish you'd heard.'

'You're not for real.'

'Oh, but I am.' Andrea smirked. 'Let's settle. We go golf together this off-season, no more pushing it off, and I'll tell you right now.'

That was . . . embarrassing. I disliked associating with Andrea, mainly because I didn't need his sleazy, one-and-done reputation rubbing off on me, also because I just didn't like him. In the end, though, curiosity won out.

'Fine,' I caved. 'It's a deal. Now tell me.'

Andrea's grin revealed way-too-white veneers. 'Palomas is

25

starting to back down. You think he's getting ready for a comeback, huh? All wrong. I heard it from the team principal himself. Cavanaugh dropped this. Palomas is retiring for good.'

'Eddie is . . . what?' I was slack-jawed. I couldn't even process it. Eddie had been in the sport for damn near a decade. Without someone of Eddie's calibre, Jolt would tank.

'Yes, Miguel. They're looking to pluck up a rookie from F2, someone different,' said Andrea, voice as quiet as I'd ever heard it. 'I swear to God I am telling the truth. Watch it unfold for yourself during off-season.'

'Hmm.' I mulled over this knowledge. Introduction of a brand-new driver to a top-tier Formula 1 team – rather than pulling a guy from a midfield constructor – was a big deal. All eyes would be trained on him. This would either bolster Jolt Archambeau or destroy them.

'Don't think too hard,' offered Andrea unhelpfully. 'It'll probably be the underwhelming son of some big sponsor again. Remember Bonham?'

I snorted. Andrea Russo sucked, but he was right. Matt Bonham, son of Bonham Plastics sponsor Reginald Bonham, had only lasted one season, and a terrible one at that. 'We are at the top, bro. We deal with threats as they come. It's nothing earth-shaking.'

Chapter Four

Diana

'What a shame, he was so close.'

My mother clicked her tongue as she wiped her hands on the dish towel, rounding the couch to sit down next to me. She shook her head at the television. She was the biggest fan of Eduardo Palomas I knew. He had been so close to netting the Championship before his accident. My entire family had sat in front of the screen with our mouths wide open when it happened, just like we did every race.

'Could this be a chance for you?' hummed Ammi with a shake of her towel.

I made a sound of disagreement. 'Not on a team like that.'

'Not even with your racing record?'

'Maybe.' I brought a leg up onto the couch, crossing it atop my other. 'But only if I'm what they're looking for.'

My mother just kept up her tongue-clicking. 'Well, you drive so nicely, *joonam*.'

27

'Not enough,' I replied. Something in me twisted and clenched itself around my heart till I felt nauseous just thinking about it. I didn't know where I'd go from here. I was in a strange position for someone in my place – F2 champion, and yet no offers for so much as a Formula 1 reserve position. I had backed myself into a corner. 'They always have an energy they want from their driver pairing, you know. Maybe they want my energy, maybe they don't.'

'They want to win,' Ammi pointed out, something I could not at all protest. That much was true: money ran this business. 'You took the title in your first season there. The doors are all wide open for you.'

If only things were that simple. I loved my mother's easy way of speaking, her clean-cut, beautiful dreams. I appreciated them, so I smiled and curled up next to Ammi. She gave me a little squeeze of her arms, as if I were still her little baby. I held few people dear, but she was different. All my life, Ammi had gone against the norms that all the other moms followed, making the possibilities for her daughter boundless. She was the person who had first opened those doors for me. The least I could do was give her hope, even in this situation where it was possible I had none.

I'd heard the news just last week. My last lifeline, a Formula 1 seat with Vittore, had fallen through, lost to a young man, probably from some European country. They had good karting schools, produced good racers from wealthy families. It made sense.

'Do you think we will get anywhere by doubting, *joonam*?' my mother went on. Her voice was a light singsong, hints of her native Persian language intertwining with English. The question wasn't to be answered as much as it was rhetorical. 'I know we lost that seat you were looking at. But we can't doubt.'

We never could, not even when I was starting to race. She'd braid my hair tight into a crown under my balaclava so it wouldn't distract me while I raced. She and Baba would make signs at home and bring them to races. When we first started to travel for karting and got odd looks, she would give my hand a squeeze and say, 'Stay with us.' She had never let me entertain any doubts, but after so many years of racing, I had begun to allow them to creep into my head.

The Formula series were different. Here, hope wasn't enough. You needed money, sway, sponsors. People thought I was just asking for sympathy when I argued that it shouldn't have been so difficult, but it wasn't just talent that got you through the racing world. I'd been signed with and dropped and signed with and dropped more times than I could count, by brands from the UAE itself. I watched every race, just like my mother did, but a pang of frustration shot through my chest when I realized that many of these men had never felt that deceit.

'We can't doubt,' I echoed Ammi's words. I didn't have the heart to do anything else.

'Who's won?' Baba called from the dining table.

'It's Peter Albrecht with the Championship.' I wiggled round in my spot on the couch to shout out the standings back to him. 'De la Fuente came in second, Russo in third. No Palomas.'

'Ah, no Eduardo Palomas,' he mused. The English melded into Arabic as he went on with his theories. 'That is sad to see. For us, for his team.'

'Baba,' I said, my voice almost warning, maybe even scolding.

We couldn't pray for the downfall of other people, hoping opportunities might open up. Something about it just felt wrong to me. I knew how much Ammi and Baba wanted this. I wanted it twice as much. I wanted to make everything they'd given up all these years count. But I couldn't fathom the notion that my chance would come at someone else's expense. It usually went rockily for the average male driver; it wasn't hard to imagine I'd have to put up with doubly as much.

Yes, I wanted a chance with all my heart. I had put every cent I had into this sport. But if I said I wasn't terrified, I would have been lying.

2022 Season

'Formula 1 is a tradition. To change this sport is to tarnish it.'

Santiago de la Fuente Sr.
#71, Rosa Dorada Racing

Chapter Five

Miguel

'"New Jolt Archambeau driver debuts in mysterious media stills that give away absolutely nothing." What is that supposed to mean, anyway? You can't even see his face.'

I was sitting on the large verandah of the Barcelona house, beside a now-graduated Jatziry Fernanda, both of us poring over the images on my phone.

'He's small,' Jatziry noted.

She was right. The new driver posed beside his car, helmet on and tinted visor down to give that air of 'hmm, who could it be?' He was lanky, reedy, and definitely small, even for a Formula One driver. I mentally ran through all the F2 guys on Jolt's feeder teams. Who on earth was that short?

Maybe Jolt Archambeau's new driver was a kid.

'This is an eighteen-year-old boy who damn near missed his chance at puberty,' I deduced. 'That's what Andrea Russo told me back in Abu Dhabi. Rookie from F2. Does this look like anyone grown to you, Jatziry?'

'Don't be mean,' chided Jatziry. 'Some people are just, ah, vertically challenged.'

'And some people see too much good in the enemy.' I nudged her jestingly. 'We're supposed to be against Jolt, not upping their self-esteem.'

'Sure.' Jatziry peered down at the phone once more. 'You know, Formula 1 could use some women . . . someone like Paula would be great. Curb this head-to-head competition where the men are always comparing sizes.'

Although Jatziry and I had begun by leaving racing out of our conversations, the passing of nearly five months of what we called very chaste 'dating' and the family called 'courtship' had changed things. Now, Jatziry had finally shaken off the nuns, and after much begging and pleading on my part, she'd grudgingly agreed to involve herself in motorsport and was slated to watch a good number of the grands prix of the coming season. I was ecstatic. Jatziry was like Paula: she was aware she'd be getting a boatload of toxicity and she was hungry to change the narrative.

'Oh, a leak from Andrea.' I hit the incoming message from him with a rapidity that surprised myself. Andrea had all too quickly become the source for all Jolt gossip as it came, due to his being in a poker club with their team principal, Theodore Cavanaugh. However, I paid a price, namely that of numerous golf rounds. 'He has a name. Daniel Zahrani. One of the UAE's, he says. I think I've heard that name.'

'You trust this man?' Jatziry said, dubious.

'Hasn't been wrong yet.'

34

She took a long sip of her tea. 'I don't know. I have a feeling he may be this time.'

'You and your premonitions,' I joked, making Jatziry scoff through a smile. 'Well, I'll know soon. All of us are invited to the cordial welcome banquet in Los Cabos, and then we'll see if Andrea has pulled through.'

Formula 1 is like the most problematic, disjointed and yet tight-knit family you've ever met. This sport is the most selective in the world; we are all competitive at our cores. F1 has a grand total of twenty seats internationally. We race to survive, to maintain our careers. That makes some guys assholes and some real diamonds in the rough. Some are only there for the money. But some become valuable friends – brothers – till the end of your career and beyond.

'Hey, Miguel! How's the break been?'

One of those brothers, Nic Necci, was the first person I spotted when Jatziry, Paula and I entered the banquet hall. Team Jolt had decided to hold this event at one of their sponsors' hotels, a lavish excursion in Cabo that beckoned all of us to enjoy one last vacation before the season picked up double-time. I wasn't too excited to have to mingle with some of these people again, but Nic was my tightest friend on the grid, so it wouldn't be all bad.

'Break's not been long enough.' I shared a complex handshake with Nic. We were, both of us, little better than rowdy teenage boys when you got us together. 'Where's Alex at?'

'He's got some engineer's cousin enraptured at the bar right now. Best leave them to it. She looks like a catch,' Nic chuckled. 'Little boy's growing up.'

I let out a laugh. 'He's seducing women now?'

'Very much.' Nic nodded to the bar. 'See for yourself.'

'Ooh,' I chortled. Sure enough, there was baby Alex with his toothy smile, eyes crinkling happily as he talked animatedly to a tall blonde who looked as if she was hanging on to his every word. You could tell he was way into her – he was gesturing like an orchestra conductor, poofy fade of curly hair bouncing with every movement. 'When are you gonna do the same, then, desperado?'

Nic just rolled his eyes with a smile. I was surprised he didn't have a girlfriend clinging to his arm, to be honest. He was your conventional charming F1 driver: always attracting women at the parties with the brown hair/grey eyes/winning smile combo, soft-spoken as he was. He took part in all the charity events that many other drivers deemed a waste of time, did all the press appearances, interacted with his fans (in his native Italian, too, which you could imagine went down well with his admirers). You couldn't hate the guy. On the flip side, though, I knew this dude well, and he, not too unlike myself, needed someone who could accept the mania that racing aroused in the average human being.

'Only the best for you, huh,' I teased him anyway. 'You'll find her eventually, man.'

'Fingers crossed, Mig.'

There weren't too many people on the grid worth wishing good things for that I knew of, but Nic was one of the few I wanted to have all the success and happiness in the world. The first year I started racing in F1, I was with Vittore Monterey, back then Scuderia Vittore, alongside Nicolò Necci, and I couldn't have asked for a more amiable, supportive teammate on and off the track.

Once Nic had Alex and his new friend in tow, we headed to our respective team tables near the stage. Unfortunately, this meant I'd be stuck making dinner conversation with Andrea Russo.

'Take a good look,' Paula reminded me. 'Check out the drivers for this year.'

I obliged, and already I made out a shuffle: Heidelberg had dropped Kowalski, replacing him with Vittore's high-performing Darien Cardoso-Magalhães, an American racing under the flag of Brazil, a quite bold move. Vittore now had rookie Byron Hargreaves of Canada driving alongside veteran Christian Clay. Otherwise, the roster swap of the season was what we were just about to witness: Jolt's child prodigy.

'Please, be seated,' Theodore Cavanaugh said from the extremely over-the-top stage set up maybe ten feet from our table. We were already seated, so it was obvious they were out to make a big show of it.

'Good evening, ladies and gentlemen, our boys of the hour, as it were. My name is Theo Cavanaugh, and you know me as team principal of Jolt Archambeau Racing,' he began, voice echoing on part of his overkill microphone.

'He runs a whole racing team?' whispered Jatziry. 'He looks like one of my *tíos*.'

I almost snorted wine out my nose.

'Jolt did not foresee these circumstances, that's for sure,' said Cavanaugh with a chuckle that rippled through the crowd. 'The departure of Eduardo Palomas was an unexpected, sad loss, but we realize it is what was best for both Jolt and Mr Palomas. With an open seat, Jolt saw this as room for improvement, room for new blood.'

'Young blood,' I muttered with a roll of my eyes.

Nic leaned back from the Griffith table neighbouring ours to elbow me. 'Play nice, Miggie.'

'We want to do what's never been done in F1. We want to leave behind a legacy.' Cavanaugh was really laying it on thick now. 'Jolt embodies the culture of pushing the envelope and soaring above boundaries. That's what we'll do this season. So, without further ado, please welcome your newest Formula 1 driver, number forty-four for Jolt Archambeau Racing, Daniel Zahrani!'

Cavanaugh hurried offstage as obnoxious pyrotechnic sparks lit up the open space, and the lights dimmed. The screen behind the stage faded into a racer's silhouette entering a track.

'What the hell is this?' Paula murmured.

'Publicity stunt,' I whispered back with all certainty. 'Too much pomp for a flop of a newbie.'

The video reel faded to black. The sparks stopped.

'Come on,' I grumbled. 'Show yourself already, you son of a—'

As the smoke cleared, a figure became visible. That same slim, short stature, a racer in full gear, helmet and all, just like in the promo photos.

'Take off the helmet, boyo!' hooted Kramer's Craig Grant, to jeers from everyone within a five-foot radius. This was pretty typical motorsport behaviour. Many of these guys peaked in high school and never descended, giving them the prickly demeanour of frat bros out to haze a new recruit.

Number Forty-Four reached up and unfastened his helmet and brace. Raucous cheers filled the room in such volume that

Jatziry plugged her ears beside me. Nic and Alex were up on their feet. This was no cordial welcome. It was a pre-season hype rally.

Jolt's newest driver finally removed his helmet. The cheering reached a fever pitch. And then, very abruptly, it all died out. Dead silence.

From beneath Forty-Four's helmet tumbled sheets of straight black hair. Warm brown eyes rimmed in kohl liner glanced across the room without surprise, despite the fact that one could hear a pin drop. The driver casually traded the helmet for a Jolt cap as we all watched, jaws to the floor.

For a split second, I could swear that her eyes landed on me, and mine on hers, sparkling beneath the bill of her cap. Daring me to say something about this twist of fate . . . this twist of fate that had taken one look at me and gripped me like an affliction, stabbed me with a pang of something I couldn't quite place in the moment.

'That's . . . not a kid,' I managed.

'Did he not say Daniel?' Alex whispered.

'Oh, no.' Nic gaped, eyes wide. 'I think we misheard.'

The team principal awkwardly cleared his throat from stage left. 'Diana Zahrani, United Arab Emirates. Please join me in, um, giving her a warm welcome.'

I turned around in my seat to meet Andrea's eye two tables away. 'Diana!' I mouthed.

He just shrugged, completely gobsmacked.

It was still quiet. No one dared make a sound. This was unreal and unimaginable. Jolt, of all constructors, had staked their future on—

An ear-splitting whistle from beside me nearly blew out my

eardrums. Paula had got up on her chair, a huge grin across her face.

That broke the spell. Hesitantly, a cautious wave of applause began rippling through an audience still sheathed in disbelief and amazement. I was absolutely floored. I didn't even know there were women in Formula 2, which, in hindsight, was exceedingly embarrassing.

'I am beyond thrilled to be racing Formula 1,' said Diana Zahrani from onstage in a voice far too gentle for the fraternity that was F1. 'So many people told me it wouldn't happen from the day I started karting, and I know that was only the tip of the iceberg in terms of the criticism I'd face, but this is what I've dreamed of. I'm ready to do justice to Eduardo Palomas's legacy.'

Jatziry leaned my way with a smirk. 'Told you, Miguel. More Paulas.'

Chapter Six

Diana

There was no way this was actually happening. All last year, I had stayed behind after my Formula 2 races and watched with bated breath as the Formula 1 cars whizzed past the catch fencing at double our speeds – so close and yet so far.

And now, Jolt.

My parents' premonitions had come true. My fears and my hopes had manifested themselves.

So yes, I had expected as much hesitation and I could still feel the disbelief radiating towards me in waves as I took the mic and said those words: 'I'm ready to do justice to Eduardo Palomas's legacy.' I looked across the tables at faces both surprised and unconvinced. My entire body was shaking. This was only the beginning of the rollercoaster, I reminded myself. I had a thousand twists and turns left ahead of me.

And so one can imagine how shocked I was when Paula de la Fuente came up to me at the bar, just as I was mustering up the courage to start making my team-mandated rounds of the room.

'Good evening.' She smiled in my direction. 'Diana Zahrani, right?'

'Yes,' I managed. Paula de la Fuente was iconic. She ruled over her brother's paddock with a fist of iron, the only female radio engineer to ever enter the post. I knew her voice well from watching the races and hearing her make judgement calls over that radio to save Revello's races.

Her straight hair was clipped half up with a butterfly pin. She wore a two-piece pantsuit in a menacing maroon with matching heels. She was one of my idols, and she was *right here*. As in, in front of me. Speaking directly to me.

'I'm honestly a big fan,' she continued.

Um. *What?*

I laughed nervously. This woman looked as if she'd stepped out of a Chanel campaign. She had the kind of analytical mind that made most of the teams on the grid shake in their shoes. There was no way she was a fan of mine. 'I know this is a little strange to say,' Paula went on, 'but I watched the Formula 2 races, and I can't tell you how inspiring it was to see you winning that Championship.'

'I'm only starting out,' I remarked with an anxious chuckle. I was suddenly so conscious of all my little mannerisms, of the trace of Arab accent that expat school hadn't managed to erase from my words. 'We'll have to see what I'm made of in the Formula 1 races now.'

Paula glanced over at the Jolt table and, as I followed her

42

line of sight, I thought immediately of their other driver – my new teammate, Kasper Ramsey. Hailing from the United Kingdom, Kasper had proved a difficult intra-team rival to Palomas, and now he looked completely unconcerned, drinking with his team. He saw no threat in me.

'Does it bother you at all that these men don't take you seriously?' asked Paula, raising a pointed eyebrow at Kasper.

'It's the game.' I shrugged matter-of-factly to quell the shakiness in my voice. 'They underestimate us for being women, but that's an advantage. They go easy on you, and suddenly, you're out in front.'

To my relief, Paula burst into laughter. 'Oh, *tía*, you'll have a brilliant season. I like you, Diana. You're one to watch out for.'

'Appreciate it.' I made to leave with one last grin, but Paula wasn't done just yet.

'Hey, Diana!' she called from paces away.

I turned back towards her.

'Did you want to meet the Revello team?'

At that exact moment, I felt something change in the conversation, the mode switch of the dynamic from friendly to business. I added two and two together as Paula sized me up. Sure, I might have been getting on well with *Paula*, but if we wanted to avoid mid-race conflicts and maintain our standing, I also needed to have a positive relationship with Scuderia Revello. She was going to try and make an ally of me, I was almost certain of it. I remembered this from the PR instruction we had received on entering F3. You always wanted more allies than you did foes. Foes made for drama, and drama lost you sponsors. So this? I needed this.

'Yes, please,' I replied.

Paula eagerly led me back through throngs of staff and engineers, to where her team had gathered at their table. Andrea Russo had lugged a slew of alcoholic beverages back for the masses. He was doing tequila shots with the pit crew, because, you know, if you did not piss on your territory, you were not a man. Another woman I didn't recognize, with pale brown eyes and dark hair tied up into a neat ponytail, looked on indifferently, helping dazed crew members into banquet chairs.

'This is F1,' Paula said to me with a roll of her eyes as we approached the chaos.

A clatter from my right caught my attention, the proud announcement of the final member of the team, unmissable as he was. My heart felt as if it had dropped into my stomach as I registered who had finally decided to join us.

Miguel de la Fuente giggled and slumped against the table. In his hands were two bottles of tequila . . . and he was utterly incapacitated.

My mother and I were unfaltering fans of Eduardo Palomas. Both of us had cheered the older driver on in every race. But for years, Palomas mentored de la Fuente, the two of them always meeting up at the end of races to exchange thoughts. Miguel was a nepotism baby, but he was a talented nepotism baby if I'd ever seen one. He raced like Eduardo Palomas, he strategized like Palomas, but something else about him now, something in his face (what little I could see of it), perhaps, tugged at the back of my mind. I wasn't totally sure why, but something about this prodigal son of the Formula 1 empire that bore his family name was gripping my nerves.

And it didn't help that the last thing I'd expected to see

Miguel Ángel de la Fuente, number eighty-eight, King of Spain, doing at this event was nearly passing out on the table.

'Uh . . .' I watched as Paula struggled to force a smile upon her face. 'Diana, Scuderia Revello.'

A couple of guys fixed their hair and sat up a little straighter. Andrea adopted a disturbingly condescending expression, coupled with a hint of smarminess. '*Che bella*. Wonderful to meet you, Miss Diana.'

My entire body shuddered, as if it were rejecting his mere presence. 'Andrea Russo?' was all I could muster.

'That's me.' He smirked. 'You really are quite beautiful, if you don't mind my saying. Why waste that on Formula 1?'

I could have *gagged*.

People loved to focus on that. I was pretty, therefore racing was a waste. And the way this man was looking at me, with greed and lechery in his eyes . . . God. I took it back. I think I could have fully *thrown up*. On him.

Instead, I said, 'Excuse me? I'm afraid I don't understand.'

'You don't have to *race*, you know, for the money. You are from the UAE, no? Lots of opportunities to marry into it.'

Oh. This, this was also not new. It was nauseating. The UAE always made its way into the conversation. The rich men, the fast cars. I had to be stupid to be passing that up for a life of sport, of course. I could be sitting at home by the pool in sunglasses with my five kids and a martini, but I was here instead. What a dick.

'I love to race. And I've spent more than I've earned to get to this point, Mr Russo,' I explained politely. I honestly wanted to vanish from the scene. This didn't bode well for a decent relationship with Revello, let alone for a foray into Formula 1.

'My family put it all on the line for me to drive because that was my passion. Not for money.'

'Well, it's always wonderful to see racers here for the sport.' Andrea winked. Disgusting. 'I know it's unprecedented, but welcome to have such a gorgeous face as well.'

Crap. I glanced nervously at Paula. She bored holes into her brother's head of messy hair with a killer glare, perhaps willing him to snap out of his stupor and save this situation. No hope. I glanced at the other woman across the table, the only person besides Paula who seemed to feel any kind of discomfort about the way this was going. I hoped my expression was pleading. *Help. Me.*

The woman reached over and pinched Miguel de la Fuente's arm.

'Ah!' He sat straight up in his chair. 'Wow.'

Mig's eyes found his sister's, but they immediately travelled to mine, doing the maths rapidly.

'Ooh.' He dusted crumbs from his suit jacket, making sure the Revello crest was in order. 'Yes, I'm, uh—'

'Miguel de la Fuente,' Paula finished before her little brother could spectacularly upend his own name.

'Of course.' I lowered my voice to a whisper that only she could hear. 'Is he feeling all right?'

'I'd bet he's not,' she whispered back. 'I am so, so sorry. He is not usually like this. None of them are. Except maybe Andrea.'

I attempted to give her a knowing smile. 'It's okay.' Then to Miguel, 'It's very nice to meet you, Miguel.'

'You a fan?' Miguel teased, leaning forward with a lazy grin. 'Come on.'

'Yeah.' My palms were sweating so hard that I had to wipe

them on the pants of my jumpsuit as I spoke to him. 'You race like Palomas, I notice. Just . . . a bit reckless.'

'Ohhh, that's harsh, Diana.' He pouted with far too much enthusiasm. His eyes drifted towards the other woman with a smirk. 'You need a little reckless when you're riding the track, no, Jatziry?'

Jatziry, that was the name of the woman standing beside him, I supposed. She appeared to be drowning in embarrassment right then and there, cheeks turning red fast. '*Madre del . . .*'

'That's my fiancée,' proclaimed Miguel happily. 'She likes them reckless. Like when—'

'Okay, Miggie.' Paula smiled as broadly as she could, concealing completely the fact that her brother's chances of a positive on-track relationship with me had just slipped to between slim and none. 'We will get you home, all right? I really apologize, Diana—'

'No need.' I grimaced out of sympathy, sweeping a dark curl from my face. 'As long as he gets some sleep. And . . .' I reached out and patted Jatziry's hand, at which the gobsmacked fiancée in question sprang to life.

'I apologize for Miguel's behaviour,' said Jatziry hurriedly. 'He just—'

'I heard nothing. Don't worry. Men are something else entirely when drunk . . . *and* when sober, for that matter,' I reassured her. 'I've got to turn in early, busy day tomorrow. Good night, guys.'

'Good night,' echoed Jatziry, still looking dazed.

And bless her heart, if 'good' was not the worst possible word for it.

Chapter Seven

Diana

My campaign manager worked furiously at the gum in her gloss-lined mouth, looking me over one last time. She placed an insistent hand on her hip. 'Honey, you need to cooperate, okay? This is the image Jolt wants, this is what we give 'em.'

I did not want to cooperate. My day had already begun on a bad foot. Barring the uncomfortable interactions of the night before, my front wing had broken in a morning run at Autódromo Hermanos Rodríguez. The livery team had reacted badly to my expressed desire to have a decal of my parents' names on my halo.

And I'd burnt my toast at breakfast.

Now I was back at the hotel, where Jolt had set up an elaborate studio for photos with my fellow driver, Kasper Ramsey. Jolt had apparently decided on the image they wanted, but it was not one that I had greenlit.

'No, no. There is no way I am going to do this.'

'That's not how these things work, Diana.'

'I am not posing with Kasper like that!' I protested. 'We are equals! I'm a driver for this team, not his woman of the month!'

The manager just rolled her eyes. 'Babe. This is what sells. "Equals" does not. If you've got issues with it, check your contract.'

I gritted my teeth. She had me cornered. We both knew that my contract stipulated I had to follow the instructions I was given if I wanted to stay on the team.

Across the studio, Kasper was working with his makeup artists. He dug right under my skin. Despite being just twenty-five with a perfect complexion, blond hair, icy-blue eyes, and a flawless bone structure, he appeared to have elaborate skincare regimens and coats of makeup for every occasion. I hadn't been kidding about his having a new woman every month, either – he wasn't a pleasant personality, reminiscent of a slightly less disgusting Andrea Russo from Revello. He certainly didn't seem to be taking me seriously. Maybe he didn't think I belonged there.

But you know what? This was motorsport. On the plus side, I was received warmly by many lovely drivers – Peter Albrecht said I was stunningly talented, which killed me because he was *so* dreamy – but there was always going to be doubt. There was always going to be stigma; there was always going to be the sense that I ought to be worshipping at these men's – these constructors' – feet for allowing me to be here. Allowing me where? In this awful position that went against all my morals? No wonder it was so hard for a woman to make it this far on the circuit. Racing was a culture built on derogatory stereotypes and a lack of support, and you just had to roll with it to succeed. For crying out loud, it'd taken them so long just to shut down the toxic 'grid girl' thing. Meaningful change was nowhere in sight.

It was sad that the campaign manager was right: this was what sold.

With far too much aggression, I pulled back the sleeves of my jumpsuit so that what was left served as trousers to my Nomex long-sleeve fireproof, before joining Kasper beneath the harsh photography lamps, coy smile plastered on my face.

'This is so exciting,' I lied through my teeth as the photographer gestured to me to get on the chassis.

'Oh, it is.' Kasper took his place sitting in the cockpit of the prop JA76. As for me, I got to lounge ever so casually across the front of the car's chassis like a calendar girl.

'Perfect!' called the photographer.

This was only for promo, I reminded myself as I held my smouldering expression. They'd already taken my official headshot – simple photo, standing, no smile – and it had come out badass. This was just a formality, after all. No one would care.

'Now with the Jolt, Diana!' the photographer instructed. On cue, his assistant shoved a bottle of the hot pink battery acid that was supposed to be an electrolyte-rich sports drink into my hand the second I was on my feet again.

Well, of course.

With a sigh, I held up the bottle uncertainly. 'Are we sure about this?'

'Yes, yes, just look relaxed!' the assistant dismissed me impatiently.

I gazed down at the bottle. It would all be over soon and, once the racing started, nobody would ask me to pose sexily on a Formula 1 car ever again.

I popped the cap. Whatever.

In one fell swoop, I dumped the entire thing on myself, eyes closed, mock happiness written across my face as the sticky beverage coated my beautiful black uniform.

'Wonderful shot, Diana, they'll love this one!'

I wished somebody had warned me about the loneliness that came with being at the top.

After ogling me as I soaked myself with Jolt Raspberry, Kasper Ramsey invited me to dinner with him at a high-end joint in the city. I politely declined, booking out the whole hotel gym for an hour so I could work out in peace, no one staring or competing or pointing out my flaws.

I loved my peace, of course, but about ten minutes in, I tired of being alone.

I wanted something like Miguel de la Fuente and Nic Necci had shared on Vittore a few years back; even when they'd lost horrendously (one in two), they had fun because they'd done it together. Here, my teammate wanted nothing to do with me. I was used to having to go it on my own, but sometimes, company would have been nice.

From my perch on the bench, I checked my phone in vain for some excuse to escape. By the grace of a higher power, I got one. Unfortunately, the more I read, the more I recoiled.

It was a rather unfortunate message from Miguel de la Fuente's personal assistant: the first red flag. In a brief summary of the two-paragraph email, it laid out a basic apology for Mr de la Fuente's inappropriate behaviour, and requested that I join said driver for a reconciliation dinner before the Revello team packed up and left tomorrow.

What a mess.

I'd seen people attempt to amend their mistakes in all sorts of obnoxious ways, but I had to admit, this was a new one. I wanted to harbour a positive relationship with Revello as much as Paula had, but this was an *email* from his *assistant*. I had no guarantee that Miguel himself would show.

Just as I was closing out the email, my phone vibrated with a text. Oh no.

Kasper Ramsey: **Sure you're not down for dinner?**

I bit my lip. I was running out of options here.

So I reopened the email from Miguel's assistant and checked all the details. Address, time, okay. Tacos. At least it wasn't Kasper. This was the lesser of two evils. Miguel de la Fuente, if he did hold true to his assistant's promise, wasn't an astronomical douchebag with entitlement issues.

Right?

Chapter Eight

Miguel

If I couldn't recover from this one, my ass would be screwed till the date of my death. First the welcome party, then Susanne sending an email on my behalf, and now tacos? What the hell?

I drummed my fingers on the table for two at the restaurant on the outskirts of Cabo, currently alone with a heaped serving of embarrassment. Why couldn't I have sent that damn email myself? Susanne was great, but this definitely hadn't been a job for her, a harsh truth I was only just coming to terms with now.

Maybe I was hazy because I was still processing last night, a saga I did not recall but about which a flustered Jatziry had told me.

'Really, Miguel?' she fumed. 'You said that about me in front of everyone *including* this new woman? What will she be thinking, huh?'

Yeah. So it had been pretty bad.

I'd just about given up hope of Diana's arrival when the door finally swung open.

Diana Zahrani slipped inside, removing her cream-coloured cap. Today, her dark hair had been pulled up into a ramrod-straight ponytail, and she wore a Jolt hoodie and black yoga pants.

I awkwardly raised a hand, and she headed my way.

Diana smiled rather graciously, given what a total fool I'd made of myself in front of her just twenty-four hours ago. 'It's great to see you, um, doing better, Miguel.'

'On the outside,' I quipped.

She let out a laugh and sat down across from me. As sad as it was, I had been too drunk at the big reveal to recall much about meeting her, so it was surreal to be at dinner together now, face to face. She was exceptionally pretty. Warm brown eyes, perfect eyebrows, straight nose, gentle smile quirking just slightly to the right.

'So, uh, Diana . . .' I cleared my throat, wincing. This was the very epitome of painful. 'I wanted to say sorry. You know, for how off I was yesterday. It's just inexcusable, especially given that you—'

'It's nothing,' she said quickly, the unconscious scrunch of her nose betraying her own feelings. 'I could see you weren't at your best.'

'Yeah.' I grimaced. 'I just thought maybe we could start afresh. Meet properly, without all the, um, work stuff.'

Diana smirked. 'Paula put you up to this, didn't she?'

'What?' I hoped I didn't appear too flustered. 'I mean, kind of, but I didn't want to leave without redemption either. How . . . how did you know?'

'The email from your PA was kind of telling.'

'Ah, yes.' I could usually hold my own in the worst of media sessions, but now I felt out of my depth: my palms were clammy and I couldn't hold her gaze properly. It was her eyes, the way she looked at me, the dark line of the kohl narrowing as she regarded me with the slightest judgement. I couldn't do anything but wipe my hands against my jeans in an attempt to steady myself. What the hell?

Ironically, Diana herself saved me. Picking up her menu, she said offhandedly, 'Do you . . . are you friends, you and Andrea Russo?'

My instinct told me to say 'yes', no matter what. See, image mattered in F1. I had to look friendly. But then I remembered Jatziry telling me how women value honesty and, for some reason, I didn't want this particular woman to see me as a total idiot. I decided to choose more wisely.

'Not at all,' I admitted. 'Andrea's a great driver, just not such a great person.'

I could have sworn Diana let out a sigh of relief. 'Yeah, he makes me uncomfortable, to say the least.'

Yikes. Jatziry had told me this, too. Andrea's remarks towards Diana had been pretty unforgivable. I might have been an asshole yesterday, but hopefully not in Andrea's league. Wait till the GPs: Andrea would be running feral, leaving Diana to play keep-away. A strand of anger unravelled in my chest at the mere thought of it.

'What about your teammate, Ramsey?' I asked.

The sickened look on Diana's face said it all. She dropped her menu, brought out her phone, and tapped at the screen before turning it to me.

I lurched back on impact. 'Whoa, this is . . . whoa.'

It had to be a crime to produce promo photos this . . . unsettling. Diana's fellow driver, Kasper Ramsey, sat triumphantly at the wheel of his car. Diana was perched on the chassis like a mermaid on a rock, faux smile plastered across her face.

'Why me?' she groaned. 'Why? I hate to say it, but Kasper makes me want to flee fast in the opposite direction. He is very Russo.'

She withdrew her phone exasperatedly. 'That should be illegal,' I agreed. 'Isn't that your title? "Driver"?'

'You'd think so.' Effortlessly, Diana put on a grin, changing modes on a dime. It was astonishing and saddening all at once. She tapped her menu cheerfully. 'Enough of that. Which tacos would we like?'

And I don't know what it was about the way she switched up that quickly, but it was as if I'd seen that before. Maybe it was an interview or something, but I think I'd have remembered. The sharp prod of déjà vu disconcerted me as I took in the broad smile on Diana's face, an expression that was both beautiful and melancholy. It made me want to sit here with her for hours, to figure out what she was hiding behind those trained smiles, not to mention why the hell I felt like I knew those trained smiles so very well.

I shook it off as quickly as it had hit me. I had amends to make. I took a look at the menu and picked out my tacos.

Chapter Nine

Diana

In what could probably be described as the most awkward dinner of all time, Miguel and I polished off our tacos in dead silence. This was not the reconciliation either he or I wanted. It was painful.

'Uh, so . . .' Miguel gulped down a sip of horchata. 'So when did you start karting?'

It was a very flat question, but it usually struck up some form of banter among the driving community since many Formula 1 pilots started out karting together as kids. At least he was trying. If I thought hard enough, I could unfortunately trace Miguel back as the perpetrator of all the events that had led to this one.

It was hard to think of him as the perpetrator of anything. He was handsome, of course – overgrown hair tousled by endless hours spent wearing helmets, deep chocolate eyes framed in thick lashes. Heralding from a rich European family, his bloodline shone through his strong, stubbled jaw, proud Roman nose smattered with freckles, and full lips that betrayed a placid nature via a contented smile. He looked as if he were a complete stranger to mischief, something I knew first-hand to be completely untrue. He was already making me feel flustered. The best I could do here was to act as normal as possible.

I decided to play along, slightly out of pity. 'Late,' I replied, taking a sip of my own horchata. 'I began karting at fourteen. I've only been at this for nine-ish years.'

'I see.'

'And you?' I smiled jestingly when I realized the irony of my innocent question. Miguel had probably learned to drive before he'd learned to walk, and I said as much to him. 'Then again, I really shouldn't have been asking a de la Fuente about when he started karting, should I?'

My joke got a chuckle out of him, releasing the tension between the two of us. 'True. It's a pretty tired tale now.'

'I'd like to hear it!' I raised my glass in protest. 'Please.'

'Okay, uh, I got in the kart when I was four? Yeah. And then I did some titles in Canada before I got into OK-Junior at, I think, twelve, a cup or two, KF2, got into Revello's academy, Formula 3 with Bianchi, F2 with Bianchi, and now I'm here, I guess. Same as every de la Fuente guy ever,' Miguel finished, maybe a bit sarcastically.

It was insane to hear these kinds of stories, at least to me. This wasn't so commonplace where I'd come from. Access was everything, and when you didn't have that, you were done for. I nodded. 'You're clearly very accomplished. Don't be so quick to sell yourself short just because of the de la Fuente thing.'

He raised an eyebrow. 'Huh. True. And if you don't mind my asking, why did you join late?'

'Sure. I was born in the UAE and we moved to Saudi Arabia shortly after for my father's work, which is where I grew up,' I explained a bit awkwardly. I got a lot of questions about home, but never about my relationship with it. 'Women weren't allowed to drive till 2018. They banned us from driving in motorsport, as well as day-to-day, and so when I started karting it was still hesitant, still frowned upon. I raced on-and-off, when I could. It was only in 2018, when the ban was lifted, that I was allowed to compete in F3. I raced for Saudi one year, and then I changed over, back to the Emirates. I'm a little behind the Jolt calibre, in my opinion. *Yaani*, Kasper is like you, with all the experience and Championships and sponsors. I'm just grateful to be here.'

'Damn,' he remarked, and I had to admit, he looked shocked. It must have been the driving ban that did it. Oftentimes, especially for well-off men from well-off families, they didn't even consider these things. Their cars were their pride and joy. 'You're from Saudi Arabia, then?'

I made a so-so gesture with my hand. 'Sort of. But I'm moving back to Dubai now since I race under the flag of the UAE. Not to mention the rules are just much freer there. That's why I got my licence with the Emirates. I just want to . . .' I shrugged, trying to find the words, 'fly free.'

'Fly free.' He repeated my words. Each syllable he spoke was almost a hushed puff of air, mingling with his slight Canadian accent. His eyes mirrored mine, slipping down to my lips for a moment that was so fleeting I could have sworn I was just seeing things. I felt that same tug in my gut as when I'd seen him at the

Jolt reveal. Something in his voice . . . something almost familiar to me. It was like having a thought on the tip of my tongue.

'I'm sorry, I know you didn't want to hear the whole lecture . . .' I tried to ease up the moment, but he shook his head.

'No, don't be. It's really amazing,' Miguel replied, gaze still searching my face. 'To see how much you put into this dream.'

'Thank you.' I swept my ponytail behind my shoulder, just a small, insignificant habit I'd had since I was young. Yet something glinted in Miguel's eyes at that simple gesture: recognition.

'Do I . . . do I know you from somewhere?' he began slowly. 'I apologize, I feel like I remember you. From before.'

My forehead furrowed. Miguel's brow creased in turn, as if he could sense my confusion. 'Not that I know of . . . Well, wait.' I leaned back in my chair. 'Were we ever together in F3 or something? I raced for Kender.'

He looked up exasperatedly, as if he'd find the answer written on the ceiling somewhere. 'It's likely we might have been, but I left F3 for F2 the year you were tapped. We logically couldn't have bumped heads at races. I doubt it.'

My phone began releasing a dastardly vibration that shook the entire table. My eyes went wide. 'Shoot. I have to be back at the hotel to meet my new trainer. So sorry to cut this short here, Miguel, but . . .' I pulled a sticky note and pen from my bag, scribbling something down on it with my left hand before passing it to Miguel.

His fingers brushed mine as he took it, sending chills up my arms and down my back. He glanced at my hand, as if he had meant to ask me something or point something out, but

I suppose he thought better of it, because he looked away soon enough, reading the note with a slight squint of his dark eyes.

'My direct line,' I said by way of explanation. 'You won't get any weird redirects or anything through this number. If you need anything, don't hesitate.'

'Same to you.' He held out his right hand. 'I'll see you at winter testing.'

I started forward with my left. Dumb as I was, I couldn't stop doing that, even though I knew everyone else in my life was right-handed. It felt doubly as embarrassing before Miguel de la Fuente, a feeling that reddened my cheeks as I offered my right instead and shook his hand firmly. Those same chills, both warmth and cold all at once, invaded my muscles, reminding me that this, something about this, was not new for me. My body remembered this.

'See you at testing.' I shot him a quick smile that I hoped concealed my nerves, swept up all my things and sped out through the door, my heart pounding at a thousand kilometres an hour.

Chapter Ten

Diana

I looked on from the paddock as Miguel's crew helped him pull his car, Revello's latest R3-71 model, from the garage. According to my engineer, he claimed this – the winter testing – was nothing exciting. Teams would attempt to log the most laps, as well as the data to be used in the fine-tuning of the car later on. Revello was already projected to do well, as usual. Jolt seemed happy with their build, and were keen to have me sit in the car and try it out. Maybe winter testing was unexciting to everyone else, but this was my first time driving *my* car. I'd done reserve. I'd run someone else's practice once. But now, I'd sit in *my* car and get out onto the track. Far from finding it routine, I was positively bursting with nervous energy.

'It's crazy, isn't it?' remarked Kasper Ramsey's latest girlfriend, a well-known British supermodel by the name of Cassandra Cavendish. I hadn't been aware he had a girlfriend; at least, the way he acted around me – and the texts he'd sent me – had suggested otherwise. As the drama could get heated, she was supposed to be in Kasper's garage and not mine, but Cassandra seemed like the kind of woman who had a habit of getting things her way. 'A woman in Formula 1 after all these years, and one from the Middle East, at that.'

I nodded with extreme cautiousness. I wasn't sure if this was her attempt at being genuine, or her being as fabricated as possible, but I was nowhere near sold.

We watched Miguel's Revello in silence for quite a while on the screens, zooming down the straights at top speeds. It was a brilliant car, but his handling was equally effortless, hitting every curve just right to maintain the maximum speed. I could have watched him drive all day.

It took a few laps before Cassandra tipped her Chanel sunglasses down to protect her eyes from the harsh daylight of Sakhir, Bahrain, where we found ourselves for this testing session. She cleared her throat before turning to me, unnerving with her massive sunglasses now gracing her face. 'Well, you rather enjoy watching Miguel de la Fuente race, don't you?'

I almost choked as I tugged on my balaclava. 'I don't know what you want me to say. He's a Formula 1 driver. He's good at what he does, isn't he? I mean, you're standing here watching him, too.'

'I'm sure,' hummed Cassandra. I tried to ignore her, to put my helmet on and lock in, but I couldn't hear anything except her voice, repeating that phrase once more. 'I'm sure.'

I'd been thrown into Formula 1 just like I'd been thrown into most series I had ever raced in. My career had been a series of lucky events, one right after another, which landed me in the Formula circuit, but left me little time to cope with the change.

I had been doing this for a while, adapting. It was how my childhood had passed me by, something I had willingly given up in pursuit of a dream that no one thought I would ever get close to touching. And now I was here, in this car for the first time since seat fitting, ready to run it, to feel all its beautiful power beneath the same hands I had been told were too small to drive.

Sometimes I paused to wonder why I chose racing, why I chose cars – the very thing that took so much away from my parents. But we often choose what we know we cannot easily have. I chose a path of hardship, and I chose a path of pride, for myself and the family that had supported me when no one else did.

That same pride swelled within my chest when I grabbed the shimmering silver halo of the JA76 with my gloved hands and lowered myself into the seat designed to fit my body perfectly. I had yet to add a couple of custom elements, stickers and the like, to this car, but already it was mine. It bore my number – forty-four – and no one else's. It bore my name on the halo: ZAHRANI. My stomach fluttered when I was handed my steering wheel, attaching it to the car as I'd done hundreds of times before. This wasn't the same, though. This was the beginning of something new. I knew it would be difficult, but just like I had known when I decided to sit in a kart for the first time, it only pumped more courage through my veins. I exhaled hard, and I pushed down my visor, awaiting the all-clear from my mechanics, the moment when I could finally give this engine what it had been waiting for.

Finally, the crew rushed away from the car, and the lead mechanic pointed to the exit, beckoning me with a wave and a nod.

I gave the car the slightest bit of throttle, and it was perfect. It responded as if I had been driving it for ages, easing into the turn and gliding onto the pit exit. Then track. Brilliant, endless track stretching out beneath an expansive orange sky, the sun burning bright as it set beneath the asphalt horizon. I could have looked at that sun all day as I drove in complete and utter bliss. Never had I felt this way in a car before. The Jolt Archambeau was a beast, and I was at the helm.

It happened all at once. I was floating across the straight with the biggest grin on my face and no indication whatsoever of any concerns, and then one of my four tyres went flying straight off the rim. My head and stomach both turned, my neck stiffening in automatic response to the strain as my wonderful JA76 spun once, then again, and – with a terrible crunch – hit the wall, remaining tyres the only buffer between the car and oblivion, causing it to bounce into the TecPro barrier. As if adding salt to the wound, the two tyres that had just hit the wall tumbled away, as they too abandoned the body of the car.

I gasped for breath, my engineer's voice over the radio yelling into my ears. 'Diana? Diana, are you all right?'

Well. *That* certainly put the 'test' in 'testing'.

'Yeah,' I harrumphed more than anything else. Oh, of course I was all right. I peeled myself from the seat and hopped out over the mess to get out of the car and inspect the damage. Great; we'd lost three of the four tyres, not to mention bent up the front wing and chassis. My face was going warm, and

I knew that beneath the helmet, I had to be turning red. Tyres did not just *depart the car*. Tyres had to have been screwed on poorly to pop off like that. Someone on the garage team had made a costly mistake on my first lap out.

I held it in the entire walk back to the paddock, even as I had to watch the safety car zoom out onto the track as my wrecked vehicle was airlifted on a crane, a sheet over it like some sort of automobile shroud.

Once I was safe in the garage, in my private room away from prying eyes, I let my fury erupt. This was one thing that had not been stipulated in my contract but was an unspoken understanding: the men could get away with certain things, such as public tantrums, that I couldn't afford. If ever I lost my temper, I made sure I had no other witnesses. I tore off my helmet and threw it a bit too forcefully onto the ground in front of me. I grabbed a pillow off the couch, smothered a scream with it, and added a 'What the hell?' for good measure.

This was supposed to be my team. This was supposed to be my home. And I didn't even have four functioning tyres.

It was going to be a long season.

Chapter Eleven

Miguel

The first race of any F1 season always had to be memorable, though the term 'memorable' meant different things to different drivers. In this case, it could be said that I had some bad blood with this year's opener. The Saudi Arabian Grand Prix, taking place in the winding Jeddah Corniche Circuit, was a sight to behold for spectators looking for action in the desert but, for me, it was a reminder of everything that could go wrong during a GP.

The de la Fuentes boasted that they were Formula 1 through and through, top of their game, and yet I'd done it – I'd proven the cliché to be wrong. I got reckless last year on a treacherous curve in Saudi; suddenly, I was hanging upside down in my car. There was a reason that this track took the moniker of most dangerous F1 street race by a large margin. You had to be driving with the utmost mental strength to make it through successfully.

Nevertheless, our crowd, filling the stands completely, was already abuzz with excited chatter; it was the opposite of the vibe in the motorhome. I hid out in my personal room, stretching my thoracic and, most importantly, doing reflex lights with my trainer. These lights, evenly spaced on the wall, were actually buttons. Whenever one lit up, I slammed it as fast as I could. It might seem like a silly arcade game, but it gave me massive amounts of stress. Reflex lights helped you practise for that last-minute turn or piece of debris; most of all, they prepared you for the second the race began, when you had to go from zero to one-eighty at the start. 'You're doing great. Good time,' Louie, my long-time athletic trainer, commended me. Since I'd started in Formula 3, got to the point where it was necessary to have someone who could provide me with dedicated regimens and ensure that I was at peak physical shape at every turn, I'd been working with Louie. He was the best, in my opinion – at least, I thought so when he wasn't kicking my butt with his exercise plans. 'Keep that up.'

As I bashed the last light, Paula popped her head in, prepared as usual with her two cents. Her hair was thrown up into a bun, and she looked as if she was positively perishing in her team polo and headset, already visibly sweating buckets. 'A talk, Lou?'

Louie nodded and waved her in. Paula ran things around the paddock, but Louie's word was final when it came to the strict parameters he set for – basically – my daily life. Only once Paula had express permission would she disrupt sessions like workouts before GP races.

'We want pole, Mig,' she said plainly. She was very upfront

like that. 'I know you can net it. We need to push and show our might from the get-go. Also. Let us watch Diana. No contact, keep it friendly. Make sure you are giving her room on-track. We don't want to sully our press image. But if it comes down to getting pole, cut her, okay? What is it the kids say? Leave no crumbs.'

'Pole. Don't hit the lady. Got it.'

It wasn't like I could make contact with Diana if I tried, anyway. We were on good terms now, and besides, something about her still seemed to poke at the back of my mind as if trying to provoke a memory. Hitting her would be disastrous beyond the media backlash.

As Q1 dawned upon us, I shifted anxiously in the cockpit of my car, and the announcements blared over the loudspeaker, battling with the sound of engines revving as some teams made their way out of the pits and onto the track.

'You're clear for the track, Miguel,' Paula said over comm. 'Do this right.'

My pit crew backed away, and I turned out of my garage, taking the pit lane onto the track. I could see the curve I'd crashed on from here. It was clear: F1 was a game of the mind. So as I set off on my out lap, I played my own games.

I cast any thoughts from my brain until all I saw were the cars sharing the asphalt with me, to hell with people. It was a dumb way to think, but it was the only way. You either raced like that or you were out of a career. I learned fast that you had no choice if you wanted to stay on the grid.

A faulty engine fired behind me, pulling me from locked-in mode. 'Who's that?'

'Clay for Vittore. Keep on going. Let's start on a flying lap,' Paula ordered.

I sprinted across the start, my time beginning as I hit the main straight with DRS wide open, one eye on my speed.

'Looking good, Mig. Good pace. Steady on the turn.'

I eased up to hit the apex of Turn One perfectly, coming out into Turn Two near effortlessly, then speeding up just enough. No reason to go too crazy burning my tyres on Q1. I finished out the track with what I felt was a decent time, confirmed by Paula.

'All sectors purple. You go P1. One twenty-nine and a tenth.'

'Good. Has Andrea done one yet?'

'Just behind you. He comes out with one twenty-nine and eight-tenths.'

Q1, the eighteen minutes of it, breezed by. I ended up P1, using very little effort. Q2 was similar. According to Paula, Diana clung to P9 to finish out top ten and get a spot in Q3, with Andrea behind me holding P2, and Heidelberg's new wunderkind Darien Cardoso-Magalhães at P3. The Q3 line-up was in, and the final heat was on.

I rendezvoused with Paula and my team in the garage. My sister crouched down beside me as the crew put up my sunshade. 'So far so good,' she said. 'Remember what I told you. We come out of this on pole, *tío*.'

'No less for my favourite *bruja*,' I assured her around a mouthful of electrolyte drink.

'I will pretend I did not hear that.' Paula cleared her throat. 'So. You have been taking it easy, now I need you to go hard. Because I suspect Diana is doing the same. There's no way Jolt took her on to replace Palomas if this is her usual calibre.'

70

'What's that mean? Do what I have to?'

'Don't show all your cards,' warned Paula. 'Play it smart. Use your DRS, but don't make any overtakes that might cause us to crash out. I know you'll do it anyway, but it can happen to anyone.'

With that advice reminiscent of what Palomas had told me in Austin, the Q3 cars aligned in the pit lane to exit. I knew the way things went, but we had some changes in drivers this time around – changes that would shake up how all the rest of us raced.

I came out onto the track sandwiched between Andrea and Peter. 'Diana a few cars away,' said Paula. 'Should not have to worry about messing with her laps.'

We finished our out lap and began the flying lap ready for some action. I pushed the car much harder than I had in the last two sessions, the new model responding perfectly to my every cue. This car, the R3-71, seventy-first of its F1 line as the name suggested, was the most recent and strongest member of the Revello family, with unparalleled speed and handling in response to the FIA's new 2022 regulations. Many a constructor had experienced a decline in the quality of their car due to these rules. Revello was not one of them.

'Go for it on the back curve. DRS on.'

I sped up into Turn Twenty-Two, unencumbered by drag, and zoomed ahead. The crowd roared in the distance, definitely in approval.

'Purple sectors one and two. Let's finish three out strong,' Paula commanded.

I obeyed, foot steady on the gas as I crossed the finish for what I felt was a stellar lap all around.

'Yeah, Mig, that's three purples and you go straight to the top. One twenty-eight and a tenth. I don't think you can be beat with a lap like that.'

'Yes, boys! Who's close?'

'Darien just finished his lap. Still P2 behind you.'

'Okay.'

I went into another rest lap on the outside as the cars still making flying times whizzed past. This pole looked certain. I was practically sitting on P1. The others were seconds behind me, anyway.

'Miguel, I recommend you go for another flying after this,' said Paula, voice hesitant.

'Try to go faster?'

'Yeah, because things are changing here. Russo has got P2. Delta point one-one-five.'

'Got it.'

I tore out of my rest lap back into the straight for a splendid flying lap once more. Q3 was going just how I would have liked by the time I crossed the start one last time, with just enough on the clock for one more flying lap, fully prepared to push even harder than I had before. Which was when I realized that the grid hierarchy was switching up right before my eyes.

'Is that Zahrani taking those turns like that? Wasn't she just struggling in Q2?'

'She is going *fast*, man.' I could hear the anxiety in Paula's tone. 'She goes purple in Sector 1, just ahead of you. Come on, Miguel! This is the last lap you get!'

I gritted my teeth and laid it all down as hard as I could. 'What was that?'

'Still a yellow sector, Miguel. Still yellow. She's heading into Two.'

'Shit!' My wheels bounced right over a curve. I was losing my composure. It was so sudden – Jolt was playing us. I couldn't believe what was going on.

'She goes purple in S2. *Vamos*, Mig!'

'I'm trying!' I yanked the car around the last turn. 'Please tell me that's purple.'

'Okay, so that goes purple.'

'All right. Let's end this.'

Diana leading the train, we soared into Sector Three and down the straight. I both prayed and cursed as she crossed the finish, and I did the same not far behind.

'Diana has gone faster—WAIT, YOU GO DELTA POINT ZERO-ZERO-EIGHT, MIGUEL, YOU BEAT IT!' Paula nearly screamed just as my front wheels crossed the finish line.

'YES!' I whooped.

I could hear the celebration from Paula's end. 'POLE!' I heard my mother yell. 'MY MIGGIE ON POLE!' It was pretty much the best sound I had ever heard.

'*So* damn close!' said Paula over radio. 'What a quali, Mig, well done!'

The grandstand too was in a twist after such a tight qualifying, but they went insane as I passed them, collecting the applause I couldn't hear through the exhilaration on their faces. I docked at the first-place sign and leaped out of the car on a dishevelled high to embrace my crew over the fence, back-thumping abounding. There was no feeling like this: the very top of motorsport. You had that advantage locked in for the race, which meant you got to worry that much less.

After the team, I met Diana's car at the second marker just as it came to a stop, the floodlights glistening against the shiny black paint of the body. She'd given me the qualifier of my life. I don't think I had ever raced anyone to such tiny points of a second, and that too on her first quali. I was short of words.

Diana flipped up her visor. Breathless, I rushed over to her, and that strange, indescribable recognition I'd felt when we had dinner that day in Mexico now flickered clearly as day in her irises, eyes that threatened to hook mine and keep me there all night. We yanked off our helmets and our balaclavas, and this woman, I don't know if it was the smile on her face, or the flush in her cheeks, or the way the lines from the helmet etched her skin, but I couldn't *not* focus on her.

'Brilliant,' I finally managed. 'You're brilliant.'

Chapter Twelve

Diana

'Brilliant,' said Miguel de la Fuente.

The way his gaze held mine made me acutely aware of the stray hair sticking up all over from the crown of braids hanging on to my scalp. My mother used to say I looked like a cavewoman when I got out of the car, all nasty and sweaty, curls matted. But it didn't seem like Miguel cared. He took me in with an expression of awe I had never seen from anyone else, stirring up a tingling in my fingers that had me pulling off my gloves to rub my palms against my thighs.

'You're one to talk.' A grin finally slipped out, a gesture I could no longer hold in. Something about that connection that had formed between us when our cars pulled up alongside one another and our eyes had met was compelling me beyond my senses. 'Mister Pole.'

'You were less than a millisecond out, *tía*!' He grinned right back. 'You are as much pole as I am.'

I waved a dismissive hand, ignoring a little hop-skip of my heart. 'Celebrate. You've earned it. Just know I will be right there beside you to take the gap if you mess up tomorrow.'

He let out a laugh, a wonderfully husky rumble that I wanted to feel rather than hear. I blinked. *Stop it, Di.* 'In your dreams,' quipped Miguel, though he was still smiling.

My eyes flicked to the cameras for just a moment. It was a lot – a lot more than Formula 2. They were everywhere on the track, getting footage of the cars post-quali and hovering around us. I thought I had moved fast enough, but Miguel caught the gesture. 'What's up?'

'Weird. They're all watching us,' I said, my voice catching with nerves.

'Watching you,' he corrected me.

'That does not help my anxiety.'

Miguel chuckled nervously. Nervous, and Miguel de la Fuente? I thought I'd imagined it, but there was certainly a tinge of something there. He turned to me, meeting my eyes directly. 'I get that it's terrifying. It always is when you first race in Formula 1. But, Diana . . . they've never seen anyone like you before. None of us have. I know . . . I mean, I haven't.'

My pulse quickened as blood rushed behind my ears, drowning out the sounds of the roaring crowd and shouting journalists. My heart was thudding against my ribs so hard that I felt it would punch a hole through my chest. 'Good thing or bad thing?' I asked.

'Good.' He exhaled, a kind of placidity entering his face as he peered at a camera, and then back at me, that hint of admiration still heavy in his eyes. 'Definitely good.'

76

The moment was quickly broken by a particularly aggressive shout from a man beckoning a tall woman through the crowd, her microphone bearing the logo of the Formula 1 series' primary broadcaster: the big leagues were here.

'Just take a deep breath and answer them honestly but carefully.' Miguel shot me one last smile. 'You got this.'

We went our separate ways, me to the reporter and him to Darien, who had made third position. Perhaps accidentally, his hand brushed the arm of my suit as he headed off. I pursed my lips, my gaze travelling to the spot that he had just touched, whether knowingly or unknowingly.

Stupid.

I laughed quietly under my breath with a shake of my head and stepped forward to answer my questions.

It wasn't as if I had any exciting pre-race rituals, which many pilots did. In that way, I was boring. I turned on some old Warda in the garage to calm my nerves, checked my layers to make sure they were FIA-approved, removed my jewellery, and warmed up: brutal squats, quick reflex activities. I didn't play any hype songs, just let Warda transport me to some quiet desert island where it was just me, and my life's dreams weren't hinging on the race to come.

I'd done this a thousand times, except now it was different. Now, I was in Formula 1. I was coming out of the gate in the front row for today's race in Saudi. I'd already seen the memes about how I was wrecking everyone's fantasy teams after my quali and – guiltily – I was elated.

I used the outside mirror to reapply my kohl right before the race (could not drive without the appropriate evil eye measures). Ever so sneakily, I smeared a fingerful of the chalky black behind the right mirror of my JA76.

Okay, so I had pre-race rituals, but that did not make them exciting. However, they had become iconic in the wrong sense. When I was karting, someone once started a rumour that my applying kohl to the car had to do with black magic of some sort, which, among many other so-called offences – including but not limited to being a woman – did not do my reputation much good. Ever since then, I attempted to be as stealthy as possible in carrying out any good-luck manoeuvres prior to the races. People would take anything you did and turn it into a story.

'All eyes on you and de la Fuente,' the team principal, Theo Cavanaugh, remarked as I checked the car. 'Ready for a fantastic performance today, yeah?'

I nodded absently, shooting him a vacant smile. He was very nice to me, obviously, but probably for the same reason he was nice to the devil incarnate that was Kasper Ramsey: because I was an investment that had seemingly begun to pay off. And either way, my mind was only on one thing in that moment. Or maybe two. Maybe my encounter with Miguel after the qualifying. Maybe—

'Could we check that all four tyres are screwed in again?' I asked a mechanic. He glowed a pale pink before nodding and calling his colleagues to fulfil the request.

'I suppose the song of the day for you would be "Hit the Road, Jack", then?' my engineer, Aiden, chuckled.

'I think I have to agree,' I said with a laugh. I hadn't known Aiden for long, but we had become fast friends. He lived in a flat in Kensington with his husband and two dogs. His favourite movie was *Titanic*, and he made the most delicious tea cakes while we were on the road. I adored him.

'I'm not gonna give you instructions,' Aiden said, forcing me to stop zoning out and give him my full attention. 'I think you know how you're gonna play this. I just don't want you going into corners with that oversteer you tend to use. Race wisely and play your aces sparingly. I'll see you on podium, speed demon.'

Aiden gave my shoulder a reassuring squeeze, which did little to ease the nerves bouncing through my body like popcorn kernels in the microwave bag.

'I don't know.' I lowered my voice. 'So many of these people have been so kind to me.' *Miguel.* 'Why does overtaking them just feel . . . wrong?'

'Overtaking *always* feels wrong, remember, Di?' Aiden smiled almost sympathetically. 'It's up to you what you choose to do in the end.'

I chewed on my bottom lip in thought. 'Yeah.'

Aiden nestled his headset atop his neatly cropped blond hair, logging onto his screens. I made my way to the JA76, pulled up my jumpsuit to zip it up, and traded my cap for my balaclava and helmet.

Prep flew by in a haze. I was out of it, sitting in the grid after formation lap before I knew it. Mind full of anxiety, I waited for escape.

As the lights began to flash on behind me and I got on the clutch, I saw the route I'd taken to get here. So many challenges, so much I had to cut through, so much red tape. My relatives' baffled expressions when my parents told them with pride that their daughter would race Formula 1 someday. The sting of the slaps from the aunties who insisted I come back to reality and look for a husband. The rocks through our windows wrapped in notes condemning our family for breaking local law. The booing at my first Saudi race, where I thought I'd have an adoring home crowd looking out for me. Every slur, every attempt to stop me from racing, every friend who left my side – all of it fuelled my anger in the moment. My car's engine roared.

This race was for all those people. Because they could suck it when my parents told them that yes, Diana Zahrani had raced in Formula 1 on the front row, in Jeddah, and the crowd had done nothing but cheered her on.

The lights went out.

I surged right ahead. I told myself that I would do whatever I had to so I could bring this trophy home. Jolt could market me as their airheaded Arab bimbo all they liked. I was, on the contrary, here to win.

I cruised along the inner after a less-than-ideal start that had me on edge, and as per Aiden's advice over the radio, I defended until I had about fifteen laps left in the race.

'You're at P5, Diana,' said Aiden. 'Kasper on your rear, so I want you to get aggressive now. Next is Peter. Let's see it.'

I tapped the gas. The car zoomed ahead, pushing one-eighty. Fences flew past as I caught up to Peter Albrecht in the next couple of laps and finally rounded him, cringing internally. All was fair in Formula 1, right?

'P4. You want podium, Diana?'

'Copy.'

'You want podium?' he repeated, raising his voice.

'Like hell!'

'Then let's pick that pace up. Come on, Diana. We want to see you cross that finish first.'

As the race wore on, it became less likely that I'd get to P1. I was almost relieved when I realized my car wouldn't get close to touching Miguel's. But P3 . . . podium. It was right there. It was right there in the form of Russo's rear vibrating just in front of me.

This is a gap. Take it.

Barring all fear, with a lap left to race, I did. I took that gap. I sprinted past Andrea Russo when my DRS opened on the main straight, and when I heard Aiden yell into my radio, I couldn't comprehend what had just happened as I crossed the finish.

'Yes, Diana, that's P3!'

'Excellent! Excellent, thank you all so much!'

'Stellar going, Diana. So excited to call myself your engineer. On behalf of all of us in the paddock, welcome to Jolt Archambeau Racing.'

That last formation lap was one of the best memories of my life. Everyone in the stands was going crazy; all the fans, not just mine. I was stunned to realize that yes, this was much more than myself. This was a woman placing podium on a Formula 1 Grand Prix after a lifetime of looking up to the ones who'd come before her, after so many others who had made it possible for her. I had this chance to show everyone what *all* of us were capable of. Especially the little girls who wanted to race but thought they couldn't. It was only a thought – that was it. And if we wore on, motivation waning at every bump in the road, thinking those negatives were reality, we would never win any race, whether that was the race on-track or in our lives.

I parked my car at the P3 marker. I took off my helmet, ran straight to the red plastic board with the huge white number three, and gave it a massive hug, heedless of the bright flashes of cameras all around me going off as press attempted to capture every second of my celebration. I didn't care how stupid I looked. I wanted to cherish everything I was feeling in this moment.

As I was disentangling myself from the large P3, I heard Miguel's voice from his place at P1.

'You're fucking dangerous!' he yelled from next to me with a laugh, the wire of his radio swinging as he lifted his own helmet to reveal eyes creased with excitement and a face shimmering with sweat. 'Damn good racing!'

I grinned wide. This was it. Young Diana, shy and reclusive, had seen hopes of this from behind the barrier separating women and the rest of the world in Saudi.

Miguel extended a hand, and I took it gladly. The mere contact, even through gloves, sent waves of warmth up my entire arm as he bumped shoulders with me. It was a typical man move, what so many of the drivers did after races, and maybe I would have thought less of it if I didn't feel his other hand at my waist for but a second.

Was I hallucinating?

I definitely wasn't. I felt that thudding of my dumb heart again, as if confirming my suspicions. Something was certainly going on. Something more than the simple fact that taking his hand was a memory I suddenly recalled as clear as crystal, a memory I prayed that, maybe, he did too. Could that have been the reason he'd got that glint in his eyes? Could it be that Miguel de la Fuente was suffering this same bout of confusion and emotions as I was?

I didn't dwell on it. I let go of my delusions and made my way over to my team to jump the fence and celebrate till I was told to do my required media duties at the interview station on the track.

The journalist that met me there, a tall woman in a red suit, was clearly ecstatic. 'Well, first and foremost, Diana, congratulations and we look forward to you claiming your trophy on the podium. Diana – you are the *first* woman to stand on the Formula 1 podium as a driver in *years*. How do you feel?'

'I . . .' Words were failing me. 'I want, I want to say I'm still processing it. We only go up from here. I wanna thank my parents, who can't be here today, but who are watching from home, and I thank Jolt for believing in me. Thank the Emirates for all their support and their funding, for letting me be their Falcon this year. Thank Lella Lombardi for scoring those very first points that allowed us to break into this male-dominated sport today. I'm just thankful, I guess, for the support.'

'Thank no one but yourself,' said the journalist with a smile. 'This is your work. You brought yourself here over the years. I can speak for us all when I say we hope to see you as a grand prix winner as well.'

I let myself run through those words as I set foot on the podium and took my place on the P3 step with Miguel and Darien on P1 and P2. I was given my trophy, which I raised high in the air above my head. Confetti hit the bill of my Championship cap, and my eyes brimmed with tears. Miguel and I exchanged a look of sheer pride and, regardless of my crying, I smiled without restraint, gripping my trophy tight. I liked to think I had the right to shed a few tears after all this time.

Chapter Thirteen

Miguel

I would have loved to spend all week rejoicing in my season-opener first place, not to mention the podium that Diana Zahrani had nabbed, but the morning after the race was unfortunately slated for last-minute team press conferences about how Diana Zahrani had snatched the podium from Andrea Russo's grasp. Revello had made a strange 1-4 with a far better car than Jolt's, and people, of course, rather than accepting the fact that there was a very talented new driver on the grid, wanted to ask questions.

Excitement was obviously still in the air, but Revello higher-ups had instructed myself, Andrea, and the rest of the team to keep an air of seriousness. See, we couldn't look *too* happy for Jolt, seeing as one of our drivers had been outperformed by – oh no! – a woman. That was what we anticipated the interviewer would lead the session with.

The Revello team gathered in the press room at that point

to watch the interview. Team interviews meant that Andrea and I would be interrogated at once, as would each pair of drivers in the other teams. Jolt had gone prior to us and, though I was hoping to get a glimpse of Diana, their team had already cleared out. A few of the other members, including Paula, Andrea's engineer, and our team principal, Cristoforo Montalto, gathered behind the camera while Andrea and I sat down before it. The interviewer, a lanky man with thick glasses, named Brian Crowberry, nodded our way.

'So, we'd first love to congratulate the boys on a great finish yesterday,' Crowberry began. 'Getting right into the points is not a bad start to the season. And, Miguel, a special congratulations to you as you've won the first grand prix of 2022.'

Andrea had apparently not received the seriousness memo, because an eye roll on his part sneaked out. It was very noticeable. I could already see it breaking Twitter.

'It's becoming a bit clearer that Jolt is a worthy competitor, as Mr Montalto has told us, but why don't you tell us about this race, Miguel?' asked Crowberry.

'Well, I would say this is only one of twenty-three. We put forward our best Revello foot, and yes, we are still learning this new car, I know I am, but we did hold up a good race,' I replied. 'While the safety car set me back a bit, I was able to recover, and I am really happy with this win, even if we have a way to go. Andrea?'

I was lying through my teeth, obviously. I knew Paula would be able to tell, at the very least. Sure, I'd won, I couldn't be too upset, but I'd gone full push, and Andrea had dropped the ball for Revello as a team: no strategy issues, no pitting issues, nothing. This guy had simply underperformed.

'Yeah, uh, I think Miguel about covered it. You know, the safety car really messed my run up. It is disappointing missing the podium, missing a one-two or a two-three, but I agree, it was a good performance. We'll show up with even more at Imola.' It was obvious that Andrea too was concealing his anger and, against the norms of sports interviews, his piss-poor sore loser attitude. Obviously, no one had expected Diana Zahrani to blaze onto the track like an atom bomb, but Andrea and his fellow backwards men in motorsport probably felt the shock more than the rest of us.

'Great. And this one is for Andrea,' Crowberry continued. Andrea visibly winced in his chair. 'We all saw the vicious mid-race overtake you suffered at Diana Zahrani's hand, and we heard something on the radio.'

Andrea only sank lower in his seat. I had a feeling he, like the rest of us, knew exactly what was coming. I held back an evil smirk.

'I have it here with me.' Crowberry read from a notepad off-camera. 'You said, and I quote, "This *redacted*! She's out of *redacted* control! *Redacted!*" End quote.'

Andrea gulped before adjusting his mic. 'Yes. Um. Emotions were running, just running a little high.'

'Ah, I see. Anyhow, I was asked to pass on a message regarding this radio from Jolt's conference just before this one. This response, we obtained from Zahrani.' Crowberry cleared his throat and consulted his notepad once more. Oh, boy. 'Her reply: "Andrea – the next time you cuss me out, call me by name."'

Cristo Montalto's mouth made a very appalled O. I pursed my lips, biting down peals of laughter that would probably make me as big a Twitter meme as my teammate.

'Next, then,' Crowberry segued awkwardly, 'to Miguel. What, if anything, does this sudden podium by Zahrani say about this season? As Paula has said, this is something she's wanted for a while, a woman driving Formula 1.'

'Yes, I'm pro-Diana,' my sister called from behind the camera, and I finally burst out laughing.

'We're both pro-Diana,' I corrected with a smile. 'I honestly cannot wait for Imola for that reason. Some people have said to me, "Oh, you should not fear a woman." But that's classless. Diana is a *great* driver. I did fight her a bit at the beginning. She fought, even though she didn't get off too well, and she was in strong form. It's a feat to climb up to the podium the way she did on her first race here.'

'So what's the dynamic between you and your sister in regards to Zahrani's addition to the grid?' Crowberry added.

'She loves Diana, but we both know that this all comes down to business on the track.' I tried to choose my words wisely.

'And, Miguel, is it true that you're rather friendly with Zahrani as well?' Great, Crowberry's calling card: tabloid-esque questions that were intended to stir up gossip. I internally rolled my eyes. 'Or so we might assume from the interactions of this weekend.'

'You people will use anything for a headline,' I said, adding a chuckle that I hoped concealed the way my voice quavered merely at the thought of this weekend.

The way my legs went weak when she looked at me like that. The way she *drove*.

'I've only just met Diana. As I said, she's a great driver, and I wholly respect that. I respect her tenacity in the face of driving bans and everything she's overcome to get here. It's only

88

common decency to befriend someone with such a bright spirit, someone so extremely—'

'Driven,' Paula helped me out, causing laughter all around.

'Yeah,' I agreed, smiling. 'Besides, that is the true spirit of Formula 1. Yes, we are all here for the trophies and the glory, but we respect each other's journeys to this grid, and that should link us all together. Make us a family.'

Cristo looked quite happy with that. With a teammate like Andrea, I had to play press darling, always representing Revello justly. I knew it was a de la Fuente thing to make the media happy, and no doubt part of why the F1 circuit kept us around.

'You handled that well,' Paula told me as we exited the press room.

I smirked. 'I've been told I do so periodically.'

'*Claro.*' She raised an eyebrow as we walked down the hall of our Jeddah hotel. We would retrieve our bags and get on our way as soon as we could, the rush of it all no different from any other grand prix. 'I have been meaning to ask, though. How did the tacos go? Very well, I presume, by the interactions I saw after yesterday's race?'

'Yes, well. Almost too well. I ought to thank you for that,' I teased her. The light tone in my voice concealed a pang of something else. Something that made me think of the weird feeling of déjà vu we seemed to share that day in the restaurant, and every time we'd crossed paths since. 'We reconnected in Mexico. Nothing but good in store for our Jolt bridges. On the flip side, it'll make it harder to try to push Diana next race. She's a real one.'

'You two are more similar than you realize,' Paula pointed out, nudging my elbow. 'The honesty, the kindness, the attitude you both have.'

89

'The attitude,' I echoed with a laugh. 'Come on, I don't even begin to approach Diana. She's got so much unspoken attitude it's almost scary. All in her eyes, so much bite. I avoid passing her before races just so I don't crap myself, and yet she's one of the friendliest people I've met.'

'Oh.' Paula snorted. 'Just don't get too friendly. You are betrothed, my dear, and you've got a reputation to watch.'

I rolled my eyes so hard that everything went dark for a second. 'Come on, Pauli, who you taking me for? You sound like 'Buelo. I can already hear him.'

'He would be all over you for fraternizing with the enemy of tradition,' she said sarcastically. Our grandpa, our father's father, as prim and proper as he was, never missed the opportunity to drop an out-of-pocket remark here and there.

'Right. And plus . . .' I pulled a velvet-covered box from my pocket.

Paula gasped quietly. 'Is that . . .?'

'French pavé. Four-carat diamond.'

'But *dios* . . . that's got to be . . .'

'Over a hundred thousand.' I almost mouthed the number, but I shrugged indifferently. It was a necessity, anyway. Didn't matter that the box had felt like a lead weight in my pocket all day, that it felt like a bandage I was trying to press to a gushing cut. 'You said it, we're betrothed. It's time for me to pull my end of the bargain. For Ziry.'

'My, oh my,' my sister quipped, quite amazed at the hundred-thousand-euro rock that her brother was casually carrying around. 'You are really serious about this, Miguel.'

Damn it. She was doing this again.

Being so much older than me, I guess Paula felt as though

90

she had seen my entire progression through life so far, the way racing slowly became my '*raison d'être*' (I didn't know what this meant, but she did, because she'd learned it in her fancy private school and brought it home to me one day). And then, eight years ago, our parents and Jatziry's parents had sat down in the living room of our home in Barcelona. They'd decided that I would marry Jatziry when I turned twenty-five. I'd been sixteen back then. Jatziry was fourteen.

'Had the two of you even wanted it?' she blurted. 'You were just kids.'

'*Vale*, Pauli, what's going on?' We stopped at our elevator. I jabbed the up button before turning her way with a huff. 'You always sound so surprised about Jatziry and me. We were young. I get that. But you know as well as I do that this is how it goes, man. I'm playing with the cards I was dealt. I'm not lying to anyone's face here.'

Part of me wondered if all her scepticism was just because Mamá and Papá couldn't get past her insistence at that age. Paula was smart – really smart – and she refused to concentrate on anything that was not auto engineering. I guess they decided they had to tie me down. And Jatziry . . . Jatziry was the collateral.

'I never said you were lying,' my sister said.

'Bullshit. You were surprised that I first wanted to go talk to her after Austin. Then, when I offered to bring her with me for a few GPs this season. Now the sarcasm about "betrothal" and "getting too friendly" and how you looked when I showed you the ring,' I shot back. 'Why are you asking if I'm serious?'

'Miguel, I think you are in that phase of your career,' Paula finally admitted. 'You are just trying to compensate for the risk of what you do, the guilt attached to it. It isn't like either of you had the arrangement on your minds till that crash.'

'That *changed* things,' I groaned. My sister had the ability to suck all the energy out of me and leave me feeling like I'd run five marathons back-to-back. I hated it. 'If I . . . God forbid, Pauli, if something happened to me, think about it, the *one* person I would not have done right by would be Jatziry. Like, come on, at least I can fix things now . . . so let me fix things, Paula!'

'Expensive gifts are not a fix,' said Paula stiffly, the tone that told me I was being a dumb little boy starting to creep into her voice. 'Taking her to the races with you is not a fix. You don't go from partying and drinking and going insane on the weekends and blacking out on Sunday nights to being a dutiful fiancé, Miggie. This . . . this is just too drastic for me to believe that you've suddenly sworn yourself to living like this. Are these really your emotions, your wishes? Is this where you see yourself once this season ends: married?'

The elevator doors opened. We stepped inside. Our security detail made to join us, but I held out a hand. *No.*

We waited till the doors closed.

'This is my *obligation* to Jatziry,' I replied through gritted teeth. 'You shouldn't judge something greater than ourselves. This is our legacy.'

'I am your sister, Miguel.'

'And Jatziry will be my wife,' I fired back so quickly it seemed instinctive.

Paula didn't push it any more than that. But I could not shake the gut feeling that she was right, and I was lying – to myself and to Jatziry.

Chapter Fourteen

Miguel

Since we had just arrived in Imola yesterday, and I tended to get heavily jet-lagged, I wanted nothing more than to jump right into bed and sleep for twelve hours straight. Instead, I smoothed one last wrinkle from my suit jacket, stifling a yawn. The only thing saving me from appearing absolutely decrepit now was Jatziry's under-eye concealer. I'd have to pray I could hold up well enough at this evening's event that no one would make out the full extent of my exhaustion.

In many ways, you could never attend anything as lavish as the Imola Drivers' Dinner. It felt like an almost Regency-era tradition, with men in suits and women in ridiculous dresses, twenty drivers and their immediate team members in the more official black-tie edition of Jolt's embarrassing pre-season launch. I was flabbergasted when Prada itself reached out and struck a deal with Revello to dress our team from now through to season's end, replacing the old policy of 'whichever suit you want, as long as you iron the patch on it'. It gave off the vibes of a Catholic school uniform, but I wasn't complaining – it was the most comfortable suit I'd ever worn.

As you might imagine, the idea of a gala made Jatziry very happy. This was good, because after Paula's words drove daggers beneath my skin – 'Is this where you see yourself?' – the uncertainty had begun to seep in. I tried to block it out. I had convinced myself that this, well, it was where both of us were meant to be.

'I'd love to try to get a place over you this weekend.'

Andrea Russo really thought he was being smart. I rolled my eyes internally. We drove the exact same cars, save for a few customizations, which meant that his shortcomings should be attributed entirely to his driving skill.

Beside me, Jatziry looked as bored as I felt, her arm through mine so the glimmering ring I'd finally worked up the courage to give her last evening was visible. She wore a beautiful red dinner gown, with ruffles like a flamenco dancer's, giving her the appearance of a high-class Spanish princess. Her hair was tied into a sleek ponytail with a crimson silk ribbon. She was gorgeous, easily outdoing the Revello men in their uniform black suits bearing the crown and shield emblem above the breast. Paula, unfortunately, had also been designated a uniform suit, but with a horrid skirt version rather than the trousers. She'd rejected it in favour of one of my mother's old dresses from when Mamá would attend galas with Papá when he raced for Vittore in its prime: a black, mermaid-style gown that stood the test of time. I didn't see her now, though, since she was probably steering clear of both myself and the topic of our sordid argument back in Jeddah: Jatziry.

'I'd love to see you try,' I said to Andrea, as if I were just joking very politely, something I wasn't actually doing. This guy's audacity baffled me.

'Oh, look, there's Diana!' Jatziry came in clutch. 'Why don't we speak with her, Miguel?'

She tactfully separated our presence from Andrea's. We moved in the direction of Diana Zahrani, who was laughing with Nic Necci and Alex Romilly.

Diana was excellent at making friends. She had that likeable nature that meant half the grid would easily count themselves as a ride-or-die for her, and a fraction of those drivers had fallen in love with her already. It probably wasn't making it easier that she looked like the true queen of the circuit. She was ethereal in a traditional blue silk kaftan dress, with borders embroidered delicately in gold and a matching belt around her waist that called very minimal attention to her, something that her natural glow did instead. Her hair fell down her back in sheets of glistening black, and her eyes contained all the attitude they usually did, offset by perfect wings of onyx eyeliner. The way she talked so happily, so completely oblivious, I still couldn't look away, and I still had no words as to *why*.

'Well, hello there, everyone,' Jatziry segued smoothly, ever the diplomat. 'Andrea is on quite the ego kick tonight, hmm?'

I hoped Andrea didn't see the dirty look I shot him as he gallivanted about with the daughter of Wilson Nitro's wizened team principal, brown hair plastered with gel, moving barely an inch in his animated, falsified conversational gestures.

'As always,' said Alex.

'He's one of a kind,' Diana remarked, eyes tracking Andrea unhappily. 'And not in a good way.'

Nic nudged her. 'Look at how far up his ass his head's gone, Di.'

'Dude! This is a gala,' Alex prodded his teammate.

'Okay, little boy.'

Such was the brotherly relationship between Alex and Nic. The tightest pair on the grid, Nic had taken an eighteen-year-old Alex under his wing when joining Griffith in 2020, the same year I left Vittore for Revello. The two of them, both Brits born out of country and raised just an hour from one another, had bonded immediately. To this day, Nic still treated Alex as the 'little brother', despite his being quite grown, which made him the baby of the pack to every other Formula 1 driver.

'He's right, though,' agreed Diana. 'This fool does have his head up his ass.'

'Talking to him was like walking on hot coals,' Jatziry added. 'He thinks he can outplace Miguel.'

'He'd have to outplace Diana first,' Alex joked. 'And he would come out with scratch marks all over his pretty face. Miguel and Darien only got lucky.'

'Hey.' Diana elbowed Alex jestingly, making his champagne slosh in its glass. 'Careful with your words, dude.'

'Aptly put from the woman now referred to as *Danger*,' said Nic with a smile. 'Remember what you said, Miguel? "Fucking dangerous", you called Diana? Turns out it's stuck.'

'As it should.' I raised my glass, my eyes flitting to Diana, and hers to me. The brief, almost bashful celebration we shared in this moment made me go totally light-headed. 'To Danger.'

'To Danger,' our little circle echoed, and we all clinked flutes.

Diana smiled my way. 'Thanks,' she mouthed.

'Don't mention it,' I mouthed back.

We sat down at the huge dinner table soon after. Naturally, like at Jolt's season opener bash, everyone was placed according to teams, and then by constructor alliances. Unfortunately, in some cases, this put teammates together. We had to contend with Andrea, while Diana dealt with Kasper Ramsey and the rest of Jolt. To my left sat Peter Albrecht and Darien Cardoso-Magalhães with Heidelberg's clan, and to my right, between our Revello section and Jolt, were Alex and Nic for Griffith.

As dinner came out, more gossip made the rounds. Darien brought up the Formula 1 video game with the glitch that made everyone's player avatar turn into Miguel de la Fuente. Something stung in my chest when I watched the way Diana and Nic, of all people, were laughing so easily over something as silly as my dumb character bug.

And then Nic put an arm on the back of Diana's chair, and she didn't protest, just smiled. She looked at him like he was the only human in the room. It was a very special ability that I wanted to believe Diana had with everyone.

Also, when Diana laughed, Nic looked at *her* like *she* was the only human in the room; this was how I realized that Nic was one of the drivers in the 'falling' category of Diana's on-grid allies. Every expression on his face mirrored hers. He was in awe of her, Nic. I felt my heart wrench the moment I realized that I was, too. I just didn't have the liberty to show it.

Anyway, Nic was a great guy, and if anyone did fall for Diana and get fallen for by Diana, all the better it was someone like him.

The event in full swing, our rotations around the room were interrupted by a blunt text from Paula telling me I was needed in Conference Room 1D. With a groan, I promised Jatziry I'd return and set back off downstairs.

'This is just you,' I noted wisely as I entered the conference room. It was true. Only my sister sat at a chair off to the side of the rectangular table.

She gestured to the seat across from her with a sigh. 'Listen, Miguel—'

'Is this about Revello?'

'No.' Paula waited as I took the seat. 'I would like to apologize. To you and Jatziry, as it were.'

My eyebrows drifted upwards. Paula wasn't an apologizer. She resolved things. She said men in her position never apologized, so there was no reason she should have to. I almost felt bad, even though I realized what she was apologizing for.

Idly, Paula adjusted a stray ruffle in her gown. 'I did overstep, Miguel. I admit it. *Es tu vida*. If you want this, I'll not complain. Jatziry is a wonderful girl. Our family adores her, you adore her. I just . . . I think I am finding it hard to accept that you're growing up.'

She looked pained. I waited a beat. And then I let myself crack a smile. 'Now that is truly surprising.'

Paula almost exhaled in relief, returning my smile. 'Mig, I'm just proud of you. I don't want to ruin that, and if I am proud of you, I guess I ought to trust you.'

'Just a little.'

'Yes.' She chuckled before her tone turned more serious. 'But . . . I still care about you, *tío*. So if something is *ever* off, even if it's awkward or stupid, please tell me.'

I let out a laugh. 'Ya, Pauli, come here.'

I reached out and gave my sister a hug. It was the first time in too long that I'd hugged her. She was inches shorter than me, which made me feel almost protective of her. Yet she was still my big sister, the person who'd go against the world if the world was against me.

I almost said it, how she was right sometimes. How I questioned this choice on occasion, how Nic's arm on that chair grasped at my lungs. How maybe, I wanted more than this predestined future. Everything had been decided for me since I was a child. What was good, what was bad. Maybe I wanted to burst out of the mould and choose for once. Fall in love rather than wait for it to come to me, like gradual relief from a bad head cold. But I guess I *was* protecting Paula from my mistakes. Because I didn't say a thing.

Chapter Fifteen

Diana

When I was signing all the fans' things the day before, upon Imola arrival, I'd scrawled my name on one girl's karting helmet. It made my heart sing to think of her wearing it. Anyway, I put my name to it, and she said, 'Can I ask you a question?'

I nodded, smiling. She didn't look any older than fifteen or sixteen, dark hair and eyes. Reminded me of myself, same colour helmet (white and chrome).

'Do you ever feel alone?'

I met her expectant gaze, still full of dreams at such a tender age. And I said, 'All the time.'

I wrote something else on her helmet before returning it to her: *Never doubt yourself.*

In Formula 3, they once had a therapist come talk to us about mental health for race-car drivers. At that time, it was something most drivers chose to ignore out of pride, myself included, until the therapist looked directly at me – the lone woman, even then. 'There's also the silent career killer: imposter syndrome,' she deadpanned.

One minute I'd be on top of the world, celebrating a grand prix podium, popping champagne all over the place, and the next, waves of self-doubt and loneliness hit hard. Why did Jolt really put me here? And, despite acceptance from most of the grid, why did I always feel so isolated? Why did writing to that girl that she should never doubt feel like a lie spoken right through my teeth?

These lies started early on, a rollercoaster of emotions that I concealed from the beginning of my professional career. It began after Baba's accident, which meant he and Ammi could no longer come to my races. I was just starting F3 at that time, and I felt as if I'd lost my whole cheering section. Even as I won race after race and smiled from P1 with the trophy hefted high above my head, as my grandstand section grew to fans bringing DECK 'EM, DIANA posters to races, I missed the people who had raised both Diana Zahrani and Number Forty-Four. My parents had always pushed me to race when everyone else scoffed. They never once buckled under the societal pressure. They were the reason I was in Formula 1. If they hadn't been there, I might as well have quit at the first sign of criticism back in karting.

Talking to Nic Necci back at the dinner was like soaring at the top of that rollercoaster. He was a development I had not foreseen prior to this dinner: a grey-eyed, brown-haired angel in the body of a Formula 1 driver, it seemed, with a heavenly smile and a wonderful laugh, gentle-mannered and observant. I didn't think he'd so much as glanced my way earlier, till I picked up on it that evening; till he sat down next to me and struck up conversation, almost sheepishly. I warmed to him relatively easily, especially considering that the nature of my career goals meant I had tended to avoid showing any warmth to other drivers over the years. Media would say things any chance they got; and yet now I thought, why not? Why not do something different?

And either way, very few people genuinely cared, and I think it was just heartening to see affection in his eyes. I hoped he saw it in mine, too, that we connected so easily. I was still learning about the Formula 1 world step by step, still learning how it felt to have Nic's arm around me. And guiltily, for reasons beyond what I could put into words, it reminded me of Miguel, of taking his hand and remembering that he, too, cared. I felt terrible when I thought things like that because of how happy he was with Jatziry, and how she, too, was struggling to figure out the intricacies of Formula 1.

I opened my suitcase and traced the print running along the leg pocket of my jumpsuit: *RAMISSA*, a combination of my dad's name, Rami, and my mom's, Elissa. People still had odd theories about the name as I'd never confirmed it. One viral tweet claimed it was my (nonexistent) daughter's name, a rumour started by the livery department when I asked them to put the same decal on the halo of my JA76, the part of the car that had already saved the lives of so many drivers in sickening crashes and might one day save mine. It only seemed fair that my parents' names should be written across it.

Again, for them, I told myself. Do it once more, and do it better than ever before.

* * *

102

I was quickly tiring of the press conferences, but I was contracted to do them, so I ended up in a pre-race interview Thursday night before practices began the next morning. And this one was Revello–Jolt–Griffith, a feast for the vultures due to the cutthroat competition between the teams that had reared its ugly head last year. Everyone was wondering whether Griffith could make up for their missed chances and climb the grid to get on Jolt's ass. I, however, was just fending off the loud thumping of my own heart as I took my seat at the panel table beside Nic Necci, who was quickly becoming my safe place.

We exchanged a smile, his much the same as mine: reluctant, bashful. I waved hi to Alex, and he waved back, perky as usual. I was jealous of his ability to be so present *sans* coffee. Further down the table, past Kasper, I saw Miguel and Andrea, stars of last season. I'd been watching the reels – no wonder Jolt were pushing so hard. They'd fallen just short of producing a champion of the world in my predecessor, Eduardo Palomas, and although Revello had faced the same problem, both their drivers landed on the podium for the Championship. Jolt had missed out, big time.

'Good morning!' Alex said happily into his mic. 'Why don't we get started, Brian? We don't want to be here any more than . . . well, I think *you* want to be here. Never mind.'

'May we start with the Imola outlook?' the interviewer, Brian Crowberry, kicked it off, ignoring Alex's bold statement. 'Right now, Revello are still the favourites.'

'Not for long,' quipped Kasper Ramsey, faking a teasing smile my way. 'Isn't it, mate?'

'So you're referring to Diana?' Miguel shot back. I could not help but let a little grin slip out as everyone laughed at that one. Miguel winked, and I think I forgot how to let air out of my lungs. I prayed it didn't show.

The chatter on Imola continued. We ruminated about our cars, about the takeaways from Jeddah that we'd carry with us to this race. This realm of conversation was safe: no controversy, just facts. It did not last, though, because soon we headed into uncharted territory.

'And, Diana, how are you doing in terms of this new environment, these new people? How's it been?'

Cameras flashed as I spoke carefully. 'It's going well. I wasn't expecting to make so many friends here.'

'Miguel, we hear that you're one of those friends Diana's made, a close one, at that,' Crowberry pushed. 'What's that like?'

'Like you and your friends, I guess.' Miguel laughed. 'I mean, I've gotten to sit down with all the guys at this table, even the baby, at some point of my racing career. I don't know what you want me to say beyond that it's a privilege to know such a resilient driver.'

'Thank you.' I forced the words out of my mouth as my brain short-circuited.

'So how did that quali, that nail-biting millisecond delta, how did that feel?'

'Infuriating.'

We all chuckled. Didn't matter who you raced, you always hated the feeling of being on the precipice like that. Any fool knew as much.

'And, Diana, what are you up to, then? Celebrating your first race, first podium in F1, or all eyes on this one?'

'Well . . .' I thought for a moment. 'Honestly, a bit of both.'

The shrewd reporter smiled. Great, he'd struck gold. 'And the fans are dying to know. Who've you been celebrating *with*? Because thus far you're quite the mystery woman.'

'And I'd prefer that it stays that way. I keep my private life private,' I replied simply. 'I've been celebrating with myself and my banned Egyptian record collection, *kanafeh*, and a cup or two of tea.'

Crowberry continued, 'But if you win podium again, Diana, P1, even, and you could rejoice any way you liked, your fans ask, what would you do?'

I pondered over this for a moment. I could give several answers to this question. I could confirm his hunch that, indeed, banned records, *kanafeh*, and tea would go all the way. Or I could entice the audience and, if it was in the interests of all parties, drop them something.

I could feel Nic's eyes on me.

'I could make up any number of crazy possibilities,' I finally gave in. 'But I'll tell you it won't be just myself next time. My next celebration plan is more or less set.'

The crowd murmured excitedly, now mid-speculation. 'Is that true?' said Crowberry with a smirk. 'Dare we guess?'

Kasper shot me a probing look.

I just shrugged. 'It's my favourite pastime to whip the media into frenzies,' Nic had joked at dinner last night. He was right. This was ridiculously fun.

The conference ended, and my phone vibrated with a message just as our teams parted ways. I already knew who it was, but my heart skipped a beat checking it anyway.

* * *

Nic Necci: **We killed her back there.**

I chuckled aloud. Kasper nudged me. 'Hey. What are you going on about with that reporter?'

Me: **So I take it you're keeping that promise?**

'Is this someone on the grid?' Kasper went on. 'Well, Diana, are you seeing someone?'

He couldn't tear me from my internal chaos. I heard the pleasant echo of Nic's voice from the gala. 'Next race, I want to take you out after. Imola is pretty after dark.'

'You're so sure we'll have something to celebrate,' I had teased him in return, concealing my nervousness. I hadn't expected it to hit me with such force. I should have been positively elated, and yes, I was excited. Yet a part of me was weirdly disappointed. By what, I wasn't sure, but it was drumming up a difficult anxiety in my mind.

Nic: **Not quite. Because even if neither of us get podium, I'm still taking you out.**

I gasped a little, chewed on the inside of my cheek to shut myself up. Oh, things were certainly happening now. *Stop freaking out. Take the win.*

'Or, you know what?' Kasper was talking to sheer air at this point, at least till he smirked my way, the condescension reaching his cold blue irises. 'You planning on doing shots with Jolt after our next podium? Finally making good on my offer?'

Ew. 'I just have other plans,' I said casually.

'Damn.' He rolled his eyes. 'Should have seen it coming. Of course, if you could celebrate however you liked, it'd be getting on your knees—'

'*What?*'

'—for that wanker de la Fuente.'

106

A stiff wave of anger filled my chest; right there in the lobby of the inn, with everyone and their PR teams watching us, I grabbed Kasper Ramsey by the arm, pulled him into a relatively invisible corner, and hissed under my breath, 'Who in your *right* mind do you think *you* are to call me a *whore?*'

Kasper spat out a laugh.

'What the hell is funny to you now?'

'Why're you so upset over this?'

I crossed my arms, stone-faced. 'You insinuate I'm going to ring in a podium by servicing an engaged man and expect me to sit by idly? I am as much a Formula 1 driver as you, Kasper.'

'Oh, Diana,' he cackled, clapping my shoulder as we moved from the corner back into the lobby. I stood ramrod straight to resist the urge to break his hand. 'You're so worked up over de la Fuente, you must already be hiding something. Is that your next celebration, then?'

'Kasper, you . . .' I scoffed, but he'd already done the damage. Disgusting. I would need to take at least five showers just to get the echo of his words off me.

You're so worked up over de la Fuente.

Yes. Disgusting.

Chapter Sixteen

Miguel

I always got the chills when I put on my racing boots, knowing my team's outcome that day would rely half on me. After all, it was almost racing tradition to place blame on the driver rather than the team. Why wouldn't it send shivers down my spine?

I'd learned to quell the nerves over the years through routine. I let my jumpsuit hang loose at the waist and popped on my white Revello cap backwards, the same way Papá used to wear his. I blasted music into my earbuds as I began the reset into high gear: all race, no talk. In those moments when they prepped the car, I circled the R3-71 like a protective parent, saying nothing, just connecting with the engine, with the chassis. The hairs on my arms stood straight up every single time, and it was no different at Imola.

As my pre-race ritual wound to a close, I flashed Paula, who was already preparing her screens at the interior wall in my garage, a thumbs-up, and I said the same thing I had said every race Paula had served as my engineer. '*Adelante*, Pauli.'

'Ladies and gentlemen, welcome to the 2022 Emilia-Romagna Grand Prix, and the grid is set here as the drivers pull in. Claiming today's pole . . .'

The announcer's voice threatened to break the sealed-in link I always established with Paula and Paula alone as the formation lap set off. Our cars circled the track slowly before approaching the grid once more, lining up in the order determined by yesterday's qualifier. Pole had thankfully remained mine. P2, Darien Cardoso-Magalhães. P3, Diana. P4, surprise, it was Nic Necci. Perhaps his rumoured flirtation with Diana was the cause of this burst of motivation placing him ahead of Andrea, Kasper and Peter Albrecht – one driver each from the Big Three. Something turned in my stomach. Must have been the Italian breakfast.

Either way, it was anyone's race.

'Let's burn it, Miguel,' Paula said. 'On the clutch.'

The lights ticked on. My legs bounced unconsciously. With a growl you could likely hear across Italy, the lights were out, and the Imola Grand Prix was in the air.

'Out front, Miguel, stay out front. Darien coming in to fight. I want you to hold out carefully.'

My car skirted ahead, already getting a jump on the pack in preparation for a solid lead.

'Diana is falling back. Darien falling back. Get a good pace in, please.'

The chaos of the start came and went after the first lap. The grid spread out. Myself, Nic, Darien, Andrea, Diana, Peter, Kasper. It was a solid layout, making for a good race.

'You now have a two-second lead. Two seconds. Well done.'

Till Lap Twenty-One, we were holding on. The lead was good, and then things began to change as the pit-stop windows kicked in.

'Darien is pitting,' Paula warned me. 'It's almost time, Mig.'

'Yeah, my tyres are . . . going. No grip. It's bad to drive.'

'Right here. Box, box.'

I pulled into the pit lane, over a speed bump that almost scared the life out of me. I was counting the seconds myself, as I knew Paula would be doing.

'Darien is out. Nic just coming out. You'll have a bit of work to do.'

We made a 2.5-second stop. I rolled out of the pits, engine growling for a fight. I could smell it. I needed it. That was just how I raced.

'Yeah, it's now P1 Diana,' said Paula anxiously. 'She has not pitted yet. Darien third, cut by Nic second out of the pits, and now you. Good gap between you and Alex. Let's keep that buffer and up our pace.'

'What is Diana on that she's not . . . not, uh, box?'

'Hard tyres. She has, though, low grip, low speed. Will not be hard for Darien and Nic to get there. Unless you do first.'

I sped up and accelerated hard to match Darien on the outer during the twenty-fifth lap. I shot forward on the curve, and I winced as the car careened, dangerously close to going wheel to wheel with the Heidelberg, but we made it.

'That is P3, Mig, P3,' my sister declared proudly. 'Let's keep going.'

By Lap Thirty-Two, I was neck and neck with Nic. I was on the edge of my seat. I pushed hard. He pushed back. I thought we, too, would be tyre to tyre. The wheels aligned, but then I saw it, the tiniest gap on the curve. If I didn't take it, I'd be stuck here for another lap, not to mention possibly lose the place to Nic.

'Run it,' I mouthed before I put on a surge of speed and darted ahead.

'Yes!' I heard a clatter over the radio as Paula presumably jumped right out of her chair. 'Keep it up. *Vamos, tío*, P2, let's show them how bad you want this!'

'WHOO! TURN UP!'

We did. We were bordering on catching Diana within the next five laps. We were coming for Jolt Archambeau hard.

'Careful on the chicane. Keep with Diana,' Paula ordered. Chicanes, series of rapid turns, could be make-or-break. We could not afford break.

I decelerated to match Diana, taking the curve with good grip. And that is when everything turned to the biggest mess I had ever seen in my life.

Diana, ahead of me, hit the chicane perfectly, except suddenly, her front left wheel stalled. On hard tyres, it was suicide. Her car instantly overshot. I had no choice but to swerve wildly, costing me visual of the drivers ahead of me, and the last thing I caught sight of was Diana's JA76 spinning off the curve.

'¡MIERDA!' Paula yelled. 'Overtake NOW, Mig!'

I did so with an ear-splitting 'HOLY . . . HOLY SHIT, WHAT JUST HAPPENED?'

'You avoided collision. P1, Miguel, safety car out. Continue as directed. It is a red flag.'

'What happened?' I repeated. 'She was UPSIDE DOWN, Paula! I need to know if Diana's all right. Did she hit the wall, is she out or what?'

My heart was going a million beats a minute. I had only seen Diana's car spin off. It wasn't enough for me. I knew enough to register that I had to keep going, that stopping wasn't an option for us. But what the *hell* had I just seen? My breath was catching as I thought of her hanging upside down in her car or something. A fire. Or worse.

'Miguel, I did not catch that footage, I did not see it. I cannot tell you what is happening,' my sister attempted to answer me.

A rustling as she adjusted her headset. And then a new voice: Jatziry's. 'What . . . is she okay?' she whispered to my sister. I realized with a shock that Jatziry had never before experienced an F1 crash live. 'Is Miguel okay?'

'Miguel is okay, but . . .' There was a lull in Paula's reassurance. 'I don't manage Diana's end. I don't know.'

Soon enough, I yanked the car into the pits, and I parked it completely crooked before jumping right out of the cockpit and running into the garage without so much as removing my helmet. 'Do you have the footage, Paula?' I shouted. I could barely even do that. I didn't think my voice would even work. It didn't feel like my legs were working.

'They will show it once they have word on Diana,' Cristo assured me.

But it did little to calm my anxiety. The next twenty or so minutes passed agonizingly; with each moment, the only thoughts in everyone's heads were the negatives. When it took this long to release footage, it could never be a good thing. Never.

And, finally, it appeared on the TV. We all crowded around the engineering station to watch, and what we saw left us horrified.

It felt as though the crash was happening in slow motion. That single tyre halted, and the car skidded, before it pitched over itself, an array of sparks flying as the roll hoop crumpled beneath carbon fibre and the halo screeched against the asphalt. It hit the TecPro barrier, bounced back against it, and at a hundred and fifty kilometres an hour, slid into the gravel pitch separating the track from the fences, ending upside down with a sickening crunch.

'Oh, Jesus,' I barely whispered.

The live feed was now displayed. Crews were still struggling to lift the car out of the gravel as an ambulance left the scene. The caption reported that the catch fence had prevented any harm from coming to the fans in the grandstand via flying debris, and either way, the first few rows had more or less run the second the car had come their way. As the JA76 emerged from the wreckage, there was a collective gasp. It was missing all four tyres, the chunk off the top that included the roll hoop, the front and rear wing, and part of the chassis.

'What about Diana?' I almost pleaded to anyone in the room who could give me an answer. Paula shook her head, turning to our team principal.

'They have her en route to the hospital,' said Cristo. 'I have heard she might have been conscious. Just hanging on.'

Part of me knew that was simply another punishment, to be conscious. If Diana was awake, she'd have to relive the memory of that nightmare crash for the rest of her life. She would remember each and every second of it.

We heard nothing more, but the wreckage was removed, and the race restarted, a standing start on the grid. My efforts paid off. I crossed the finish line first. But after a crash like that, a crash that had stopped the hearts of everyone watching, it didn't feel the same. It felt just like Eddie Palomas's incident, and I had no idea how to react.

'That's P1, Miguel, P1.'

'Great job, guys. Really well done.'

My celebration was subdued – flat, even. 'Any word on Diana?' I asked. It was all I could think of, all *anyone* could think of.

'Hospital has said she is conscious still. No other information. It's all okay, Mig,' Paula tried to comfort me.

And yet, even as I sprayed Nic and Darien with champagne, I was not proud of how I'd won. I tugged my podium cap a bit lower and took my leave after the mandatory interviews. I was quiet as I retreated to my personal room, which I knew was abnormal as hell for me, whispering only a few hushed words to a rightfully concerned Jatziry, reminding her I was all right. My team let me take my time, because I'd still have to face the media in the TV pen on my way out of the track complex.

This was Formula 1. Winning was so sweet. It elevated you to the status of legends, it exhilarated you, it set all the atoms in your body on fire.

What they did not tell you, however, was how much it hurt to win at the expense of someone else.

Chapter Seventeen

Diana

Once I was discharged from the large hospital in Bologna, to which they had flown me in a helicopter with far too much drama, I sat down in the back seat of the company car, still lacking some feeling in my legs and neck, upped beyond belief on painkillers, and let myself be driven back to the inn like a guilty child.

It felt like one big walk of shame, no ending in sight. The walk into the hotel, the way the fans' cheers blurred into white noise. I took the elevator up to my room. I locked the door behind me, and I sat down on the ground. I ran over the letters of *RAMISSA* on my suit over and over again, remembering how I had been at one with the car until something had gone wrong, and suddenly, I wasn't any more. I saw sky and ground and sky and ground, and then I was stuck, my head pounding, begging me to pass out and give in as my engineer barked orders into my earbuds, my legs unfeeling, leaving me with the fear that once I got out of this car, my Formula 1 career would have ended as soon as it began. I prayed that maybe my parents had missed this race. I kept my phone tucked behind the TV so I wouldn't have to talk to Ammi if she called.

When I stood, I finally let myself out of the jumpsuit. I peeled off the heat-protective Nomex long sleeve I wore underneath. I turned the shower to as cold as it went and absolutely blasted myself, washing away all the guilt and the embarrassment. Or, at least, I tried to.

Yes, this was only one crash. This was not be-all – or end-all. But I couldn't help thinking that even though it was an error in the car, I could have made a save. I could have done something to prevent it, and instead, like a fool, I froze and allowed an incident to follow; let the car sustain millions of dollars' worth of damage. I was so new to Jolt, I couldn't afford to lose my seat.

I had spun out before, just never this badly. I let the cold water shock me to the reality of this situation. Replayed it in my head time and again.

The car careened, flipping over itself till my head snapped back as I collided with the TecPro and ended upside down, my roll hoop discarded in the gravel beside me, my neck barely able to hold up my head. I was on the verge of tears that wouldn't even come out as I heard scream after scream from Aiden's end of the radio, and I tried my hardest to croak out words. 'Okay,' I managed, even though that was a lie. Every inch of my body felt as if it had been dismantled and taped back together as hastily as possible. I couldn't move – whether that was because of mental shock or some sort of spinal cord injury, I didn't know, nor did I want to find out.

I would look like an idiot, a careless, ditzy excuse for a woman in F1, who had refused to pull over and retire when it seemed like something was going wrong, who couldn't take control of the car when something *did* go wrong. I had been in the lead. That could have been my first victory. And yet . . .

I remembered the girl whose helmet I'd signed. *Never doubt yourself.* How could I not?

I changed into an old Archambeau Junior Team shirt that was far too big and fraying on the edges with a pair of running shorts, and I curled up on the couch, cocooned in a sherpa blanket from home. I turned on the TV and accessed the on-demand feature, logged into the auto race streaming. Formula 1, I searched. I selected the Emilia-Romagna Grand Prix.

And I watched.

It was just my crash again and again. Spin, flip, TecPro, flip, and gravel. Pulling the blanket over my face, I groaned over the announcer analysing it all. 'And this is the crash, the footage of which was just released now that we know Diana Zahrani is en route to the hospital. Absolutely terrible. As she tries to spin into the crash, save the car, the wheel there gives out, car goes upside down, and there's that roll by the TecPro – and you can see, you know, that halo doing what it's meant to. But I've still never seen anything like it. What a, what an unbelievable end to Zahrani's run at Imola.'

The beep of the incoming radio sounded. Now my voice, dazed: 'For . . . for [beep] sake. I . . . sorry.'

'Are you all right, Diana?'

'Okay.'

'Diana, are you all right?'

'Something wet in . . . the car.'

'Hang on. Hang on, Diana.'

'Can't really feel . . . feel my legs.'

'The medical team is on its way.'

A shift in camera view. I watched from the perspective of Miguel as my car skirted right off the chicane inches from his. He didn't see any more than that, zooming ahead before debris could fly and ruin his race.

'HOLY [beep]! HOLY [beep],' he yelled. 'WHAT JUST HAPPENED?'

'You avoided collision,' Paula's voice replied. 'P1, Miguel, safety car out. Continue as directed. It is a red flag.'

'What happened?' His voice was tinny, like he was gargling with bees. 'She was UPSIDE DOWN, Paula! I need to know if Diana's all right!'

I didn't remember the rest of what I watched, them helping me out of the car and into the ambulance. Part of me didn't even want to look. This sport was ruthless; the expectations were crushing. When you were a woman, they demanded double of you than the other guys. *What do you want from me?* I wished I could ask them. The answer was stupidly, glaringly obvious: more. More, even if you are in hospital with an oxygen mask over your face, huffing life back into your body after a dance with destruction.

'She is a risk-taker. She's aggressive. She plays the game in a way none of our drivers have before. If the stakes are high, Diana goes for it anyway,' Cavanaugh had said in the press conference Jolt had held shortly after they'd signed me. I wasn't there, but I'd seen all the videos. Because for me the bar was not just high, it was, as always, towering, monumental.

Onscreen, the race continued. My car was removed from the track, its husk of a body lifted out of the gravel by crane just in front of the fences. I could see from here, even though it was ever so tiny on the screen, the way my parents' names had been scratched off the halo, and I thought to myself, *Damn. You could have done better*.

The pace did not let up after my crash. A standing start resumed the action. Miguel finished P1. Nic got P2, which made me feel immensely proud of him. Darien swung P3. Kasper had apparently been unable to pick up the slack I had left behind and bring in a podium. I listened to the radio as Miguel crossed the finish line.

'That's P1, Miguel, P1.'

'Great job, guys. Really well done. Any word on Diana?'

'Hospital has said she is conscious still. No other information. It's all okay, Mig,' said Paula, a lingering anxiety still tingeing her voice.

A crackle that sounded like an exhale from Miguel's end. '*No es lo mismo, Pauli, sin Diana. Nada.*'

'*Yo se,*' she replied, '*pero esto es la carrera.*'

I didn't know Spanish, but the eerie weight of their voices over radio pulled me to my feet and away from the television screen. I wished Nic were here, which I would have loved if it weren't for the second place he'd won and my twentieth. The competitive demon inside me growled to let myself wallow in my failure. I didn't deserve to celebrate Nic's success, nor should I.

I pulled my phone from behind the TV set: missed calls, most (forty-nine) from my mom, a few (three) from Ramsey, one from Cavanaugh, and a gentle text from Nic.

Nic: **How are you? You need me to come upstairs?**

I sighed. He knew how these things went because, after all, he'd had a few such incidents last season. I just needed time to reel, to process my situation.

I was embarrassed to admit to myself that I wished it wasn't just Nic checking in on me, of all the drivers on the grid.

Me: **I'm okay. Picked up some head injury, whiplash or whatever. Wanted me overnight but you know I wouldn't have. And thank you, it's all right. I just have to, you know**

Nic: **Go over what happened on your own**

Me: **Yeah. I'm so sorry. I know we had plans**

Nic: **Don't be. I'm glad you're OK. Rest. I don't want to see you discombobulated next race**

The laughter that escaped me caused my neck to protest immediately, making me wince. I procured a cold water bottle from the minifridge and pushed it to my upper vertebrae. Ugh.

Me: **HA. Won't be. Goodnight and congrats Nic. I'm impressed**

Before I could check for a reply from Nic, or if I'd had messages from anyone else, a knock at my door turned my attention from the screen of my phone. I lowered the volume of the race on TV. Most everyone knew to leave a humiliated racing driver to her own devices, but apparently someone hadn't got the memo.

I cracked open the door, wary of looking like a distraught teenager. I blinked away the daze from the whiplash to take in the face of my visitor.

Miguel de la Fuente blinked back at me. 'Diana?'

'Miguel?' His name came out like a rasp. Did my voice really sound that bad?

'I'm sorry, I know you have to sit in your own headspace and contemplate these things, but I just wanted to make sure you were, um, fine.' He extended a small paper bag my way. 'Not sure exactly what you like, but I think you said something at the conference, and these were all I could find.'

I accepted the paper bag tentatively, opened it up to reveal a lidded plate. A smile spread across my lips. A slice of *kanafeh*, that Middle Eastern pastry I'd mentioned at the interviews. My absolute favourite.

'Where did you get this?'

'There's a little family-owned place in town, actually, that makes them.' Miguel shoved his hands in his jeans pockets awkwardly. It made me chuckle a little how this aggressive driver, this typical alpha F1 guy, now stood before me with the demeanour of a wet paper towel in straight jeans and a team windbreaker. His hair still stuck up at funny angles from wearing the helmet; it peeked out from beneath his ears. He looked like he hadn't shaved all weekend. His eyebrows were knitted in worry, deep brown eyes searching me for surface injuries. His hands moved to the pockets of his jacket emblazoned with the Revello crest and a handful of sponsors.

'Thanks.' I grinned, but I grinned too hard. It turned to a grimace as my head began to pound furiously. I pushed harder on the water bottle.

'Are you hurt?' Miguel asked. His eyes did that puppy-dog thing again.

'Whiplash. The bare minimum.'

'And . . . is that the race playing?'

'Maybe.'

Miguel's expression turned almost to pity. 'Oh, Diana, why? Turn that off. Turn it off.'

Reluctantly, I hit the off button on my remote. 'Fine.' I raised the bag containing the *kanafeh*. 'But tell me. You went all the way across town for this?'

Miguel just shrugged.

I gave him a look. 'Come inside. You have the right to eat some of it, too.'

'Well, I've never actually had it before.'

'So?'

'You can't guarantee I'll like it,' Miguel pointed out, though he walked inside as he did. I could tell he was messing with me, trying to cheer me up, even though anyone worth their salt in racing knew that nothing could lift you out of the abyss except practice, endless and torturous laps on the sim.

'You won't know if you don't try.' I sneakily switched the TV back on. 'Welcome to my pity party.'

Chapter Eighteen

Miguel

I knew Diana's pity party all too well.

When I entered Formula 1, I learned the crushing weight of true public humiliation. The first time I crashed out of a race, I lost my bearings completely. It happened to the best of us. We effed up, we holed ourselves into hotel rooms, and we ate, cried and overanalysed. We went into it thinking we were the exception and, like Diana, like any human being with a conscience, we crumbled a little.

Okay. A lot.

Maybe it was stupid for me to have joined Diana, or that she let me, or whatever, but I just felt awful for her. Her shunt stung like my first F1 crash and, frankly, I couldn't revel in a win knowing that it was in part due to someone suffering a near-fatal crash through no fault of her own.

Diana set her pastry down on the coffee table. I noticed she had turned on the TV again. For the millionth time that day,

I gaped at the screen as the crash played out from my point of view.

'You are lucky I didn't take you with me.' Diana read my mind as she procured two napkins for all the bits of *kanafeh* that would make their way onto the table.

I couldn't help but choke out a laugh at that. 'My survival's all thanks to the way you steered out into the spin.'

She sighed. I figured I couldn't praise her handle on the situation to get her out of this one. 'I don't always do everything right, Miguel.'

'You didn't do anything wrong in this,' I replied quietly. 'And for the record . . . no one does everything right.'

Diana nodded slightly, then pulled the *kanafeh* from its bag and broke it up into two pieces over the napkins, holding one out to me. 'Here.'

I accepted it, and we sat down on the couch, the TV now running an extended crash analysis. 'It's not something you can escape. Everyone slips up eventually.'

'When did you slip up, then?'

I thought. 'Austrian Grand Prix, 2019. My first season, I was with Scuderia Vittore. With Nic. Cutthroat competition, Nic Necci, both of us young and reckless. It was a back-of-the-field team then, so normally the public couldn't care less about us, but when I spun out, it was awful. Everything I'd done was leading up to my nabbing a higher seat, a Revello seat, and I thought I'd blown it. I thought I was the bane of the whole damn grid. I ordered five pizzas, locked the door so my athletic trainer would have no hint—' Diana laughed, making me laugh, too. 'I blasted Guns N' Roses like an emo middle-schooler, and I watched race reruns all night long.'

I didn't mention the awful pressure, the pressure too raw to admit to anyone. I remember feeling like I wasn't worthy of my own last name, that I'd never fulfil the burden that came with the blood in my veins. And that was crushing. Racing was crushing.

Diana nodded. 'We are all the same, aren't we?'

'Yeah. We are, in some ways.'

She chewed on a bite of *kanafeh* in thought. 'This is really good.'

'For real?' I pulled apart a piece from mine. 'Then here goes nothing.'

I stuffed it in my mouth. It was . . . new. Cheesy, nutty, crunchy and creamy, all those things and more. 'You're right. This is friggin' delicious.'

'Isn't it?' Diana took another bite. 'So. What's middle school?'

My jaw almost dropped. The way she'd said the words as if they were in a language she had never heard in her life baffled me. 'You don't know middle school?'

'Well, we were not Saudi. My father is Egyptian and my mother Persian. Baba is Coptic Orthodox, Ammi Zoroastrian, so I couldn't go to a Muslim school. I went to the same expat school for years one through twelve,' she pointed out.

'Like . . . a boarding school?'

'Yes, except I didn't live there.'

'So not at all like a boarding school.'

She shot me a look. 'More like the academies at the convents, then.'

'Wow. You missed out on the horrors of public education,' I teased her. It was actually kind of funny, the fact that I went to Canadian public school. I think it was because I was too

125

bad a student to top my class like Paula, and so no boarding school was willing to accommodate both my abysmal grades and my karting crap. Public school was great, though. Weird stuff happened often. Once, some kid streaked through the halls naked with a bong in one hand and a blunt in the other.

'Anyway.' She pulled her blanket up to her chin, concealing the logo on her T-shirt: Jolt's junior team. 'When did you get over it?' she asked. 'The humiliation?'

'Is it cliché of me to say that I still feel it?' I said. 'I feel the shame all the time. I overshoot one turn, and suddenly, the media is on my ass. It just, I don't know, makes you so . . .'

'Helpless,' Diana said, echoing my thoughts. 'Alone.'

I exhaled, a heavy breath laden with the weight of the sport that both gave me life and poisoned me slowly. 'Yeah. Alone.'

In the background, I heard myself talking onscreen. '*No es lo mismo*,' I was saying over my radio. '*Sin Diana, no es lo mismo*.'

I didn't grow up using my Spanish. Canada forced me to learn French as a Québécois, a language Paula never really took to. More than our parents, it was Paula who mommed me on these counts. '*¡No ingles!*' she would command, with all the fervour of a teacher at the chalkboard. '*¡Dimelo en español!*'

Despite her efforts, Spanish only came out when I was stressed, upset, or otherwise in my feels. Sometimes it happened over the radio in races, because what I wanted to say just couldn't be expressed in English.

'What does that mean?' Diana asked. It was an innocent question but, to me, so loaded.

I watched the cars pull in, killing time before I had to answer her in this game of questions that was quickly becoming more and more dangerous.

'It's not the same without Diana, I said,' I finally translated. 'And Paula said, she knows. But this is the race. That's how it works.'

The silence that followed was deafening. Neither of us spoke for a long minute.

As if she sensed the tension, Diana grabbed the remote and changed the channel.

I wasn't even sure what she changed it to, but when something new appeared, I recognized it immediately. I laughed aloud. '*Roman Holiday*, Diana?'

'I didn't know how to choose something else so fast!' she protested. We both went quiet to listen to the movie, garbled as it sounded. I leaned towards the speaker and, pretty soon, I realized what we had on our hands.

'In *Italian?*'

At long last, Diana cracked up, falling back onto the couch in shock. 'Oh. I can't understand a word!'

She and I devolved into giggles as Gregory Peck and Audrey Hepburn conversed in badly dubbed Italian. I really didn't remember laughing this hard at anything in so long. Formula 1 was go, go, go all the time. I'd forgotten what it was like to stop and actually laugh about something stupid, not for the media, not respectfully.

'Everything is in Italian!' I choked out. 'We don't know any Italian!'

'You're on an Italian team! What do you mean you don't know Italian?' Diana chided me as we gasped for breath. I thought she was equally awash in hysterics, until I opened my eyes long enough to see that she was clearly in pain.

She squeezed her own eyes shut. 'Shit, man. Pass me the meds from the dresser.'

'What . . . for your head?' I sobered up right away, snatching the bottle as quickly as possible. One glimpse of it, however, betrayed the answer to my question. This was heavy-duty prescription painkillers, well beyond a headache.

'Diana, what happened in that car?' It was my turn to question her. 'Did the car . . . did you have a fuel leak, was there fire? Did you get burned? You know how dangerous that can be, it's—'

'No,' she assured me, her expression pained. 'I had no fuel leak, no burns, don't worry.'

'Then what . . .' My mind compiled all these details about the crash. The broken roll hoop, a small piece of it they couldn't find. Diana's radio: something in the car was damp, and it wasn't fuel. Suddenly, it made sense. I turned abruptly to Diana, my head pounding as I took in the severity of just what could have happened in that car. 'It wasn't just whiplash . . . was it?'

She shook her head. 'It's nothing. It's just some part of the roll hoop that got me and—'

'Where?'

Diana sighed in thought, as if she was debating whether or not to push this any farther than it'd gone. Then she moved so her back was to me, and tossed her long ponytail of black hair over her shoulder with one hand, tugging the neck of her T-shirt down with the other. There, just below her cervical vertebrae, was a large pad of dressing taped to her skin, starting to soak through.

A small gasp left my lips. 'Diana . . .'

'It's okay. They put stitches in. I'll be fine.'

'Fine,' I echoed in disbelief. She'd been stabbed with a part of the roll hoop. That could have taken out her spinal cord. How was she fine? 'Your bandage is wet.'

She let her hair back down, curls and snaggles unlike the sleek look we normally saw at grands prix and press sessions. I noticed a tattoo on the side of her wrist as she fixed an errant curl: a falcon, sort of like the one on the back of her helmet. 'I'll live.'

'You're supposed to change it when soiled.'

'How would you know, Dr de la Fuente?'

I raised an eyebrow. 'Any driver knows.'

Diana looked at me with an exasperated glare. 'Fine. Can you help me? I can't reach it.'

'No, I absolutely will not help you.'

She tilted her head.

'I'm kidding. Come on. Where's the dressing they gave you?'

'On the counter over there.'

I grabbed the new gauze and tape. I wasn't afraid of blood, or any kind of wounds; in fact, I was well used to them. But my hands did shake a little when I realized that this wasn't as simple as fixing a cut on my own arm. This was Diana, who was somehow trucking through the fact that a part of her own car had impaled her and left a gash in her body. I went and washed my hands very thoroughly before returning to Diana, who was primed with instructions for me.

'They said to—'

'Centre the gauze, don't touch the inside, tape four sides. I got it, don't worry,' I said as I sat down behind her on the couch. 'Move your hair again.'

She swept her curls over her shoulder, but she missed one tendril of hair. In the most awkward manner possible, I tucked it to the side with the rest of it, so that her bare skin was exposed to me, avoiding touching her back as much as possible so this didn't get more intimate than it needed to be. I cringed to myself. Of course, I couldn't do this normally.

'You're being weird, aren't you, Miguel?' She read my mind. It was infuriating.

'No, I'm—'

'Miguel, this is not that deep. I need your help. And you're the one who said I should change my dressing.'

'Okay, okay.' I gingerly started to remove the tape ever so slowly. Diana's skin was so soft that I thought I'd wreck it if I pulled. 'Almost there.'

'Throw it out and put the new one.'

'I know.'

'Uh-huh.'

I was kind of freaked out, to be honest. I know I'd said it didn't usually do that to me, but the gash that streaked across the lower part of Diana's neck was terrifying. Her healthy tan got sallower around the wound, which couldn't have been anything good, and the cut itself was sealed shut with, if I was counting right, almost twelve stitches. I tore off the rest of the tape and got rid of the dressing, centring the new rectangle over the stitches. I taped it on all four sides, the same way we'd been taught as teenagers: basic first aid. My fingers hovered over my hack job of a gauze application for just a second more, before I decided better of it and let my hands fall.

'Thanks.' Diana moved her hair back over her shoulder so it fell down her back. Without any makeup or any fancy outfits, no glamour whatsoever, she was even more stunning. Nic was lucky. So, so lucky.

We sat back down on the couch, and Diana brushed something from her cheek.

'Did I rip the tape off too hard?' I asked nervously.

She let out a laugh wrapped in a sob. 'No.'

'What's wrong?'

Pulling her knees up to her chest, Diana looked my way, tears in her eyes. 'You know why women don't get into this sport? It's because no one wants to sponsor us. We sell our . . . our reputations for sponsors. They isolate us from everyone else in this rat race. And they still want more from us. Just this one crash – just one – and they'll say I'm incompetent. Miguel, the track, it is what it is. But I fight *myself* every minute of every day.'

'Diana . . .' I steadied her by the shoulders. The lack of faith in her eyes was astounding. Was this what we did to our women? Crippled them with so many expectations that they crumbled at their own hand? 'You are extremely competent. Your first race was a podium. So few drivers can say that. And this was not your fault, you hear me? You couldn't have prevented that kind of collision. But you don't need me to tell you any of this. You know it. I want you to stop giving damns about everyone else and give one or two about how powerful you are. Crashes happen to every powerful racer. It's the best ones who can forget about that, go back out there, and win.'

Both of us uttered no words for a moment. Then Diana said, 'I think I needed to hear that.'

'I agree.'

'I'm not alone.'

'You aren't. You have family, friends.' I wanted to say, *you have me.*

Diana wiped away the last of the tears. She made to rub her eyes, but I smacked her hand away. 'Don't. You need good eyes to drive, remember?'

She scoffed. After a beat. 'I don't really talk about this because the media would make it my fatal flaw, but I trust you, and . . .'

I picked it up right away. 'Your family. I've never seen them in your motorhome. Are your parents . . .?'

'No, nothing like that,' she assured me. 'It's just that . . . my father was in an accident just before I started F3. He's paralysed below the waist. He can't walk, can't do many things we take for granted. My mother cares for him every hour of every day. It's a miracle my sponsor money at that time was just enough to let them both live comfortably without working. That's what matters most. But since then, they have not been able to come to my races, and . . . they're my *parents*. The fact that they can't see me race . . . when everyone else turned away, they stuck by me, Miguel. So ever since F3, I've struggled. I miss them. I don't know who else to believe sometimes.'

I imagined returning to my garage: no Paula, no Mamá, no Papá. I couldn't. 'That's . . . I'm so sorry.'

Diana leaned back against the couch. 'Thank you. But I don't want pity. I want pain relief. Which I'm getting now, but still.'

'I'd say alcohol, but we don't want you crossing drugs, passing out, and starting a scandal.'

'Oh, no,' she chuckled with a yawn.

Part of me wished I could be Diana's pain relief. I wanted to give her a hug and let her know that she could believe me, that I'd be behind her no matter what. I didn't even know quite why. I could be an unaffectionate person, a frustrating person

132

at times. But I knew that I'd smack down in a heartbeat the first reporter to ask Diana how she felt about her career after that crash. I couldn't fathom how everyone who interacted with this brilliant woman didn't feel the same way about her.

I thought about this for a few minutes, as Italian *Roman Holiday* played on. It took me a while to realize that Diana had actually fallen asleep.

She was snoring away, slumped against my left side, exhausted from what had to be the longest day of her life. I stood slowly, gently lowering her head onto a pillow so she was on her side, and pulled her blanket over her. I turned off the TV.

'You're not alone,' I whispered, even though I knew she wouldn't hear. I took one last look at Diana, completely placid and slightly loud (no, she snored like a chainsaw and a screaming goat had a baby), and I smiled a little as I slipped out, closing the door quietly behind me.

Chapter Nineteen

Diana

Qualifying in Miami was beautiful. I could not have asked for anything more. I fell onto second position for the race grid, which elated me. Miguel pulled in next to me for his third straight pole position of the season, Peter in search of an advantageous start in P3. But at every chicane of this vicious new city track, scenic as it was, my heart seized. The fact that I had bounced back felt too good to be true. All of it did.

But this was real. As I answered a question with one of the official reporters post-qualifying, a familiar voice said from behind me, 'The queen comes out on top again.'

I turned around to meet Nic's eyes, wary of the camera. 'Well, you are P4. Not far off, right?'

'Not far. So you gotta watch your rear tomorrow.' Nic smiled slyly, and before I could comprehend it, he pulled the right shoulder Velcro strap on my uniform clean off, cackling as he trotted off ever so triumphantly.

'Sorry,' I said to the reporter, concealing my grin beneath the concentration of fixing my shoulder strap. 'He can be a child sometimes.'

The reporter laughed, slightly obnoxiously. She was dressed to the nines, decked out in a hot pink pantsuit and Louboutins. I'd seen her earlier in the day, doing a little too much bicep grabbing with the Heidelberg guys, which had made me think she was one of the WAGs, meant to be kicked back in the paddock rather than armed with a mic on the pit wall. 'I assume you two are good friends.'

'Yeah.' I couldn't help but glance in Nic's direction as he stuck his tongue out at me. I remembered how Miguel told me to stop giving damns about what everyone else thought. And why should I care what they had to say? If it was not in bad taste, then why should I dedicate myself to being an angel all the time? After all, I clearly wasn't one on track.

Across from us, I was met with quite a strange sight, and possibly even a sign. Paula de la Fuente was doing a Revello video with her brother, cutting loose for the first time since I'd met her. They both had sandwich cookies on their noses, heads leaned back, playing that game where you had to scrunch your face to get it to fall into your mouth first. Something must have been in the humid Miami air – Paula very rarely stepped out into the media's eye, much less to wiggle biscuits into her mouth.

I mean, there was little to it. If the guys could prank each other and flip off the camera and say things their principals would wash their mouths out for, there was no reason I couldn't as well. Stop giving damns.

135

I looked right into the camera. 'You know what? Give me a minute.'

Nic was now waving to the Griffith camera. The F1 one trained its lens on me as I crept into the frame behind him and swiped the royal blue cap right off his head.

The Griffith team burst into peals of laughter, most of all Alex, hunched over in stitches beside his teammate. 'What the hell?' Nic patted his hair in search of the cap. Still concealed from Nic's view, I donned the hat myself and casually stepped out to Nic's other side.

'Well, I believe Jolt Archambeau will indeed demolish Griffith this race,' I deadpanned ever so seriously, darting out of the way of a grab from an amused Nic.

'One moment,' he said to his press team. 'This is war.'

Alex was already prepared with his phone. He recorded the entire thing as I evaded Nic in a match of superior reflexes (difficult among two Formula 1 drivers).

'You're not gonna get it,' I laughed, holding tight to the offending hat, attempting to lift it above Nic's head.

With an impish grin, Nic faked me out and regained control of the cap at last. 'Don't jinx it next time,' he teased.

'That's unfair. You're five inches taller.'

'Nice excuse.' To my surprise, Nic reached back out to me and fitted the cap back on my head. 'Will that dinner of ours ever happen, Miss Zahrani, if you do decide not to crash again today?'

'Now *you're* jinxing it.' I adjusted the strap, letting my fingers brush Nic's for just a moment. 'Assuming I don't wind up wedged between the wall and the fence, though, I would love to follow through on that.'

The cameras were right up in our faces, but at this point, I was used to it. Besides, I felt it in the air. This was going to be my redemption race.

As expected, it all came up roses for Jolt Archambeau.

The start was admittedly awful. My reaction time was delayed, Aiden told me, and I fell back to P4. But I wasn't about to let the voice in the depths of my brain hinder me. I drove hard, the only way I knew, and when I crossed that line on podium, splitting the two Heidelbergs, career best result, glory in Miami, I felt that the work I'd put in on the sim following the crash, the mental stress, the pact to let nothing stop me from bursting right onto the scene, was very much paying off. P1 and P3, Peter and Darien successfully orchestrated a double podium and a double shoey for Darien's home race. Unfortunately, Miguel did not fare so well, falling from P1 due to terrible strategy and a start slower than mine to end P5 below Nic.

I made a note to repay the favour and talk to him later on, recalling the way he'd stopped by with my favourite food, got my mood up when I felt absolutely hopeless, listened to my stories. And I know, I know I said it was platonic, but the feel of his fingers against my skin . . . I had to push it away. I didn't need that now.

In the moment, the *Carmen* 'Prélude' began with pomp, as all three of us set down our trophies in favour of expensive bottles of champagne. We whipped our bottles every which way, sending froth flying across the stage. I got even more soaked this time than my first podium in Saudi, owing to the fact that Darien dumped half his bottle on my head.

'SHOEY!' the crowd chanted.

'YEAH? You want a shoey?' Peter Albrecht yelled back. 'You'll get a shoey!'

Peter turned my way, mischief in his hazel eyes as he reached down and untied his shoe. I hoped I was not blushing, fangirling, or gagging too hard. Alas, I couldn't hide the fear on my face. 'Oh, no.'

'You ready?' he asked, an eyebrow raised as he removed his racing boot and dangled it by a finger. It was unbelievably hot and disgusting all at once.

'Uhhh . . .' I lost the ability to form words. Peter gave his shoe an expectant little shake, and Darien raised one of his own, all smiles.

Peter tossed his boot, catching it with a smirk. The fans only roared louder as they realized that a triple shoey was in order. 'C'mon. Don't let all these people down. Drink from your damn shoe, Di, just this once.'

'I don't know.' I cringed away from the shoe just slightly, glancing down at my own in disdain. 'I prefer my champagne in glasses.'

I laughed, thinking this was the end of it, but my eyes went wide as I realized that *Peter friggin' Albrecht* was *getting down on one knee* in front of me, racing boot extended my way.

'Diana, love, I would appreciate it if you could complete my life's desires and just do a little shoey from your boot for me.'

I quite literally freaked out, covering my face with my hands, more due to the shoe than anything else.

'Okay, Peter, I will do a shoey for you.'

The fans went absolutely berserk when I gingerly loosened my shoelaces and wiggled out of my right boot, filling it to the brim with champagne.

'Three,' counted Darien. 'Two. One!'

On one, we brought our shoes to our lips. I squeezed my eyes shut, and without making any physical contact with the edge of the shoe, dumped the champagne into my mouth. It spilled all down the front of my suit as oddly tangy alcohol hit my tongue, but I chugged it till it was gone, and triumphantly, fighting back bile, I raised my shoe in one hand and my P2 trophy in the other.

'That's how you do it!' whooped Peter. 'I love this woman!'

It was all well worth it. I'd never heard a sporting crowd this loud or felt this utterly high off my own adrenaline before, though that may have just been the shoe sweat. I had just been proposed to by Peter Albrecht after placing podium in a grand prix. To hell with ladylike. This was a dream come true.

'And after, he came to me, and he goes, "Here's to many more, Di." I was like . . .'

I pantomimed an explosion for Nic, thoroughly entertained as he was. 'Like, what? *What?*'

'You, Danger, are on your way,' said Nic with a smile, raising his wine glass.

I clinked my own with his in solidarity. 'As are you. A P2 and P4 for Griffith? Expect a new contract soon.'

'Knock on it.' He rapped his knuckles on the table.

'Would you stay with them? If you got one from elsewhere?'

'I mean . . .' Nic looked up in thought. 'I'd hate to leave Alex . . . but it would be huge for my career to move up, you know? To a top team.'

'It would be,' I agreed, lighting up at the thought of it. I set my glass on the table and took the last bite of my lava cake. 'I could see you doing that. Driving for, like, Revello or Heidelberg or Jolt.'

'Jolt?' Nic raised an eyebrow. 'You think we could drive together?'

'You do deliver every time,' I remarked. 'Kasper has been slipping. I've heard talk about it. The fact that you beat him, that's a benchmark.'

So not everything came up roses for Jolt, actually. Ramsey finished P10, just barely in the points and nowhere near the calibre Cavanaugh wanted. This wasn't new. Even before me, Eduardo Palomas carried the team. Kasper's performance was not exactly commendable.

'Sure.' He grinned. 'But forget that. Maybe even forget that we race, just for a moment.'

'Forgetting.'

Nic locked eyes with me, his stormy-grey irises boring into mine. I could discern every little strand of brown hair that brushed his eyelashes, every smile line of his face. 'Thank you, you know. For taking a chance on me. I'm just glad I've met someone as remarkable as you, Di.'

That melted me. Nic did that, the sweet talker that he was. 'Oh, Nic, I say the same. You made me feel at home on the grid, and really, don't thank me. I'm just as grateful for a rival like you.'

Nic's laugh filled the room. I was banking on the private table we had on the balcony of this modern restaurant in the Art Deco district to keep us away from prying eyes and media. Nic could laugh all he wanted, and I could feel the companionship I so desperately needed.

So we topped up our glasses and treated ourselves to just a

bit more wine on the balcony, taking in the neon city below us. It was a perfect end to a perfect weekend. But, depending on how you saw it, the weekend was either about to get much better or much worse.

'Can I . . .'

I chuckled. 'Take it.'

He squinted at the caller ID, then picked up. 'Hello?'

Whoever was on the other end spoke. Nic replied periodically. 'Yes. Uh-huh. Uh-huh.'

As this went on, his face broke into an expression of bigger and bigger disbelief. His jaw dropped, eyes widened. 'Sure. I'll . . . I'll follow up. Yes. Good night.'

Slowly, Nic lowered his phone, turning to me. The man was in complete and utter shock.

'What happened?' I asked, worry cracking my voice. 'You okay?'

'Diana.' He reached out and took both my hands in his shaky ones. My heart began the agonizing elevator descent into my wedges.

'Oh . . . is it bad?'

'Diana,' Nic repeated. 'I've been offered a seat by Jolt.'

Chapter Twenty

Miguel

Two weeks after what was undoubtedly a humiliating race, I reclaimed P1 at Melbourne, forcing Darien, who was on the rise, to P2, and Diana to P3. I was extremely satisfied with the race outcome but, same as everyone else, I had only one thing on my mind the day after the Australian Grand Prix: unbeknownst to us during the race, that had been Nic's last ride with Griffith.

I watched the news next morning from my hotel room, as baffled as the rest of the motorsport world. Mid-season trade-offs just four races in were a rare occurrence, especially between high field teams. They simply didn't happen.

'Yes, everyone, Melbourne 2022 was the last we will see of Nicolò Necci as a Griffith Lion for now. Jolt Archambeau Racing has signed a lucrative swap with Griffith, giving the latter Kasper Ramsey, whose performance had been declining steadily for the last year, costing Jolt points and hundreds of thousands in damages alike,' the National SportsHub anchor was gushing. 'In return, Jolt will be receiving Griffith's brilliant upstart driver, Nic Necci.'

I pulled on my shirt and popped in contacts as the anchor went on. 'Jolt Archambeau Racing will return in a week's time for Spain with the perfect dream team, and arguably the only team with realistic chances of a one-two, with two drivers who are incredibly skilled and both very softly spoken. With this advantage, will Jolt show up at Barcelona? Only time will tell as Necci has a record of placing highly in a severely disadvantaged car . . .'

'Damn it, Nic,' I mumbled, turning off the TV. I'd expected Andrea to go before Kasper, in all honesty. And at least, if that happened, we would have Nic's fantastic driving on our side. Instead, Jolt had moved even faster and come out of the tussle with a team that could easily destroy the Scuderia.

I tapped at my phone in a furious bid to check the points standings. I quickly realized Jolt could very well screw us over. They were third in the Constructors' Championship, having netted ninety points. Revello was sitting at first, just ahead of Heidelberg, the former with a cushy hundred and sixteen points. But that disadvantage due to Kasper Ramsey, the same disadvantage that had been allowing us to remain in the lead, was gone now.

'Ugh,' I groaned.

I was on the verge of switching off the phone so I could just get breakfast in peace before we packed up and left, but an incoming call from Jatziry flashed across the screen. I picked it up right away.

Jatziry had flown out last night. She'd be attending her

cousin Lupe's wedding in Guadalajara the weekend of the Barcelona race and, due to family obligations, would be spending the next week there. I'd miss her during my home race, but in a weird way, it took some of the edge off. My parents, watching me uphold the pride of España or something, was enough pressure as it was.

'Hey. Where you at so far?'

Jatziry's sigh crackled through the speaker. 'Stopover in Atlanta. We have been waiting here. How are you?'

'Freaking out.' I let out a nervous laugh. 'You seen the news? Diana and Nic will both be driving Jolts in Barcelona.'

'Ay. Miguel, no racing for a week,' sang Jatziry with tired bliss. 'Keep your Formula 1 away from me. This is my little vacation.'

'Okay, okay. Well, everything's okay, right? Just a check-in call?'

'Yes. Also an I-miss-you call.'

'I miss you, too,' I chuckled. 'I'll run to breakfast, Jatziry. Call when you get to Jalisco.'

'*Claro, amor*. Stay well.'

Amor. I swallowed a little at that word. She said it so easily, and when she did, the nerves crawled in, telling me I had to say it, too; that was how those things worked. Except I couldn't, not even now, not even when she could. We hadn't ever mentioned love between the two of us. *Amor* suddenly held so much weight.

I hung up and promptly tossed my phone to the side. A new worry to contend with, and it just so happened to be during what was potentially the single most stressful week of my career. This was going to be fun.

* * *

144

Hours later, Revello was back on the road (read: in the air). Also, it was technically only half of Revello. Andrea was going back to Calabria for some performance meetings, which were an embarrassing way of the team telling you that you were wasting their time and failing to bag them the points they needed. No one wanted to sit through those. I felt just slightly bad for him.

I, on the other hand, would be making a beeline to the house in Barcelona to hide away from Jolt, who'd unfortunately also be taking the early route directly to Spain. They were already cooking up promos for their new line-up and, naturally, they would party like there was no tomorrow because they now held the key to sweeping the Constructors' Championship in their own hands.

Racing aside, I kind of couldn't wait to be home. I'd got acclimatized to Québec for a time: of course I loved it there. But there was nothing like Barcelona; lazy, warm days spent training and hanging around at the tapas bars. They'd also be bringing my car here, which meant I had full liberty to rove about in it with the top down and greet my local fans. So long as I could stop worrying, it would be great.

As promised, on landing, my car was already waiting beside Paula's. She drove a Heidelberg Hybridge Chaser sedan (traitor). I promenaded the streets in an unmissable black Revello Catanzaro 202.

The Catanzaro was the sum of my wildest dreams. My father always told me that if I wanted a nice car, I'd have to earn it myself. Driving that car, I felt like I had finally made it on my own. People often said that my name was the only reason I'd gotten into F1. I said I wouldn't be winning grands prix and pulling up in a $900,000 convertible if that were true.

'Not too much bluster,' Paula lectured me the second our feet touched solid ground in the airport. 'At least pretend you're hiding. This isn't like Québec. Everyone knows you here. Careful taking photos, people will steal things. Don't wear your Rolex out in public, *please*. No reciprocal flirting with fans. No winking. No singing. No dancing. And keep your cap on' – she flipped my hat around so that the bill was no longer backwards how I liked it – 'the normal way.'

I flipped it right back. 'This *is* the normal way.'

'Let's stay covert.' Paula reached out and readjusted the cap. 'Just be normal. Okay? Let's try and keep a low profile. Jolt's vacation here is enough. We need to remain dignified.'

'By which you mean tea party and wedding planning with our parents.'

'*Verdad.*' My sister smiled sarcastically. 'You could have gone to Guadalajara with Jatziry, but you chose España. Face the music, *tío.*'

She opened the door of her parked car and disappeared inside, leaving me to panic. If I had to spend a week straight with Mamá and Papá, I might just lose it.

I remembered how Paula had roasted me back in Saudi Arabia. Her remarks were so foreign to me, till I just then began to realize she'd been right. I was in Spain. I wanted to do all of the things, but those obligations I'd fought Paula over had to come first. I had to honour my promise to do right by Jatziry, and yes, that meant tea parties and wedding planning sessions with our parents.

I slid into the driver's seat of my Catanzaro. The purr of the engine beckoned like a temptress. *Party. Tapas. Alcohol. Fans. Beach. Gym.* All slipping from my grasp.

With a groan, I pulled out of the lot, leaving the airport behind for the countryside roads that would take me to my very first home.

It was not very long after I was born that we moved to Canada. Mamá had me three weeks after the last race of Papá's final Formula 1 season. Shortly afterwards, we relocated to Canada, with the intention of getting away from the attention that our father's former career attracted, and so that we could receive a good upbringing, a good education. What my parents got instead was one child who loved Spain so badly that she returned to the country to attend university, and another who fell for Spain so hard he decided to move back there for good.

I had no recollection of Barcelona as a kid. Therefore, I automatically hated the thought of home being anywhere that wasn't Québec. Then, during the summer break at the end of one karting season, when I was sixteen, we took the first trip to arrange my match with Jatziry. I was a goner. I begged my parents to stay one more day. One day turned into a week turned into a month. I stayed the whole summer and swore I would return to Spain.

When I was tapped for F3, everything fell perfectly into place. A home base in Barcelona was ideal for so many of the races that were scattered throughout Europe. I enrolled in college in Spain through a reciprocity agreement; since then, I'd spent most of my time on the road, alternating between Canada and Spain as I saw fit.

I followed Paula's car up the shallow hill near the old church onto the roundabout driveway, to where our house sat, haloed in meticulously trimmed bushes. A terracotta-coloured fountain, reminiscent of those in the Alhambra, was positioned out front, set among sprays of vibrantly coloured flowers. Both retirees, our parents loved gardening to death. Gardening and golf and horses, they couldn't live without.

The estate, a Spanish Revival stereotype in and of itself, held some of my more prized recent memories. Here, we'd held my engagement party to Jatziry just last year, in the courtyard formed by the peach walls, lights strung across their muted surfaces. On my first trip, I crouched at the bushes with Mamá and helped her plant her favourite flowers (pomegranate flowers, bluebells, lantanas), as I confessed to her that I wanted to spend the summer in Spain.

Paula and I parked on the drive, exchanging a knowing look as we got out. Our parents were wonderful people, but they had a very particular idea of how things ought to work, what with reputation and money, particularly our father, whose time in Formula 1 had earned him high prestige in Spain. Santiago de la Fuente Jr. was, after all, the second Spaniard in history to win a Formula 1 grand prix. Santiago de la Fuente Sr., his father, had been the first.

I removed my cap and tried my best to fix my hair, vainly attempting to hide the fact that it now grew both over and past my ears.

'Give up now,' laughed Paula. 'It is doing nothing for you. Besides, your hair is nothing to them. You just won a grand prix. *No te preocupes.*'

I rolled my eyes as we walked to the front door together. 'Here we go,' I said, deadpan. 'Let's start the week off right.'

Chapter Twenty-One

Miguel

'And in that last lap – damn, he was close to beating the woman from Jolt for fastest time!'

Papá was beside himself with Revello's Melbourne performance. Every race, he boomed with all his might that his son deserved a place among the greats, for within the family it was the great expectation that I would do what he could not: be the World Champion in Formula 1.

This time, though, it was a bit different, I could tell from the way Papá was fixating on a driver other than myself, and it was almost a relief.

'Wish I'd been there to see it in person,' he went on. 'You were fantastic as usual, Angelito, brought home our P1, but Jolt . . . I cannot even begin to conceive of it.'

'You have to think broader, Tiago,' Mamá said with a smile. That was my mother in a nutshell – thinking more broadly. Among Spanish high society, she did what she wanted, wore what she wanted and said what she wanted. People had gossiped among themselves like crazy when my father got married to her, saying they would not last because she had too much attitude. They were completely wrong. Papá and Mamá had lasted, and, of course, they had had us. In my mind, it was Paula who took after Mamá the most. *A team is only as powerful as its engineers, Pauli*, Mamá had told my sister when she'd first got the job. *And Revello, I can tell you, needs your power.* Paula definitely got her brazen attitude from our mother. 'This is a new age.'

'I'm only surprised the gravity hasn't snapped this lady driver in half!' Papá retorted.

I couldn't help rolling my eyes. 'Papá, come on, she has trained for this, too.'

'Clearly!' Mamá helped me out. 'You said it, Tiago. Look at how she races. *Es una, como se dice, supermujer.*'

I looked to Papá expectantly.

'She's good,' he admitted at last. 'Very good.'

The rest of us burst into laughter. I never thought I'd see the day Papá, firm in his ways, would acknowledge that a female driver might be skilled at her art. 'Yes!' Mamá declared triumphantly. 'And from a place in which women could not drive till 2018.'

'Till 2018?' yelped Papá. '*¡Qué lástima!*' What a pity!

We continued to laugh at his complete and utter shock, though inside, I felt pretty shocked myself. My dad knew so much about cars and driving and racing, working on a team that garnered international recognition, that sold cars to countries like Saudi Arabia itself, and yet he hadn't been aware of the issues for women around the right to drive. It was a painful kind of irony.

Once the laughter had subsided a bit, Mamá spoke up. 'You karted with her as a kid, no? You and Diana, her name is? The face looks so familiar.'

I raised an eyebrow. This was a new one. 'Karted with her?'

'Hmm. Wait just a second.' Mamá bustled down the hall and up the stairs.

'I wonder what she's on about now,' mused Papá, as our mother re-emerged soon after with a massive book – an album. She sat back down on the living-room couch and riffled through it before opening it and laying it flat on the coffee table, sliding it my way.

'*Míralo,*' she said, eyes ablaze with nostalgia.

The three of us did. I did. And all I could say was, 'No way.'

We were looking at the childhood equivalent of the now-iconic photo taken after Saudi quali. And it wasn't only one picture – it was many. They were dated 2012. In one, I offered Diana Zahrani a gloved hand as I helped her from her kart, just like in Jeddah. In another, the both of us held podium trophies high, Miguel P1 and Diana P2. And then it was 2013. I was fifteen now, and Diana and I embraced each other as confetti rained down around us. The last photo showed us post-hug, and the unspoken words between the two of us, in teenage eyes now grown up. I grinned sheepishly in my slightly oversized sponsor-laden suit, Velcro undone, hair wild, completely lost as my gaze met Diana's exhilarated one, haloed in what was then curls . . . I was in disbelief. This old set of photographs, particularly the last, it held volumes of emotions.

'I don't think I remember these,' I murmured.

'You were in the thick of your karting career at that time.'

Paula ran her fingers over the kart picture. 'You were driving and driving back then. You stopped to recall very little.'

My attention stayed on the 2013 pair, even as my sister peered at the earlier photos. 'Mamá, you took these? You kept them?'

She nodded, beaming. She was getting older: you could see it in the definition of her smile lines, and the grey in her brown hair, but how happy this made her; it aged her backwards, as beautiful as she was either way. 'I didn't think you'd remember how much fun you two had when you karted together, so yes, I kept them.'

'Wow.' I slipped the last photo from its sleeve. It felt as if I was holding a part of me I hadn't realized I was missing. Everything trickled back to me: the feeling of déjà vu I got when Diana did certain things; those little habits that struck a chord in my brain, and – more than that – in my heart. Maybe I had never seen her again after those karting races, but she had never really left.

'Damn, Papá, you remember? In this 2013 one, she beat me, and you said you would also drink from my shoes if she made it to Formula.'

Papá went pink. 'I said that?'

I chuckled and passed Mamá the photo. 'Is this for real? Man . . .'

'Of course, it's for real!' Mamá let out a little laugh as she took in the picture for herself. 'This *I* know clearly. It was only a few races. You didn't know one another well, at least, not as well as I would have liked, but you two would be joined at the hip at races. More you. You were like a fan of hers, Angelito. Just see this look on your face. Part of me thought we had better tell Jatziry's parents you would only ever be able to marry another driver. You had it so bad for this girl, this Diana.'

'Oh, Ma.' I buried my face in my hands like an embarrassed schoolboy. And I'd thought this couldn't get any worse for me. 'I remember. I was such a dud. I was so stupid around her.'

Papá laughed his booming laugh. 'A true de la Fuente.'

Mamá tried to conceal a snort and failed. I looked up at the ceiling with a sigh. 'Mamá, what if she remembers what an idiot I was?'

Our mother just gave me a typically warm smile. 'I find it absolutely adorable that you still care what she thinks.'

'I mean, of course. She's . . .' I exhaled, grinning that same grin as my younger counterpart. '*The* coolest driver I know, honestly.'

Papá shot me a look.

Paula laughed out loud. 'Our dad is right here – take that back while you still can.'

'You get what I mean,' I said with a roll of my eyes. 'Like, what if she knows and has just been quietly laughing at me this whole time?'

'Doesn't seem like it.' Mamá raised an eyebrow, tapping the photo of young me holding a hand out to Diana. 'Seeing as she willingly recreated this moment. Oh, I had goosebumps when I saw it. It felt *como el suerte*.'

'Destined,' Paula echoed, driving her shoulder into mine.

I just waved a dismissive hand. 'C'mon, that's just in fairy tales.'

'Everything happens for a reason,' quipped Mamá. 'Maybe Diana is back for a reason.'

She didn't push it any further, just let it simmer with me.

Paula obviously sensed it, too. Something else was going on here. And I wasn't sure just yet if my mother, for all her superstitions, was right. Maybe I was a little nervous, too.

What if this was *suerte*?

Chapter Twenty-Two

Diana

The evening of our first day in Barcelona, with very few outstanding obligations on my end, Jolt let me out of my enclosure to go sightseeing for the night (without security, which I was pleasantly surprised about). Nic would be staying in to do papers and meet the team, though I wished we could go out together. It wouldn't be much fun all alone.

Resisting the sweatpants urge, I rooted through my bag till I found a pair of mom jeans. I paired them up with an oversized T-shirt and my Jolt-colored Air Forces. If anyone recognized me, they might say I looked sloppy, but at least I would be comfortable. I grabbed my purse, swiped on my kohl, and headed out onto the town.

Barcelona was almost labyrinthine, which brought me endless happiness. Going exploring was one of the things I couldn't do back home but had excuses to do out here. I'd already planned out my travels: everyone told me to do La

Sagrada Família, but I asked around with the locals, and I decided to go see Santa Maria del Mar instead.

I walked through weaving streets, past lights flickering on, artistic structures and mosaics in all the colours of the rainbow, as the sun prepared to set, and the tourists came out in search of an aesthetic vantage point. It took me some time to find the basilica. I was not bright at directions. I made a U-turn, checked the map on my phone, and interrogated shop owners. At last, I found it: Santa Maria del Mar.

It was a wonder of Gothic architecture, something that might sound a bit tedious if I described it minutely, but which was stunning in person. The stained glass glittered in aptly positioned floodlights, spires reaching upward like giant sewing needles. It was definitely more flamboyant than any churches we had in Jeddah, that was for sure. I walked up to the path and entered the doors below the arches.

My breath left my chest in a gasp. The interior was absolutely brilliant. The rose window was even more mesmerizing from here, a kaleidoscope of multicoloured petal-like shapes. The pews appeared to go on for ever, all the way up to the altar in the front, where the statue of Santa Maria del Mar stood. Above me, high arched ceilings met in domes that made the church feel truly like a sanctuary. The dim light of the sconces transporting me to a time before electricity.

I crossed the aisle in the middle of the church, taking it all in. Could you imagine getting married somewhere this magical, this pure? It was a far-off dream, but I turned in a slow one-eighty to absorb all of it.

Only then did I become aware that – though the cathedral appeared empty – I wasn't alone. Someone – yes, it was a priest, rustled about at the altar. I slipped primly into the pews. I wasn't adventurous enough to risk gallivanting around the cathedral in front of a man of God, unfortunately.

So I did what was socially acceptable, and let the enduring tenacity of it all wash over me in silence. I even clasped my hands, bowed my head, and said to myself, *If I could just get one sign, Mother Maria, one sign that this Formula 1 chaos will be all right and that I've found my safe place. Amen.*

When I got up, I went to light a candle. The priest looked my way as I set my own flame for my prayer. He smiled kindly. 'Everyone lights one for a reason,' he said in a lightly accented voice. 'Do you have a prayer?'

I nodded, a bit sheepish. 'Somewhat. You think Santa Maria hears it?'

'Of course,' the priest replied. 'She will. All in its own time.'

Time. I thanked the old priest before I left with that word in mind. I felt as if I had used up so much time already. How much longer would I wait till my questions would finally be heard and my sign finally delivered to me?

I stepped back out into the city, now slightly aimless. I got stopped a few times for photographs and to sign hats and pictures, but I soon realized that the more I walked, the more confused I got.

And then I got *really* lost.

The street I now found myself in was the exact opposite of the tranquil backstreets I'd been looking for. There were tourists and pedestrians every which way, traffic jamming the road shut, modern buildings juxtaposing the high-spired churches.

I did a quick about-face before turning to the left, where

the crowds seemed to thin out farther down the sidewalk. Safety. Okay. I had to move fast before the media hit.

'*Diana!*'

Oh. No.

I made the fatal mistake of turning back towards the voice that had just yelled my name, and there, toting cameras as if they were loaded weapons, was a clutch of paparazzi.

I liked to say the paparazzi were a myth. I'd never encountered them in F2; they couldn't have cared less about me, though the Championship garnered some traction for my public profile. I didn't think I'd ever run into them, but now, suddenly, here they were.

Before I made any more rash decisions, I spun towards the emptier sidewalk and pumped my arms and legs in as brisk a walk as I could manage. I heard the photographers behind me, a backdrop to the sound of my own heart beating. I didn't know my way around this city, but I had no choice but to try and find another route. I made a sharp right turn into the space between two churches, whispering a hushed prayer to the higher power and, as I bustled in the other direction, the sound of the reporters dimmed until I could no longer hear them shouting.

That was too close.

I was safe. Except I had no idea where I was.

I dug my hands into my hair with a groan. I figured I was hopelessly lost when someone said from behind me, 'Oh, wow.'

I moved to rush away at first, but I exhaled in relief as soon as I saw who was there. This was Miguel de la Fuente's home turf, so he looked entirely comfortable here, even though he was panting. I was just glad to have run into someone who knew their way around this maze of a city. 'Thank goodness.'

'Fancy seeing you here, too.' Miguel looked to be as out of breath as I was, his hair slightly tousled, eyes wide in surprise. 'What the hell are you up to?'

'Unsure.' A group of already drunk guys stumbled down the pavement beside me and, unconsciously, I took a few steps closer to Miguel. 'I've just . . . run from the press, I suppose. No idea where I am right now. I came from a cathedral.'

He raised an eyebrow. 'La Sagrada Família?'

'Santa Maria del Mar, actually.'

Respect danced in Miguel's eyes. 'Smart tourist.'

'Why are you . . .' I gestured up and down his well-built form. His shoulders still moved with amped-up breaths. Even without any context, it was obvious he'd sped off from somewhere just as fast as I had.

'Fans.' The right corner of his mouth quirked up and he shrugged, as if to say, *Oh well.* 'It happens at home.'

I shuddered. I loved my fans with everything I had, but if I had to be chased down in my wonderful Dubai, I think I'd scream. 'Wow.'

'I mean. It's over now,' he said with a half-hearted chuckle. 'So, anyway. You went to Santa Maria?'

Something about the way he sounded so delighted by my choice of destination made me go slightly giddy. 'Yes. A couple of people I asked here recommended it.'

'You liked it?'

'I loved it.'

Miguel grinned, and with his cheeks still slightly flushed from his fan-evading escapade, his freckles just barely discernible, I had to hold back my own smile. 'You know, if you're enjoying Barcelona, if you're up to it, there's a great tapas place not too far from here.'

'I can't even tell my ass from my head,' I said, 'so that would be the ideal course of action.'

'Okay, c'mon.' He laughed as we began walking side by side, two F1 drivers undercover in the busiest city in Spain. 'You're pretty close to La Boqueria. It's this big public market, has some great food. But I can get you to the really good places. The holes in the wall, as they say. Cross here.'

We continued across a road and, as we went, the crowds thinned out, making way for a more folksy feeling, traditionally decorated buildings with colourful flowers juxtaposed against old architecture. Miguel led us into one of the smaller places, beneath a pink awning, and into a dimly lit room I guessed was some kind of bar and/or restaurant.

The place seemed very small. Everything was wood panelled, and the lamps were frosted and just a touch dusty. I forged onward, trailing uncertainly behind Miguel. There were no customers or anything, no place to sit. Miguel called something to the woman at the counter in Spanish, and she replied with a broad grin. We approached a set of doors in the back of the bar, if I could even call it that.

'Ready?' he asked.

I was still assessing this new environment. 'Uh, yeah.'

'Don't dismiss this place out of hand yet.' Miguel turned the door handle. 'Right this way.'

Still dubious, I obliged, and suddenly, we were in a massive courtyard. I must have audibly gasped, because Miguel chuckled. 'Told you.'

'Oh . . . this is beautiful.'

160

We stood in a courtyard which was walled on all sides but one. From that open side, you could see the rolling hills of the countryside, the firefly-like lights shining as dark fell. With a start, I realized that this was not just a courtyard. The entire place had been built on some sort of peak, perhaps the top of one of those rolling hills. The little restaurant was abuzz with activity. There were people eating, many young couples chatting in animated Spanish at tables overlooking the stunning view, surrounded by the glow of oil lamps and the city itself. Planted all around the courtyard were pots full of brightly coloured flowers and towering trees. Vines climbed up the walls unchecked. Nature had been allowed to grow unhindered here, it appeared.

Miguel gestured to a table perched right at the edge, fit for the kind of idiots who gambled their lives on open-cockpit race cars. I was still completely awestruck as we sat down. I had never seen anything like this. Nothing I'd experienced living in the city could match this tranquillity.

'Tía Catalina will be out with food and drinks soon, but for now . . .' Miguel reached into his pocket, 'I wanted to show you these.'

I wasn't sure what I was expecting, but it was certainly not four old photos.

Miguel spread them out across the table for me and sat back, letting me take it in. At first, I didn't completely understand, but then it hit me that they were *us*, kids in go karting uniforms, together. It appeared that our story had begun nearly a decade ago. Here we were, racing together once more.

And with that, I remembered everything.

'We were babies!' I let out a laugh coupled with relief, holding up a photo in which Miguel and I were hugging after the karting cup in Monaco, when we were all so new to the circuit that we felt like huge celebrities being in Monte Carlo. I had beaten Miguel that day for first place, but only by a hair. 'Miguel, where did these come from?'

'My mom.' He smiled, now a bit shyly. 'I know this is stupid because I'd only seen you at a race here and there, but . . . I was a huge fan. Of you.'

I picked up the next photo, glancing down so he couldn't see my cheeks going red. I wished I had words to tell him what this was doing to me, and to that feeling of recognition that had been unnameable until now. Memories resurfaced in my mind, snapshots of just a few moments with that boy I instantly shared a camaraderie with upon our very first race together, that boy I thought I would likely never see again.

In this photo, we held one another at arm's length, eyes meeting. Miguel and I both had a certain starstruck aura about us. He wore the same mischievous smirk as he did now. I glanced up at him, peeking just above the upper edge of the photo. All at once, I felt starstruck once more. Miguel's overgrown black hair was tousled and yet neat, drifting carelessly with the wind. Shards of pale brown and green danced in his dark eyes. I noticed that smattering of freckles across his nose, almost untraceable against the natural tan of his skin. Just a bit, so slight it was inconceivable, his strong, stubbled jaw shifted as he, like myself, attempted to make sense of this strange moment, this anomaly in time. I lowered the photo, knowing I could no longer hide my own hesitant smile.

'*Suerte*,' Miguel said, the understanding passing between us the same way it had in that picture. 'You believe in destiny, Diana?'

'Well . . . not really.'

'Me, neither.' He cracked a grin. 'That's a load of lies. But you . . . I don't know. I just feel like we've been brought back on the track together by . . .'

'Something else,' I finished slowly.

'Sounds crazy, doesn't it?'

'Just a little.'

'Whatever it might be . . .' Miguel shrugged, and I envied his blissfulness in that moment, detached from everything else. 'We're here now.'

That much was true. This place was gorgeous, a jewel of perfect peace tucked away to preserve its innocence, a hidden wonder in this bustling city. The countryside untouched, the courtyard completely tranquil.

And yet today, it wasn't Barcelona that took away my ability to speak.

Chapter Twenty-Three

Diana

I hadn't really felt it before, but I was beginning to experience some pressure racing alongside Nic. The rate at which he had taken over the track in the JA76 was terrifying. No one would outwardly acknowledge this, but every single F1 team had a number one driver, the better performer, the title winner, the celebrity, and a number two driver, who served primarily as insurance, occasionally outperformed and continually defending their seat. It was only Nic's first race with Jolt, but I had to pull out all the stops. There was no way I could fall into this number two trap.

I slid into the seat of my car, bracing myself with the halo as I settled down. The team checked everything, and made sure the tyres – I now demanded two walkarounds to be certain – were screwed in properly. I couldn't take any risks.

'Check them again,' I called from beneath my helmet. 'Once more, please.'

I was glad they could not see the look on my face. Then they would know just how frightened I was.

The Spanish GP began with a bang – literally.

Right on to Turn One, lights out and away we went, there was a massive three-car collision that resulted in a premature yellow flag. It was the Wilson Nitro driven by Michael Cade, spun off the tracking, taking Ben Kittington's Burgess and Jonas Hauser's Misaki with him. I groaned as the flag went out, still trapped in P2.

'Ugh, this flag,' I said to Aiden.

'Give it some time,' he replied, immensely level as usual.

The flag felt as if it was out for all eternity. It was finally withdrawn, and I didn't wait. I pushed as soon as I had an opening, gritting my teeth against the force of the turns. I slipped in front of Nic without remorse, holding in P1.

'Get a good lead, we don't want DRS behind you,' said Aiden. 'Good one second delta. On your rear now, Nic P2, Miguel P3, Darien P4, Peter P5.'

'All right.'

I sped down the straight, leaving Miguel well behind the one-second DRS detection window, thankfully. I had a tactical advantage. I had to keep it.

It looked beautiful till about Lap Fifty. The top three were the same: myself, Nic, Miguel. I took the chicane after the first straight, car responding perfectly. And suddenly, the rug came out from under me. The front left locked up, just like it had at Imola. Except this time, it was all on me. I'd braked too hard, causing my wheel to catch.

I swung onto the curve hard, my whole car bouncing as I ran over the kerb.

No, no, no, not again. 'Damn it!' I yanked the steering wheel with all my might. By some miracle, I forced a recovery. But I'd lost time now. I knew it. I had Nic in my mirrors.

'Let's get right back on track, Diana. You're still in P1.'

'Is there damage?'

'No, no damage, Diana. You're running on newer tyres than Nic, but now this evens you out to about the same, that's all it is.'

I put up defence on the back straight, still keeping Nic just out of DRS range. He could not pass at this point. All I had to do was hold on.

'Hold, right?' I said. 'How is my pace?'

Silence from my lifeline on the other end.

'Aiden, how is my pace?' I repeated, worried now.

Finally, he replied. What he said, I wish I had never heard.

'Diana, keep your pace. I have a team directive from Cavanaugh.'

'Keep my pace?' I echoed incredulously. 'But then Nic will—'

'Yeah. That is what he's saying.'

I wanted to yell in that moment. It took everything I had to pull back my emotions and stay professional over the radio. I couldn't believe my ears. What the hell was going on?

'Diana,' a new voice came on. 'This is Theo, Diana. I think it's best you hear it from me.'

Cavanaugh on my radio? No way. 'What is there left . . . for me to hear?' I wrenched the words out of my mouth as I jerked around the back chicane.

'I know you were defending very well, but, Diana, we will invert the cars. Easy does it.'

166

'Confirm, Theo, you want us to do what?'

'No, listen to me, Di. Let him by.'

'Is it the spin?' I almost pleaded. 'The car has no performance damage. I can keep this, I really can. I can keep P1.'

'Pushing *will* damage. Nic has a better P1 defence.'

The words punched me in the chest. 'Um, okay. I am holding pace. He can overtake now.'

Never had I felt like more of a failure in my professional career than when I watched Nic Necci pass by my slowly paced car, when I'd let my own mistake give Jolt leeway to wrestle me into compliance. Of course, they did have a reason for inverting the cars: I'd nearly gone into the wall, my car was missing the facilities necessary to secure a safe, cushy P1 with many seconds between the next driver, and that meant Nic could defend better, so the odds of him leading us into a victory were better, on and on. But my sportsmanship had officially cost me what could have been my first P1. Was this Jolt's way of telling me I was going to be their number two now? After all, I'd mishandled the car. It wasn't a technical error this time.

Yet there was a feeling I couldn't shake. The car was still *there*. I still had the power I needed to race. Aiden had said there was no damage after my pirouette. I could have held out. Did that mean, then, that Jolt thought I would not put up a fight? That they could use me as insurance for Nic?

'And that's P2, Diana, P2. Excellent job, mate,' Aiden's voice crackled as I whizzed past the chequered flag.

Forget about that, I wanted to say. This P2, this was not what I had raced for. I could have earned a P1.

'Thank you,' I said instead.

* * *

I didn't want to approach anyone after the race. I didn't even want to speak to Miguel about it, regardless of the fact that after Imola and the tapas bar in Barcelona, we were beginning to get much closer. Maybe people thought I was crying from the way I kept my helmet on all the way back to the cooldown room, but I was seething. I wanted to strangle someone.

I could have done it, achieved P1. It was right there, just within my reach. It echoed in my mind as I got into the cooldown room first, swapped my helmet out for a podium cap. *Let him by*. The radio message that would soon spread like wildfire across the internet.

I gulped water as I watched highlight reels from the race, waiting for the other two to come in. I realized that Nic probably didn't even know what had happened, likely assumed that my car had been damaged, so he had had to take the lead.

My mother and father had taken me to the Jeddah Corniche once when I was much younger, before Baba's accident. Ammi had grabbed a handful of sand from the ground near the coastline and poured it into my own palm.

'Look, *joonam*,' she said. 'Open your hand.'

I'd stretched my fingers out, and suddenly, the sand had gone right through, gone as quickly as it had been deposited into my grubby child's hand.

'Sometimes, you will get these amazing chances, Diyana,' she told me. 'These chances to do something, to have everything your heart desires. And they will slip through your fingers, just like that. That's how the world is, *joonam*. Not everything is meant to last, because otherwise, what is the reason to live? What is the reason to keep trying?'

What *was* the reason to keep trying? I had driven this entire race in P1, and at the last second, Nic got to take the glory, to take credit for the race I had led the entire time. This, I should have held on to tighter.

'P1, baby!'

Soon enough, Nic and Miguel were in the cooldown, already celebrating Nic's very first victory, completely unaware of my feelings. It was probably better that way. Inversions were a fact of racing, but could poison the grid with dangerous rumours.

'Congrats, guys.' Miguel collapsed contentedly on the couch as the highlights rolled on. 'Ooh, this start.'

'This was so bad,' groaned Nic. Onscreen, Cade flew across the track and hit the wall. At least I hadn't done that again, I thought.

We watched until I nearly spun out. 'Fantastic save!' Miguel nudged me. I forced a smile in return. My stomach did a slow somersault as I realized what was about to happen. I prayed they wouldn't play the radio.

It came on anyway.

'Keep your pace,' said Aiden.

Nic looked on intently. Miguel's eyebrows knitted together as Cavanaugh joined in. 'We will invert the cars.'

'Confirm, Theo, you want us to do what?'

I pursed my lips and glanced away. All three of us were deadly silent.

'Is it the spin? The car has no performance damage. I can keep this, I really can. I can keep P1.'

Either way, I made myself look at it. Nic overtook me with little trouble.

It took a moment for Miguel to speak at last. 'What . . . the hell?'

'Oh, Diana.' Nic shot a look of pity my way. 'That must have been tough. When our cars suffer that kind of damage, the aftermath is *always* tough. But thank you, you know. For playing for the team. It's because of you that we got the one-two.'

'Don't thank me,' I said stonily. 'You can thank Theo. As he must have thought you were more formidable in P1 than me to invert.'

'Di . . . really,' Nic went on, patting my shoulder. 'It's a great thing you did as a sportsman today.'

'Sportswoman.' I stood up and adjusted my hat. 'You're most welcome.'

I knew I shouldn't take my anger out on Nic, but he was behaving as if I'd just done something really saintly for Jolt today. He was just . . . why couldn't he see it? They would check my car and find there was no substantial damage. What would it take for these kinds of race politics to be exposed?

'I don't know,' said Miguel slowly. 'Doesn't inversion feel . . . unjust? Against the spirit of the race?'

'It was for the team,' Nic replied. 'It's whatever gets us those points, bro.'

I struggled to conceal the disgust on my face. 'Yes. For the team.'

Nic spread his hands, leaning back against the couch. 'C'mon, it happens. Could have just as easily been me out in front after the spin and letting you by.'

'Sure, it could have.' I shook my head.

'What's that supposed to mean?'

'That you already know I'm going to have to sit down for a "talk" with Cavanaugh.'

Miguel shifted uncomfortably. 'You followed the team order, though.'

'It's never over,' I said, voice catching. 'Once this kind of thing starts, it never ends.'

Chapter Twenty-Four

Diana

The inversion during the Spanish Grand Prix was all that the grid and everyone else, now not just in the motorsport world, could talk about. Some were saying it was a tactical move due to a less powerful car out front, and others saw it as typical toxic auto culture. Jolt seemed to have more faith in their male driver than a woman who, in her first year of Formula 1, had brought the team four podiums and would have grabbed a first place if not for the team order.

As I waited outside the conference room for the panel, my legs felt as if they were going to crumple beneath me. I knew I was going to receive support, but I would also be getting a backlash. There would be people out there who agreed with the team order, and people who believed I was inferior to my teammate. If I wanted to make a point, it would be difficult. I would be talked over, my media coach had warned me. Speak clearly and speak kindly was the advice. There was little more I could do about the situation.

Just beyond the door, a press intern called out to me. 'Miss Zahrani? You're on.'

I took a deep breath. It was time to bow to the inevitable.

It was not just me who would be at this panel. Up at the front already sat a contented-looking Theodore Cavanaugh, no doubt armed with answers to any probing question he might receive. I looked away the second I saw Nic, face unreadable, approaching from the other side of the room. The final member of the conference would be our strategist, who was the last to enter, right behind Nic.

'So, a one-two at last,' the interviewer began right off the bat. I had barely touched the chair when the question left his lips. 'That's brilliant. But we hear, Mr Cavanaugh, as everyone has, that there was a team order inversion on Lap Fifty-Three. Walk us through that one.'

Cavanaugh had been waiting for this question, rehearsed for it, because he remained emotionless. He took a sip from his silver Jolt tumbler. 'Well, Lap Fifty-Three was a difficult decision. On Fifty-One, Diana did have a lockup that nearly sent her into a spin, and she recovered actually very fast, but our view at that point was that she could have problems with the car, would be unable to carry the race home in a stressed car, and she had not that, uh, strong history in Formula 1 that Nicolò has had, so we banked on him. We have solid data that Nic paces very well, is very reliable, and we would rather have him P1 than have Diana suffer a malfunction and maybe take out both cars. So we decided it was safer, because then we could also have Nic's slipstream carry Diana a bit in case her pace slowed. It was a necessary strategic move.'

Necessary. I bit back words for both the audience and my team principal.

'Certainly,' replied the interviewer. 'And, ah, Nic, how does that P1 feel, then? Any different?'

'Honestly, it does not feel right to invert with anyone,' he began primly. 'I can't imagine what such a tough decision was like for Diana, but, um, I do think that it was tactically justified. To keep us in the lead and keep us safe, right, in case anything happened to Di's car. I, uh, I've been in this circuit for a while longer than she has, acquired some more skill and race craft, and I think the outcome speaks for itself.'

I fought the urge to shake my head in disapproval. He sounded just like Cavanaugh. Could this man not think for himself? I'd seen so much of that in him – so much *thought* – and yet here, it was just gone.

I wondered if Miguel was watching, and if he felt the same way. He had known Nic such a long time, raced with him; they had become close friends, like brothers. What irked me was that it was possible this shift was due to their friendship. Nic had never had an opportunity till now to get ahead, to race for a big team, while Miguel had nearly won the Championship just a year prior. And now that Nic had enjoyed his first taste of victory, there would be no turning back. The jealousy, the comparison, it had him in its fists.

'Now for Diana. How do you feel? Think you perhaps could have won that race?' The interviewer chuckled. 'After all, that's what so many people are saying. Even Kasper apparently believes you could have had P1.'

'Maybe I should have had P1 then, since he thinks so,' I quipped, prompting laughter and camera flashes from the crowd. I could have thought that through a little better. 'I will be very frank. I see the tactical reasoning. But hearing the words "let him by" come from your principal is every driver's worst nightmare. What that is saying is "Hey, let our number one through." It's only five races in, only one for Nic, and the lines are already being drawn. It is heartbreaking to be shown your true status in the eyes of your team. It really is. I don't want to have to fight against both my team and all the others to achieve some level of success in this sport, but I guess there's nothing I can do about it.'

Someone in the front let out a low whistle.

'That's . . .' The interviewer trailed off. 'That's a bold statement.'

I picked up my water bottle, slowly unscrewed the cap, and took a small sip. 'I know,' I replied.

There was a moment of silence that lasted no more than a second before all hell broke loose.

The press corps was yelling, cameras clicking madly, journalists pushing up against the ropes with microphones and handheld recorders and even notepads. They were rabid. They had smelled drama, and now, here it was.

'Let's get out of here,' the media officer to our left whispered. 'Diana, you first.'

'Get out of here and what, leave all their questions unanswered?' I shot back. 'We need to be honest about this. At least, I feel that I do.'

And I knew I didn't have the luxury of behaving how I

wanted to and getting away with it. I knew that was true for all nineteen of the others, not just for me. But in that moment, I decided I had to stand my ground. I pointed to the reporter closest to me with a nod, and I said, 'Yes, please.'

Chapter Twenty-Five

Miguel

I raised an eyebrow Jatziry's way as she stood and fixed herself a glass of ice water from the kitchen. We'd been watching the Jolt press conference – a painful ordeal for everyone involved. To see this kind of behaviour from Nic was something I never thought I'd have to contend with, but we were here now, with him playing puppet to Cavanaugh and Diana left to fight for herself. It was a disaster.

But Jatziry, for her part, had been quiet. She'd been quiet since she'd returned, to be fair, yet I had to wonder. As much as this situation wasn't one we'd chosen for ourselves, we cared about one another, and that compelled me to ask her: 'Hey, Ziry, what's up? Be real with me, you've just seemed . . . off.'

She sighed. 'Put racing away for one minute and ask me how the wedding was, Miguel.'

'Sure. How was Lupe's wedding?'

'Horrible!' she admitted at last. My jaw fell slack. *That* wasn't at all what I had expected. 'No one will stop asking me where you are, Miguel. Not even my own mother. It's like I am only half a person without you. Everyone wants to see Miguel de la Fuente, number eighty-eight, Scuderia Revello, and when I show up without you, they pounce on me and then ignore me altogether. Not to mention that *I* wish you were with me. It feels like a chore alone, Miguel, and I do not know what else to tell you.'

I was quiet for a moment. I blinked. I processed.

That was a lot.

'Wow. Okay. Wow. Jatziry . . . if I'd known that was how you felt, I would have gone with—'

'That's the thing!' she put in. 'You realize after the fact, Miguel. There is no next time! There is no redo! Lupe will not get married again! Just . . . just make some effort, Miguel, to see what is going on here. With us. Miguel, we may be *together*, but we do everything ourselves. What is this, hmm? Tell me.'

'Jatziry.' I took a deep breath. I think she realized she was rattling me, which was fair. Because all this time, I'd rattled her. 'When I asked you, you know, back at the end of last season, if you were ready for this, I meant the race. Racing comes with me. It's a package deal. My team is as much my family as my parents, Paula, or you. And this is my living. I signed a contract promising I would live and breathe the Scuderia. The travel and the work and the media and the crashes. Sometimes I will have two weeks for a wedding. Sometimes I won't.'

'And that is the problem.' Her voice was quiet and yet even. 'You get that. You get your two weeks, you get your race. That is what you've always wanted. But no one ever asked me that.'

'Asked you that?' I echoed. My bluster had faded away, replaced by a sort of guilt.

Jatziry. Who was Jatziry? Did I know who she was? What did I even know about her beyond what everyone else did? Beyond the things our families had told us? What had her passions been, what had she loved? Had she given things up to be here? I'd never so much as thought about it. Just like she didn't know me outside of my races and the grands prix.

She shook her head. 'Because listen, Miguel, I know what else you want. I know, I can tell, and the more I think about it, the more . . .'

I prayed she wouldn't say it, and yet it hung in the air. I tried my best to steer around it. 'Racing, it's a part of me. It's been a part of me for the past twenty years. It won't just go away. I know you hate how much time it takes. That's just a fact of what I've chosen for myself. I just want to race, and it's costing you, I feel that. That's true.'

'Then why are you wasting your time planning your wedding with someone from outside this racing world of yours?'

'What?' I was stunned. She'd said exactly what she was going to earlier, and the blow wasn't any duller, 'Jatziry, what do you mean?'

'Is there something I don't know, Miguel, about your history with Diana?'

The question kicked the breath out of me. 'We were in karts together a couple times as kids,' I finally stuttered. 'There's no history to speak of. We barely remember it.'

'Oh, Miguel.' Tears welled up in her eyes, and as I watched her struggle to keep them at bay, they began to prick mine as well. 'You wouldn't be able to live with a wife who hates racing. And I don't think I'd be able to live with a husband who loves it more than me.'

'That's okay, though. Love can come with time,' I tried. I was grasping at straws. This was fatal. I'd never felt this helpless in my life.

'It will not. It will not for either of us, because I know I can't say it.' She swallowed, meeting my eyes. 'Can you?'

She waited. I waited, too. I waited for the words to come, a waterfall of emotion that would overtake me and send the three syllables rolling off my tongue. This should be so easy for me, I thought. After all this time, shouldn't it be easy?

'Can you?' Jatziry repeated.

I didn't know what to say or do. She just looked at me so guiltily, with the implication that it was me who we ought to feel sorry for in this moment.

'We should give this some time' was what she said.

Some time? We had just uncovered the biggest crack in our relationship, a gaping hole, and giving it some time would mend that? Why did people always say time would fix things? Time was no bandage. Time was not stitches.

'I have to be in Calabria tomorrow,' I said anyway, my voice threatening to break. 'I think a few days apart will do us good.'

Later that evening, before I left for the airport, I dug out some of my very old karting videos from ten years back and played them.

In the videos so old that they were stored on discs, with fading labels written in permanent marker, I found what I was looking for. Canadian Junior Karting Cup, 2012. I watched as I crossed the finish line first in the race, and the video cut to me celebrating among a sea of confetti, the first-place trophy held high.

There she was beside me. Second place, but she looked so unbothered as she congratulated me. She looked so young back then, so carefree, before the stress of the career had gotten to her. The two of us locked eyes and smiled, and I read her lips: *You did so good.*

As we laughed and talked and rejoiced on the television screen, all the hope slipped out of my soul. Jatziry was right. Look at us. Then and now. What if I needed someone who could race with me, keep up with me as I soared through life at three hundred kilometres an hour?

What if everything I had trusted my family to know was completely and utterly wrong?

It was true. I already knew things had gone from shaky to unsalvageable before I left for Calabria.

No matter how hard I tried, I started to see signs that Jatziry saw right through me. We spent such little time together. We treated time with one another like a chore. Like any couple, we went through rollercoaster phases, up and down, over and over, except the downs never completely went away. We didn't talk things out, didn't do anything but expect issues to vanish over time. When talking to Paula, I had called Jatziry my 'obligation', our conversation becoming more and more vivid in my memory as I realized Paula's predictions had all come true. Overcompensation, trying to build something I didn't have the strength for. Now, I was stuck with the aftermath.

I trudged through meetings and debriefs at Revello HQ, counting down the minutes till I could return home and end this misery. I didn't know what would happen. I just knew I wanted it to be over.

* * *

181

'We had a few good times, right?'

Across from me, Jatziry shook her head, smiling sadly. Her eyes held an unnatural amount of melancholy, which contrasted sharply with her usual happy-go-luckiness. 'No, Miguel, think about it. You conjured all of it. Neither of us can even say we love the other.'

'But—'

She let out a sarcastic laugh, an emotion I wasn't used to hearing from her. 'I don't even know your favourite colour.'

'My favourite colour . . .' I trailed off. 'Jatziry . . .'

'No – I do know it.' Her eyes looked only dejected, humourless. 'Revello red and green.'

I gritted my teeth. 'This is . . . Jatziry, you're sure? You don't want to save this, save us? Our families have waited for nearly a decade, and we just . . . give up on it? Why?'

'We do not live for our families.' Jatziry twisted her ring idly, the one I'd given her in Imola. 'We were supposed to live for ourselves. You live for the race. I need to find that for myself. Whatever makes me *live*.'

It was so final. I didn't know what to say.

'I saw some old videos from your karting cups,' said Jatziry, voice just above a whisper. 'You left them out after you left. Did you fall for her back then, Miguel?'

I hadn't even admitted it before. Though I had momentary feelings for Diana, I had never once cheated on Jatziry. I hadn't chosen to accept the truth. But now that she'd laid it before me, I couldn't just dismiss my emotions as awe or admiration any more.

'Things from when I was young – I don't take them seriously,' I finally spoke. 'But . . . I did. I did, and I don't know, but . . .'

I may still be falling, I wanted to say. I didn't need to; Jatziry's face told me that she'd heard those silent words anyway.

She took a deep breath. She seemed so small in her white day dress, hair falling down past her shoulders in perfect waves. She was innocent and, for that, I felt guilty.

'Thank you for your honesty.'

She slipped the ring off her finger and held it in her right hand, stared at it as if she were deciding. Then she set it down on the coffee table.

'You know I wish you only the best, Miguel.' She patted my cheek, and her smile was so broken that I wanted to pick up the pieces and glue them together with those tears that fell from her eyes. 'I will go back to Madrid and tell my parents. It is not your job to worry about any of that. And . . . I will keep watching what I can on TV.'

'You . . . you don't have to,' I managed.

She shrugged. 'My habits continue to compel me, you know, to cheer on the only pompous, big-time race-car driver I ever cared about.'

The last event that Jatziry and I appeared at together before she moved out and away for good was a private concert in Sevilla. Flamenco rang out through the amphitheatre as the most esteemed guests from across Spain sat and enjoyed the show, live music, dance and drinks.

We pretended to be exceptionally happy. We smiled for all the cameras and acted like we were laughing at something the other one had said. In a way, it wasn't much different from what we had been doing before.

It would be the photos they took at that event which

appeared in the news when the word got out: our engagement had officially ended, and not with a wedding.

I sat in the Barcelona flat we shared, now just me.

I watched as the articles rolled out over the next few days. 'Where has the love gone? De la Fuente fiancée car missing from lot.' 'Rumours that Jatziry Fernanda Calderón Blanco is back in Madrid.' 'Will we see Blanco at de la Fuente's next race?' I did not at all want to go to them and confirm it. Instead, I waited eagerly for the Monaco Grand Prix, where I could let go of everything and just feel perfectly in place behind the wheel. It was true: for me, racing was my constant. Everything else came and went, and without knowing it, Jatziry had proven that.

The night before my Monaco flight, I called Mamá back. I'd dodged her calls since Jatziry left, and I was replying days later. My mother would hate me for this.

I listened to the busy tone till she picked up.

'It finally happened, hmm?'

'Um, Mamá, I'm sorry I didn't call back—'

'Oh, Miguel, it is not even that!' My mother groaned. 'I knew it all along, you knew it, we all felt that you two were not at ease together. And yet you played with that poor girl's heart, ya, Miguel!'

I nearly fell off the couch. 'What – you *wanted* this?'

'Paula told you!' Mamá snapped. 'That this isn't like you, this living for someone else's wishes. You did not listen to anyone!'

'But everyone was counting on this. I literally cared about Jatziry! It's not like I tried to hurt her!'

'Men!' I could practically see my mother massaging her forehead. 'I said from the start. You were, what, such a cowboy from childhood. When your father insisted on this match between you and Jatziry, I told him it would not work. You would never be able to love someone who would not come down to a hundredth of your lap time, *chico*. Never.'

'Mamá . . .'

'Well, figure it out, no? And only when you do, tell me. Grow up, Miggie!'

With that, Mamá hung up and, as usual, I was back at square one. Time to 'figure it out'.

'This might even be good for you,' Paula assured me on the jet to Monaco. 'Remember how last season was? You had fun.'

I very much remembered, and maybe I had a little too much fun. As everyone was so fond of saying, both my racing and my presence had known no limits. I lived like every other crazy young driver, because every other crazy driver did not have fiancées from arrangements made with prestigious families with a bit of a grievance against the circuit (which was how my thought processes went at the time). Now I no longer had said fiancée. How the tables had turned.

'I put myself through unnecessary torture attempting to enjoy the days before a race weekend,' I corrected my sister. 'I'm surprised my trainer didn't give me the paddle for all the trouble I caused last year.'

'Well, that's because you had Ben before, and now you have Louie,' she offered.

'Louie is pretty relentless.'

'Yes, he did devastate you when he swapped all your American microwave mac and cheese dinners with controlled protein bowls.'

'Come on, apples? Oats? Couscous, he thinks I'll eat couscous?'

Paula cracked a rare smile. 'This is what I mean. Who cares about Louie and his protein bowls? Eat some powdered cheese, *tío*. Do what makes you erupt with joy.'

'Like you have.' I smirked, gently changing the topic. 'That Revello challenge with the cookies was a tell-all. And you tweeted just the other day. *You* tweeted. And you stopped putting your hair in those scalp-damning ponytails, Paula, what is going on?'

'You know, Mig . . .' She shrugged. 'As a girl, I just . . . I wanted nothing more than for our parents to put me in karts alongside you. When I watch you race, sometimes I wonder if it could be me, if things had worked out differently. The status quo has already taken so much from me. Why let it continue to control my life?'

'Huh.' I guess I'd always seen my big sister as unwavering, determined and focused. I didn't realize that determination was partly due to her own demons. 'Then you can start with this.' I leaned back in my leather seat, slung a bottle of champagne from the bucket of ice opposite us, and set it on my tray beside my flute. 'No one tells Louie.'

Paula laughed, extending her own glass. 'All right, champ. One drink. Nothing more till you bring home that grand prix this weekend.'

Chapter Twenty-Six

Diana

Monaco didn't typically have any preference for Formula 1 teams. They tended to cheer on their home driver, Jules Beaumont for Burgess. Yet I watched as hundreds of fans crowded the airport upon our arrival, most bearing Revello flags, wearing the Scuderia's livery colours, holding up posters and phone cameras. I waited for my luggage inside as the crowd of hundreds turned to over a thousand, desperate to get one glance at the beleaguered drivers who had just touched down in Monte Carlo.

I squinted to look through the window. 'Why are there so many of them?'

'It's Revello,' Nic replied with a chuckle. 'There will be this many of them everywhere you go.'

I wasn't sure how Nic and I were faring at the moment, but all hell had broken loose after I insinuated that Jolt might have been setting me up to be second to Nic. So, of course, I had to behave as if it were only momentary anger, a product of my stubbornness and all. Nic and I didn't directly address the matter. It just seemed to fade a little as we got lost in Monaco prep, though I, for one, still held more than a bit of resentment. Nic was being far too casual in the grand scheme of things, which only got further under my skin.

Miguel and Andrea plus their team came down into the lobby, carrying white suitcases complete with the green and red stripe. Andrea approached the windows and waved cheerfully at their absolutely feral fans.

I wasn't sure if there was now bad blood between Miguel and Nic, mates since day one, but if there was, they didn't show any signs of it. Nic extended a hand, and Miguel took it as they pulled one another into a brutal back-thumping hug. 'Hey, amigo, is it true?'

They pulled away from each other. Miguel nodded ruefully. 'Yeah, I mean, it's some stuff that happened. But I guess it was for the best, for both of us.'

Miguel, as rumours had suggested, was allegedly here post break-up with Jatziry. I didn't want to believe it. The two of them were always so effortless together. But I was also conscious of the worm of guilt that wiggled into my heart when I thought of how well Miguel and I had clicked in Barcelona. I held myself back from feeling *anything*, even as we'd looked at those old photos and laughed in the courtyard. I could tell he cared deeply for Jatziry, and I could see it in his appearance now: hair unruly, sporting a pair of darkly tinted Ray-Bans and stubble that bordered on a beard.

'Probably true. You know how this sport is, like a damn parasite,' quipped Nic. 'At least there's not that tension between you two any more. Focus on the race. And hey, Monte Carlo, best place to be after that kind of thing.'

'Why's that?'

Nic lowered his voice. 'The *babes*, Miggie! You don't remember how you used to run it before? Absolutely wild, this guy,' he said to me now. 'You wouldn't recognize our daring little heartbreaker.'

I raised an eyebrow. 'Line up the other nineteen of you, I couldn't tell any of you apart. You all think the same, act the same. What with the booze and "babes" and such.'

'Aw, Di. You know I'm always loyal to my best girl.' Nic nudged me playfully, but somehow he didn't feel like the same man I'd met at the start of the season. He was changing. He had in common with the rest of them just one more thing I'd forgotten now: title chaser with a flair for the dramatic, in whose world everyone else played a supporting role. *Team first*. What about the teammate he had said he was so grateful to have met?

Miguel, though I couldn't make out his eyes, chuckled in an almost sardonic manner. 'Didn't seem like it when you justified taking P1 from your best girl on bogus team orders.'

'Hey.' Nic pointed Miguel's way in sudden warning. I assumed he was jesting till I saw the deadly seriousness in his stormy eyes. 'That's my team. You can have your drama and I'll have mine. Or else we can just as easily talk about gimmicks like you banging Bernelli's daughter.'

'Watch your language, Nic,' said Miguel, with the exasperated demeanour of a tired parent. It was odd. I tried to process both this bit of kindling Nic had just dropped and the fact that he never usually fired his mouth off like that . . . ever. 'That wasn't even while we were on Vittore.'

'Who's Bernelli?' I asked.

'Our old team principal.' Nic smirked. 'Apparently, Vittore Monterey's car isn't the only thing Miguel took for a ride.'

'All right, that's enough.' Miguel rolled his eyes. 'I was new to F1, and stupid, too. The fame went to my head.'

'Yeah, and I bet the controversy did as well,' pushed Nic. 'The press said you only left Vittore so it wouldn't seem weird when you boned Antonia.'

I pursed my lips. 'Tone it down. As much as I'd love a full-length lecture on Miguel's sex life, we have places to be, guys.'

It would've been reasonably funny if the two of them hadn't exchanged such dirty looks in parting. I waited for it to blow over before following Nic outside.

The city track itself was known for being ridiculously narrow, but the streets of Monaco were perfect for cruising about and enjoying the ambience. I drove to the hotel myself, through scenic streets with the top of my Porsche down to wave at a few fans here and there. I was really starting to love this place.

Our hotel was probably one of the most luxurious of the season, complete with a tempting casino. I settled down in my room prior to team dinner and photos for a bit of peace and quiet. I put on my favourite Fairuz, made a cup of hot water, and took out one of the tea bags stocked in the cupboard above the fridge. I kicked my feet up in the patio chair with my tea, closed my eyes, and forced myself to relax. Monte Carlo was beautiful, and this race would be, too.

Once I'd drained my cup, I changed into a black dinner dress, pulled on my heels, got all done up. Presence was key. I couldn't let anxiety show in front of anyone on the team, and

I had to be buddy-buddy with Nic. For that, though, I figured we had to at least attempt to clear the air.

We met in the lobby, already awash in entourage members. I kept my voice low as we walked. 'Are we playing nice again?'

Nic smiled broadly as Cavanaugh's wife passed us by and waved happily. 'When were we not?'

'When you act like you care about me, but then justify inverting me for no logical reason all at once, it's hard to trust you, Nic.' I pantomimed Nic's overly large grin. We were, both of us, excellent actors.

'I thought we'd decided we were different.'

'Doesn't mean it feels any different when you stab me in the back.'

At that, I saw a hint of the Nic I'd first met at the beginning of the year – a glimmer of vulnerability in the furrow of his eyebrows, a twinge of pain in his eyes. But he'd become adept at hiding these things now. Whatever I had seen was replaced by a mask of indifference in less than a split second.

We ran into a few fans on our way to the banquet rooms. I dutifully readied my pen, as did Nic. 'Listen, I don't devalue you, Diana. But F1 is business. This is how things go. Sooner you learn, the better.'

We nodded, smiled, and signed autographs before moving on. 'Right, then,' I said. 'Sounds like it's impossible for teammates to be any more than friends is what you're saying. Just as hurting me by rationalizing my being collateral and then calling me inferior on live television is just business.'

'Diana – look, I didn't mean that. Things between any set of teammates is always rough,' Nic tried to reassure me. 'Even Alex and I had our spats.'

'Sure.' I bit my lip, holding back nastier words. 'Alex didn't feel the way I do about you. And that's what makes it hard.'

'Diana—'

'Let's be friendly. Put on a good front.' I stopped walking, and he followed suit. 'For the sake of things, I won't hold any grudges.'

'Hey . . . does this mean you'll give me a chance?' For a moment, I heard a hint of the Nic I'd first met. Genuine, caring, true.

'I think we should stay at arm's length, Nic, if we want to race together.' I looked down at the utterly uninteresting tiled floor. 'Without hurting one another.'

He was quiet. I was quiet. We resumed our walk through the doors to the banquet room. At last, he said, 'That may be best.'

Chapter Twenty-Seven

Miguel

I couldn't quite tell how I was feeling about this race. I'd said lots of things to the media, of course, in expressing my excitement, but I couldn't tell where I was lying and where I wasn't. I knew I clearly looked different – forgone a haircut, shaved less so you could see the shadow of a beard now, had someone say I looked 'a mess'. It didn't stop people from swarming me, from congregating outside my hotel and my car and the track. Everyone wanted a piece of Miguel de la Fuente, but no one cared if I wanted to give away a piece of myself.

I got out onto the track in Monaco for Q1 with a bit too much of that anger in my driving. 'Watch your speed,' Paula instructed me as I started my out lap. 'You know anything can happen here.'

It could. Last year, I'd nearly crashed on the hairpin just before the tunnel and could have forfeited my race. It wasn't awful; after all, this track was one of the most dangerous on the grid. Crashes here were nothing new. But it took precedence in my mind, back when it had happened and ever since. I didn't think much in the moment, dumb as I was, but after the fact, I couldn't stop glancing backward and promising it wouldn't happen again after going over every possible scenario. So yeah, maybe I was a little nervous as to what my emotions might do to me in this state, on this track, and Paula definitely was. 'Give yourself time to be confident,' she always told me. I'd been terrible at that since day one, and I'd never felt more alone than I did now: Monte Carlo, no Jatziry.

I managed to make it around smoothly, though. At that point, I said, 'Let's go for a flying lap, Pauli.'

'Good. No traffic ahead. Hit a good pace but take care with the car. Super narrow.'

'Got it.'

As I crossed the start, I went hard on the straight, which immediately went into Turn One at Sainte Devote. Paula muttered in hushed Spanish, probably resisting the urge to bite her nails as I entered the second sector, taking the Loews Hairpin before making my way into the tunnel. 'Easy. Ease up on the gas. You'll exit too fast,' she instructed.

'I know, Pauli.'

The speed on my steering screen dipped slightly. She exhaled as I made a clean exit. 'Bring it home, *tío*.'

I was running a perfect lap down to the last sector. Almost at the finish. Max push.

There was a clatter from my sister's end as she whooped. 'There it is! We are back, baby.'

'We keep moving forward,' I said to her.

Needless to say, it was set. I soared through Q2 and Q3 and

took pole seemingly effortlessly, then victory lapped before meeting the media, with whom I used my rusty French to convey my feelings, a painful effort I committed to twice a season for the fun of the fans. '*C'était bon. Lâcher prise, non. C'était vraiment bien.*'

It was all fun and games, sure, but inside my sights were on tomorrow. If I didn't keep locked in on the race, I would go soft. And if I went soft, my season was as good as over.

It became evident the next day in the race. Paula clucked her tongue as I yanked my car into the lead after a rocky start, trailed by Nic, Andrea and Diana, in that order.

'Ease up, you're far too sharp, Mig,' she almost singsonged anxiously.

'I know what I'm doing' was my retort.

I pushed the Revello to its limits. I could feel that I was pushing it in the way the car shook beneath my grip. But Nic, who had been behind for twenty laps, was now gaining, too. Every overtake on this track was hell – we all knew it. 'Stay ahead. Don't let him in the pocket. You are currently one tenth faster,' Paula updated me.

It was agony. I felt my breath leave my lungs every other turn. Nic was breathing down my neck. Only once I met with the chequered flag in P1 did I regain my composure.

'*¡Vamos!*' yelled Cristo Montalto, hijacking my poor sister's radio.

I laughed, a release of nerves and tension. 'Let's go!'

I could hear everyone celebrating on the other end, even our parents, probably clinging to one another and cheering bloody murder.

Paula, though. Paula wasn't celebrating. The second I got down off the podium, trophy safe in my arms, she pulled me aside, gesturing widely to the crowd. 'Maybe *they* don't see that something is wrong, Angelito, but I do. You are many things – a thrill-seeker, an icon, one of the best drivers in the world – but you *are not* reckless. And never on a track like Monaco. Never in such an obvious way. You don't throw smoke and go flying, Miggie. What are you driving like? You can kill yourself driving like that on this circuit! There is only *one* DRS zone, Miguel, this whole thing is not one big straight!'

'Isn't that the point?' I clapped my sister's back with far too much enthusiasm, taking a swig from my champagne bottle. 'No more obligations. No one tells me how to drive.'

'Miguel—'

'I'm fine,' I said, grinning ever so broadly.

'I don't think you are.'

'That's okay. Because I am.' I tipped my podium cap her way. 'Nothing's stopping me from getting World Champ this year, Pauli. You said it yourself. I can make this good for me.'

Chapter Twenty-Eight

Miguel

The Monaco win drove everyone crazy, and that was just how I wanted it.

Already almost fifteen points in the lead, I kept on opening up my gap. Onlookers were astonished by the level of aggression I'd gotten away with in the narrow streets. No one to tell me no, I cut completely loose, drove the kind of race I knew would turn heads away from the Jatziry gossip and back to F1. Sure, Paula was pissed. Sure, she knew me well enough to tell that I was being stupid, but I needed this. I wanted what I had before. I wanted to forget that anything else had ever happened.

And it worked. The next race in Baku, another scenic street circuit, I zoomed into P2, pushing so hard I almost had a DNF on an especially sharp turn. That didn't matter. I felt as if I was peaking again. The roars of the grandstand told me all I needed to know, so I made it a pattern.

Austria: P1.

France: P1 and Fastest Lap.

Hungary: P1 and Fastest Lap, culminating in a celebratory lap complete with tyre burnouts that had the mechanics in tears, netting a total of one hundred and two Championship points in the past four races.

'Pain is key: Miguel de la Fuente's emotion-fuelled race story so far.'

Antonia Bernelli turned her magazine my way. It must have been one of those sports tabloids, as if I'd care. It was surprising enough that Antonia had turned up at a race all the way in Canada, but the fact that she held reading material was even more astonishing.

Being in Canada was pretty iffy as far as a lot of racers were concerned, usually because of the weather and the surprise animal appearances that often graced the track. But although I didn't race under this flag, Montreal was home, too, so I had no issues. I was on a streak. The season was going great, I had time to kill, and distractions couldn't hurt. Distractions like, I don't know, my old on-and-off fling with the Vittore principal's daughter, Antonia.

I pushed the hotel bed comforter off my face with a yawn and took a look. Yep, sports tabloid. The cover bore a dramatic still of me standing atop my car in France.

'You look good.' Antonia tossed the magazine aside and did a mirror check. She was already dressed for press conferences, in a white jumpsuit, brown hair tied into a painful ponytail, pale skin coated in makeup. 'Though that may be because I've seen more than *Sports Illustrated*.'

'Could be.' I sat up blearily. 'What's today, Thursday? FP1 tomorrow?'

'Uh-huh.' Antonia did an about-face. 'Do my eyebrows seem even to you?'

Out of spite, because they sure weren't: 'Yeah, they're even.'

I rolled out of bed and pulled on my team shirt and jeans, still discombobulated from whatever alcohol I had consumed last night. 'Ugh. Don't know how I'll drive tomorrow.'

'Neither do I,' remarked Antonia. 'Which is good for Vittore. I'd say make this a habit to dampen your performance and let our team through.'

'Aha, so maybe your daddy should make you team principal, Miss Bernelli.'

'I prefer the benefits without the work.' She shot me a cold smile. 'See you later, Miguel. Perhaps we can meet up after the weekend. Celebrate your more-or-less certain win.'

Antonia slipped out of the room. She was right – my winning was pretty much assured. I had no shame in saying it.

I didn't have a lot of shame at all these days. But every so often, I'd come across Diana. We hadn't really hung out since Barcelona, since everything changed, and she would just give me this sad look, as though she didn't recognize me. In those moments, I'd feel terrible. Even after I convinced myself that it didn't matter because I was winning, the terrible feeling hung around.

The press conference was due to be held at noon. This was good. I wouldn't have to run into Antonia and possibly have something slip to the media. I put on my team windbreaker, jeans, a clean pair of white tennis shoes, and the Rolex that was a pretty permanent fixture on my wrist. I'd taken the liberty of reading the 'Pain is Key' article earlier, and it praised my tidy media appearance. If there was any façade I particularly excelled at putting up, it was that.

As I walked into the press room, I noticed Nic, dressed quite similarly. We were brought up in F1 the same way – to appear neat and clean whenever a camera was in front of us, with leeway given during and after races. He had charisma, I had to give him that much.

Myself, Nic, Andrea, Kasper and Alex sat down to wait for Diana, who arrived right on the dot of twelve. She took a few liberties with the typical team gear; she had on black jeans, custom Jolt Dunks in the team colours, a black cami, and a light wash denim jacket, with patches of the Jolt logo and its sponsors cleverly placed to match the windbreaker. I got the feeling she picked and chose these things pretty carefully; the touches of black, white and purple suited her perfectly.

I leaned forward to grab my water bottle, and I couldn't help but give myself an extra second to take her in; how effortlessly good she always looked, the way she always glowed. Her eyes caught mine for just a second, contact that sent me backwards with a start so quick that I almost tipped out of the chair.

'Nice to have you all here in Montreal,' the interviewer, back to Crowberry, began. 'And all three teams running close in the Constructors' and Drivers' boards. Let's start left to right. So, uh, that's Nic. You're here in Canada, you flew out the gate with Jolt. What do you see here for you?'

'Yeah, I feel I will have a better idea after practice. I've always had good results here, though. Last year a P5. Hopefully we'll beat it this time,' he replied.

They went on to speak about Nic's P5 with Griffith a year

ago. Kasper yawned. His media coach was definitely going to smack him after this.

'All right, thank you, Nic. On to your teammate far from home here, Diana Zahrani,' continued Crowberry. 'Tell us, we are moving along in this season, creeping towards that break. Do you have a plan in place for the remainder? What will your game look like for the rest of 2022?'

Diana just raised an eyebrow, sweeping a curl from her face. I had to turn to look at her because *jeez*. Attitude.

'Well, my game plan's not the sort of thing I'd discuss in front of my rivals here, Mr Crowberry.'

The crowd hooted, the bunch of us sitting on the panel laughing, albeit somewhat nervously. Diana just grinned obliviously, adding a little shrug, her stunning eyes crinkling with genuine humour.

Once Crowberry had recovered from his twinge of embarrassment, he moved to me. 'Miguel de la Fuente. There's a lot of questions for you, but I'll select a few. First off, this run of success. It seems boundless. What's the reason, if any?'

'I mean . . . I don't like talking about personal matters,' I began carefully. 'But I feel that much of it is due to those. I drive best unrestricted. I don't think I would attribute it to forces beyond the natural. It's just this team, putting in the hours on all the parts of the operation. And, because of them, I have this wonderful car that works well with me every time.'

'Yes, certainly. Speaking of driving best unrestricted, this style we see from you is very reminiscent of your Vittore year. Some might even call it dangerous. How is that working for you?'

'Very well. No intention of stopping. You get back what you put in, you know? All on the line.'

'So you must be bracing yourself for another good result,' said Crowberry. 'In your second home, too.'

'Would be great, yeah.'

'Indeed.' The interviewer read the next question. 'Now, this one's a bit loaded, as we know you tend to veer away from personal discussions. But what are they like now, your races? We know your parents catch a race or two, but it appears your paddock building currently consists just of staff at most GPs. Who's in your personal cheering section?'

My jaw stiffened. What were they doing? Calling me out for being alone at races? It wasn't anything unique. Lots of drivers were solo.

I couldn't think of an answer. Fortunately, one of my fellow solo drivers spoke up.

'I'm aware I don't actually sit in there, but his paddock isn't just staff.' Diana leaned forward to reach her mic. 'I'd be in Miguel's cheering section whenever he needed, if he would have me there.'

Hopefully, she could see the gratitude in my eyes when I met hers. Her smile was warm, apologetic yet supportive. Smiles like that were so rare in this business. Smiles that pure, and smiles that beautiful.

'I'd have you there,' I confirmed.

Crowberry looked caught off-guard. 'Oh? And, ah, that's very positive camaraderie between two members of rival teams there.'

'We *can* be friends, remember?' Alex put in. 'Besides, those two are on the same wavelength. Watch this: guys, name an animal that starts with "G".'

'Giraffe,' I said.

'Gorilla,' Diana said at the same time.

'Okay.' Alex nodded. 'I take that back.'

A moment of friendly laughter for the crowd. Diana beamed as we shared a look, a welcome change from her more disappointed glances, the ones I'd been seeing through my past few chaotic races. I could tell she was hurt, and not because I was winning, but because I was endangering myself.

After the conference, we filed out from the panel and into the hall through a back door.

'Tell me they did not just ask me what I'd do if an animal crossed the track.' Andrea was rolling his eyes. 'That is the most evil "would you rather?" ever!'

'I mean . . . depends on your lead.' Nic tried to amend it. 'It's not necessarily bad that you said you'd keep going . . . over the animal.'

Russo went on groaning about the roadkill dilemma. Beside me, Diana winced just slightly, arms hugging her midsection like she'd been knifed in the gut.

'Hey. You good?' I asked. I don't think I'd ever really seen her visibly in pain in broad daylight, other than in Imola, so I had to admit it concerned me now.

'I'm good,' she assured me. She didn't look so good.

'Come on, you saved my ass back there. Let me help,' I offered anyway.

Diana sighed. 'Do you have any Brufen on you?'

'Bru-what?'

'Ibuprofen.'

'Why? Wait, are you in pain? Did you get hurt?'

'Miguel, trust me, I haven't been shot or stabbed or had my

organs rearranged.' She shifted uncomfortably. 'I just *really* need a painkiller.'

'Whaaat? A painkiller? Are you all right, mate?' Alex piped up.

Diana glanced my way with murderous intent. 'I'm fine. Just having some aches is all.'

'Suck it up!' called Christian Clay as he passed us on his way to the conference room.

'Your uterus isn't rejecting itself, asshole!' she yelled back. Clay nearly tripped over his own feet. I almost did, too, and it seemed the other guys were no different. '*You* suck it up!'

Clay quickly disappeared from our sight. We stood in the hall, totally flabbergasted.

Diana slowly turned back to us and crossed her arms, miffed.

'I, uh . . . can't you, like, take something to just, not?' Kasper said hesitantly.

She just stared at him.

'So that's a "no"?'

Diana shook her head before resuming the walk, as if to say, *This can't be happening.* I suddenly really wished I had ibuprofen to offer the woman.

'Is it true it hurts more than a heart attack?' Nic asked.

'Not everyone gets cramps. But in my personal opinion, yes, I wouldn't be surprised if that were true. However, I have never had a heart attack, so that question is objectively unanswerable,' she said bluntly.

It was so weird. In karting, we grew up in this utopia where you raced nonstop, through allergies and fevers and colds. We didn't talk about what women went through . . . they just drove. So over time, we accumulated all these questions we never thought we'd be able to ask.

'You just drive for two hours . . . while having an abdominal heart attack . . .' Alex trailed off.

'Not to mention all the humidity. Sitting in your race suit in the car baking while you just, you know. Bleed.'

Andrea gagged.

'There's no way for you to just hold it?' said Kasper.

We all stopped to glare at him. Diana turned around stiffly.

'Jeez, well, can you hold it when you're bleeding, Kasper?' Diana replied exasperatedly. 'Can your body just decide to take a pause, and oh, no more blood?'

Alex snorted. I bit down hard on my tongue to hold back laughter. Kasper went hot-pepper red.

'I'll get you ibuprofen, Diana,' I finally said after a long silence, allowing the chuckles to escape. 'It's the least I could do.'

She nudged me. 'You know, you could also admit when you are in pain. It'll do you good.'

I wasn't sure what to say to that. I just kept walking.

Chapter Twenty-Nine

Diana

I lounged in a beach chair set up in my garage on race day, cucumber slices over my eyes, feet up on a pile of tyres. The entire team knew better than to disturb me. This far out from season start, they still struggled even to speak to me at times. I don't know if it was because I scared them, or that they just didn't know how women worked. I pretended I couldn't hear a word they were saying as the sound of old Egyptian music, my Warda records, piped through the garage and out towards the paddock.

'She's starting to scare me,' one of the mechanics remarked. 'She just sat there like that yesterday as well, falling asleep next to her Victrola, and not an hour later, she qualifies P2. It's terrifying.'

'It's women,' Theodore Cavanaugh said with a chuckle. 'They're like this all the time, but it's only this bad once a month.'

Laughter rippled across the garage, interspersed with *rabab* music from my record player. No wonder women didn't want to race in the pro leagues. The others didn't even understand what it was like to deal with something as natural as being on your period, just laughed about it. Kasper had asked if you could *hold* it. The world sucked.

I watched the reporters pass by the Jolt garage. One snapped a sneaky photo of 'Zen Diana' to immortalize later. As much as I knew this was what I'd signed up for, I could not help but hate it sometimes.

Either way, we suited up for race start. I was going to be in P2 on the grid, and Miguel, obviously, was on pole. With both him and me in front, it would be a tough race, but that wasn't the worst of it. Nic would be starting in P3 behind the both of us, and he was bent on being the one to end Miguel's streak of ones and twos.

We lined up, tyre warmers taken off, and the formation lap began. Everyone swerved, getting heat into their tyres. I concentrated on the glint of the white Revello chassis beside me. I had to turn the tide.

The wait for the lights to go out felt like for ever.

Five, four, three, two, one . . .

And we were racing.

It was going perfectly. I got away from Nic in P2, got good headway. The traffic was minimal. It was all ideal.

Then, just in front of me, Miguel turned a hair too quickly, his wheel on the verge of grazing mine, inching ahead steadily to keep his position. He held on to P1 going into the turn. I struggled to match his pace behind him.

Suddenly, a puff of smoke emerged from beneath Miguel's right rear tyre – it had popped straight off.

'Shit!' I yelled into the radio.

Miguel slid right across the turn, and his rear wheel knocked my front wing. My car lurched back, and I saw it coming before it even happened. I flew into the side of Nic's car, and the both of us went flying at a hundred-some kilometres an hour.

I was bracing for a collision against the wall, but instead, Nic buffered me as he pushed Andrea off the track. Andrea decked Peter to the side. Peter crashed into his teammate, Darien. Darien's car took the final blow of the entire accident, flying into the TecPro and breaking clean through the front of the chassis, front wing officially departed from the rest of the car. And just like that, the entire high-field had been effectively eliminated from the Canadian Grand Prix, no roadkill required.

'No way.' I laughed from my stranded position in the gravel as the red flags went up. I was still deciding whether that was an upset laugh or a sheerly amused laugh. This was the end of my run, my attempt to snag a P1, but it was also the end of Nic's run, not to mention Miguel's. This was a development.

'Holy *crap*,' Aiden, my engineer, said. 'That is six DNFs with Heidelberg, ourselves and Revello out of the race. Midfield's wildest dreams. Alex P1.'

I watched the remaining cars stop before our mess in formation, unable to proceed through broken cars and all sorts of debris, including – but not limited to – wings, tyres and side mirrors. Oh, this was bad, but come on, it had to be kind of funny. All six top cars out? Who'd have seen it coming?

We disentangled ourselves from our vehicles with thumbs-up all around to show the others we were okay before lining up for the walk of shame back along the left of the track. Although today there was really no shame, more amused acceptance.

What had I said? Nic wanted to break Miguel's streak. That had definitely happened, just not how I imagined.

'Well, Miggie, your crew screwed us all over today.' Andrea clapped Miguel on the back.

'Yeah, don't worry.' Miguel just rolled his eyes, eerily calm for someone whose pit crew had incited the DNF of the top three teams. 'I'll have a word with them after. Surely Heidelberg and Jolt will, too.'

Nic snorted. 'Bet on it. Revello's about to get obliterated.'

'Technically, we've all been obliterated already,' Peter pointed out smartly. It was true. The carnage to our cars was greater than anything the season had seen so far.

'Some more than others.' I gestured to Darien's car, practically snapped in half against the TecPro. 'I wonder how they'll repair your Jenga tower of a chassis.'

'Ah, thousands and thousands in damages,' he said dreamily. We couldn't help but laugh at that. All our teams were probably banging their heads against the pit walls right then.

'Thought this one would be a moment to remember, huh?' Miguel said to me.

'Surely it will.' I returned his look of amusement with my own. 'I'll remember six DNFs and Alex winning for Griffith.'

'Romilly for P1!' Darien hooted through cupped hands. 'He wins, we all go nuts in the paddock so the media gets confused.'

'Agreed,' I said with a grin. 'The docuseries camera guy will be even more confused when he goes looking for rivalries.'

Miguel grinned. 'Only rivalry here is me and my mechanics, Danger.'

Chapter Thirty

Diana

The lost opportunity in Montreal spurred me on as I struggled with new car mods in Silverstone. I pulled through to finish third. I could hardly believe how fast the season was progressing. We had two races till summer. The upcoming weekend would test our limits on a brand-new track, force us to brave conditions reminiscent of the Sakhir circuit that it had returned to replace. The Indian Grand Prix was back. This time, it would go down in the streets of dry, sandy Jaipur, Rajasthan.

The notion was foreign to us all. Press conferences abounded in the days before we left for Jaipur. We would be racing in the vicinity of beautiful traditional architecture unlike any other, relics of ancient times meticulously preserved, with roads narrower than Monaco running through the city, and a gorgeous palace that served as the residence of the revered royal family. I found myself unable to get any sleep on the jet over.

We were met with unbelievable pomp. Dust hung thickly in the air and a posse of cabbies attempted to drag our luggage into their cars, but the fans here were hardcore and super-welcoming. I let them garland me with jasmine and marigolds. They showered us in flower petals. Someone passed me a beautiful pink silk dress, with sparkling gold fringe, as well as a red box of sweets. These people were celebrating the return of a sport that they thought they would never see again in their country. *This* was the magic of racing, its ability to bring together humans from across the globe.

'This is crazy!' I shouted over the roar of the crowd hindering our getaway from the airport, hoping that Miguel could hear.

'I know! These guys are the best!' he remarked, as a group of women had him crouch down so they could wrap his head in a turban of bright pink fabric. Locks of his wavy hair peeked out from beneath, refusing to cooperate.

'I am never leaving,' I agreed, beaming at the older woman placing a platter bearing flowers, nuts, and a clay lamp before me. She reached into a small pot on her plate and pressed a finger heavy with vermillion powder to my forehead, just above the spot between my eyebrows. A blessing? I wanted to cry a little bit as she passed the platter to another women beside her, brought her hands to the sides of my head, and pulled them back to hers in what I assumed was intended to ward off the evil eye. 'Thank you,' I said to the woman, hoping she understood my words or, if not, my smile.

She must have, because she grinned at me with eyes full of the same sort of pride I saw in my mother's, giving the dress in my arms a little pat.

We finally approached our cars, assisted by the security

staff's efforts, though part of me wanted to stay longer. Miguel and I shared a grin. He looked so goofy, so out of his element in his turban with the end sticking up flamboyantly, freckles prominent in the harsh sunlight. His eyes held mine just a moment longer. 'I hear our hotel has all these places to explore. Care to join me this evening?'

'Oh, of course. Seven sharp in the lobby.' I grinned. 'You can keep that on if you want.'

'Funny.' Miguel glanced upward, as if trying to scope out his new headwear.

I reached over and tugged on the little ruffles sticking out at the top of the turban. 'It's still on your head.'

'Ha-ha.' He smiled, heading off to his sleek Revello. 'See you then, Di.'

At seven on the dot, as we'd agreed, I arrived in the lobby of the Jai Mahal Palace. Miguel was already there (no turban), casually kicked back on one of the couches arranged around coffee tables in the middle of the atrium. Owing to the extremely scorching summer climate of Rajasthan, he wore a short-sleeved button-down and khaki shorts. It was a hallmark old money outfit, but Miguel made it look a bit too good.

For my part, I had heard that it was a local norm for women to avoid showing too much skin, something I didn't usually do, anyway. I stuck to a longer floral dress with flowing long sleeves, silky white fabric printed in dark blue designs.

As I drew closer, Miguel stood up in recognition. 'Lots to see,' he said once we had met halfway. 'This place is literally a palace.'

And he just smiled, this dopey look on his face rendering

me unable to reply. He took me in, as if we weren't in a beautiful hotel that begged for our attention, something I couldn't quite understand, but that sent me blushing ridiculously hard.

'Anyway. Are you a garden kind of woman?' he asked.

'Stop.' I raised an eyebrow. 'There's a garden?'

'There is a garden.'

'Well, we've got to go.'

We wove through the palace lobby, a welcome distraction from the tension that stretched between the two of us. Eventually, through the back doors of the hotel, I could see the garden. It was huge: perfect green grass as far as the eye could see, pristine brick pathways carving a maze through clean-cut shrubbery. It all seemed to glow as the sun began its descent to the horizon.

'There.' Miguel pointed to a traditional rectangular gazebo in the middle of one section of grass. 'Let's check it out.'

It was characteristically hot out, but at this hour, there was a slight breeze. We opened the doors and took a huge outdoor staircase down to the level of the garden, before following the brick pathway to the gazebo, where a futon-like porch swing stood, padded with colourful cushions stitched in artisanal cloth and small glass mirrors.

Miguel jumped right onto the swing. The whole thing shook so hard that I thought it was going to fall. He patted the spot beside him. 'Room for two, Miss Zahrani.'

I accepted, taking a seat. Our legs brushed each other's as I pushed my feet out to take a big swing. In the distance, traditional horns and drums sounded. There was some kind of procession going on in the larger gazebo a few grass plots away from us.

'Is that a wedding?' I squinted. I could barely make out a couple with a red sash between them, circling an altar, a fire, maybe.

'I've been to, like, one Hindu wedding in my life, but yeah, pretty sure that's it,' Miguel confirmed with a smile. 'Isn't it cool?'

'It's beautiful. What a beautiful place,' I said. 'Everything feels so untouched. Like in a hundred-some years, nothing has changed.'

'Bizarre,' agreed Miguel, adding his strength to swing us even higher. 'Isn't it cool, though, all the travel we get to do in this career? What we get to see?'

'We're blessed.' I squinted at the sun as it began to dip below the horizon line, silhouetting the ongoing wedding against the endless skies. 'We are lucky. It's a dream that we've made it this far.'

'I knew from the moment you beat me in Monaco all those years ago that you would.' Miguel shot me a smile. 'Not to mention the way you gave no craps in karting. And you still don't, you demon.'

'Neither do you.' I smirked. 'I hear you chewed up Revello on that Canada weekend . . . you know, for the . . . boom.'

He chuckled, pushing a hand through that runaway hair of his. 'Yeah . . . I did yell at the mechanics. Maybe a bit much. But come on, I went right off the track and took you with me.'

'That was unpreventable,' I reminded him.

'Yeah.' He gave me that puppy-dog-eyes look. 'Sorry.'

'Oh.' I laughed, nudging his shoulder with mine. 'It's technically your team that dragged me down with them, not you.'

Miguel grinned. 'Is that a rule? One of us DNFs, the other DNFs too?'

'Hmm. Sometimes wrecking the car is better than having to endure another finish behind Nic.'

'I mean, if it's any consolation . . .' Miguel scratched the back of his neck awkwardly. 'You're working a *lot* harder than him. You have all our respect. I mean, I know you have mine. You . . . you didn't just make me a fan, Diana. You have something that no other driver does, this humble charisma about you that just screams to me that you'll bring home your P1s very, very soon.'

My heart skipped a beat. 'That . . . Um, thank you.'

'Sure. You're literally the only person who puts me in my place on-track. Of course, victory will be coming your way. Don't give up now.'

'The only person. What about Paula?' I teased him.

'Not the way you do.'

I sighed, smiling. 'At least I'm putting someone in his place. Because Nic . . . I'm getting nervous about racing with him. I don't know. His attitude has been making me anxious. Drivers like that *always* try something on the track, and it never, ever works out. What do you say to that?'

'Asshole, maybe.'

Miguel waited a beat to gauge my reaction before he burst out laughing, which rocked the entire swing.

'Careful, careful!' I couldn't control the snorts that emerged from me and only made Miguel laugh harder. He collapsed onto my side of the swing, his head falling into my lap, wavy black hair flying every which way. Part of me wanted to run my hands through that crazy hair of his, but I held back, the same way I always did.

Then Miguel let out a little yelp, raising his hand from where

215

it had been against one of the pillows. He rolled over, looked up at me with an innocent smile, and held out the offending finger, which, naturally, he'd cut on the corner of one of the sharp mirrors on the cushions.

I could make out the splash of freckles across his nose in the light of the setting sun. His eyes crinkled with the sting of the cut, his expression like a guilty little kid who'd just spilled all his juice. 'Oops.'

'Mm-hmm.' I bit back a grin. I took his hand in mine and helped him sit up, facing him on the swing. 'I have something, don't worry.'

From my purse, I grabbed one of the two bandages I fortunately had sitting in my arsenal, more due to the sometimes-aggressive by-products of broken acrylic nails than anything else, and a tissue. 'May I?'

Miguel nodded, extending his finger, and I pressed the tissue to it with a fair amount of force before bringing out the bandage, which I wrapped gently over the cut.

'All done.' I looked up, and Miguel's eyes were rapt, completely focused on me, holding a hint of pleading. I wasn't sure what had just happened, but all I did know was that – with that one look – he had me as hooked as he was.

We just stared at each other for a moment as if we had only just met, and then I finally let go of his hand as he used a push of his legs to send us swinging yet again. I found myself sneaking glances at him, hoping he wouldn't see. It was so stupid, and yet, I craved this stupidity. I craved the way he made my body go completely weightless. The blood left my feet, and I could scarcely stand up. My muscles lacked tone and my mind lacked sense, and all I could think about was *him*.

The last of the sun fell below our vision. We swung and listened to the buzz of the wedding. I exhaled, letting my head droop onto Miguel's shoulder.

I was vaguely aware of him peering at me – somewhat curious, somewhat content – before turning back to the sky, tinted with stunning reds, oranges and golds that you couldn't get anywhere else.

Chapter Thirty-One

Diana

I'd seen Jaipur on the simulator, but in reality, it was a completely different ordeal. The track was both captivating and deadly. It sucked you in with sights, like a siren's scintillating song, and then it hit you with full force. Jaipur was reminiscent of Monaco, but rather than having a section of curves as in Monaco, there was another DRS straight. You had to both think before you made moves and be prepared for wheel-to-wheel action at top speeds. Then there was the scenery: building after building of historical architecture, whose stones lent Jaipur the nickname 'Pink City', which had become the easy shorthand for the race itself.

'Oh, this track is the seventh ring of hell,' groaned Kasper, elbowing Alex. 'Ain't no way Griffith will finish Top Ten, mate.'

'C'mon!' Alex raised his fork. 'Just 'cause you crashed in FP2 doesn't mean you can't gun it tomorrow. Quali still awaits.'

'I'm shooting for top fifteen,' Andrea put in unhelpfully. 'That itself would be a surprise.'

After an exhausting first two practices, the entire grid, even Craig, huddled up to get dinner at a traditional food place in the hotel. Our digestive systems might not thank us the next day, but it was worth it. The food was delicious and, honestly, the spices had me a little homesick. All twenty of us were left feeling like we'd each eaten for the entire grid after the meal (probably not a great idea the day before a race).

'You got one thing right. The track.' Benji Kittington slumped backwards in his chair. 'I'm going to DNF so hard.'

'Aw, chin up,' I said. 'You drove good today! In the ten both sessions. Don't let Kasper's mood sink you.'

'Says Miss P1,' pitched in Craig aptly.

I raised my hands as if to say, '*Hey, what can I do?*' The track was difficult, that was granted, but this challenge had been working in my favour. I had placed P1 both free practice one and two today. Something about the Pink City just sat right with me and my car.

'Right, dude, she was driving like it was second nature.' Byron leaned forward ominously, a mood that his goofy grin ruined. 'So, Diana, did you or did you not come down last night at two a.m. and drive this entire track at least fifty times to figure it out before we did?'

'Maybe.' I glanced around in mock-suspicion. 'There were no witnesses. No one will know.'

The bunch of them cackled as a waiter passed by the table and placed a platter of assorted sweetmeats before us for dessert. 'Bro!' hooted Darien, already pulling out his phone to document the spread for his Instagram feed. 'Check these out.'

'Aww.' Nic loomed over them before plucking up a little pink one. 'These are cute, right?'

'Is that . . . foil?' Jules squinted.

'Nah, man, it's just, like, some edible silver leaf,' said Peter. He popped one of the diamond-shaped sweets topped with 'foil' right in his mouth. 'Yup, edible.'

'Di, catch.' From across the table, Alex launched one of the little desserts my way.

I caught it with my mouth. 'Ten out of ten!' I declared around an Indian sweet.

'To the first pole of Jaipur!' called Miguel, raising his sweetmeat. 'Diana "Danger" Zahrani. May many more P1s follow you this weekend.'

The nickname made me laugh as the others followed suit, tapping their petite treats together. The sounds of our happy chatter filled the outdoor dining pavilion – along with something else.

An erratic squawking turned our attention to the nearby shrubbery. I gasped. 'You guys, a peacock!'

The creature in question spread wide its massive train of tail plumage, revealing a display of brilliant blues and greens. 'Just out here in the middle of nowhere?' said Peter in disbelief.

'That's common here,' Banyu laughed, taking out his phone. 'Dude, it's dancing!'

I grinned as the peacock hopped from foot to foot in its prancing 'dance'. 'Does seeing a peacock mean podium tomorrow?'

'I actually know this one.' Miguel smiled, a sly gesture that he directed my way. I felt my chest flutter like the hopping of the peacock. 'It does stand for good luck and fortune. It also serves as an omen that someone you've been searching for might be right before you.'

I pursed my lips to stave off my own smile, and met Miguel's eyes for only a moment before looking back to the peacock. Was he saying what I thought he was saying?

'Oooh,' Alex howled from beside me. 'Who've you been looking for, Di?'

He flicked his gaze at Miguel. I pressed a finger to my lips with urgency, and Alex's right eyebrow rose.

Really?

I nodded. *Shut up.*

'We'll need to discuss this in depth later,' said Alex with a straight face and a dearth of humour in his big blue irises. 'But for now—'

I swear to you, this kid got up from his seat, stood across from the peacock, and began to 'dance battle' it. I have never seen an animal appear so confused as that poor peacock did when Alex started doing the Running Man. Mind you, he was a rubbish dancer, but every one of us was in tears from laughter. Miguel's eyes locked onto mine, and we laughed and laughed, because at least to me, it felt like we were sharing this unspoken secret meant just for us.

Chapter Thirty-Two

Miguel

I trained my gaze on the five lights hanging above us after formation lap: tunnel vision. This was a pretty nasty start. Timing would be extra important. I was starting P4, with Nic P1, Diana P2, and Andrea P3 after a close quali. I'd thought it would be her sitting on pole but, once again, it had just slipped from her grasp.

'Take a deep breath,' Paula reminded me. 'You've got this, Mig.'

I did. Just cars, I told myself. Not drivers.

And yet, as I watched the rear wing of the Jolt in front of me vibrate slightly, I couldn't think of anything but its driver. Her head on my shoulder as we sat on the swing, the way she laughed at Alex's peacock dance, that smile of hers that told you she'd let you into her circle, and her eyes, sometimes shy, sometimes bold; the little toss of her ponytail when the hair got in her face. In that moment, she ruled over my thoughts as the royal family did this city: a single look at her would leave me helpless. This, in racing, was an instant fatality. I had to be able to overtake Diana, and instead, I was choking.

I pushed the clutch as the first light finally glowed red, engine purring. 'Come on, Miguel,' I muttered under my breath. 'Just go racing.'

Five lights. Lights out.

I shot forward immediately, flooring the gas.

'Easy, easy on the start, you have Turn One up ahead. It will be sharp,' warned Paula.

Her words echoing in my head, I cut in front of Andrea on the turn in one of the ballsiest moves I'd made this season. Just in front of me, Nic and Diana's front wings nearly touched as Nic darted inches ahead.

'You have a gap on Diana!' Paula urged me. 'Take it!'

It went against everything I had been thinking before lights out, but I did it. I slipped on through the opening and slid in front of Diana, directly on Nic's tail.

'Excellent. P2,' my sister said.

We rounded Turn Five, the entire pack holding in position as we went through one of the old city gates. I wanted P1 now, but it would take another lap or so to get within striking distance.

'Go for it now.'

'Going.'

I cut round the outside, sweeping around Nic in a daring move on the chicane. I thought that was the end of it until – not seconds later – Nic began to speed up, preparing to hit back for the win.

'I accelerated, how is he still there?'

'No idea,' groaned Paula. 'He's on you, though.'

'Yeah, that's what I'm seeing!'

I don't even know what happened in that moment. I definitely didn't anticipate the move from Nic, but there was no gap, not even a bit, and suddenly, something hit my back left wheel. I tapped the brake out of a sense of panic. It was too late. The spin thrashed my head from side to side before I finally slammed into the TecPro.

'He-he just checked me,' I managed. 'In the back.'

'Nic has damage, Miguel, but we need you out of the car. This is a DNF.'

'Damn it!' I cursed, smacking the wheel. No way. There was no way Nicolò Necci had just ended my grand prix run. This couldn't be happening.

The press got to me faster than Nic did.

'Miguel! Miguel!' a reporter yelled, leading a crowd my way as I attempted to find the Jolt motorhome so I could confront Nic. 'Did Nic take you out of the race?'

I ignored the questions, even though my PR manager would have my ass for it later. I burst into the Jolt backrooms, water bottle in hand, and already standing in wait was Nic, hair still sticking up, indentations from the helmet marring his face. At least his hadn't gotten bruised from blunt force.

'What the hell?' I said in disbelief. 'Nic, what happened out there?'

'You brake-tested me, why don't *you* explain?' he shot back angrily. 'There was clearly no opening for that!'

'I brake-tested *you?*' I was appalled by his nerve. 'Last I recall, Nic, it was your front wing that hit my tyre! At least you came P11. This ended my race, man!'

224

'Well, I apologize—'

'Thank you.'

'—but it's not something I could have prevented if it wasn't my fault to begin with! I got that damn five-second penalty, all right? Is that enough for you?'

'Come on!' I finally exploded. 'I'm just telling you exactly what the stewards will say, all right?'

'So am I. What was your reason, huh?' Nic took a step forward, more hostile than I'd ever seen him. 'You *literally* tried to throw your car back at me!'

'You hit the tyre! I felt it!' I pushed. 'How else would my car go off the track like that? You think I'd do that willingly?'

'How've we gotten on these past few weeks, Miguel? It's like you hate me for getting this seat.' It felt like we were gaining on each other now, every word of ours louder than the last.

'I hate you for *using* your seat, Nic. You've defended race politics and you've stopped giving a crap about the people around you,' I spat. 'Just like today. But I would never intentionally hit you. I just want the brother I used to know back. I'm tired of this.'

Rather than replying, Nic turned to the podium. Peter and Andrea, on first and third, stood on their steps. Diana Zahrani smiled at both of them from second, the grin on her face stretching ear to ear, ponytail bouncing behind her head.

'At least Jolt still got a podium,' Nic said coldly.

But that wasn't my focus.

'I race because it's how I make my bread and butter. Every win is a step up.' Nic tipped his head at Diana. 'It's the same for her. Same for you—'

225

'You don't get it, Nic.'

'So why? Why are you striking back because I want to play the game?' he continued. 'You have to grow to place first, Miguel. You of all people should know that.'

'Not like this!' I ran a hand through my hair. 'Doesn't it matter to you that you're hurting your team as much as you help them? Hurting Diana?'

He let out a frosty laugh. 'Why should it? Doesn't matter to her what I do. So what if Jolt is a team? We're independent drivers on-track. This isn't doubles go-karting.'

'No, but—'

'And aren't *you* only causing your team more grief?' Nic taunted. 'Every reckless race you drive, you make your mechanics work double-time. Your sister's blood pressure shoots up, and you're millimetres from crashing so hard that not even TecPro would save you. All because your fiancée figured out that you were more in love with racing than with her and left you.'

My hands unconsciously balled themselves up into fists. 'And what would you have done? Anything to win? You'd hit me off the track? Invert with your teammate? I don't know what's next, endanger her life with a brake test?'

Nic's jaw clenched. 'You know what? If I had to, I would.'

I was at a loss for words.

I turned to look at Diana, gaze trained upward as she raised her trophy to the heavens as if to say, *This is a blessing from you. Thank you.* She was beautiful, intelligent and humble, all attributes that drew me to her like a moth to a flame. I couldn't help it; I was tumbling closer and closer until – and I knew it was a matter of time – I would singe my wings.

226

Suerte. She'd come back for a reason.

'You wouldn't, would you?' said Nic.

I nodded silently without moving my gaze.

'Would you lose out on a P1 for her?'

'Nothing is keeping me from strangling you right now,' I sighed.

'Well?'

For a moment, I didn't know what to tell him. I'd been pushing so hard for the wins I had gotten over the last few races. We'd been told this since we were kids: your goal in motorsport is simply to come out on top. But seeing Diana now, something struck me when I realized it wasn't just the podium that mattered. It was the person who was standing there right now.

'A million P1s. I would give her all of them.'

Nic just looked at me like I was crazy. I knew how drivers like him thought. Who would sacrifice victory – winning, of all things – so easily? That was our career. The more we won, the longer we drove. Right?

'Not everything is always about the race,' I told him as I watched Diana spray Peter with champagne. 'Wish I'd learned that earlier.'

Chapter Thirty-Three

Miguel

Next was COTA – the Circuit of The Americas. Heading there after Jaipur, and the strange fever dream of the incident with Nic, Diana glowing up there on the podium the way she always did, I wasn't sure exactly how to feel. So much was hanging in the air, and my sister being my sister, she tried to get right to the heart of the matter with me. I, of course, did not cooperate.

'Mig, what is up with you?' Paula asked after *she* beat *me* on the F1 PlayStation game.

'Nervous for COTA,' was my simple response. I didn't want to push it, honestly, and I didn't flash back to the Palomas incident of last year, so at first I left it at that, and Paula dropped her attempts to wring information from me. It only took five minutes for her to give up.

'No, actually,' she kept going, 'I know you're nervous. But this isn't just a COTA thing. You have stuff on your mind, don't you?'

I didn't reply, only kept driving. Unfortunately, I ran my car right into a virtual wall, after which I finally caved, collapsing against the couch as dramatically as I could. 'Man, Paula, this thing with Nic, and . . . Diana, dude.'

'So you finally admit it?'

I shot her a defensive look. 'What?'

'Remember that day at the gala when I said you could be honest with me?' She smirked. 'I knew from then. I am your big sister, Mig, there are very few things you can keep from me.'

'Sure.' I drew the word out with a roll of my eyes. 'Real talk. How do I even tell her? How do I do this without siccing the media on us or ruining our friendship?'

Paula just laughed.

'What?'

'It's funny how clueless you are.' She snatched the controls from my hands and turned to me purposefully. 'All your life you've either a) had relationships created for you or b) had women automatically fall to your feet. And suddenly, you actually have to try. No?'

I scoffed. 'Okay. Yes, I admit it. *Please* help.'

'Hmm.' She grabbed a pillow off the couch and leaned back. 'How would you go about it if Formula 1 was not in the picture? If you were just normal people working normal jobs and whatnot. What would you do?'

'I . . . would . . .' I thought for a moment. 'Ask her out, I guess.'

'¡*Vale!*' she replied. 'Easy.'

'Easy? We have such busy lives. Always travelling, racing, team stuff, press, promo,' I retorted. 'When can we somehow magically get time for a date in our schedules?'

'Do you have a Plan B?'

'What do you mean, "Plan B"?'

'If you can't ask her out, what else could you do so that she knows how you feel?'

I sighed. 'I don't know. Do people still buy flowers and chocolates?'

'You are horrible at this,' my sister declared proudly. 'Twenty years in your cars and you have lost any semblance of social skills.'

'It's that bad?'

'Come on, Mig. You have to think "unique"!'

'We're going to Austin, right?' I paused to think. What was unique there? 'Would a cowboy hat and boots be appropriate?'

'Ay, Miguel.' Paula held me by the shoulders and gave me a brisk shake. 'Gifts and trinkets, anyone can buy those. You need to show her that you care, and affection isn't something that can simply be bought.'

'Affection . . .' I trailed off. 'Maybe I can work with that.'

She patted me on the back. 'Good. Then no buying cowboy boots, for crying out loud.'

Sure enough, a welcome line of Dallas Cowboys cheerleaders and rich folks in cowboy hats greeted us the second we stepped off the jet onto the steaming asphalt. This was Austin, Texas: home to the Circuit of the Americas.

'I hate this,' Andrea Russo said from my right as we walked to our waiting cars.

For the very first time, I had to agree with my teammate. He looked like he had back in Jaipur, dishevelled from all the excess heat. I doubted I appeared any different, and they hadn't even made us wear the hats yet. 'Me, too.'

Austin was much more city than one would expect. The hotel was in the middle of it all, so I drove us past scenic skyscrapers and storefronts cut by a beautiful blue river laden with bridges to get there. I liked this feeling of the US, the bustling business vibe paired with a touch of something more creative, which was why I was so glad we still had one more American race on the calendar after this.

'Now I want to eat brisket,' I beseeched my sister as we turned into the hotel lot.

'Don't you dare,' my personal trainer, Louie, said from the passenger seat. 'Don't you even dare, Miguel. Last time you had barbecue, your ass was throwing up your stomach's complete contents in the motorhome bathroom minutes before we got you in the car.'

'It's so worth it though,' I groaned. It was. We didn't get that kind of stuff in Spain, and if we did, it was nowhere near the same. 'Don't you ever just want, like, a nice All-American meal of some of that In-N-Out or Kentucky Fried Chicken, or whatever?'

'Hell, no,' Louie immediately replied.

'I might accept,' Paula offered.

'Even Paula!'

'You could not pay me to so much as touch a bucket of American fried chicken.'

'I will feed you myself, Louie. You should be fed. You diet every day.'

'No, Miguel, that's the point—'

'You will eat good. In America. Brisket for the whole team,'

I suggested with a mischievous grin. No one could say no to brisket on me. 'Come on, now.'

'I refuse.' Louie was adamant. 'It's fried, Miguel.'

'Only eat one!'

'It's still fried!'

'Everything is fried here, Louie.'

'Okay.' Paula laughed. 'Eat whatever you like. As the people here can't seem to stop saying, it is a free country.'

Nevertheless, Louie gave me the entire dietary regimen lecture once more as we headed to our hotel room and then immediately to press, as we'd unfortunately touched down late. Today's panel had me paired with Alex, Nic, Darien and, for no particular reason, Christian Clay.

'This will be interesting.' Darien read my mind as we entered the press room, set up with folding chairs like the ones those Hollywood directors sat in while they yelled at the cast.

'Strange combo,' I agreed. 'I wonder what awful logic they had as to Clay.'

'Felt,' replied Darien. 'They put Di with Andrea *and* Kasper too. Can Peter save her?'

'Ugh.' I shuddered. 'He'd better.'

'Let's start with the questions,' Seth Berkeley, our interviewer for the day, began, signalling for silence as both of us took our seats with the others. Anxiety punched around in my chest. After the way things had become so heated following the race, being on a panel with Nic made me fall into a weird limbo where I wasn't sure if I wanted to fire shots or run the other way. Something would slip out, that was for sure.

It was okay at first. Alex spoke a little about the pressure of winning in Montreal, and carrying it through with high points at Silverstone, in Jaipur and – hopefully – Austin. Something about a spin Clay took, and from which he'd recovered flawlessly, was also discussed – a difficult trick, especially on city tracks. Darien put in a polite word about the competition within the team with legend Peter racing alongside him, and about how they supported each other anyway, each cheering the other on, which – I had to admit – had me rooting for Darien as well. Then they got to the situation between me and the guy who was allegedly my closest friend on-track.

'That was definitely one of, if not the most controversial accident of recent years,' said Berkeley. 'Miguel, tell us a bit about what happened.'

'This was all addressed, uh, through the footage and during the race.' I cleared my throat awkwardly. 'I guess Nic saw that opening there, and when there wasn't room, he got forward a bit, which took out my tyre. There was pretty much no way to recover from that spin.'

'And that's been confirmed by the stewards,' Berkeley added for effect. 'Nic, anything to add?'

Thankfully, Nic merely shook his head. 'No, ah, I think that's more or less the situation. However, I'd say there was a gap, and the last second, Miguel closed it on me. Though I served my penalty, so what's done is done.'

I almost opened my mouth to say something, but I thought better of it. I tightened my grip on my microphone instead, attempting to suppress my temper.

'Of course. One more thing to ask you, Nic. You have historically always performed very well at COTA. You took that opportunity last year to seize fourth, even with a red-flagged race. What can we expect from you this time around?'

'Uh . . .' Nic laughed. 'I know this is a rigged question, seeing as this track is also of significance to my teammate, as that get-to-know-the-grid video seems to have said . . .'

The infamous grid video had been filmed at the beginning of the season and released about two races in. It provided drivers an opportunity to introduce themselves through a series of casual questions, try to gain some favour with the fans. One question tackled our motives for driving: a moment where we realized we wanted to be in Formula 1. Diana's story had looped in the United States Grand Prix in a particularly significant way.

'Just the track that Diana's father had always dreamed of seeing her race at; you know, the only race she ever watched live,' said Alex casually, stirring chuckles from the crowd.

'. . . but winning, that's my priority,' he finished. 'I'll do whatever it takes. I understand, trust me. Taking that P1 home would be a crowning glory for her, but it would be for me as well.'

Christian Clay cleared his throat. 'Anyway, someone's parental pity party shouldn't be an excuse to let them into P1. As you said, Nic, we all watched the grid video. Good story, but that won't do. Old Pete earned his prize the hard way last weekend. Why shouldn't Diana?'

Some onlookers nodded in approval, but others were clearly unsettled, as was I. Now Clay's inclusion made sense. The press already knew they had a dumpster fire brewing with Nic and I together. Adding Christian Clay made it even better: a *misogynistic* dumpster fire.

'Not everyone is born with a silver spoon in their mouth,' Peter pointed out. I was immediately grateful for his interference. The anger was starting to bubble up in my chest, and if I said something, I was afraid it wouldn't go as well coming from me as from his calm-and-collected persona. 'So how we get here and who we honour is just as important as what we do on-track. It's not an excuse, it's simply reasons we do what we do. And, either way, would we be shutting down Nic if it were him in Diana's place? If he had a personal story?'

'Oh, damn,' muttered Alex.

'Well, Peter, going back to that initial question Mr Berkeley had asked, there was clearly intent to *shut down* Nic,' Clay pushed on. 'To vilify him for simply performing better than his female teammate in strength and skill.'

'Whoa!' Darien whistled. 'Whoa, whoa, whoa. Where was that energy when Nic's superior "strength and skill" took out another car last race?'

Clay shrugged. 'Nic doesn't seem to be using his parents to garner fan support. Let's face it. You've seen the news articles, haven't you all? Not to mention what Diana said in that video. Called her financial situation as a child in karting "complicated." The Zahranis' finances are not "complicated". They've got everything they need and then quite a bit. Any driver makes a handsome sum. This one races for the *Emirates*. She's got to be swimming in money, but the audiences always pull for the pauper.'

Nic just shifted uncomfortably. Damn it, when would he say something? I was almost shaking. This dude was calling the Zahranis, people who'd struggled for something as small as their daughter's right to drive, liars. I'd heard the way Diana talked about the three of them – a tiny family, as steadfast as they were loving. There was no way Christian Clay could blow smoke like this and get away with it.

I finally sighed wearily. 'Christian, did you hear Darien? If you watched the entire grid video, you'd know that almost every driver has a similar story. I have a similar story regarding Spain. Even Andrea never made that a bigger deal than it is. He would go watch Monza every year with his family – that's his story, and I don't have a go at him for that. The sentiment we grow up with – not pity – is what shapes our drive to win, which to me sounds like a good thing. Everyone needs the right motivation to thrive in Formula 1. Maybe that's just Diana's motivation, and if it is, it's none of your business.'

'I mean . . .' Nic finally spoke. 'You were born into this.'

The audience went quiet. I sucked in a breath.

'What?' I said.

'You were favoured on Vittore even when you underperformed. You went to Revello, didn't you?' he continued.

A pressure settled on my chest as I searched for a reply. He wasn't wrong about my name. I knew that much was true. But I didn't *underperform*. My spot, like everyone's, had been earned, not given. 'What does that have to do with the question?'

'*Family* is how you thrive in Formula 1.' Nic's eyes were so cold that I could find in them no trace of the old friend who had become a part of the de la Fuente family over the years. I wanted to scream some sense into him. 'Whether that's teams or races or what. We're not living in a utopia. Names matter here. Your name gave you what you have in this sport, and yet you preach motivation.'

Just like that, the bond between both of us shattered completely. I could almost see the thread of destiny that connected myself and Nicolò Necci snap, as disbelief and pain entered my body. I could not think of any words to say in reply.

I had trusted this person with my life on the track, and now he'd abandoned his principle completely.

'He's right. You never really needed sentiment to put you in a Revello,' prodded Clay.

I was quick to retort. I wasn't back on my feet, but I couldn't just sit and take punches like this. 'I wouldn't have gotten anywhere if I didn't love this sport, man. And I admit it. There are flaws in the system. But no one bought me a seat. I earned it through years of racing, through practice. So I do believe I have the right to claim passion and *dreams* as motivators in my career. Now, sir, are there any other questions for me, or can I go brush the manes of my ten horses and order my humble servants to polish my throne now?'

The tension in the room slowly subsided, and the audience tentatively began to laugh. I was relieved. I couldn't always pull off jokes well – that had never been my thing – but this one, thankfully, did the job. Yet the expressions of the other drivers didn't change. I risked a glance at Nic. There was not an ounce of remorse on his face.

Chapter Thirty-Four

Diana

No one had expected Austin, one of the most fun, flamboyant races on the calendar, to turn into a competitive mess, but here we were.

The sun shone bright on race day, beating down brutally to give us a track temp upwards of a hundred degrees in the local Fahrenheit units. The grid had been set: Miguel would start first, Nic second, Darien third and myself in a fourth I was not all too proud of, especially given the ongoing drama.

I'd turned on the TV the night prior, just to unwind before the big show. It had already blown up: 'Watch Formula 1 USGP interview where all hell breaks loose.' Talk-show hosts speculated, sports reporters pontificated, and tabloids splashed explosive headlines. Clips of it were everywhere, including that stupid loaded question about my personal experience, which most platforms agreed was inappropriate, and the one where Clay went to town on how I grabbed at pity to paint myself as some damsel in distress. They brought up my family's finances and called it a media ploy. And then poor Miguel spoke in my defence.

My animosity towards Nic grew a hundredfold.

Nic had been so on edge with Miguel as he brought Revello consistent P1 and P2s. It was obviously only a matter of time. Yet something of this magnitude . . . no one had seen that coming.

Once I finished my stretches and had practised with the reaction lights in the team building, I slipped out of the garage for just a moment to meet Miguel outside his. He was waving to the gathered fans, as he always did. I was glad they weren't taking the rubbish interview as gospel, but were still showing up armed with flags and banners.

'Hey,' I called.

Miguel turned abruptly, a lock of his wavy black hair flying out of place. 'Hey, Di. Oh, man, I've been wanting to check in on you—'

'Not the first or last time I take shrapnel. But you, Miguel, how are you?' I exhaled, taking him in. He wouldn't admit it, but he looked worn out. All of this was taking a toll on him, too. 'You didn't have to stay on that path, but you did, and Nic . . . what a mess.'

'Yeah.' He let out a mirthless laugh. 'But what can we do? The race goes on, right?'

'Right.' I tried for a smile. 'Well, best of luck.'

'Back at you. And also,' Miguel added quickly. I watched in surprise as he glanced at his shoes bashfully. Bashful and Miguel de la Fuente . . .? 'There's a surprise waiting for you in your motorhome. Nothing insane, I promise.'

I raised a sceptical eyebrow. 'A surprise? You didn't have to . . .'

'I definitely did. You'll see,' replied Miguel with a smile that only caused my curiosity to grow.

After that intriguing announcement, we parted ways. I walked calmly to my garage, resisting the urge to bolt. I peered around the corner of the open door.

I could not believe it.

Aiden was pointing out the parts of his engineer's dashboard, the intricate windows of his screen, to a short woman, green-eyed and curly-haired, youthful despite the grey in her small ringlets, and a man in a wheelchair. He was bearded, bald, and dressed vaguely like an American professor in a sweater and slacks.

I knew I should have remained composed. Yet, there was simply no way.

'Ammi!' I cried. 'Baba!'

My parents' concentrated expressions transformed into huge smiles as they caught sight of me. I ran right to them like I used to after karting tournaments and, before my very eyes, they aged backwards. I saw my father standing, his arm around my mother, happiness overflowing as they drank in the sight of their pigtailed daughter lugging along her massive helmet.

Now, all these years later, my mom and I crouched down to the level of Baba's wheelchair. Fighting back all my emotions, I hugged them both tight.

The United States Grand Prix was the first and last race my parents had taken me to see. We got passes to the USGP as a gift from a relative living in Texas. Our plane tickets were even cheaper than Abu Dhabi passes, where you had to empty your pockets just to stand. It was 2009. I was ten years old. We stood in the sweltering heat for over three hours. I fell in love.

After Baba's accident, we knew it was impossible to return to where it had all started, or, for that matter, any race. Round-the-clock care that my mother could barely provide, no airline able to accommodate Baba's needs, much of the barebones money I was making in the lower Formula series still going towards paying off tuitions from the expat school, and Ammi absolutely terrified to fly. So I couldn't comprehend that – for the first time since I started F3 – my parents had travelled halfway across the globe to watch this race so dear to our hearts.

I struggled to form these very words. 'What . . . how—'

'We couldn't miss it,' said Baba. 'I told your mother that – damn my problems – we had to come see you back here. Then came something else – a godsend.'

'A godsend?' I repeated.

Ammi nodded. 'A jet with a full-time flight nurse, another special nurse for Baba . . .' She gestured to a blonde lady in jeans and a pink blouse who was conversing with the media manager. 'All free of charge. A gift from our guardian angel.'

'Does this guardian angel have a name?' I was astonished. These things were no small matter. Even my sponsors had not been willing to help out this way. The hiring of a good nurse was an overwhelmingly expensive deterrent. And anyway, they had been paying me enough back in F3 and F2. They had no reason to shell out any more money.

Then I remembered Miguel's warning. The surprise.

'A friend of yours.' Ammi smiled. 'Said he knew what this meant to you and that he owed you at least this. Miguel.'

I pressed a hand to my chest, attempting to quell the rapid beating of my disbelieving heart. 'Miguel brought you here.'

Part of me wanted to cry. People assumed that as Formula 1 drivers, we craved the material: speed, trophies, costly gifts. Miguel had brought me my parents for the first time in almost five years. He owed me nothing. I owed him everything.

'Oh, Ammi.' I choked back tears as I held them both tight again, my life in its purest form.

The events of that first pity party came to mind, the one after I'd been injured in Imola, at which Miguel had joined me. He'd asked about my parents. My answer had clearly hit a nerve for him, but I didn't think he would remember it, really. My story was one in a sea of equally sad driver come-ups; all of us had fought demons and slayed Goliaths to get to this point. I was perfectly fine with that. But Miguel cared enough to give me my parents on a race weekend, to fill both my own empty paddock and my heart.

'So, now that we came all the way here, *ya albi* . . .' Baba smiled. 'Do your best, *lah?*'

I laughed. 'The competition is excellent. It will be a lot harder than that.'

Ammi patted my cheek. 'We know, *joonam*. But you never cared how hard it was.'

She held up her phone. The lock screen was, in true Ammi fashion, my first karting cup win. My curls, the mirror image of hers, flew everywhere as I held up my trophy with a toothy smile, cap about to fall off.

'You had the worst car,' my mother told me. 'It was your first year. Someone had tried to kick us out, it was about to rain, and you'd lost your bag. Everything that could go wrong

242

did. And look at what you made from it. Look at this little girl. Look at your career.'

I met my own eyes in the photo. I had no cares back then. I raced without abandon, but I had left a part of myself in that kart. Ammi was right. I needed that part back now.

'For you.' I gave my parents one last hug. Then I grabbed my helmet and clicked it on, locked in. It was time to pick up the pieces and drive as a whole again.

The moments before the start of a race caused a palpable anxiety like no other in me.

What if I lost? What if I went back to my parents without a trophy?

These rational fears were the enemy of every driver. Returning empty-handed plagued us at every race. Today, these fears were coming over me in relentless waves.

My car shuddered beneath my feet. I felt every vibration flow through me as I clutched the wheel.

Look at this little girl.

I closed my eyes and let myself breathe. Instead of drawing on all the bad things, all the reasons to prove them wrong, I did what my mother had told me. I remembered what made me love this sport so much.

The first time I sat in a kart at a local fair. That was the clearest memory in my mind. The wind tousling my hair as I went down the little chicane, kart whipping me this way and that. *Again*, I couldn't stop saying. *Again, again, again.* My parents gave in. I kept going till I could lift my first trophy high, and the adrenaline, man, was unlike anything I'd ever felt before. I know I said I fell in love the first time I watched a race, and that sounds clichéd, that sounds vague, but oh, I truly fell. I had an addiction to that kind of speed. Nowhere else could a girl in the Middle East find so much power at the tap of a pedal.

Maybe Miguel was right. Maybe destiny, fate, all of that was real, and it had led me to my one true love so many years ago. Where had that love gone now?

Every beat of my heart was a thump against the straps of my seat belt. The final red bulb went on.

Lights out.

At one with the car, I knew right away when it was time to hit the throttle. I accelerated harder than I ever had before. Every good race begins with an excellent start. I made sure my start was seamless.

I surged ahead and got a jump on Darien to press Nic going into the first turn. And from there . . . when I tell you we raced, we raced.

I let go of the notion that I was here only to complete a job and walk away with a pay cheque. I drew on those days when I raced and trained and forced myself to the brink of physical collapse, unable to so much as walk back home, all because I couldn't live without the sound of the car firing up as I led it through the throngs at the start. I pushed so hard that I got within striking distance of Nic towards Lap Five, and Aiden said those magic words.

'Team says you're looking more competitive. Go for it.'

I gritted my teeth and put everything into chasing this car down. Nic swerved and darted just out of reach after the second DRS straight. I knew I wouldn't be able to get him easily. I would have to overtake on a corner.

'You'll use the next turn, Diana.' Aiden echoed my thoughts.

'Yeah.'

I pulled the steering wheel to yank my car around the outside of the turn and, despite a wheel-to-wheel exit that had me questioning whether I'd finish the race in one piece, I came out of it ahead of Nic.

'You are now P2, Diana, P2.'

'Let's keep moving forward. Gap to Miguel?'

'Delta already three seconds.'

I tried my hardest to catch Miguel before pitting, but I ended up ducking out still in second around Lap Twenty-Four. It was better than expected: I came out in fourth place. Then Darien pitted, then Nic, then Miguel . . . I was P1, but not by much. Miguel exited the pits just half a second behind me. I'd got the advantage. It was time to secure it.

Even as he crept up on me, I defended hard, watching turns to make sure there was no logical gap. I tore past to create my lead, until we were mere laps from the end of the race.

I was ready for it. I was preparing to push on the straight, and then, suddenly, the yellow flag came out.

'Safety car, Diana. This could turn things. You had about two-second delta from Miguel.'

'I was close, man!'

'I know. Let it roll.'

Positively on edge, I sat through the safety car, maintaining my speed behind the green sedan leading the pack. It was killing me. I *was* close. I had to finish this. Except now, Miguel would resume racing right on my tail.

'Ending now,' said Aiden.

So close, Diana. Right there.

'Safety car is in, let's go!'

Miguel's engine growled behind me. My pulse pounded in my ears. Could I do this? Could I do another lap at this pace? I was not sure.

'Bring this home, Di. Bring it home for your parents!'

The image of Ammi and Baba waiting in the motorhome was all I needed.

I absolutely floored it and, arcing sloppily around the next turn, I darted ahead. Inches of track to spare, I surged forward to take the chequered flag.

'THAT IS P1, DIANA, YOU WON AUSTIN!' Aiden nearly screamed.

'OH, THANK YOU!'

'NO, THANK YOU!' Aiden cried. 'THANK YOU, DIANA!'

'Aiden. Aiden, we won Austin. We won at COTA.'

'Yes, we have!'

'The States. In the States, we won, Aiden. Thank you. Thank you.'

I only grasped the depth of these statements as I rolled by the fence to pick up the flag of the United Arab Emirates, handed to me by a crew member. Stunned, I waved it through my victory lap until I pulled up to my place marker. I could scarcely believe that the big number one now stood before my car. Number one, for the very first time.

It took a moment for me to gain the sense to flip up my visor and wipe away the seemingly endless tears.

After a good deal of awkward clambering, I planted my feet on the chassis of my car, and I hoisted myself all the way up, arms raised. The cheers were absolutely feral. '*Joonam*,' my mother's voice crackled through the radio. 'We are so proud.

Win or lose, we are always proud to be your parents. Hold your head higher than ever, Diyana Zahrani. I know we will.'

The tears continued to prick my eyes when I took my spot on the podium, holding the Emirati flag high. Someone threw me a rhinestone-studded cowboy hat, and a security guard made to grab it, but I held out a hand. I pulled off my podium cap and took the cowboy hat, tugging it on for the fans. Hopefully, they wouldn't want it back. I was absolutely disgusting, filthy with sweat.

The opening notes of my country's beautiful anthem played over the speakers and, as I removed my hat, clutching the flag close to my heart, I couldn't control my emotions any longer.

The anthem came to an end, and applause and cheers filled the air when we accepted our awards. My first-place trophy felt so light in my hands, I could scarcely believe that it was there at all. First place. Formula 1.

I pressed a huge kiss to the side of the cool metal and lifted it high above my head, giving it a good shake as if to say, *Yes, we've finally got here.* Seeing dreams was one thing. Seeing reality was another entirely. I'd always had to make room for myself in this sport and, finally, it would have to make room for me. This trophy was more than just one first place, and as the champagne flew and celebrations abounded, I could feel it as Miguel and Darien sprayed me with their bottles, the cold liquid sobering me to the fact that this was very, very true. I had the chance to be the beginning of something new and necessary to diversify a space that had resisted change for ages, and I was going to take it.

I brushed tears and champagne from my cheeks, laughing

as we set down our huge bottles. This was everything my parents had ever dreamed of, and the best part was that they were *here*. They were watching it and, for all I knew – which I did, because they were as soft-hearted as anyone I'd ever met – they were crying just the same.

Which reminded me of my guardian angel.

I turned to Miguel, and he immediately picked up on the gratitude in my glance. 'You liked your surprise?' he asked with a laugh.

'I loved it, Miguel,' I said through an embarrassing little sob. 'Thank you. Thank you for bringing them here. You have no idea how much that means. My guardian angel – that's what my parents called you.'

He reached out and squeezed my hand in his strong one. The touch sent a warmth spreading across my skin and up my arm, until it made its way into my chest. I felt my eyes widening as I realized what was going on. 'You've done it. You've won the United States Grand Prix, Diana: how's that for giving your parents a surprise in return?'

The crowds were going absolutely crazy as Miguel drew closer to me. They pushed against the barricades to get closer to our podium platform. Cameras flashed around us, eager to capture all the chaos of this moment. I couldn't believe this was happening on the podium. 'More – more than enough,' I managed.

Miguel looked up at me from the P2 spot, and suddenly I could hardly stand. I felt completely unrooted. I didn't know if I wanted to feel that way, not with the world watching us. The feelings I had for Miguel de la Fuente, words had not yet been invented for them. Did I want him to come closer? Did

I want him to stay there? I had no idea. I just stared at him, unable to move. What was the matter with me?

'You . . .' I could see the conflicting emotions flicker in Miguel's irises as he, like me, struggled to make sense of this moment. 'You're just . . .'

'And you . . .' I tried to find words, but my nerves overcame me. 'With everyone here, I just . . .'

That emotion in his eyes? I pinpointed it as longing, framed in thick eyelashes and a smattering of freckles only I could make out, a feature that felt more intimate than any physical contact to me.

He leaned towards me ever so slightly, stepped towards me, his hand still in mine. He was close enough that I could feel his breath on my skin.

I thought of all the horror stories I'd heard early in my racing career: men lure you in, they take your reputation and tear it to shreds. Let a man get in your head, and you lay the foundations of your own downfall. The doubters will find reasons to take you out of this sport. For the men it's not the same, but for you, all it takes is a split second.

It doesn't matter how much you want him. You can't allow yourself to need him.

The pit of my stomach was filling with warnings and fear and anxiety that countered the brilliant warmth in my chest. I could not let that split second spell the end of my career. I had to resist. And so, eyes wide, I stepped back with a start, more instinct than anything else.

Stupid.

I stepped awkwardly, onto the corner of the slippery podium step. My body felt it before my brain registered it. My foot turned at an unnatural angle, and pain shot straight up my ankle.

I think Miguel saw it, but I could never be sure. I recovered quickly, with what I realize now was his help, his arm pulling mine back up towards him. I placed the majority of my weight onto my good foot, and bit down on my tongue to silence the curse I was holding back. This couldn't be happening.

His own gaze was full of worry, distracted by how quickly I'd startled, letting go of my hand as fast as he could.

I blanketed my shock in a tight smile and a nod. 'I . . . I'll see you.'

I rushed off the stage as fast as my painful ankle could carry me, hoisting the trophy and champagne aloft a couple of times for the sake of the fans before turning the corner to stumble down the stairs behind the podium.

In the quiet area behind the stage, I let out a shaky breath and a muffled cry as I yanked off my racing boot, pressing a hand to my throbbing ankle.

'Oh, no,' I murmured, looking up at the perfect blue skies of Austin.

Oh. No.

Chapter Thirty-Five

Miguel

'Man, she is . . .'

Beside me, Darien just chuckled. 'You're stalling, Miguel.'

'But actually. She's *everything*, dude, and I scared her away. How do I even get within feet of her right now?' I sighed.

Diana positively glowed, in the same rhinestone-studded hat she had picked up on Sunday, paired with a white fringed jacket stitched with roses over a black tank top, flared jeans, and matching black cowboy boots. The way her hair kicked up in the breeze and her face lit up with that huge smile as she signed autographs on her way to her car made me feel like I'd been an idiot to misread the moment yesterday. That was a *podium*. In front of the world and their mothers, I'd made the mistake of literally overstepping. After that, I just felt too shamefaced to approach her in the Rosa Dorada. She was so loved, so out of my league, and I'd managed to mess it all up, in the moment of her greatest triumph, too. How would I even begin to make amends?

'Come on,' Alex urged me. 'You're running out of time. Get a move on, otherwise you won't see her for another month.'

He gave me a little nudge down the row of barricades, and I shuffled gingerly towards Diana. 'Hi,' I managed.

Alex stuck out an arm to push me even further and, as Diana turned, I nearly smacked right into her. She caught herself against my chest with a clearing of her throat. 'Well, hey, Miguel.'

'Hi,' I repeated, completely lost for words. Her scent of amber and vanilla drifted gently my way. 'Summer break, huh?'

We awkwardly disentangled ourselves from one another. 'Yes.' Diana nodded with a hint of confused hesitation. 'Break.'

'Where you, uh, where you going?' I coughed out the words.

'Probably Dubai.' She glanced down at her feet, as if they were the most intriguing part of this conversation. 'I'm starting to move in for good now, so I'll finish that over break. And you? Barcelona, right?'

'Yeah. Barcelona. Family and all.' I cleared my throat. 'Uh . . . bad time, I know, but about yesterday . . .'

'What about it?' Diana gave me that same forced smile she'd thrown my way on the podium yesterday. 'Nothing happened. It's okay. Don't take it home with you over break.'

I felt my face go warm. Funny how close to forty degrees Celsius in a car didn't faze me, but every interaction with this woman had me sweating buckets. 'No, no, it's just . . . are we good? Are *you* good? Your foot—'

'Is all right,' finished Diana far too quickly, glancing towards her car as she bit her bottom lip in thought. It was way too attractive for the amount of weight this conversation held. 'Relax over break. Recharge. I guess I'll see you in Spa, Miguel de la Fuente.'

She waved goodbye with yet another small smile that compounded more than eased the tension in my heart, and then she hurried towards her car, passing a tip to the valet.

I watched completely helplessly as the most wonderful human being I'd ever met hopped behind the wheel and drove herself away in her Porsche Panamera.

Well.

'What'd she say?' Alex immediately asked me, Darien not far behind. 'What'd *you* say, mate?'

'I . . . uh . . .'

'Huh?' said Darien.

'She . . . it's weird,' I managed. 'She's going to Dubai. I'll go to Barcelona. And we'll see each other again. At Spa, you know.'

Alex just glared at me. He blinked. And then, finally: '*Mate!*'

'It's not anything legitimate!' I shot back almost defensively. 'It's just *off* between us. I told you, I'd messed it up too hard to—'

'Go to her!' Darien chimed in, clapping me on the back with a brotherly kind of insistence. 'Dude, you know you can't just sit here and sob about screwing up. You clearly care too much about her for that. So *please*. For our sake, don't make us watch you mope over break. Go win that woman over.'

Go to her.

I clung to those words as the summer break began with shutdown, and I lounged around Barcelona in between training and all the media crap. A week passed by, then two.

'Why are you on your phone, Miggie?' my mother called from the bushes across from me, her arms full of the flowers she'd just cut from her garden. 'I'm telling you. It is Darien who spends too much time on Instagram and not you.'

Mamá tossed her secateurs aside, turned my way. 'Are you texting Diana right? *Tío, texting* her? Really?'

'Ma!' I groaned, burying my head in my hands. 'No, of course I'm *not* texting her. You saw what happened in COTA. I can't face her again. She won't forgive me for messing up like that.'

'Does she seem like the kind of girl who wouldn't forgive?' Mamá shot me a look. 'Miggie. Go into town. Take a walk. Maybe when you return, you'll realize texting isn't enough and you need to go *find* that woman. *¡Vamos!*' she added, for that little touch of Spanish mother on the warpath. I would have insisted that I wasn't texting her, but I didn't want to get thrashed, so I obeyed.

I wasn't in the mood to get mobbed by tourists, either. I skirted around Sagrada Família and took an emptier footpath through the edges of the city, around the older churches and houses, the more authentic parts of town. I watched a flamenco dancer and traditional musicians perform in the square, the massive crowd rapt as the dancer glided across the pop-up stage. I had some tapas and bought an artisan bracelet for Mamá. It was a good distraction.

After all that, I decided to head back home the way I'd come. You could see the sun setting now – it demanded my undivided attention as it painted the sky in glowing oranges and pinks. It had my attention, up till I remembered something else about that gorgeous Barcelona sunset.

It was stunning on its own. It brought us hundreds of

thousands of tourists from every corner of the globe. I could watch it a million times over and never tire of it. But when I'd watched it with her, I'd realized just how much I had been missing all these years.

That sunset would never grip me the way it had before, not now that I'd sat across from her and watched it halo her curls like she was some sort of angel. 'Guardian angel,' she'd called me. It was all her. She painted the skies of Barcelona with all the colours of her laughter and her smiles and her gentle teasing, and man, I was *not* going to let her think I'd just let everything that happened in Austin go without making amends.

I tugged my phone from my pocket and opened the search engine. Into the bar at the top of the screen, after a couple of frantically mistyped attempts, I managed to stab out the correct words at last. *Dubai flights tonight.*

Chapter Thirty-Six

Diana

'Jolt's going to be like, what did you go and do to yourself? This is not good.'

'No, no! You look the same.'

'Ammi.'

'Okay. It is just a little bit of an accident,' my mother gave in. 'You have the boot, *joonam*. It could have been much worse.'

'It was embarrassing,' I corrected her with a groan. 'Ammi, if Jolt finds out, I am *dead*. My reserve driver will have to pick up the slack for the return race if this isn't "okay" by next race. And going forward from there? Who knows if they'll even want to renew my seat? This is such rookie behaviour from me.'

'You aren't silly for wanting to put yourself first,' Ammi assured me.

'I'm silly to have sprained my foot on that podium!' I protested, jabbing an insistent crutch her way. 'Now I can't even go full throttle.'

'I did wonder,' Baba added from his wheelchair, 'how you slipped so badly, *albi?*'

I grumbled under my breath. 'I don't exactly know. Probably because I was riding a wave of ecstasy from the P1 while fighting nerves and attempting to keep my career alive. Those things don't go too well together.'

'Well,' said Ammi, 'as far as I can see, you had a good excuse to have Miguel at your beck and call. You could have suggested he come here for break, you know.'

'Ammiiiii,' I groaned again.

'What? Is this because we have to stick to your side now?' my mother said with a teasing smile. 'You don't want us making sure you don't slip and break the other leg, champion?'

'One mangled foot is more than enough,' remarked Baba, fully intending to shame me, but with no licence to do so.

'Baba,' I mumbled, throwing my head back against all the pillows my mother had piled on my bed. It was ridiculous. I looked like a sickly Victorian child. I'd sit in bed and wait for my home trainer to come and move the ankle around until I wanted to sob of pain. Then she'd make me get *out* of bed and do reps in the gym, and then, as if it wasn't enough, she stuck me in the ice bath. It was misery. Necessary, but miserable.

Still, I knew there was a reason for what I'd done. If I hadn't taken that step back, my heart would have made the next decision, and I would have regretted that for the rest of my life. But I regretted *this* anyway. I regretted the look of guilt in Miguel's eyes when I left COTA so abruptly. I wanted to turn around and wrap my arms around him so he knew just how close I wanted him to be.

And yet. My mind tried its hardest to reason against my irrational desires.

'Ammi, can you close my blinds?' I asked my mother, before she wheeled my father out of my room.

She raised a perfect eyebrow my way. 'Close your blinds?'

'What if someone sees me like this?'

'No one will see you.' Ammi laughed. Then she winked. *Winked?* 'Besides. You should look outside. It will make you feel better.'

I scoffed. My parents could be so corny sometimes. I couldn't be upset with her, though; she was trying. Maybe this was just her idea of being helpful. It was hard to tell sometimes. 'Okay, Ammi. I'll look outside.'

My parents left the room, Ammi closing the door behind her, and I turned to the stupid window with a sigh. My place in Dubai was not even in the city – those had been too expensive. I was just outside of Dubai proper, where I could live in a quiet residential area and have just enough peace to sequester myself away and recover from what was apparently a tendon injury.

'Why don't you actually show me something interesting,' I said to no one in particular, 'and maybe I'll finally leave this stupid room.'

The universe must have heard my plea for once in my life because, as if on cue, a stone hit my window.

I started.

What?

I must be delirious. Maybe I was truly embodying the persona of the sickly Victorian and suffering a fit of the vapours while I was at it.

Yet another stone, or whatever it was, hit my window. Twice, three times. The tapping on the glass sounded insistent, and I threw back the bed sheet in annoyance. Why couldn't a woman wallow in her humiliation undisturbed?

I shot up from my bed, exasperated, and thundered over to the window, at which point I tore it open with a shout: 'What on Earth is—'

'Hey!' Miguel de la Fuente called up from the front yard of my small house.

He was red in the face, flushed from the brutal heat of the Middle East's oven-like climate. It irked me that he was still as handsome as ever, with his effortlessly untamed hair and his jeans and sweater – jeans and sweater, in Dubai. He had to be roasting out there.

'Why don't you come in?' I yelled back.

'Wait!' He reached down to the ground near his feet, where a stack of boards lay, and picked up the first one. I squinted to read his enormously scrawled letters.

SORRY.

He flipped it over.

DIANA.

I wasn't sure if I should laugh or cry. What was this guy doing? Had Miguel watched *Love Actually* on the flight over and gotten struck with a bit too much inspiration?

He tossed the board aside and grabbed the next.

I KNOW I WAS AN IDIOT.

Flip.

I DIDN'T MEAN TO.

New board.

HURT YOU.

Flip.

SO YOUR MOM HELPED ME.

I had to laugh now. He was sorting his boards to find the final one so hurriedly, with a little furrow of anxiety on his brow. The gesture in itself touched my heart, of course, but something about his demeanour made it feel as if it were melting.

Last board.

MAKE THIS FOR YOU.

Fumbling to chuck the poster board to the side, Miguel held up a brown paper bag, from which he withdrew a plastic baggie. Of *kanafeh*.

'I'm sorry I couldn't get you something more!' he shouted. 'Customs is a bitch here!'

I clapped a hand over my mouth to keep myself from snorting. Miguel de la Fuente had just come all the way to Dubai to deliver me *kanafeh* he'd made . . . with my parents.

'You should come down!' Miguel told me. Oh, he was definitely in on my mother's plan to get me out of the room, and this was working a little too well.

'It's going to take me a full ten minutes!' I retorted.

'I'll wait as long as you need me to!' was his full-volume response.

I just shook my head and covered my face with my hands, turning the other way so he couldn't see how red my dumb cheeks were getting.

By the time I got down the stairs, Miguel was sitting outside on the little back patio of the house. His jaw dropped as I drew the sliding door open, before grasping my crutch with an iron grip once more.

The words started to bubble out of his mouth. 'Oh, no. Oh, no, no, no, I didn't . . . I can't believe I . . .'

'It's not your—'

Miguel was still shell-shocked. 'You have a boot. And crutches, you have crutches! All because I decided to act like an idiot. Diana, this *is* on me. What about the next race?'

I shrugged.

'Oh, no,' he repeated, rushing over to help me over the threshold. He didn't stop fussing over me, walking slightly behind and to my weak side, ushering me towards the chair at the small outdoor table until I was seated. At that point, he collapsed across from me and threw his head back, groaning into his hands. 'Diana. I'm so sorry.'

'It's not your fault,' I tried but, if I was being honest, I could tell it did little to convince him; the guilt in his eyes told me he still felt responsible.

He pushed the plastic bag of *kanafeh* towards me. 'Please. Have some.'

I couldn't help but smile at that. He'd made this with his own hands for me. Obviously I would have some.

I reached into the bag and broke off a piece, took a bite, chewed, and yes. Realistically, it was what you expected for the first time someone made a pastry that took years to perfect, but this came with a little something extra. It was, without a doubt, the best *kanafeh* I'd ever had.

'How is it?' He drummed his fingers on the table a bit too quickly to be anything but nerves.

'It's wonderful.'

I stifled a giggle as Miguel exhaled hard in relief. 'Good. That was *way* too crazy to make.'

'I really appreciate it.' I bit back a much broader grin than the one I'd allowed myself to show him. 'This means a lot, Miguel.'

Now it was he who was beginning to turn red, and this time, it wasn't just the heat. He beamed, grabbing a piece of *kanafeh* for himself. And we just ate and exchanged glances. We didn't need words to express what was happening between us.

Once we had finished the desserts, Miguel cleared his throat, meeting my eyes. 'So, Diana, I wanted to ask. Would you . . . could I stay here till break ends?'

I almost choked on my last bite of pastry. 'What?'

'I want to stay.' He seemed to begin a sentence that didn't quite come out before restarting. 'I owe that to you. Whatever you need while you recover, I'm here. We'll stay out of the media's way, whatever we need to do. I just can't in all conscience go back to Barcelona and pretend you're not here, with . . .' He waved towards my crutches.

'You want to stay here?' I echoed his request in disbelief. Miguel did not strike me as the kind of person who would enjoy playing nurse's aide for two weeks, during which he could have been doing anything else he wanted – wining and dining other women, clubbing, travelling, swimming, relaxing by the beach. But his eyes were wide, filled with a kind of desperation I knew I had no chance resisting.

He nodded with the purest determination, his jaw set. My heart soared.

Miguel de la Fuente was going to stay with me in Dubai this summer break.

* * *

I had one guest room, next door to mine, which Ammi helped Miguel get set up in before she and my father returned to their house. 'I told you,' she said with a knowing smile, before she got in her car. 'Sometimes it is worth opening your window and taking a look outside.'

The next day, Miguel and I had a lazy lunch in the house before freshening up for the very first thing any good tourist did in Dubai. I changed into a sky-blue full-length dress with billowing sleeves. Miguel, poor thing, finally traded his sweater for a short-sleeved button-down patterned with little white dots, and ditched the jeans for khaki shorts (what was it with this man and his khakis?).

Miguel refused to let me go down the stairs until he was in front of me. He ensured I didn't topple down the steps, holding his arms out dramatically as if I'd fall straight on top of him at any moment. He chose the moment my feet were on solid ground before telling me, 'I like your shoes . . . oops, sorry.' He grinned. 'Shoe.'

I rolled my eyes at his feeble joke, glancing at the single Air Force taking most of my weight. It looked insanely tiny set against the boot protecting my ankle. Time to see how long I made it walking around Dubai in my monstrous footwear.

Miguel drove us through the city with the top of his rental car down. It was still daytime; we wouldn't quite get the lights yet, but Dubai was sparkling with life. We pulled into the Dubai Mall, from which we entered the Burj Khalifa unnoticed, emboldened by the sunglasses that constituted our perfect disguise. In truth it was a miracle that no one pointed us out, though, likely because they were so used to seeing us in our team colours and suits. We went through the line just like everyone else, and then we reached my new worst enemy: the two elevators to the top.

I groaned as we approached the doors. 'They will put us in this metal box with fifteen other humans, Miguel. Or more.'

He just chuckled. 'Is it me, a foot thing, or are you . . . scared of elevators?'

'I don't like them,' I corrected him with a shiver. 'I take stairs when I can. Lifts freak me out. And no, the leg doesn't help matters.'

'Don't worry about it,' Miguel offered.

'Don't worry?' I echoed in disbelief.

'I don't know . . . breathe.'

'Breathe? That's even worse than "don't worry"!'

'Come on.' He gestured to the elevator as its doors opened.

I tentatively clopped into the small space. With every tourist that followed us inside, my heartbeat increased a tick. It was an irrational fear, which made it all the more impossible to stop. Perhaps Miguel noticed my shoulder tense beside his, because he threw a smirk my way. 'So it's true, you do have a fear of elevators.'

'Strong dislike,' I corrected him as I struggled to compose myself. This was utterly stupid.

'Why are we even here, then?'

'Well, I wanted you to see it!'

'I could go without, Di. I have you,' he quipped, smirk now a smile.

The elevator jolted, signalling the start of our ascent, and one of my crutches slipped an inch. I would have been fine, but in a speed true to stellar racing reflexes, Miguel's hand flew to hold me still.

I didn't need a mirror to know I was the colour of the stripe on the R3-71 now.

I could feel the warmth of his body around mine, detect every note of his cologne. For thirty seconds I kept myself from losing it – either because of my discomfort about the elevator or about Miguel's proximity – before we were able to get out and move to the second elevator. At long last, after what felt like ages, I was given respite when the doors opened and we stepped out onto the highest floor of the Burj Khalifa accessible to the common tourist.

'Thanks,' I managed, once we were out.

'No, thank *you*.' Miguel grinned and looked around like a kid in a candy shop, absolutely enraptured. 'This is friggin' *awesome*.'

The uppermost floor had windows all around, and was in a sort of doughnut shape circling the centre. Modern couches and coffee tables were scattered about. Waiters milled around with trays of macarons and fruit juices. I grabbed an OJ in an attempt to concentrate my skittishness on a mundane activity. Miguel immediately sought out the macarons.

'Wow,' he said as we approached the windows. 'Am I actually high?'

I chuckled. 'Miguel, you are very, very high.'

He shot me a smile that told me he'd understood my little dad joke. 'Look at this. I mean, it's not new to you, but look how vivid all the colours are.'

I did look, and he was right. I'd never thought of it that way. The blues of the water were oh-so-turquoise, the buildings sparkling like diamonds on the neck of a bride. It was, I said only to myself, how I saw everything when I was with Miguel.

'Can I ask, Diana?' he said. 'Why does your dad call you "elbow"?'

'*What?*' I burst out laughing. 'Elbow?'

'Elbow, right? That's what I heard. I saw you guys back in COTA. He called you elbow.'

'*Albi*,' I corrected him, smiling. 'It means "heart" in Arabic. But only Baba calls me that.'

'What does everyone else call you?'

'Ammi calls me *joonam*. Persian for "dear". And everyone else . . . I guess they call me by my Arabic name. My actual name. Diyana.'

'Uh . . . your Arabic name is . . . Deena . . . but your name is also . . .' Miguel struggled to make sense of this.

'The westernized spelling, D-I-A-N-A, is what you know. But the name my parents gave me, D-I-Y-A-N-A, is one of many Arabic variants,' I explained. 'When I started karting, they would pronounce *dee-ye-neh* like Diana. So it stuck.'

I could practically see the wheels turning in Miguel's head. 'So . . . Diana, uh, *Diyana*, what should I call you?'

'Depends. What do you want to call me?'

'Diyana,' he repeated. My name, my real name, sounded like liquid gold in the huskiness of his voice. I could have listened to him say it a million times over. 'That's crazy.'

'Guess my parents wanted me to be a little crazy.'

Miguel smiled shyly. 'It's a unique name. It's beautiful. Maybe motorsport doesn't like it, but I do. It's cool.'

'Thank you.' I let out a breath in relief. I had never really told anyone else. Some people had said Diyana was too Arab for me, too Islamic, so it had seemed easier to go along with the westernized name. Till now.

'You're welcome . . . Diyana,' he added.

We spent the rest of the day eating junk food, walking the aquarium, and nearly getting lost in the Dubai Mall, with an insouciance that would have horrified our teams (particularly as Miguel somehow got into the Kid Zone and nearly broke a tiny seesaw).

The highlight, however, came when we found a *pani puri* stand out near the exit of the mall. We'd already blown way too much on food, and we certainly didn't need any more, but the second the shiny stand caught my eye, I was gone.

I nudged Miguel to get his attention. 'Mig. Mig, look.'

He followed my gaze to the stand, his eyebrows rising. 'Oh? What's that?'

'Let's have you find out.' I was already making a beeline for the stand by the time the words left my mouth. It took me less than a minute to exchange words with the vendor and grab two bowls, one for Miguel and one for myself. *Pani puri* was one of my favourite Indian foods. It wasn't something that I had grown up with in my household, but I remembered sharing it with the girls from my school when their parents would drop them off: baggies of crispy *puri*, little fried discs that you poked a hole in, and then loaded with potatoes, chickpeas and onions, plus the spiced *pani*, a minty-flavoured water that the girls would bring in a separate tiffin. My acquired obsession for the food had followed me ever since then.

I passed Miguel his paper bowl bearing a single *puri*, which

I figured would be more than enough for him to try. 'Here. Try this, I swear.'

He gave it a look as if sizing up an opponent's car. 'Is this gonna be spicy?'

'Not more than your tapas,' I assured him (lie) around a bite of my own. I closed my eyes in bliss. '*Wow*. It's delicious. Trust me, you have to try it.'

'Okay.' With one last sceptical glare at the puri, Miguel finally picked it up and took a bite. 'Okay. Okay, this isn't bad, it's—'

The spice hit him, and I'd never seen Miguel run faster than he did in that moment. I was shaking with laughter, trying to keep up with him on my crutches as he headed directly for the nearest ice-cream vendor and came away with a massive milkshake the size of my head. I laughed and laughed as he downed the thing, handing me his bowl of *puri* with a groan of relief.

'It's that bad?' I giggled when he finally parted with his milkshake.

'Yes,' he mumbled, his scepticism now turned to full-on disdain directed at the *puri*. 'The food Spaniards eat is bland as hell, Diyana. That . . . that is a loaded missile in a really small bowl.'

I tried not to laugh again, but I couldn't stop myself. A snort escaped my mouth, and I chuckled while Miguel cleaned out the entire shake on the walk to the Dubai Fountains.

It was a relief to be outside. We stood among a crowd of tourists who were squeezing against the banisters for the best view of the dancing fountain doing Nancy Ajram's 'Shik Shak Shok', the unofficial title track of the Middle East. No one would point us out or take photos of us when there was something much more worthwhile to concentrate on. We were fully safe here.

'It's stunning!' Miguel bobbed his head to the beat as the opening notes of the song struck up and the jets lit up, spraying water in complete synchrony. 'But I'm sure you already know that.'

I smiled. 'It's not the same when you watch alone.'

He met my eyes with a grin. 'So it would not seem this beautiful, if I were to visit on my own, Diyana?'

Diyana. The fact that he was using my name, my actual name, so easily, plucked the strings of my heart, awakening butterflies within its cage. I couldn't muster much more than a shy glance at my crutches.

'I'm not glad I made you risk your foot,' he went on, his eyes still not leaving me, 'but I couldn't be more glad I'm here right now.'

I looked up. My chest was a flurry of feelings that I still couldn't quite sort out, but I knew this was real. Every bit of it was.

'Me, too,' I said.

Our shoulders brushed as Miguel pointed upward, to the largest of the jets, the lights illuminating his irises as he beamed. 'Look at that.'

I looked up, and the jets shot straight up with a loud *boom* and a rush of water, glowing the colour of Dubai's famous gold.

We watched on, rapt, and my soul soared with the jets of water. Maybe I still hadn't worked up the courage to say this much to Miguel, but I hoped he knew that there was no way, none, that I would rather be anywhere but here, with him, right now.

Chapter Thirty-Seven

Miguel

Over the two weeks we had together, we stormed Dubai completely. At Diyana's insistence, we went to the Miracle Garden and Global Village to take photos, watched a crazy fire-breather show, got swindled by the shopkeepers in the souk and, as the cherry on top of our antics, decided we wanted to see Atlantis. We dressed up in the cheesiest tourist disguises we could find, complete with floppy hats and sunglasses, and took tacky photos with weird fish. It was in our last hour in the city that we decided to do what we'd truly come here for.

Diyana beat me to the driver's seat, ridiculously fast even in the sand. I gestured to her leg. She just shrugged. 'Come on. Give me this little bit of freedom.'

I rolled my eyes with a laugh. 'Sure. Sure, this is definitely the right place to give you that freedom.'

We were quite literally in the middle of the desert. We had rented out a Jeep, and apparently, Diyana was about to take us dune bashing, though that hadn't stopped her from ensuring she got some photogenic desert shots once we were far out enough that all you could see was sand and sky. She wore a long-sleeved dress as white as the clouds that didn't seem to exist here; it fell down to her ankles. Her hair had been swept into a loose ponytail at the nape of her neck for the sake of comfortable driving. Her one available foot was dressed in a Birkenstock sandal. Forget me as the guardian angel: she looked like a real one, the one that had saved me from getting my head crushed in all my stupid racing crashes.

She gripped the wheel and switched to drive. The sleeve of her dress slipped back, revealing the falcon tattoo on the side of her wrist. 'Ready?' She smirked.

'When am I not?'

'Now.'

'Oh, shit!' I swore as we shot forward abruptly, bouncing so hard that my head nearly hit the roof. '*Diyana!*'

She jerked the wheel sharply to the right, sending us over a hump of sand and me nearly into the window.

'Are you *trained* in this?'

'I am a Formula 1 driver!'

'No, *this!*'

'Not a bit!' she replied, laughing carelessly, and throwing her head back in abandon as we slid into a mountain of sand that sprayed up around us. The Jeep clung to the side of the dune, skewing first one way then the other. I held on for dear life, and finally, after ten minutes of this hell, Diyana parked up, beaming giddily.

'Fun,' she said.

'I'm so glad we don't have two-seaters in F1.'

She smacked my arm. 'You wish.'

We got out of the car, Diyana very carefully, without her crutches, and we just gazed around for a while. There was nothing for miles, just sand. You could see the heat waves coming off the dunes, radiating and contorting our view of the cloudless blue skies. If you looked carefully, it seemed like the desert never ended, just kept going forever. It was absolutely remarkable.

'I wanted to take you to the Bedouin camp a bit off the beaten track, to avoid all those tourists trying to get the full "Arabic experience" or whatever,' said Diyana, 'but we don't have any more time.' She put on a faux pout. 'You have to leave.'

'Yeah, after this . . .' I gestured around me, to her. 'You've been the craziest, most entertaining, most *gorgeous* tour guide. I'd stay here for ever if I could.'

The ponytail holder had fallen out of Diyana's hair, and it whipped into a wind-induced frenzy, flying back so I could see the pink tingeing her cheeks. 'Do I get a five-star review?'

'Seven-star.'

I felt her fingers lace themselves through mine, finding the gaps and filling them perfectly. She gave my hand a squeeze. 'Thank you for this break, Mig.'

'Sure. Thank *you*.' I returned her gesture, running my thumb across her knuckles as I smiled, if not a little nervously. 'But just so you know, I wanna spend more time with you. The past two weeks, learning about your city, learning about the things that make *you*. I wanna give you the same in return. Show you around my world, maybe.'

'Is that a formal invitation?' she said, eyebrow raised.

I shrugged, my heart stampeding as her eyes locked right onto mine. 'So, Miss Zahrani, we all have the same questions on our minds this race weekend,' I mimicked the nosy reporters. 'A woman as beautiful as you would have a man under her control, would she not? Do you?'

'Mmm, some might say I'm in talks with a certain Revello driver,' Diyana answered casually, her smile too broad to conceal. She brought a finger to her mouth in a 'shh' gesture, and unconsciously, my gaze fell there. 'Don't tell anyone.'

'Promise. I won't.' I held out a pinky.

She linked her little finger in mine and gave it a tug. 'Done deal.'

She leaned her forehead against mine, and her hair enveloped both of us, just skimming my cheeks and keeping the beating sun out of my eyes.

'Am I your favourite driver yet?' I teased.

'Senna.' She smiled. 'But you might just be second.'

'Ah, second place.'

Diyana laughed, a laugh I caught when I pressed my lips to hers, and she closed her eyes. I wrapped my arms around her, and her fingers brushed the nape of my neck. We let ourselves destroy one another in the middle of the desert, alone, with no one to take this moment from us in the form of unsolicited photos or headlines. I fell for this brilliant woman all over again, as stunned as I had been since the first day I'd met her.

Chapter Thirty-Eight

Diana

The bliss of the two-week summer break wound to an unfortunately quick end. By about a week into factory restart, I no longer had the boot, and my foot, wrapped up in plenty of physio tape, was regaining its normal function. But at that point, my injury was the least of the things floating around in my mind.

I had kissed him. I had kissed Miguel de la Fuente, and the scariest part about it all was how perfect it had been. I could still feel his hands in my hair, his breath on my cheek. I knew this was something that could ruin me, this kind of relationship. Yet my resistance had been dulled as I walked around Dubai with him, watching him guzzle a chocolate milkshake to cure himself of the *pani puri* curse, and lose his mind over the aquarium like a small child seeing a fish for the first time. Everything he did, whether he knew it or not, slowly whittled down the barrier I had been forced to build over years in this sport. It gave me hope that we could keep this quiet. We could still chase our fantasies if we stayed silent in public. And, as much as I suspected that would simply be impossible, I chose to believe it.

Even as I scrolled through Formula 1 news articles on our team jet en route to Spa, the next race and the first one back, I continued to choose to believe it. I convinced myself that this could work, even as headline after headline passed through my screen: 'No seat for Zahrani?' 'Where is Danger in 2023?' 'Still no renewal from Jolt next season for Diana Zahrani.'

Miguel had to be exceedingly excited for Spa-Francorchamps. Here, he'd won his very first race on the high-speed track full of potential overtake zones; here, I'd have to return from break with a bang loud enough to wake up my own team and offer me an extension on my contract. I'd already waited with bated breath every night of the break, anticipating being startled awake by some aggressive midnight notification blindsiding me as regards my Formula 1 future. I couldn't believe it was happening in the first place. I thought I'd done all the things right – winning in my rookie year, podium after podium. Except, evidently, something was missing, and a part of me knew exactly what that was.

As we touched down in Belgium, my brain picked up where the season had left off. Nic's scorching retorts and the controversy around his friendship with Miguel. My first victory in Austin, and Nic's tussle with Miguel on-track prior to that. What happened now?

Naturally, a press conference.

We'd all signed contracts. We were all aware of what was expected from us in terms of the media. But these conferences only got more and more ridiculous. Walking into the Spa boardroom, we saw that these interviews were grouped by the top and bottom five constructors: ten of us all at once, seated in a UN-like setup with name cards, flexible mics, and pads of paper (why?), the desks ascending up two stair-like levels.

I mean, we weren't exactly Nelson Mandela, nor were we on the cusp of solving world hunger. On the contrary, we deafened innocents, polluted their air, razed their forests, and emptied their pockets. In the grand scheme of things, we were hardly heroes.

Nic – who I still hadn't spoken to since Austin – and I took our seats on the same level as Darien and Peter. At the far end would sit Miguel and Andrea and, below us, Kasper, Alex, and Burgess's Jules and Benji – Revello, Heidelberg, Jolt, Griffith and Burgess all represented.

Once we were all gathered to wait for the interviewer, the speculation started. After all, silly season was in full swing. Perhaps the most stunning revelation thus far was that Byron Hargreaves, the best lower-field driver on the grid, who'd brought his soapbox of a car into the top ten on several occasions, would no longer be contracted with Vittore. Even more odd, it was possible Andrea's contract would also not be renewed, setting up a possible swap meet between sister teams. Miguel was confident that Revello would come good regarding his own rumoured extension; with a nervous smile, he admitted to me that he was anxious to find out who'd be next year's second Revello driver. I was glad no one was discussing the future of Jolt. It was better for me that way.

The reporter, a portly man named Richard Foster who'd been winding drivers up big time for the last twelve years, began by congratulating Darien on his lucrative contract, his 2026 deal the most sought-after due to the clause that allowed him to stay on even longer if he so wished. Then came Alex's one-year extension with multi-year potential, the same for Jules Beaumont, and Miguel's rumoured contract that was said to be worth millions and would keep him on for the next six years. Of our little media group, that left myself, Nic, Kasper, Benji, Peter and Andrea still unsure about our destinations for next season. Foster, of course, started picking us off one by one.

'So, Benjamin, let's start with you. What's the word on next season?'

Benji, though he was a kind-hearted human who had the habit of doing whatever it took to make the people around him smile, could not be cracked by the reporters. His expression remained impassive as he shook his head. 'Sorry. Can't disclose that. All I can say is something's in the works.'

Foster hemmed and hawed, but Benji refused to cave, and eventually he moved on to Andrea. The man had driven for Revello since before Miguel joined. He once served as Leon Villena's ultra-talented complement, racing at the calibre of a future champion. Now, his four-year contract had run out, his skill was deteriorating, and all that was left was for Revello to officially close the door on him. I despised him, but the precarious condition of his seat, like Kasper's, had taken me aback.

Foster said just that. 'Been a good ride at Revello, has it, Andrea? Will this be your last?'

'Ah, well . . .' Andrea scratched the back of his neck, a nervous tell. 'I'll admit it, I've gotten the heads-up from Cristo, and yes, I am currently in talks with a few teams. I will be racing next year. It's still unclear as to whom I'll be racing with.'

Foster's next victim was Peter, who looked shockingly unbothered when he announced that Heidelberg Hybridge was not going to be renewing him. His contract being out surprised me. He'd been in good form all the way till now, winning them a Championship, proving that if anyone was worthy of staying on at his team of so many years, it *was* him. He didn't seem as if he was in any doubt about his ability to retain a Formula 1 spot, though. I agreed with his assessment – he was talented enough that he'd certainly have a place waiting for him on another top team.

Foster then proceeded to shake down Kasper. I disliked the guy from our time as teammates, but I respected him as a sportsman, and I had to admit that he'd had a pretty impressive career so far. I looked on in vicarious discomfort as Foster prodded Kasper about the loss of the seat he'd only had for half a season, and he finally cracked open about his Griffith place going to Byron Hargreaves. He would be bouncing back to Kramer to fill the spot of Craig Grant, who'd announced in the first week of break that he'd be retiring at season end.

Then Foster moved to Nic, Kasper's mid-season shift counterpart. 'And Nic Necci. Subject of all the talk this week. We've been hearing things, and we'd like for you to give it to us straight. What is the situation on your contract?'

I glanced towards Nic for a split second. This was the person in whom I thought I had found a confidant, and who had nearly run Miguel off the track before mouthing off about me and my background in public. The mere sight of him made me feel nauseous. I swallowed hard before looking away.

'That's good timing on your part, Richard,' said Nic jestingly. He cracked a smile that made me sick to my stomach. It was proud and excited and optimistic, and I knew that smile could mean only one thing.

'I can now state with certainty, and the announcement will likely be out right after this, that I have taken the chance to extend with Jolt until the 2024 season,' Nic went on, but I hardly heard him, as his words became a jumble in my ears.

I would like to say I felt confused, but in fact it made all the sense in the world when I considered the time we had shared on Jolt Archambeau this season. As far as Jolt was concerned, this little experiment – letting me muck around a bit in their car, an Arab woman driving in Formula 1 – had gone miserably wrong, because they could only keep one of their two hot-headed drivers, and it was clear which one they had chosen. I wasn't sure if I was genuinely shocked, or simply hurt that they hadn't thought to tell me before slapping me with the news *I* had been waiting for in the middle of a press conference.

It got even better when Foster turned my way with a broad smile, as if he could reach into my brain and pull out my thoughts. 'Last but not least, Miss Diana Zahrani. What can we expect to hear from you?'

'I didn't know of Nic's extension,' I started off carefully. 'Haven't heard anything on mine.'

Miguel looked completely shocked. Even Nic seemed a bit baffled.

'I thought they extended you!' he said, frowning.

'As I said, I have not heard anything.' I sighed. *Don't let the emotion in*, I pleaded, but I was struggling like I had never struggled before. I was usually strong in front of the media. Now, I could scarcely hold up my own head. 'Pretty sure we know what that means at this point in the season, but we race hard enough, we'll see results.'

'Indeed. So you are confident you'll get a response from your team?'

'I'm waiting on news, sir. Good or bad. I'm up every night waiting for that email or that phone call.'

'Hmm.' Foster raised an eyebrow. 'Now, Diana, you are both the greenest and the most prolific driver in her first season who is up for grabs at the moment. If Jolt *doesn't* renew . . . do you see another option with a top team here?'

Andrea. Peter. Their seats. Foster was asking if I felt I could win their seats.

'There are always options,' I finally said. 'But in F1, those aren't under your control. You just race as hard as you can, and let the cards fall where they may.'

Chapter Thirty-Nine

Miguel

S pa was my very favourite track, aside from my home race in Barcelona. I was certainly biased, as Spa was also the circuit where I'd won my first victory, but it was true. So many of us loved Spa-Francorchamps because it was a contest of raw, unbridled speed.

So it was fitting that we returned from our break for this grand prix. The practices had me cautiously optimistic, with P2 and P1, then another P2 in FP3. Now, we geared up for Belgian quali – arguably one of the fastest days on the calendar.

We'd also done some crucial redecorating prior to quali. Just yesterday, the news had come out of a devastating school shooting somewhere in California, Darien's home state, and he had subsequently affixed a new decal to his halo: a white dove carrying a ribbon bearing the colours of the grieving elementary school. You could imagine the backlash he got from traditional fans and media corps who believed the sport was best left the way it was – without humanity, of course – but many of us, not about to let him go it alone, attached the same decal to our chassis and halos, placed intentionally in the view of onboard cameras. To my knowledge, Andrea and I had both donned the sticker, as had Peter, Diyana, Alex, Jules, and others. Even Kasper, who normally couldn't be bothered to give a rat's ass in matters of solidarity, had the dove on his halo.

The most surprising reaction was from Nic. I'd always known him to be a fierce advocate for safety and human rights, even if that meant taking a stance on the touchiest of issues. I knew he was anti-gun from all the programmes he'd contributed to, but on this issue he was equivocal – he didn't seem to . . . *care* any more, I guess. He had his mechanics apply the dove minutes after FP3 ended because, rumour had it, he didn't need another decal setting his car apart from Diyana's.

'You are not here for him,' Paula reminded me pre-quali as I stretched in my personal room. 'Don't let it bother you. He doesn't deserve your attention. He'll be floating on the high of his own little contract extension. But Miguel, Mamá and Papá and I are here. Your Cavalieri are here. We are going to perform for *them*, Miguel. *¿Entiendes?*'

I nodded, rising from a stiff squat. 'Yeah.'

'You do not look so sure.'

'Well . . .' I exhaled. 'I'll be fine. I know the track like the back of my hand.'

'Sure you do.' My sister gave my hair a ruffle. 'Now. Let me leave before Louie gets back. He will have my head for distracting you.'

Paula returned to the pit wall, and I finished my warm-ups

with Louie before getting prepped and in the car. It was fairly mild out at the moment, typical Belgium weather, nothing to fear. It would be a clean qualifier.

Make it count, I reminded myself as one of the pit crew members removed the stopper from the front of the car and waved me out. I mustered a perfect safe release, just behind Andrea and ahead of Peter.

As I did my out lap, I mentally reviewed the points totals. The Championship, missing jewel in the crown of the de la Fuente family legacy, was virtually guaranteed to be mine. I had a thirty-odd point lead over Diyana, who'd sprung into second. But the Constructors' was our renewed focus. We were just nine points behind Jolt. It was max push now if we wanted Revello to come out on top once more after years of drought.

'You are clear for a flying lap,' Paula told me.

I floored it over the grid as I crossed the start. I knew Paula would be wanting me to keep it neat, but I couldn't help it. I blew around the numerous high-speed curves that constituted Spa-Francorchamps with the kind of adrenaline coursing through my veins that a driver only felt on his favourite track.

'Time takes you right to the top,' reported Paula when I made it to the finish. 'Now please, don't drive like the big-city Americans any longer.'

As usual, we made it into Q3 with the regular effort. It looked good for me from the practices, but the moment of truth would only come as we exited the pits one last time.

And there it was: pole position and a new track record at Spa. We would take Belgium yet again. Nic could stew in his garage for all I cared. I was going to run the race till the end.

* * *

283

'It could get bad tomorrow. Rain, they're saying.'

Andrea appeared about to combust, making laps of my hotel room. I could tell he was at his wits' end. For the first time in ages, Revello had a *front row lockout*. Andrea had vaulted himself into P2 to start alongside me at the race. Unfortunately, he was one of those drivers who didn't perform too well in the rain.

'What's a little sprinkle?' I stuck my legs up on the coffee table, loosening the zipper on my team fleece.

'You know I can never find the dry line,' groaned Andrea, sounding like a cranky four-year-old.

'Well aware,' I said.

He shot me a death glare. 'Sure. Well, Miguel, I don't know – if it rains—'

'You have to stop expecting the worst.' I threw a stray sock at Andrea. He flinched away, unamused. 'I know you're nervous because you've got to prove to the other teams that you can bring them the points. But you have to put the work in, man. You gotta try.'

He kept on pacing. This guy.

'What?' I prodded. 'What are you on about?'

'What's the use in trying,' he said bluntly, 'if nothing comes of it?'

'Meaning?'

'Look at Diana.' Andrea was an asshole, but now, I noticed, he was nervous. Anxious. 'Stellar driver. Could be out of a seat next year. Nothing means anything in motorsport any more.'

I felt my jaw stiffen just slightly at the thought of Diyana leaving so soon. If she was out of a seat . . . it was highly possible I might never see her again. That we'd go our separate ways. I'd heard exactly what everyone else had at that conference but, up till now, I'd forced myself to suppress it. Forget about it. She'd get a renewal. Of course she would, with the amount of talent and dedication she had. Jolt would have to keep her on.

'You can't say you're so positive.' Andrea looked down at me. 'You won't be able to race, will you, if Diana leaves? And you get separated again?'

That took me aback. I glared at him. 'What? How do you even—'

'Someone found old karting tapes.' His expression baffled me, and then I recognized it: pity – for me. 'I saw that, Miguel. How you looked at her. You won't cope with leaving her again.'

'We hate each other,' I replied, for clarification. 'Why are you being so sympathetic to me now?'

'Because it's all gone to pieces.' Andrea sat down across from me, eyes fraught with stress. 'And at the end of the day, we're teammates.'

I shrugged, but he was right. It *was* all going to pieces. Diyana's seat. Nic's impending reign. Jolt on our asses. If there was any moment Revello needed to pull themselves together, it was now.

And to answer Andrea's question, no. No, I wouldn't be able to leave Diyana. Not now that we were finally acting on what had been for all these years. I just wanted some comfort, that pocket of normal. We all did.

'All right.' I held out a hand. 'Let's shake on it.'

Andrea looked surprised, his blue eyes wide. Nevertheless, he gave my hand a firm shake. 'Thank you.'

'Yeah.'

285

'Also, mind a bit of advice?' Andrea said.

I raised an eyebrow. 'This may be stupid of me, but I'm intrigued.'

Andrea smirked. 'Funny. Well, in all seriousness . . . you're quite lucky. The universe gave you Diana not once, but twice. Show her all the care and affection you can. Think of Eddie.' He sighed, a deep one, that made me pause. 'Because you don't know, Miguel, when it will all come crashing down around you.'

Despite it being Andrea who had offered it, the advice rang in my mind as I braved the rains at Spa. The clouds came in patches, spitting at random intervals and sending cars spinning. In all the chaos, Darien's car skidded my way on Les Combes and, just like that, I was scrambling for grip down in P9.

I didn't hate Darien for it, obviously, though it caused a few unflattering f-bombs to fly Paula's way. But I couldn't afford this mistake.

It was an abysmal finish in the same place, earning me just two points. Andrea swung into P5 to net ten points; twelve in total for Revello. And Diyana and Nic made a 1-3, bringing home forty-one points counting fastest lap. If it weren't for Andrea's advice on behaving and making the rest of this season count for more than points, I'd have thrown something.

Damn it. I wanted to throw something.

Chapter Forty

Diana

I wanted to throw my hands in the air and yell happy nothings. I'd made first place in abysmal conditions, done another disgusting shoey with Peter, who'd nicked second, closed the WDC gap and opened one in the Constructors' Championship. It was all so brilliant. This would show Jolt that I deserved my seat as much as, if not more than, Nic did his.

But with Miguel this upset, I couldn't bring myself to do any of that.

We were at a secluded little bar in the Spa hotel late at night after the Rosa Dorada party, and I could tell he was trying to hide his feelings. We neatly avoided addressing the obvious topic: what had gone down in our own race. I didn't care that we weren't talking about it; I just didn't want to remind Miguel of everything that had gone awry for his team.

He beat me to it anyway. He turned my way, scrunching his nose at the foul taste of the non-alcoholic tequila that was clearly doing him no favours, and peered at me from beneath his long lashes. 'You haven't mentioned that I finished ninth, Diyana.'

'I don't want to remind you,' I replied, apt to deflect. I began to take a very sudden and very deep interest in the ruffles of my dress, today a red wine colour with puffy sleeves, a low neckline, skirt stopping just above the knee, and a back held together by big bowlike ties. It was a nice dress that my team had helped me find, but I didn't care all that much about it. What I cared about was that it didn't feel good analysing anyone else's shortcomings – after all, the only race we drove was our own.

'It's not about salt in the wound.' He raised an eyebrow. 'I'm not gonna be that overly competitive guy who has to have complete and utter control over every woman within five miles to protect his ego. I don't want to forget it. You shouldn't be glossing over the fact that you won, just because I had a royal screwup.'

'It was not a royal screwup.'

'You give me too much credit.'

'I give you the credit you deserve.' I took the empty shot glasses from in front of him and pushed them aside. 'Now, it's getting late. You have to fly tomorrow. If you don't sleep, it'll have your head pounding.'

'Okay, Mom.' Mig rolled his eyes, grinning goofily. 'Really. Thank you. You do too much for too many people.'

I smiled. Sometimes, I thought maybe he didn't understand how all-encompassing my feelings were. These days, he seemed to consume my every waking thought.

We stood up from our barstools and took the hidden route

outside to get back to the hotel rooms. Hiding, as one might expect, was turning out to be somewhat of a pain in the ass – at least for me.

'Very secretive, this sneaking around.' I nudged Miguel. 'You don't suppose it's actually working in keeping them off our trail, do you?'

'No one's said anything yet. I'd assume it's a success.' He shot a grin my way, and my heart skipped about five beats. I'd watched Miguel de la Fuente race from afar. I still couldn't believe that this beautiful man was right here before my eyes.

'Does it all ever strike you as unreal?' We stopped at my door, a hall away from Mig's to deflect any suspicions about our relationship status. 'All of this. All of . . . you.'

Miguel cracked a smile. He reached over and tucked the stubborn strands of hair that hung in front of my right ear behind it, the tips of his fingers just brushing my neck for a fleeting moment. 'Sometimes, I want to ask you that.'

I pressed my card against the key, grinning just a bit stupidly as I opened the door behind me. 'Is this good night?'

'Shh.' Mig eyed the space between the door and the frame and immediately slipped inside.

My eyes widened. 'Mig! What if—'

He turned me slightly towards the full-length mirror across from the dresser. His arms held my waist with a gentle yet firm touch, and I looked back up at him, my hands linking with his. 'What's this?'

Mig nodded towards the mirror. 'Take a look.'

'At us?'

'At how goddamn good we look together.'

I rested my head against Miguel's chest, taking in the smell of his slightly spicy cologne, the hint of aftershave. 'Don't tease me so much that the evil eye finds us.'

We shared air that ran thick with tension for a long minute, Mig's face inches from mine, our bodies warm against one another. Part of me wanted this fool to kiss me, to end me right then and there, but the larger part knew that herein lay the challenge. I had to hold out against the big, gorgeous eyes and the dopey yet soft smile, because if I didn't, there could be hell to pay. We'd give ourselves away. Both of us.

But what . . . what if we did?

I let my eyes flutter closed. All it would take from here was one more centimetre, and then, it could be chaos on every front. This could destroy us.

I wanted it to.

And so did Miguel. He leaned down and kissed me ever so gently, the opposite of what you would expect from a Formula 1 driver. I could tell then and there that he, like myself, was tired of staying clear in public, of stupid little glances and fake smiles. Both of us had been starved. Both of us just wanted to feel each other.

His lips brushed my jaw, and my head tilted in instant response, every touch daring me to prompt another. I felt his hands sneak around me, his fingers quickly finding the ties of my dress. In a movement so fast I could barely register it, the whole thing was open from the back, and his left hand was on my ass over the silky fabric of the skirt.

'So you're not scared I'm here any more,' he said, his voice a rasping whisper that unleashed butterflies into the pit of my stomach. The butterflies took flight when I felt him squeeze just slightly with that left hand.

'If you leave now,' I breathed, 'I will personally make sure you don't finish the next race.'

He shook his head with a smile. 'Diyana, I'm not going anywhere.'

'Good. Then finish this first.'

'Yes, ma'am.'

I cut off the tail end of his sentence with another kiss, my eyes squeezed shut for fear of losing this moment, fear that he would realize I was, for some reason, not the woman he had fallen for, or that I was simply dreaming. Because this felt just like a dream.

I didn't bother with buttons, yanking Miguel's dress shirt off so hard that I thought I saw one of them fly to the side. My touch searched his body: sculpted muscle, all lean biceps, and abs that tensed beneath my fingers. For all of Miguel de la Fuente's trophies and records and fastest laps, I found it funny that I had this enormous power over him.

I let him push the sleeves of the dress off my shoulders as we found our way over to the bed. Miguel leaned right back, falling onto the overly plush comforter with a mischievous smirk, pulling me down with him.

I wanted to feel him, and I did, I felt all of him; then his hands were sneaking under the hem of my dress, his kisses pressed to my collarbone, and he was hard against my thigh. The slightest scratch of the stubble on his jaw, his eyes holding mine in their coffee-coloured depths. I felt every little thing as we rolled over and Miguel brought the sheets over us. From there, the dress didn't make it for long; it took little more than a minute for it to become a puddle of deep red fabric on the ground, right next to Mig's slacks, which had been discarded as quickly as the dress.

His chest heaved against mine as his lips travelled down to my sternum, to my ribs. 'Ready?' he whispered.

'Of course, I'm—'

I couldn't get the words out, because suddenly his lips were even lower than that, and all I could do was tangle my hands up in his wavy hair, and his name was the only thing I could find the syllables to form because I could barely even breathe unless it was in the form of sporadic gasps of air. I let out whimpers so atrocious that I hoped the entire hotel hadn't heard. When you spent all day working to make other people happy, walking on eggshells so no one was upset, something like *this* felt insanely liberating. And extremely good. Because I knew we trained our hands as Formula 1 drivers, but this, this was something else.

By the time Mig had returned to eye level with me, I was a mess, breathing heavily through every word I managed. 'Miguel.'

'Yeah.' He grinned, pushing my hair off my forehead. 'Miss Zahrani, do you know how incredibly hot you are like this?'

'I'm . . . definitely overheating.'

'Let's see if I can fix that.'

I felt him slowly move the strap of my bra, felt his breath on my cheek, then on my shoulder. His back moved slightly beneath my hands, new yet familiar terrain. Then, with a sharp snapping sound, he froze abruptly, hands behind me.

'Mig,' I sighed.

He held up the carnage in question: my black lace bra, the hooks in the back completely snapped.

'Sorry,' he mouthed, silly puppy-dog eyes meeting mine.

I just laughed and laughed with abandon, my hair splayed against the pillow. I wrapped my legs around Miguel, pulling him as tight as I could to me, and he groaned into my neck. It was that power to tease Miguel de la Fuente endlessly that flooded me again. I brought my leg around to position myself on top of him and pushed my hips up against him ever so slowly. Now, he was completely devoid of control and a husky 'Diyana' escaped him, my name the way I had never heard it before, expressed with so much need, so much desperation.

'Please keep doing whatever the hell that was,' he said, panting. 'Please, Diyana.'

I leaned down and kissed him, my fingers playing with locks of his perfect hair. 'I just might,' I whispered.

Mig's strong hands gripped my waist, hot on my skin. 'You want to do this?'

'I wouldn't be here' – I took his hands in mine and squeezed them firmly – 'if I didn't.'

My world crashed in upon itself completely when I felt him inside me. My back arched involuntarily, and each breath was a shudder. Miguel's grip on me didn't falter for a second, his hands jumping from place to place, drawing a map across my body, as he managed to exhale my name over and over and over again. I threw my head back to quell the way my entire being pitched with each thrust, with the way my name sounded in his voice, rough and yet pleading. And then a feeling better than the top step of the podium, bliss so great that I didn't think even a title could surpass it, the most ecstatic finish line I had ever reached. I had little power over the loud moan that I had to muffle with Mig's arm, and he had not had any, either, to judge from the gradually slowing rise and fall of his chest.

'Fuck, Diyana,' he murmured into my hair, holding me close

to him, his thumb tracing circles on my back as we regained our breath, spent and sweaty. I could hear each beat of his heart from where my head lay. 'There's no one like you, *cariño*. No one.'

How goddamn good we look together. The world would yell about ceding the racing line and going easy and being in the sport for no good reason. Our careers would essentially be over. The world would never look in that mirror and see something as beautiful as we did. Yet now, that didn't matter. I had felt it myself. I felt it now, with each thud of Miguel's pulse.

This was ours, every bit of it.

Chapter Forty-One

Diana

Keeping our relationship quiet proved a lot harder than we had expected it to be.

How did no one see us? We couldn't keep our eyes to ourselves during press rounds, made banal little conversations about the weather in public, exchanged badly hidden smiles, made subtle attempts to leave space between us. Over the next two races, I wondered how no one had found us out, with the tension so plainly obvious whenever we were anywhere near one another.

We didn't meet up again until the weekend; when we did, it was like trying to suppress instinct. Now, in Singapore, we tried to conduct what was supposed to be an innocuous chat about tyre temperature on the paddock walkway, already surrounded by cameras, except Miguel's body was dangerously close to mine, to the point where his thigh brushed mine on every step. Both our minds were in indecent places, and avoiding revealing that was a Herculean task.

One that neither of us was up to, it transpired, because it was just minutes after we turned into the walkway towards the Jolt building that we stumbled through the back door into the hall. I shoved the door to my private room open and locked it behind us, laughing against Miguel's lips as we tore the team windbreakers off one another.

'They're so obtuse!' He cracked up as I tugged my black tank top over my head, biting back a snort. 'My hand was about this close to your ass.'

'Now *that* hurt me.' I breathed as his hands travelled down to my waist. 'You held out for far too long.'

'Except we're here now.' Miguel gripped my thigh, sucking in a breath as I pulled him closer to me. 'Technically . . . I didn't.'

'Me, neither.' I kissed him greedily as he undid the button on his jeans, his fingers quickly moving to the one on the front of mine.

'How the *hell* do I get these off?' he groaned against my neck.

I burst out into giggles. 'It's not that hard, come on! Hurry up!'

At that very moment, the phone in the back pocket of my jeans decided to blare with an obnoxious vibration that had us frozen on the spot, Miguel's hand quite literally in my pants.

'Oh.' I rested my head back against the wall in exasperation, pulling the phone out to see who the *hell* was trying to call me during a race weekend (more importantly, while Miguel's hand was in my *pants*).

I was too late to answer the call, but a message was waiting for me when I unlocked the phone. And I did not at all expect it to be the text that it was.

'Oh,' I repeated.

'What's up?' Mig asked, pressing a palm to my cheek. 'You good?'

'I'm good,' I assured him as I reached for my shirt and yanked it back over my head. 'I apparently . . . have a meeting.'

'Right now? Before practice?' Miguel grabbed my windbreaker from the physio table, holding it up so I could slide my arms in and pull it on. 'Who's got you like that?'

'That's the thing. It's Jolt.' My entire body was shaking. This could be either a hit or a miss for me, but that text message was everything I needed to fill up with fear. 'Cavanaugh wants to talk to me. Immediately.'

Mig ran a hand through his hair. 'Wow. You think this is your contract?'

I shrugged. 'Maybe. I think? I don't know, I just . . .'

'Go,' he said with a chuckle, giving my arm an insistent squeeze before I could stall the wait any longer. 'Go find out.'

Theodore wants to talk in conference. Be there in five minutes.

I rushed out of my private room and up the motorhome stairs to the large upstairs conference room. I took a deep breath in the hallway, fixed my hair and steadied myself. Then I knocked, two short raps on the door.

'Come in,' my team principal's voice called from inside.

I obliged, creeping inside tentatively, unsure as to what – or who – I would find waiting. What if he'd assembled an entire squadron of Jolt higher-ups to execute whatever this decision was? But the reality was even more frightening than that. It was just Theodore Cavanaugh.

He looked as faux-calm as ever. The man was always put

together, greying blond hair neatly combed, icy blue eyes reminiscent of an older Kasper Ramsey (something I had never been a fan of). It was all a façade, which I knew hid treachery and a strategy that I'd been at the receiving end of earlier in the season. He gestured to the chair across from him and smiled politely. 'Please, Diana, have a seat.'

I nodded and pulled out the chair, sitting down stiffly. I placed my hands flat on the table, the way I always did at meetings, out of nervousness: it was a tell I hated about myself.

'Diana, I'd like to speak to you about something that has recently come to the attention of the Jolt team,' Cavanaugh said.

And that was when I knew I was done for.

'We are aware you were in Dubai . . . during the summer break, correct?' he asked, although it was more of a statement. My palms went clammy as if on command. They knew. How much did they know?

'I was,' I replied simply. 'With my family.'

'Yes.' He drummed a single finger on the tabletop. I could barely breathe as I waited for the hammer to come down. 'You were in Dubai with Miguel de la Fuente.'

Not the hammer I had expected, but it smacked me in the chest nevertheless. 'Excuse me?'

'Diana . . . good relations are good relations,' Cavanaugh picked up seamlessly. 'We would love to have our ties to Revello in pristine shape, but you have to understand what this looks like for us. This isn't just diplomacy, is it?'

What this looks like? I swallowed down a string of curses, instead choosing more careful words. 'I don't believe my personal life is team business, Mr Cavanaugh. I'd like to keep it that way.'

'That's not how Jolt sees it.' His eyes bore into mine with cold accusation. 'We had an excellent strategist here two years back. Aurelia Avella, absolutely stellar. Was the genius behind Eduardo Palomas's 2018 wonder season. We had that talent locked in for us. Until she got engaged to William Breckenridge.'

'From . . . wait, you mean Will from Hybridge, way back in—'

'That's exactly who I mean.' Cavanaugh's tone was a warning. 'Aurelia left the team the following year. Now she's got a newborn child, she and Breckenridge are mucking it up in IndyCar, and she's never going to have the time to sit in a paddock and crunch out strategy again.'

Oh, my god. Was he really doing this?

'Diana, we can't be pouring resources into someone who will so easily make decisions that entail *outs*,' said Cavanaugh almost robotically. 'In and of itself, this can cost us the integrity of our team.'

Integrity. As if he hadn't destroyed the integrity of my commitment to Jolt with nothing but a couple of misogynistic words. If you are a woman, you leave. If you leave, you aren't worth it to us. But this team was my lifeline. If I didn't have Jolt, I would be screwed for the next season. As Formula 1 drivers, we didn't have *options*, skipping from team to team. Everyone had their opinions about me, and I couldn't predict who was thinking what, except for Jolt. Every member of their team was nothing but a number in their ledger, something they could gain and something they could lose. They had to do whatever it took to keep the numbers ticking upwards, and it was me who would have to make the sacrifice.

* * *

Singapore Free Practice One and Two went pitifully. I fell behind Nic, finishing fifth and seventh in the practices. Did it matter, though? Jolt no longer gave a crap about me, and if I'd been holding out any hope about them possibly seeing something worth keeping around in me, something to prove I hadn't gone weak, it had dwindled down to nil. Cavanaugh had implied that the state I was in before our discussion – my relationship with Miguel – would affect my ability to race, but my feelings after that meeting took my mind out of my car to an even greater extent. I wasn't mentally present during the practices, and I wouldn't be mentally present during the qualifier.

The words Cavanaugh had left me with at the end of our meeting rang in my head as I pulled into the garage at the end of the night, my eyes welling with tears when I realized what I had to do. I had only one option if I wanted any sort of chance at keeping my seat.

'I hope you understand what you need to do here, Diana. It's best for the both of you.'

I did. I did. But I didn't know if I could do it. I didn't know if I was strong enough for this.

The doubts had crept in.

Chapter Forty-Two

Miguel

The Singapore Grand Prix Qualifier was an exciting affair for Revello, bringing us a 1-2, redemption for myself and Andrea that had us going absolutely nuts on the podium. We splashed champagne over the heads of our pit crews as the bunch of us laughed and took photos up on the stand. Meanwhile, I saw that Diyana had finished in sixth. It wasn't terrible by any means, still deep in the points, but it was certainly out of form for a driver who'd been a regular on podiums up till now. Her practices had been equally out of character.

I'd had this nagging concern in the back of my mind since she'd gone to her meeting on Friday, and I hadn't had a chance to catch up with her since. I decided I wanted to wait till after some of the chaos died down, see if I could get hold of her post-race, before we headed to Rosa Dorada for the night.

I waded through throngs of reporters to get to her garage

with a 'sorry' every which way, fielding the congratulations with quick smiles. I was excited for the team, obviously, but I had tunnel vision. I couldn't care less what was going on around me as I nudged through the doors to the Jolt Archambeau motorhome, my earbuds still swinging, fireproofs still damp with sweat, nothing on my mind but my Diyana.

It took a couple of wrong turns in their maze-like building, but eventually I came out in Diyana's now-empty garage, the door already rolled down to keep the public out. When I saw her in there, she was polishing her halo, feet still planted in the cockpit, hunched over the front of the car. Her hair had yet to make it out of the braid crown, tufts of black and auburn-red sticking out all around.

'Hey, Diyana!'

She turned my way in surprise. 'Oh, Miguel! How did you end up in here?'

I wanted so badly to believe that it was just a genuine little greeting she was giving me, but I knew her better than she thought. I could see the puffy red circles under her eyes, the way they glistened a dull shade of their usual brown.

'Diyana?' I echoed, my voice a tone quieter as I took in the default smile that was beginning to fall from her face. 'You okay, *tía*?'

'Miguel, I think . . .' The smile was completely gone now. It had been replaced by a look of guilt. *Guilt?* 'We need to talk.'

'We . . . yeah. Yeah, of course.' I was confused, but she sounded so distressed that I didn't question any of it. She stopped cleaning and climbed out of the cockpit, adjusting the sleeves of her race suit as they hung at her sides before sitting down cross-legged on the ground beside the front right tyre. I joined her, taking her hands in mine. I traced the bumps and dips of her knuckles as she chewed on her lip, searching for words. 'What's up?'

'Jolt.' She worked her jaw, frustration spilling through into her words. 'That meeting I was called into Friday, that one-on-one with Cavanaugh. He's . . . he's not happy with me.'

'Not happy?' I struggled to find a reply to that. Diyana Zahrani was a force to be reckoned with. I'd never seen a rookie putting in this kind of a performance. I'd never seen *anyone* put in this kind of performance. How was that asshole unhappy with the diamond in the rough his team had landed? 'You've only raced months in F1. You're beating Nic in the World Championship. That's your seat.'

'I just need to stay in.' Her gaze travelled to my hands clutching hers the way they did the steering wheel. 'I've staked everything on this. If I don't get that seat, Mig, there's no security. Reserve driver, maybe. Back on the waitlist.'

'You *will* stay in. You'll prove them wrong.'

'I wish it were that easy.' She gave me this melancholy smile, and something in my heart shrivelled up when I realized I recognized it. It was the exact expression I'd seen on Jatziry's face after Barcelona when she'd taken off her ring and given it back to me. 'It's what he's unhappy about that has made it so difficult.'

My jaw was beginning to go slack. 'Difficult' was an understatement. I took in the gravity of her sentence, the meaning woven beneath it. This would be a hell of a lot worse than difficult. 'What's he unhappy about?'

'I am their investment, Miguel.' Diyana squeezed my hands tight, blowing a hair from her face. 'And anything that undermines your investment is a threat.'

'So you're saying . . .' I trailed off. I didn't need the rest of my thought to be complete for her to hear it.

This couldn't be true. What had I thought, that my mother's *suerte* was real? That this girl was everything I'd dreamed of and more? That the world stopped moving at two hundred kilometres when she lay next to me, her head on my chest? That I felt like I was finally home when I was with her?

'We can't continue like this,' she said quietly, blinking away tears. 'And I can't do this to you. I'll cost you your own seat, too, Mig. This, us, it's going to pull me down, and you're going to come with me, and you are more to me than points, Miguel, I care too much about you now to do that to you.'

'Would you do this?' I whispered, my voice cracking. 'Would you still do this to me if you care about me that much, *cariño*?'

She choked back the tears that were filling in her eyes, nodding slightly. 'It's all I can do. I don't have a choice.'

Diyana dealt me blow after blow with each of her words, every punch harder than the last. I tried to think of some alternative, some way we could get around this. Yet I couldn't, and I realized it was because if I were her, I'd be no different. Backed into a corner where all I felt was shame, as if it was something I'd been doing wrong the entire time, left with no other solution than to undo it all to prove something to the people in whose hands my fate lay. Racing was everything to me. To live in a world where it was denied me without reason would crush me whole, just as it would Diyana.

That was what I kept telling myself as the tears slipped from Diyana's eyes, as they started to fill mine. It didn't numb the pain, though. That much didn't change as I pressed my lips to hers with all the greed in my body, every ounce of what I felt

304

for her pouring from my soul into hers. When I pulled away, she pushed the hair back from my forehead, her hands shaking as she said to me, 'I am so, so sorry.'

'You don't get to apologize.' I took her face into my hands, her cheeks warm and damp with salty tears. 'You don't get to apologize because this world isn't ready to evolve.'

'I do,' she said through a sob that pulverized what was left of my heart. 'I'm letting you down, Miguel.'

She rested a hand against my chest, exhaling a puff of air that kissed my neck. I thought she had to say something, wanted to admit something more, until she stood up and stepped away, and her hands fell from me. Before either of us could double back, she turned and walked out of the garage, always the smarter of the two of us.

Her words hung in the air and gripped my heart somehow, crept into the crevices as if trying to convince me that I was chasing ghosts. They tugged at memories from the Barcelona bar, from our night together at the Spa hotel. From the swing in Jaipur and the weeks we spent together in Dubai.

I felt like I was completely alone. I felt like a driver with an empty paddock.

I picked up the stray cloth Diyana had been wiping down the halo of her car with, and as I did, caught a glimpse of her sponsor-laden car halo: brands, her parents' combined names, the dove from Spa . . . and a new sticker.

A white silhouette of two people in helmets, one sitting in her car, the other with his hand extended, a hand that the seated driver made to clasp. No one else would understand why it was there, what it meant.

You are more to me than points, Miguel.

I gripped the halo tight over the sticker till the blood left my knuckles.

I knew it was true. She was more to me than points, too. But now, I had no time to think about that. I had to forget, in order to finish what I had come here for. I needed the title.

Chapter Forty-Three

Diana

D espite everything, how I had been raised, to lift my chin and stay quiet, I cried a lot. It felt as if I had lost a limb. '*Ghorbanat beram,*' my mother used to tell me as a child, her eyes brimming with pride and her smile overflowing with happiness.

If only I could have said those two words to Miguel once, to sum up how I felt about him: *I would sacrifice myself for you.* And now, I would never get that chance.

Sitting in my private room in the motorhome, I drew my knees up to my chest as tears rolled down my cheeks. I wiped them away as fast as I could. *No. No, no, no. Your soul is stronger than the pain you endure.*

I had never once wavered in my support of Jolt. Never said or done anything that a bad sportswoman would say or do. How could Cavanaugh put me in this position? And, worse, I wondered if I had put myself in this position. I went over everything that had happened this season. Where had I gone wrong? What about my nature had made my team think I would desert them, just like that?

I tried so hard to never, ever get upset. To stand by every team I was on. I buried my anger deep down and refused to let it surface. As Baba often said: act out of hatred, and you've burned two souls. He was always very philosophical when he got the chance. That was one thing. But how I felt about Miguel? That was another.

In this sport, you had to be able to separate yourself from your feelings. I remember I had never struggled with that. I had been unflinching in my motivation, even in Formula 3, when I had my first race. Just before I'd hit the track, I found out my parents had been in that accident, the one that claimed all movement in my father's legs. I wanted so badly just to *feel*, but I knew what I had to do. I drove without thinking, and I drove to my first podium.

And then Miguel came along and complicated things. I could put anything aside in order to get the job done on track, but he was the exception. Not only did he share the asphalt with me, but he also shared my headspace. Now more than ever, I couldn't let him. Little did I know, I would be tested on my ability to hold fast sooner than I thought.

I made it through the qualifier of the Japanese Grand Prix just a week later mutely, at least. Starting P2. Except he was P1. We would fight on the track tomorrow, and it would no longer be the same.

Forget the photos, of course. The memories that I felt were such strong ties that they could not be broken even if I wanted to. The promises to hang on this time around. The feeling of his body against mine. The backlash we had endured for one another throughout the season. How I would still suffer it all for him. None of it could matter any more. Not if I wanted to keep my dreams alive. Not if I wanted his career to remain intact. Truth be told, that worried me more than my own risk did. I would not be able to live with myself if Miguel ended up out of a seat because of me.

I adjusted my earbuds and shuffled my Fairuz playlist. I raked my hair from the braids, back into a simple ponytail, and took a deep breath.

Where did I go from here?

I started my car, and I raced.

I didn't let it faze me – well, I didn't show it. I took the wheel for the Japanese Grand Prix with a carefully crafted grin on my face, concealing the fact that I didn't actually know how to feel yet. Deceived, maybe? As if I were still allowed emotions and I had not had that right snatched from me just a week ago?

And so my start was less than ideal as these things bounced around in my head. I fell off onto Miguel's rear wing, the last thing I wanted to see. Aiden urged me to try to close the delta now, while I could use the chaos to my advantage.

But something still stopped me. Some sense of understanding that this was not just a race any more. If I took the gap, I changed everything. That change, that loss . . . I was afraid that it might be permanent. That it might cement everything Cavanaugh had said to me in that meeting, and that it might cost me my humanity.

'It's hunt or be hunted,' my coach would tell me when I

used to chicken out of overtaking in karts. 'Tell me, Diana, which will you do?'

I narrowed my eyes, forcing myself into tunnel vision. My team principal's words scalded the very surface of my skin: this was what was best for both of us.

'I will take the gap.'

'Affirming, Diana. You are clear.'

We came up on the chicane. It was tight and narrow here. I was chasing hard; I would have to be careful. But that was none of my business now.

I slammed my gas and shot forward on the next curve, rightfully using my racing line. No remorse, I slipped around the inside of Miguel's Revello and made a jaunty exit out ahead.

But I wasn't in the clear yet. Miguel pushed alongside my right, not backing down. He pressed hard on the next turn, nearly clipping my front wing. We were angry and confused and in pain, and we knew nothing else. We were Formula 1 drivers. We tucked away the words we did not want the rest of the world to hear behind exhaust and smoke and sparks.

He turned in towards me.

I don't want to lose you.

I was so close to his front wing that we were centimetres from contact.

I can't keep you.

My car surged forward, and his matched mine perfectly.

But I can't let go.

'It's getting tight.' Aiden hummed over the radio. 'We may have . . . I'd say cede it to him, Di. Let's cede P1, let him have it.'

'I can get through.'

'You can . . . what?'

I was done playing nice and listening to every little thing I was told. I had done enough, sacrificing my own happiness to keep this seat, with still no word on my fate next season. It was time for me to step out and take a chance, and if Jolt didn't want this, I didn't know *what* they wanted from me.

I gripped the steering wheel and sped up, damn the risk of it. We went wheel to wheel on the track. Sparks flew from beneath my car. It was max push, the kind of acceleration that made your vision go spotty.

We came up on the next turn fast. 'Diana!' yelped Aiden. 'No gap!'

'I'll make us one,' I muttered.

I floored it, keeping the car steady. I had the inner advantage, and I used it to hit the apex of the curve perfectly, pushing myself out into first.

'Oh, shit,' Aiden whistled. 'You had me pissing myself with worry. Tell me what the hell that was?'

I laughed without an ounce of humour. 'You'll have to go ask Theodore Cavanaugh.'

The mild Suzuka afternoon brought me a P1. In the cooldown, on the podium, we exchanged no words. It tore at everything I had to remain civil with Miguel, to keep the emotions from flooding the stage the second my eyes met his as we shook our champagne bottles at one another with fabricated smiles.

Of course, the second I stepped off the podium, a broadly grinning Cavanaugh stood jubilantly at the steps, showering me with praise on the win and the razor-sharp move that had earned it. He couldn't say I hadn't done exactly what the team wanted. Ended my relationship, won the race. A nagging doubt

311

tugged at my heart, though. What if, after all of that, they *still* weren't ready to offer me the seat?

'Very well done, Diana,' Theodore Cavanaugh said loudly, beaming as he patted my back in congratulations. 'That's our Danger, right there.'

The Jolt celebrations occupied much of my attention, and yet I couldn't help but think about Miguel. I saw him talking to Paula about the race, watched her reassuring him. That was my bit of solace in this entire situation, that Paula would understand what had made me so helpless as to ruin everything this way, and would provide Miguel with some comfort. I tried my best to avoid noting that Mig's eyes were full of pain regardless.

Once I was back in my garage, back in the private room, away from prying eyes, including those of my trainer and my wonderful Aiden, I finally lost it. Maybe it wasn't ideal, but I reckoned I had just as much right as the temperamental men to show my emotions. I felt as if I had been used and thrown aside in the span of less than a season, and by the team I thought I could trust, as well. Their attention faded in and out, based on how well I followed the orders that Nic had no concern about.

Rebelling against everything my brain was telling me, I let my heart speak, throwing my helmet against the table and crying out in a yell of frustration and pressure that had been pent up since March. Because I could not stop now. I still had to race. I could not allow myself to drown in my emotions. My work would have to carry me the rest of the way.

And so it did when I repeated the feat in Mexico. Another P1, complete with fastest lap, gave me that much more edge in the standings, not to mention within Jolt. I had more fight in me yet. I could possibly take this whole thing home with me.

But I still retreated to my hotel room after that race and sat out on the balcony with a cup of tea, waiting. Waiting for a hint of hope, a glimmer of goodness, something to tell me that this was nothing but a bad dream, or some kind of test that this horrific team was putting me through; that I hadn't spent nearly a decade of my life dreaming about this suddenly unreachable future with this suddenly unreachable man.

I knew it was stupid. But I couldn't believe that it was. I just wanted him back.

Chapter Forty-Four

Diana

I thought I'd messed up again when I was called in to my second team one-on-one of the weekend just before leaving Mexico.

It had been a chaotic race, with a situation that left us no other option than to undercut Revello and overtake both their cars in one fell swoop. I didn't want to speak to anyone after the podium, but this changed when I was stopped by a decidedly unfamiliar team principal in the paddock.

'And that moment where your tyre *just* nearly got the kerb . . .' one of my mechanics was narrating the race in an ominous tone that was met with laughter as we passed champagne around, everyone loose with intoxication.

'Miss Zahrani?'

'Hmm?' I turned to face whoever had pulled me from the celebrations. It was none other than Cristoforo Montalto, Revello team principal.

'I apologize for interrupting your fun,' he said with a chuckle, 'but I've been meaning to speak to you. Would you be willing to join me in the motorhome for a moment?'

I glanced around at the mechanics, who were far too occupied with the champagne to notice anything. I, myself, was completely drenched in a mixture of bubbly alcohol and sweat, an unpleasant concoction, but I couldn't skip this. Montalto coming to me could only mean one thing. My heart had already begun to pound in anticipation.

'I would.' I nodded. 'Yes, why don't we head that way? Thank you, Mr Montalto.'

'It's no problem at all,' he replied as we walked towards the Revello building. Montalto was a flamboyant character, of course, in common with most of the team principals, but lacked the pomposity and hubris of Theodore Cavanaugh. I had heard him brief the drivers much like a mentor would: giving them pointers, suggesting strategy, accepting new plans for coming races in his stride. It was an unusual leadership style for someone coming from Jolt.

'So, Diana, I gather these past weeks have been quite the ride for you,' started Montalto as we took a seat in one of the smaller windowed rooms in the motorhome. I'd only been in here a few times, and never in a conference room. The red, green and white screamed tradition and pride. It was a more timeless version of what I'd seen on the grid, one of my favourite colour schemes, and not solely because it partially matched my home country's. 'Has Jolt offered anything?'

I was not sure if this was something I was allowed to discuss, but something in the concern dotting Montalto's tone brought the answer out from within me. 'No,' I admitted. 'No, it's just been hard. Harder than it needed to be, in my opinion.'

'Well . . . I'd like to make it easier.' Cristo Montalto gave me a tentative smile. 'As you may know, we've got an open seat at this team come next year. We need new talent, fresh talent, someone who is willing to take risks and think *with* the team rather than *for* it. You've been exemplary this entire season, Diana, and I don't see any reason I shouldn't offer you this seat.'

I blinked. It took me a moment to register what he was saying. The environment was so casual, the timing so abrupt, that I had to process this information for half a minute before responding. 'Oh.'

'Yes.' Montalto looked amused by my shock. 'I hope that's a positive reaction.'

'It-it is,' I choked out. 'Oh, my goodness. You aren't being serious?'

'I am completely serious,' he replied, pride in his tone. 'We would love for you to be a part of Scuderia Revello, come 2023, as one of our two drivers.'

I thought my heart would fly out of my chest and through the massive windows. I felt the blood rushing behind my ears. I had a seat.

'This would be Andrea's seat?' I asked in complete and utter disbelief.

'Ah!' He raised a finger to stop me. 'Not Andrea's. We have decided on what will become of that seat already, I should say, who will be in that seat. You would be coming in to take Miguel's seat. See, it's that mid-season run that worried us. We lost money with every kerb he ran over and every wing he clipped. The mechanics weren't happy with the last-minute fixes and midnight jobs. He's always been a bit . . . well, a bit of a risky driver. But seeing it in excess this season was different. And with his contract coming to an end . . . you know how these things go.'

His contract.

Nothing was ever simple in Formula 1. It was only 'yes, but . . .' or 'of course, however . . .' Dreams came with fine print. And now, mine was no different.

Miguel's seat.

You aren't with Miguel any more, I thought to myself as my eyes widened unconsciously. But it was just like making that first overtake of the season. Something about it felt deceptive. To take his seat after leaving him like this, leaving him because I thought it would be the better option for both of us. What was I doing? What was right and what was *wrong*? Because accepting this sport as 'grey' was no longer enough for me. I needed black and white.

'You'll have time to think this over,' Montalto assured me. 'We appreciate this kind of decision cannot be made overnight. We would, however, like to know by season end. Just so that we can have the appropriate conventions in place to prepare for next year.'

I made a sound that I hoped conveyed acknowledgement. I was still dumbfounded, even as I shook Cristo Montalto's hand and we parted ways.

I left the Revello motorhome, my racing boots squeaking on the shimmering floors, and then scuffing the concrete as I stepped onto the hot sidewalk, the sun beating down on my hair as if in accusation.

'Damn it,' I whispered, turning back towards the Jolt motorhome to rejoin my team.

Chapter Forty-Five

Miguel

Forgetting about Diyana was easier said than done.

Not when I watched her up on the podium in Mexico, her smile wide but her eyes sad, the brim of her cap hiding the same hurt in her eyes that I held in mine, when her hair flew every which way as she lifted her trophy, pressing a hand to her heart as if to calm it down, pointing to her team, calling out, *You, it's you, I couldn't have done it without you.*

I returned to my garage after all the podium chaos, sat down with my back to my car, and let things be quiet for a minute. I never liked quiet. I liked loud, I liked parties and people and surrounding myself with all kinds of noise to drown out the thoughts in my own head. But now, all I wanted was my thoughts. I wanted my memories of her, the ones that were still so strong that it was like playing a movie behind my eyelids when I closed them. Every colour and touch preserved, each dip and fall of her melodic accent intact. A wiser man might have told me I needed to get mad about her, or even at her. I just couldn't, though. Didn't have it in me, not with the situation her team had put her in.

The most I could do was race. There was no time to think when you were racing – it was just split-second decisions at breakneck speed, until I got out of that car, and all I wanted was her.

I knew I'd have to get up eventually. It would be time for the mechanics to pack the car up to take back, but I sat there for just one more minute before hauling myself to my feet with a groan and heading back out the motorhome exit, through the narrow hall cutting through the middle of the Revello building.

The place was abustle with our engineers and strategists, already in the middle of dissecting the race: the good, bad, ugly and horrendous.

'The clutch today on Andrea's,' one of them groaned as I squeezed past him.

'Oh, terrible. We have to fix that,' another chimed in.

The cacophony of voices post-race was nothing new – you got used to it. We liked to call it the Sunday scaries.

I passed the corner conference room on my way out through the main doors, the one no one ever used – except sometimes on Saturdays, if one of the strategists was really upset with our practice results. Today, though, someone was inside. Maybe the Sunday scaries had got a little extra-scary this time around, maybe because of Andrea nearly running both the wall and Byron Hargreaves on Lap Forty-One.

'. . . be a part of Scuderia Revello come 2023 as one of our two drivers,' I heard Cristo Montalto saying.

Wait . . . what the hell?

319

I slowed down and backed up just slightly. Okay, so I was eavesdropping, but this surely warranted it. Cristo and who? Who was he about to make an offer to? I'd known Andrea's spot was up for grabs, but I had no idea things had moved this quickly. Last I heard, Cristo had a contender but no winner.

Another voice. 'This would be Andrea's seat?'

That was Diyana's voice.

I squinted, trying to see through the frosted-glass windows, but no give. Damn it. My arms suddenly felt numb, my feet wobbly. This was it, Diyana would get her seat. And maybe, maybe if she got away from Jolt, we had a chance. My chest flooded with a warmth I'd been aching to feel for weeks.

Cristo was talking again. Saying something about the seat, probably. I moved closer to the door. '. . . decided on what will become of that seat already, I should say, who will be in that seat. You would be coming in to take Miguel's seat.'

My heart stopped.

My seat.

No way. My pulse boomed in my ears like the pounding of a bass drum, each beat threatening to blow out my hearing. No, no. Everything had looked perfect for next season. No one had ever had any doubt in my ability to swing an extension, right? This couldn't be happening.

I backed away from the door, nearly stumbling on my own racing shoes as I retreated down the hall, into the throngs of team members griping about our race pace and our pit times, back to the garage, back to the car, where my footsteps echoed off the high ceilings and no one but my R3-71 could hear the curses that left my lips when I realized how quickly this had turned on me.

'There is no trust in racing,' Papá would tell me and Paula when we were younger. He'd have us sitting on that old Persian rug by the fireplace, telling us stories about his crashes and his victories as if they were fairy tales. 'No trust.'

It was one of his famous quips that he'd pull out when he was around the media. He had these dumb one-liners, things that the men around the track at the time agreed with instinctively. Paula flashed a glance at me, the most stubborn ten-year-old I knew even then, and rolled her eyes so hard you could see the whites.

Papá didn't notice. He was too wrapped up in his monologue to care. 'There is no "fool me twice" for us, Angelito, Paulita,' he went on. 'The first time you are deceived is the last time. That is where it all ends for you, *vale*, the second you let your guard down.'

Then Mamá would bustle into the sitting room toting a storybook, fuming at our father in rapid Spanish, curling up on the rug between me and Paula, holding us close and telling Papá how we were young and we didn't need that kind of foolish *mierda* in our heads, cracking her book open and reading us something about wizards and dragons.

But wizards and dragons weren't real. Trust was. Or, at least, it was supposed to be.

'No trust in racing,' I said to Paula later, the second I caught her outside the big computer room in the motorhome where the engineers had gathered to watch footage.

I'd expected her to be upset. Maybe slightly miffed, maybe raging, but some form of angry. I mean, come on! This was my seat, this was everything I'd worked for, and she'd seen it.

She knew how hard I fought for Revello, and against Revello, resenting our family name for tainting the way that people saw me in this sport. Now, she stood before me with her arms crossed, her expression completely unreadable. She tilted her head. 'Miguel.'

'What? Are you really going to say this isn't fatal for me, Pauli?' I shot back, my voice low. 'Think about it!'

'I don't know.' She raised an eyebrow. 'Maybe you need to think about it.'

'*Me?*' I spat. This was my future in the sport, and it was on me?

'This is a chance for Diana, Miggie,' said Paula evenly. 'This is what you wanted for her, isn't it? So tell me. What do you want with all your being right now, Miguel: Diana or Revello?'

I sucked in a breath, regarding my sister warily. 'You don't mean that.'

'Oh, I do, *tío*.' She patted my arm before heading towards the door of the computer room. 'Like I said. Think about it.'

Chapter Forty-Six

Diana

We touched down in Rio de Janeiro early in the morning, just a week after Mexico City. It was the perfect distraction for me. I had been to Brazil, but never Rio, and vacationing there had remained a distant dream till now, when I stepped off the plane and was met with nothing but sunshine.

The time between races had me going stir crazy. I couldn't sit with this bombshell from Revello for a moment longer. My nerves were frayed. I needed this reset to keep going and maybe, just maybe, snag the title.

It would be close. The motorsport world were chewing their nails down to stumps over it. Fortunately, before any of that could go down, I got a few days' holiday in Rio.

Until we shifted to São Paulo for the race, I had a room booked in the Grand Hyatt Rio de Janeiro. I'd pored over beautiful photos for hours; in real life, it certainly impressed. I approached my dream come true with the top of my car down, absolutely floored by the sight. The glassy oasis of a hotel overlooked a huge pool deck right alongside the beach. Perfect green grass and frond-heavy palm trees stood in contrast against the beautiful blue sky and aquamarine oceans.

I exhaled, smiling as I surrendered my car to the valet and rolled my bags up to the check-in. I tried my best to ignore the mandatory security entourage on my tail. These three days would be sheer escape. There was nothing to worry about. It was gorgeous, and I would be just fine.

I relished the tranquil quiet of the lobby, save for the gentle splashing of water, as the attendant handed me my card. So wonderful, so very peaceful.

And then the sound of caterwauling. The sound of hundreds of women falling head over heels in love as the man of their dreams set foot in sunny Rio de Janeiro, right before their eyes.

No. I let out a groan. Why? Why could I not be the only one here looking for a happy little getaway?

I craned my neck to see out through the glass doors. Throngs of screaming girls had descended upon a black convertible belonging to Darien Cardoso-Magalhães, who frolicked happily among all the chaos, scrawling his name in marker across shirts and caps and limbs alike.

It was official. I would be getting no peace until this season ended.

Maybe the Americans appreciated California-raised Darien, but the Brazilians, of course, worshipped him. Born in Santa Teresa, he was their own prodigal son, the apple of their eye, and the object of many younger fans' desires, of course. The country had stood by Darien since he began karting at the higher stages, and they hadn't stopped since.

I stood among my bags in disbelief, anyway, as this rather unwelcome intrusion continued. Moments later, Darien finally disentangled himself from his screaming fans and ambled into the hotel, hooking his sunglasses onto the collar of his shirt. 'Diana! What are you doing in Rio?'

'This,' I said, stone-faced, 'is supposed to be my self-care week.'

'Ah, perfect! Me, too.' Darien grinned his stupidly blinding grin. 'Let's reset together, then.'

I gestured to the crowd of women still assembled at the doors. 'You have ended my peace and quiet, Dar.'

Darien snorted.

'Darien. What is so damn funny?'

'Oh, man, if you think I've ruined your peace and quiet, just you wait!' He sniggered.

'What is it?' I demanded.

He shook his head. 'Not telling. Either way, I'm unpacking and heading straight out. You gonna come with?'

I gave him a death stare. 'Only because I don't want to get turned around trying to navigate this place on my own. I'm never good in new cities.'

'You think the media will have a field day with that?'

'Oh, absolutely.' This I found funny. Darien and I were quite literally 'bros' in dynamic (his words), but we were also a man and a woman close in age and, I had to admit it, Darien was a handsome guy, which explained why the whole of Brazil was in love with him. He obviously had the dazzling smile that easily reached his friendly brown eyes. He was a ball of energy with a deep honey tan, a chocolate-coloured undercut highlighted blonde at the top, and the name *Nico* with a set of angel wings tattooed across the side of his neck. We got along well; I appreciated his vibe. However, especially with the sudden shift in dynamic with Miguel, I figured – as Darien did – that the tabloids would jump to paint our friendship as something else entirely. It was pretty funny to watch them chase their tails, though. We took whatever comedy we could get when the media loved to hunt us down at every turn.

'Perfect. Wait, you've never been here!' Darien was so excited I thought he'd start jumping up and down. 'Diana, you're gonna *love* it. I'll have to show you all the best places. This city is awesome . . .' He trailed off.

'Hey.' I waved a hand in front of Darien's face as his eyes glazed over. 'Darien.'

'Your bigger problem is here,' he whispered.

I followed his gaze back to the hotel lobby entrance, and immediately fought the urge to punch somebody.

Miguel Ángel de la Fuente was in Rio de Janeiro. And if Darien had jostled my bubble of calm, Miguel's arrival had just popped it completely.

'Come *on*!' I elbowed Darien. 'A heads-up would have been nice, Dar!'

'Don't blame me!' he said, hands raised in defence. 'Listen. Even Craig was surprised when you guys started putting up this cold front. We can't take it any more, whatever it is, and hey, I know men are dumb, it's probably Miguel's ass that messed everything up, but we're over it. You guys need to talk this out.'

'You don't get it.' My voice was steel. 'Put your hands down.'

He did. He looked hurt, but it was true; he couldn't understand. 'I'm sorry. It's a tough situation,' I amended myself with a sigh. 'Trust me, Darien, neither of us, neither me nor Miguel wants to be in this situation, and the more I think about it, the less it will benefit us. Just trust me.'

'Okay. I get that.'

I took it back. Darien looked so devastated that I couldn't stand it. 'I'll try,' I gave in. 'Why don't you invite Miguel to come explore the city with us, and that way, you can be our neutral party?'

He nodded, face brightening. 'Yes, there we go. I can do that for you.'

We wound up on the most awkward walk of my life.

I'm sure it wasn't much better for Darien or Miguel. Darien led the way through Rio de Janeiro, pointing out Christ the Redeemer in the distance, surrounded by the brush of the Tijuca Forest. I couldn't help but laugh when we walked by one of the murals of Darien in his signature pose beside Ayrton Senna.

'Dude,' Miguel said with a snort. 'The juxtaposition here is absolutely crazy.'

Darien rolled his eyes. 'Come on, I like this mural!'

'Do the pose,' I pleaded. 'Please do it.'

He sighed like someone's exasperated grandpa, but he obliged, raising both hands in the 'hang loose' gesture and striking the most on-point frat-boy smile I had ever seen, just long enough for me to take a photo. It was too funny to pass up. I wondered what Senna would think of this young Brazilian American with a penchant for disobedience and daring tattoos representing the country in Formula 1. That only made me laugh harder.

We passed Copacabana coming out of the more crowded city, beaches occupied by hundreds of people and their umbrellas and towels, and made our way to Ipanema. The sun was just beginning to set. The way the light hit the buildings and the water was absolutely stunning. We walked down to the coastline, picking through the sand and around a beach volleyball court.

'I'm gonna have to leave you folks here,' Darien said. 'I've got family I was supposed to drop in on, uh, yesterday. So give me, like, half an hour and I will be *right* back.' He looked at each of us in turn, brow creased with worry. 'Please don't bite each other's heads off.'

I made to protest, but Darien was already rushing back toward the city at a surprisingly high speed. No way would we both get through 'like, half an hour' without tears.

We were both silent for a few minutes. It was just the sound of the ocean splashing, wind rustling the palm trees, people chattering excitedly. I was incredibly surprised when Miguel spoke.

'I owe you . . . a great big apology.'

'You . . .' I turned to him. He looked as innocent as he had when I'd left him in the garage, except now he wore those stupid khaki shorts and the button-down, hair tossed about in the breeze. The sun here had brought out his freckles, but his eyes were completely dull. 'You don't owe me anything,' I told him.

'I know it won't fix everything.'

The wind kicked up as my frustration did, sending the hem of my dress flapping. I flattened it down exasperatedly. 'Miguel, you should *hate* me for all of this. Nothing will fix it all, and yet you are trying to say sorry? I want to clean up this mess. I don't want you to become a part of it. Even though . . . I gave you this part of me that no one had ever seen . . . and you gave me . . . gave me so much . . .'

'Diyana.' Miguel met my eyes dead on. I could see the pain there, the pain I had caused him. I couldn't do it.

'Diyana, look at me.'

Hesitantly, I did.

I wasn't sure what I had been expecting, but it was not what Miguel said next.

'I know what Revello said to you.'

My heart caught in my throat. That conversation with Cristo Montalto. How had it got out? Suddenly, I couldn't move. I could scarcely think. Miguel knew everything. If he'd not hated me yet, he certainly would now.

I prayed the ocean might wash over both of us and cleanse us of our wrongs, of all the poison we had filled one another's wounds with. Maybe that would undo it all and return our love to some pure standard, the crystal-clear fairy tales children grew up dreaming of. But it didn't.

'I don't know if I'll take it yet, Miguel,' I whispered through a deep breath. 'I don't know what I'm going to do.'

I saw a foreign emotion on Miguel's face in that moment. It struck me hard when I realized his eyes were filling with tears. Tears in the eyes of a de la Fuente.

Neither of us had any words, so we just stayed there. I let my mind take me back to the desert in Dubai. This same feeling, this same proximity. There had been a smile on my face as Miguel laughed, and I with him. What had happened to us?

I could still call back the earliest memory I had of this teenage boy, so sure of himself, so charming, as he got into his kart. When that race ended, when he held his hand out to me, I was gone. I remembered talking and joking and racing together until, one day, I never saw him again.

Then my hand was back in his. I couldn't let go. Not of the only person who could fight my lap times and balance my temperament perfectly.

I closed my eyes, and I let go of all those memories, all those things I could not put into words, hoping they would find their way to Miguel somehow, hoping he knew that all these things that were happening didn't take away how I would always feel about him, not for a moment. I listened to the beach and inhaled the salty air.

Miguel sat down in the sand. I did the same. We were both quiet beside one another on the beach in Ipanema that day. We didn't exchange words or look anywhere but the horizon.

We simply coexisted. We reflected.

'What is the reason to keep trying?' Ammi had said after the sand fell through my fingers at the Corniche.

I couldn't take it. I was too little to understand that I could not have everything.

'That's not right,' I protested. 'Why is it like that? Why can I not have something I want?'

'Well, *joonam*,' she'd said, crouching down so that she was at my eye level, 'sometimes the universe has not written that for us. It is not in our fate. And when that happens . . .' She smiled. 'I do not want anything falling through your fingers, my love. I want you to hold on tight and fight for those moments of beauty. You have to make your own destiny.'

Chapter Forty-Seven

Miguel

The circuit was set, and São Paulo had gone totally festive for the grand prix. The track was surrounded by stands bursting with colourful signs and get-ups alike. It was blue skies as far as the eye could see. Quali had got me on pole and, today, the beautiful weather felt like a good omen.

As we warmed the tyres out on the grid, I caught sight of Darien's glittering helmet emblazoned with a pair of Spix's macaws, the beaks coming together to form a heart that revealed the Brazilian flag in the background. Below the image on the top were the words '*We only have one – treat her right.*' There had been a lot of great designs all year, but Darien's might have been my absolute favourite.

Ten points, I thought to myself, refocusing while the crews worked on removing our warmers. They darted off-track just before countdown. The crowd roared, ready for some wheel-to-wheel drama. The red lights went on overhead.

Ten points. We can do this.

At lights out, the powerful engine roared beneath me, and we were off. Darien had got a good start, too, but I battled him hard and slid ahead, just across his front wing.

To be fair, I hadn't actually enjoyed a race quite as much as I ended up enjoying Interlagos. The weather was stunning, I was getting only clean air out front, everything was running smoothly. I couldn't remember the last time I'd just soaked in racing, and here, it felt like there was finally no stress, no worries, nothing. I let my situation with Revello – and Diyana – fade into the background as I pushed my car to its comfortable peak and cruised along the scenic track.

Things continued this way till it was time for my first stop.

'Okay, Miguel, you'll box, box now,' Paula said over the radio.

'Yeah.' I made to take the pit lane in.

I was front wheels across the line when I heard, 'No, no, no, no, stay out, stay out!'

'What?' I spat. 'I'm already inside!'

'We don't . . . we—'

I pulled into our garage lane. What I found made me want to get out of the car and pummel the person responsible myself. A crew of shell-shocked mechanics were scrambling to ready both their tools and the tyres.

Tyres.

There were no tyres.

I suppressed all my anger as they replaced my lefts, then ten seconds later, my rights. I was practically counting each passing unit of time. I couldn't yell at my pit crew, though. I had no idea who was at fault yet.

I zoomed off before the last drill was disconnected from my

car, leaving it swinging from its cord behind me. 'NO!' I finally yelled. 'Why did I just get sent in with *nothing* ready?'

'Miguel, that is on our end. Not sure exactly who. May be a garage error.'

'*Error?* That's our Championship! Error doesn't win Championships! Where am I right now?'

'Well, Darien, he pitted right after you . . . Albrecht going in now, Zahrani still running up ahead of you and behind Darien . . . you've come out P3 at the moment.'

I was just astonished. How the hell had someone managed to screw up a simple pit stop so badly? The team would be a joke. I'd be a laughing stock. 'P-frickin'-three? Then tell Montalto to fix this right now, Pauli! Please!'

She couldn't, and neither could anyone on the team. The damage had been done. To top it off, I'd been put on hards, and Peter, when he came back out, picked his way up to me on the soft compound. I was completely screwed. There was nothing I could do.

My race from heaven turned into hell just like that. Crossing the finish in fourth was agony. Diyana had gained a six-point advantage, leaving four. Four points and one race between the Championship.

I watched from the sidelines as Darien raised the Brazilian flag, clambering atop his chassis and pointing upward. He tore off his helmet. '*Para você, Papai!*' he shouted. I could make out the tears streaming down his face, even from here. The guy deserved it, and I was enormously happy for him. But for me, this was an episode out of the ordinary. My team had shot themselves in the foot with mere points to make in the Championship. Darien's maiden win was in my rear-view. All

I wanted was to storm into the motorhome and demand an explanation.

After the podium and media circuit, I did. I needed answers. I was livid. I flew past the photographers outside our garage and stomped inside. 'So whose fault was this?' I called through gritted teeth.

The team had already assembled in the 88 garage. No one looked particularly pleased; in fact, most of them looked as upset as I did.

'Now, let's be civil.' Cristo Montalto finally stepped in. 'Let's think about how this can be fixed for the next—'

'It's the *last race*, man!' I blurted. 'What's there to fix? We can't lose points, Cristo! We're moments away from losing this thing to Jolt!'

Everyone was dead silent as they now trained their gazes on Cristo, including Paula. She was the only one who knew what was going on with my seat, the only one who knew the extra weight that this situation held for me. So I was glad that she caught on.

'Why don't you go take a walk, Miguel?' she suggested, only her tone made it evident this was not a suggestion.

I obliged gladly, found the nearest exit, and pushed the door open to cool air on my face.

This was supposed to be my season. This was going to be the year I finally brought that Championship trophy home for the family, once and for all. But now, it might become Diyana's swan song.

Diyana.

I felt the warm press of the sand against my feet as we sat there in total silence. That was either the end of something old, the beginning of something new, or both. I didn't know which yet and, to be honest, I didn't know how to feel. I wasn't sure what I would do if she crossed that finish line before me and took that title, then took my seat next season. All I knew was that I had to do my damnedest to make sure that did not happen.

Chapter Forty-Eight

Diana

It was hard to leave, but the team had to pack up and get out of São Paulo early Monday afternoon. The final race of the season, the reckoning I had been waiting for all my life, would happen in one week on my home track.

I figured it would be low-key. It was, after all, a Monday, and the flight wouldn't exactly be short, so it would be late Tuesday morning when we touched down. I decided to forgo dressing up, threw on a vintage Eduardo Palomas T-shirt and sweats with my fluffy slippers, and kicked back in preparation for the sixteen hours I was to spend in this metal canister.

The crowd I was greeted by when I arrived at Emirates Palace in Abu Dhabi was beyond belief. To get my car through was enough of a feat for the driver, but when I got out between the barricades, I was left slack-jawed.

There were thousands of fans, screaming and pushing towards the barriers they had put in place, toting signs, wearing my team shirt, waving the Jolt Archambeau and Emirati flags alike. They extended all the way back to the gorgeous courtyards and around the hotel on both sides, camped out beneath palm trees and parasols.

'Thank you all!' I shouted as I did a three-sixty, still amazed. '*Alf, alf shokr!*'

I proceeded down the forest green carpet laid out to lead to the entrance, embarrassingly enough still in my sweatpants and slippers, signing as many items and taking as many photos as I could. A lot of drivers could do it faster than I did, but I liked to take my time, probably also because I was so new. One little girl passed me a photo of myself from Formula 3. I was with my very first teammate, fellow driver Oliver Tottington, and we stood back-to-back, throwing up finger guns. Oliver and I were still in contact. He was probably the first driver I'd come to truly trust as a close friend. I grinned down at the picture, scrawled my name across the bottom, and drew a little falcon off to the side.

As fun as it was to interact with my home base of fans, it was also, to me, a stark reminder: I was carrying on my shoulders the weight of this country, of the women in this region who had simply been told 'no'. There was no margin for error this weekend. Either I won, or I went home without the title. I had no other options.

I told myself this as I spent all of Tuesday morning in the gym. My trainer ran me up the walls. It was likely for the best, as my schedule looked abysmal afterwards. I had media duties in Dubai on Wednesday, all day. My track walk was Thursday morning, along with year-wrap-up interviews later. Then, it was all cylinders firing going into the race weekend.

After lunch, I was swamped with press and photography, plus a Jolt YouTube challenge with Nic. Our afternoon wore away, posing for promo pics and playing one of those games with the jellybeans that look okay but taste like vomit, all for the camera. By dinner, we were ready to cleanse our palates. I joined Nic to eat in solitude at the Emirates Palace's resident gourmet Chinese restaurant.

It was, in fact, one of the hardest things I'd ever done.

We were great at faking banter for the games and challenges, but when you took that away, there was nothing left. The tension returned in full force while we sat waiting for our meals, and Nic said, 'So . . . you leave Jolt after this.'

His tone didn't give anything away. I could not get a read on him. Was he being sarcastic or sincere? 'Yeah,' I said simply.

He waited a beat. 'Will we keep hating one another?'

I sighed. 'Nic, I never hated you.'

'Don't lie.'

'I never did,' I protested. It was true. I would sit and watch our old videos from the beginning of the season, holding out hope that something would strike, and I'd get that Nic, that reliable friend to everyone in his circle, back. 'Maybe I got angry at you. Maybe we had rough patches, maybe I don't agree with your choices. But I do not hate you, Nic.'

'Are you sure? Even after, you know . . .' He gulped. 'I want to be honest with you, Diana, about what I did—'

'I know you badmouthed me and my family on live television,' I said. 'I still do not hate you.'

He still didn't look convinced, and that actually made me let out a laugh.

'Is this the Nicolò Necci version of starting afresh?'

'Yes. No. Okay, yes,' admitted Nic. It had been ages since I'd seen him let his guard down like this. Last I remembered, we were still somewhat 'together' when he let me see this side of him, all sheepish and goofy. What had changed? 'I didn't really . . . I didn't play the part of your teammate as well as I should have this year. And now we could be splitting up, you're on the verge of a title in your very first season, but you might be leaving. Wherever you go, I don't want to lose touch. We connected at first, I just . . . screwed it up.'

I almost couldn't believe what I was hearing. I smiled. 'Nic. Don't lie.'

'Seriously.' He chuckled. 'I'm for real. I feel awful. I can't undo it all, can't get you a seat for next year, but I can offer an olive branch.'

Nic reached a hand across the table. 'Friends?'

I couldn't say no. If I was going to leave the sport, I didn't want to leave it so bitter. That was the thing about Formula 1. Our careers were about as long as the lifespan of the common mayfly. We raced, and suddenly, it was all over. You never knew when you would see the inside of a cockpit again. There was no time to harbour hatred here, only to relish what we had built.

I met Nic's eyes and shook his hand. 'Friends.'

'Great. Now, I need to tell you something *as your friend*.' Nic got straight to business, reclining in his chair, fingers steepled, his expression stern.

I raised an eyebrow. 'Don't push it.'

'Something has come to my attention.' He pursed his lips. 'You broke up with Mig because of Cavanaugh and this team, huh?'

My heart skipped a beat, thinking back to that horrific meeting. 'Cavanaugh gave me an ultimatum. It was like a threat, what he said. He had my seat in the palm of his hand.'

'Did he give it back to you, though?'

I shook my head. 'I never heard anything.'

Nic snorted.

'What's so funny?'

'Diana, it's me who's supposed to do whatever the team says!' He burst out laughing. 'I was *horrendous*. I followed their crap to a T. I literally inverted with you, called you the inferior driver; what did I *not* say wrong to you in the name of this team? I almost hit you one or two times, I got so aggressive on the track. That's not your thing, Di – your thing is to do *better*. You prove people wrong. That's your thing.'

I had a strong desire to begin hating Nic for real now. This guy was really going to try to mansplain the behaviours of his own kind. But in a weird way, some of it made sense. Why was I going against my nature? What, now, was stopping me?

'Okay, here.' Nic took a bit of a breather, back in his more serious mode. 'Remember when Mig and I screwed up and had that incident in Jaipur, Turn Five-ish?'

'How could anyone forget? You decked him right out of the race.'

Nic coughed awkwardly. 'I'm well aware. But after that race, Diana, we watched you take the podium. And it's the way Miguel looked at you . . . I asked if he'd surrender a P1 for you. He just kept looking with this kind of reverence, like someone standing at the altar in a church. He said he'd give up a million P1s for you. Said he'd give up all of them. I didn't know *that* guy had a rebellious streak in him.'

'He would . . .' I was lost for words. Lately, I felt like there was no way Miguel would ever put me above his career, not when it was his seat that I could take next year. This perplexed me completely.

'He would.' Nic shrugged. 'So, you know. Give it some thought.'

Normally, I would have loved to visit Dubai on my own, but this wasn't like last time, when I'd come to the city with Miguel. 'The Diana fever is heavy,' my PR director had told me. 'We can't let you go unattended.'

Nevertheless, I was excited. Something had leaked in the news about the city having surprises for me, which had me giddy with anticipation. Nic would be joining us but go his own separate way, while I'd spend most of my time with a handful of the Sheikh of Dubai's personal team attending in his stead. I put on my best abaya for the occasion: a silky beige with wide-legged white pants and a matching white blouse, along with a pair of black flats and my mother's thick gold hoops. I was practically shaking in my abaya, I couldn't even wait.

We left early in the afternoon and arrived in time for a cordial lunch in the Burj al Arab hosted by the prime minister and his associates. After this, I was turned over to the Sheikh's team, with whom I would be doing my civic duties as an athlete of the Emirates: walks around the city, stopping to talk to families and take pictures with children, a panel with government leaders, and last, the surprises.

Of course, my city was absolutely beautiful. I loved taking photos with passersby, just making casual conversation. It reminded me of before I'd jumped into Formula racing, before everyone started to see me as another Sheikha to this city. I knew a Sheikha had her duties, but above all, she treated her people with love and care. That opportunity to retain some semblance of connection to what really mattered was the most meaningful to me. The people here, in my eyes, were the most beautiful part of Dubai.

My government duties were surprisingly intriguing. I sat in on a panel regarding Emirati women in sports. As I was only visiting and thought I wouldn't be able to say much, it took me aback when I was asked to speak. I can't lie; I enjoyed the experience, but I was hoping they couldn't see all the sweat creeping through my blouse and exposing my nerves.

I found respite when my new entourage of men in *thobes* and *shemaghs* led me out to the Dubai Mall. We got the perfect vantage point from a built-in balcony, overlooking the fountain and lining straight up with the Burj Khalifa.

I remembered coming here with Miguel. He had been so amazed by it all, this look of wonder on his face. *Stop*, I told myself. *This is no time to lose your head.*

'Will there be a show?' I asked my cluster of confidants in Arabic.

'A special show, yes,' the highest-ranking adviser replied with a smile. He was the leader of the pack, but he was also quite vague and answered all my questions in riddles. Very amusing.

The music started up: traditional Arabic lute and drums with a hint of modern dance music. Water shot up from the fountain jets in a wave of gold. It was stunning, but what caught my eye was the Burj Khalifa up ahead.

The side facing us was illuminated with the image of a blue

sky in the desert, and then, a falcon, swooping down with wings outstretched till it landed on a gloved hand. The colours of the Emirati flag filled the screen: red, green, white, black. The tower shimmered, and suddenly, there it was.

My team photo for Jolt Archambeau filled the screens, the flag in the background as I stood at an angle, arms crossed, looking far too upset in my black and purple suit.

'Oh,' I managed.

I held my hands over my mouth as the massive tower played more videos. My first podium place in Saudi, clips from this past season, glimpses of my car, and even videos so early on in my Formula career that I hadn't known they existed. My very first Formula 3 race and subsequent win, where I pointed at the camera and yelled that this was for my parents, as hours prior, I'd learned of the crash: Baba in critical condition. Me hugging my mom and dad after COTA. Holding up the flag of the UAE on my victory lap. Huddling with my F2 friends when I learned of my Jolt contract. Blowing the stands kisses prior to the new Miami GP.

I gasped aloud when the jets of the fountain blasted full height, the lights turning to the colours of the flag. On the Burj Khalifa, I raised my fists, eyes shut and tears flowing down my face in bliss post-race, standing on my chassis in full gear.

WELCOME HOME, DIANA appeared beneath me in Arabic. DUBAI STANDS BY YOU AT THE ABU DHABI GRAND PRIX.

The crowd watching from the main levels screamed like crazy. I fought the urge to do the same. Never had this expat girl struggling to find a kart and a coach in Jeddah dreamed of her photo being projected up on the Burj Khalifa, of an entire nation behind her in such an insane journey.

'Go win that title,' said a new voice from behind me.

I glanced back, and immediately, I froze to my spot.

It was the Sheikh. Flanked by security and staff, of course, but it was him. My breathing faltered, my eyes snapped wide. My hands shook at my sides. What did people do when they met the Sheikh?

'Your Highness, I . . .' I laughed nervously. 'I have no words. Your city's support is such a great honour for me. I can't believe any of this, thank you . . .'

'It is *your* city,' he said with a smile, pointing to the Burj Khalifa. 'And I thank you. I know you will bring victory home to us this weekend, Diyana. You are our falcon, after all.'

Chapter Forty-Nine

Miguel

'Greetings to you all, then, at this final press conference of 2022.'

The relief was palpable. Even though we had the devil's spawn Crowberry conducting interviews, it was almost over. That was something to celebrate.

Diyana, Darien, Andrea, Alex and I sat side by side in casual folding chairs.

'So I think it would be appropriate to ask, how has this season felt to you all?' Crowberry began. 'What, at this point, is your takeaway? Let's start with Darien, left to right. Well, you just had your moment of the season, mate.'

'Yeah.' Darien chuckled. 'To represent like that was a different high. It was crazy, it's been a great season in the car. This season was just so much better for me. Got to work with a great teammate, an awesome team. The flow, the dynamic is

345

probably what felt best. Hope we keep going that way and that next year gets us even more competitive.'

'We certainly hope the same for you, Darien, and for Heidelberg as well. Next, Miguel?' Crowberry moved on.

Takeaways? Lately I couldn't seem to draw any good from the season. But I smiled and fibbed as I'd been trained to. 'I think this season has taught me to adapt. Clearly this sport can change with the drop of a hat. You have to be ready for that, to respond immediately if you want that trophy. We will work on our response readiness next year for a fact. Have Plan Cs for our Plan Bs.'

Crowberry nodded. 'I'm sure that certainly applied to your last race.'

I shifted in my seat. Hell, no. 'Definitely.'

Thankfully, he didn't push the matter. He turned to Diyana and grinned a TV anchor's false smile, way too much tooth on show. 'Then, on to our star rookie, Diana. Already in the running for a Championship title in your first year of Formula 1, thrown into the game after an unexpected accident left a seat vacant. You've taken it in your stride. And I believe we've all seen the spectacle Dubai put on to see you off to battle this weekend. What has this season meant to you?'

Diyana sighed. I watched her crack her knuckles as she thought, a nervous habit. She smiled almost wistfully. 'So many things. This season gave me friends and family. It gave me a platform in my country from which to inspire change. It brought me close to destruction and dreams alike. But most of all . . . it allowed me to grow as a driver and a human. At first, I came in thinking, damn, no one wants this, no one wants a woman here. Possibly *I* don't even want this. Then I

346

realized that the world may not have wanted it, but my heart did. It knew it would only be happy behind the wheel. That's what this season has been to me. Happiness.'

Everyone sitting on that interview panel knew as well as I did that this season had not just been happiness, especially for Diyana. I looked at them but, to my surprise, they didn't look as dubious as I was feeling. They, too, were beaming with nostalgia.

I thought of Diyana's first P1 at COTA. I remembered how she'd thanked me for her bringing her parents there. And our great big grid family: eating together in Jaipur, laughing over the multi-car pileup that got Alex his first win, screwing the interviewers over in conference, birthday cakes and candles, a sticky note assault on Kasper's car (we don't talk about it). Maybe, in some ways, this had been a season from which we could all glean some happiness.

Before I knew it, the last race weekend of 2022 was upon us. Things started to look up for me on Friday with a P2 in FP1 and topping FP2 – it seemed that the post-Brazil events in the garage had worked magic on Revello's disorder. FP3 sealed the deal, with another P2 for me and a P3 for Andrea. We still had a chance at this thing, a great big one.

We went into qualifying beneath the Abu Dhabi sunset, emboldened with passion. The tension in my shoulders loosened as I drifted from Q1 to Q2 to Q3.

'I've got you a nice empty stretch. Make this your best push lap,' Paula commanded me with a minute to go.

I came in with the best lap I'd ever driven in Abu Dhabi. I beamed as I braked late and slingshot myself around treacherous turns. I crossed the finish and ended the lap soaring. If this wasn't the one, I wasn't sure what else was.

'PROVISIONAL POLE!' yelled Paula.

'WHAT?' I yelped.

'NO – POLE! IT'S OVER, YOU'RE POLE!' she shouted.

'NO WAY!'

Revello was back, just like that. I almost felt relieved as I brought the car around, I can't lie. All the speed bumps along the road up till this point, they'd had me doubting my ability. But I hadn't lost it. I still damn well had it. I only had to hope I had it together better than Diyana did.

Chapter Fifty

Diana

I knelt in the garage. My mother and father held me close to them, all of us huddled together one last time before the race of my lifetime. The race that, only a season in, would define my career.

Baba's lips moved in silent prayer. I already knew the words. *Protect my child*, he always said before I drove. *Bring her back to us safe and sound.*

'Amen,' whispered Baba.

'Amen,' Ammi and I echoed.

We stayed as we were for just a moment more before I stood, taking a deep breath.

'Elissa, talk to her,' said Baba to my mother with a smile.

Ammi returned the gesture and pulled me aside. Just as I had a few, this was her pre-race ritual. Before COTA, she'd given me a talk, before all my karting races. And now, when I needed it most.

'You may always be my *joonam*,' she started, 'but we've given you to this greater purpose now, to these people. You are their pride and joy, too.'

Ammi gripped my shoulders. Perhaps she'd give me the biggest pep-talk ever – I would listen. I would listen to whatever advice she had to give me because, as I learned once I got older, she tended to be right. But instead, she only met my eyes with her bright green ones. She said, 'Bring this home.'

I had never entered a racetrack with more pure lightning in my veins than I did now. We lined up on grid after a formation lap in the beautiful sunset. The crowd was chanting, cheering. The stands were a sea of flags. It had all led here. All the long practices, the travel, the odd jobs, the tears, the ER trips, the heartbreak, every ounce of pain I'd endured, each gram of gold we'd sold for these dreams. Abu Dhabi's Yas Marina Circuit pulsed with energy, the beating heart of my world in this moment.

My family. My fans. I was no longer alone in this pursuit. A million others were at my back to keep me going. They shouted my name. *Yallah, Diana*.

I trained my eyes on the track ahead of me through my halo. We were racing at home today, and if I didn't defend my home, I would have let this crowd down.

Lights out.

I was told later that it was my best start all season. Instinct kicked in and took over. I drove like it was second nature. Miguel, just beside me on pole, zoomed ahead, but I stayed level, nudging myself into a good speed and keeping to his tail.

As the grid spread out over the next few laps, I lost some ground. 'Delta over two seconds,' said Aiden. 'Let's try a notch faster, shall we?'

We sped up, and soon, the gap began to close. I wasn't chasing yet, but it was good progress. With about a second and a tenth between us, I pitted for hard tyres. The crew pulled off one of their quickest stops all year and sent me back out, engine roaring.

'Miguel coming in to pit. So you are just behind Darien now, Diana.'

'Sure. I'll get him.'

I did adore Darien, my favourite flamboyant wild child as he was, but this was strictly business. Overtakes were overtakes.

'He's not making it easy,' I grumbled as I attempted to go wide. The intention was to force Darien into a defensive position and get an opening out of it, but he wasn't responding. He stayed right where he was.

'Don't you dare do it again,' warned Aiden.

I grinned under my helmet, speeding up into the next turn. I slid past Darien on the inside and went nearly wheel to wheel. But it paid off – I emerged in P1. 'Did it.'

'You're absolutely bonkers.'

'Well aware. Where is Miguel?' I asked.

'Just coming around the other side of Darien, too. He'll be right on your rear,' Aiden answered. 'Let's hold our pace.'

I made it to about the thirty-fifth lap in my lead, at which point the second stop ensued for hards. Abu Dhabi was sweltering; tyre deg was at an all-time high, and I was losing speed quickly. This time, though, we gambled to pit after Miguel. As I rolled into the pits, Aiden reminded me that the hope was I could use my new-tyre advantage to take the lead.

But I was starting to get worn out by the heat. My mother's voice reverberated in my head: 'Bring this home.' Miguel in

P1 though, he was suddenly unbeatable. With him performing at his very highest potential, besting Miguel was a pipe dream.

'Push harder, Diana, you've got fuel,' Aiden urged me. 'Ten laps and still out of DRS range.'

I was struggling a lot. I didn't have the experience racing in these kinds of conditions and at this speed. By the time I got my car its first dose of DRS, I was two laps out.

'Delta point five and narrowing. Take the gap when you see it.' Aiden's voice held nerves I'd never heard before. Even my unshakable engineer was starting to worry.

My heart thudded against my rib cage as I realized what this was. It was only right that in the race of a lifetime came the test of a lifetime. My parents were in the paddock. Miguel was milliseconds ahead of me. And now, the biggest victory of my career was at stake.

Fear gripped me. I clutched the steering wheel as my breathing grew rapid. There were no what-ifs, only winning and losing. I was on this track with nineteen men in a sport designed for them.

'*Ya albi.*'

My breath caught as that race flooded back to me. Jeddah, the single-seater junior series. My first defeat, and I had been inconsolable. I was silent the whole way home, and when we got back, I locked myself in my room and cried. I was only fourteen. I had nothing to lose but that race.

But my father, as gently as possible, had knocked at the door. Like an engineer through the radio, I listened to his voice.

'Diyana?'

I wiped the tears from my face. 'Baba?'

'Listen to me. This is not the child we raised. I know that child, and I know she does not let her fears win. You absolutely cannot let yourself be scared of them,' my father said to me, each word even and calculated, 'when it is they who should be scared of you.'

'Of . . . me?'

'Of you, *ya albi*. One race, one loss, it will not define you. It will make you stronger, and it will make you fearless. Do you understand?'

I nodded, forgetting that he would not see it.

'Do you understand, Diyana?'

'I understand, Baba,' I had said at last, voice quavering.

Now, I pressed the gas straight to the ground going into my next turn. I had to do it. I could not let myself be scared of them. One more bitch overtake, for the title.

I'll bring this home.

I braked as late as I could and launched myself around the inside a final time. My car lurched, bottoming to such an aggressive extent that I could see the sparks fly out to the sides. I gritted my teeth against the force on my neck as I evened out and shot forward even faster, accelerating with Miguel right beside me. He inched forward. I responded.

Cursing under my breath, I slammed the throttle down the straight. I was almost two tenths from him now. My right front wheel nearly touched his left rear. Our wings threatened to scrape one another. I exhaled, pushing the car so hard that my head went woozy, Miguel's rear before me turning to a blotch of white and red. Every cell in my body was telling me to stop, but I didn't. And once again, just like that very first podium in Saudi, it came down to the final stretch.

I gave it all the gas I could. The eyes of thousands of Emiratis were on me, thousands of women, the ones who watched on TV sets behind closed doors with the volume on mute so their families didn't hear. My parents, my old friends, the girl whose helmet I'd signed at Imola. And I hoped and prayed that the powers that be had an eye on me, too.

'DIANA! DIANA!'

It was Aiden. I caught a glimpse of sparks, more of them, overhead. What happened? Had I crashed? I could not possibly have; I was still driving.

No, I was definitely in one piece. And those weren't sparks. They were fireworks.

'I didn't . . . I didn't happen to—'

'IT'S YOU, DIANA, IT'S ALL YOU!' Aiden practically screamed, piercing my eardrums. 'YOU CRUSHED IT!'

'Diana, this is Theodore Cavanaugh,' a new voice chimed in. Our team principal, the one responsible for this mess I had gotten into. This time, however, he wasn't here to invert me with my teammate or warn me of my fate in the sport. 'What a drive, Diana. What a drive. I'm honoured to witness that. Honoured to have you as my driver.'

'YOUR WORLD CHAMPION,' I heard the loudspeakers boom. 'DIANA ZAHRANI, CAR NUMBER FORTY-FOUR, JOLT ARCHAMBEAU . . .'

The crowds were absolutely euphoric as I attempted to wave to them as best as I could. I made it back around the track to the main straight. Aiden came over the radio again.

'Wreck that car, Diana.'

I whooped and yanked the wheel to the side. The air filled

with thick smoke as I looped around and around in doughnuts, both hands off the wheel, in the air.

By the time I parked, my head was spinning. I felt like every rope tying me down to this world had snapped, and I was free-floating on this endless plane of dreams.

I fought my own body just to get to a standing position on top of the chassis at first. It was all so loud, so overwhelming. By the time I found my footing, I could barely raise my arms in ecstatic bliss. Someone handed me the Emirati flag. Feebly, I attempted to hold it up. All I could do was cry.

When I got down from the car, I immediately fell to all fours on the ground and sobbed ugly, hiccuping sobs. The surface of the asphalt was grating against my gloves, but it felt familiar. An old coach once told me that what you give the asphalt, it gives you in return. I had given it everything I was able to since I had known that this was my sole purpose in life. It had showered blessings back upon me.

My parents were the first ones there, Ammi pushing Baba along in his wheelchair. They were in tears as I was, as all three of us cried together.

And then a wave of black and silver and purple crashed over us. The team flooded the track. I wanted to thank them all, but I couldn't move from the ground.

'Get up, *joonam!*' I heard my mother shout distantly. She tapped the side of my helmet. 'You are a champion now!'

She took hold of my hands and brought me to my feet. I pulled off my helmet and balaclava, and I screamed a primal scream from the depths of the knot of pain and sacrifice in my chest.

* * *

The podium celebration ended me.

To hear the live band play our national anthem yet again, I could scarcely believe it, this time with drums, *rabab*, a choir of children, and all. This was the Middle East's first World Championship – the first time we had heard our wonderful 'Ishy Bilady' sung, as one of our own stood on the top step of the podium as Formula 1 title winner. I blinked back more tears. Cameras flashed, and my fellow Emiratis cried in celebration with every lyric, roaring as the band came to a crescendo, the anthem ending, and I raised the flag behind me.

I accepted my trophy with shaking hands. We grabbed our bottles. For the last time that season, the *Carmen* 'Prélude' played and, before I knew it, I'd been absolutely drenched by Miguel and Darien. We laughed together as I shook my trophy in the air and, at the end of it all, as the fans took photos and screamed in excitement, I sat there on the steps, baffled by what I had just been a part of. It still did not feel real.

And then I felt a hand on my shoulder.

I turned with a start. 'Miguel?'

'Diyana.' His voice cracked as he said my name, just quietly enough that only I could hear it. I pursed my lips to hold back a cry.

'Miguel—'

'Diyana,' he said again. 'We're gonna talk. Right here. Now.'

Chapter Fifty-One

Miguel

I was in pain.

We de la Fuentes, we were arrogant. We always had to be the best, and when we weren't, we didn't know how to deal with it. We didn't know how to lose.

The doughnuts were fun, and all the chaotic end-of-season revelry in our cars. Yet the entire time, I felt nothing but my heart sinking as I realized this was another year gone by without doing my part to uphold the family name, and worse, another year gone by without *winning*. No Drivers' Championship, no Constructors'. Jolt had gotten both.

But then I saw her up there like I always did. She was crying these tears of happiness as her people called out her name, waving the flags and making little hearts with their hands when she held up the P1 trophy.

Paula's words began to make sense.

She sat on her step of the podium, looking up at me with

surprise in her red-rimmed eyes, the irises appearing to glow as the bright LED display behind us played her victory reel. Her wet hair was still in its braids, matted with champagne, curls beginning to sneak out of the clear pony bands. Her racing boots had been set beside her, resplendent in a puddle of their own.

'I mean, first, congratulations,' I told her as I sat down beside her on the step. 'You drove one hell of a race out there.'

'Thank you.' The look didn't leave her face. 'Are you okay, Miguel? I know how you trained so hard and . . .'

'I'm fine.' I exhaled. It would be a while, but I'd be fine again.

'Are you upset at me for winning it?'

Such a bold question. It could be seen in so many ways, her asking that question, but her eyes, innocent and wide, concerned, betrayed her intentions. She was still putting me first, still worrying about me when it was only her success she should have been relishing.

I raised my gaze to meet Diyana's. She glanced away, towards the bottom of the podium stage. It was a hard question. Of course, her winning had me angry.

'I am a little upset.'

Her forehead furrowed, and she looked down at her hands.

'But I wouldn't *dare* be upset with you. It would be with myself, because in all this dumb competition, I forgot that one of the most important things I learned this season was how to support *you*.' My shoes squeaked on the flooring as I made to face Diyana. 'You never complained. You gave me all the love you could. And you didn't ask for anything in return. So I would be extremely upset if I let myself be the man who should revere you but instead doubts your tenacity. Because if I do that, Diyana, it won't matter to me what happened with today's race, if I won or you won. I'll have lost a long time ago.'

Diyana trained her eyes on mine. I thought that was it. She would get up and leave – that would be her decision. That would be the end of it.

She didn't leave.

She laid her head on my shoulder and exhaled. I could feel the distress leaving her body, smell every note of the sandalwood she used in her hair. 'Miguel . . . I just don't want you to suffer here because of me. I know you are so, so talented, and if I take your place, it's—'

'No. You're taking my seat.' I took her hands and stood up and, though she was confused, she stood with me, swiping a curl behind her ear and adjusting her hat.

I stepped down from the podium, down so that I stood below her, and looked up at the woman who had driven away with my heart over the course of this insane season. I removed the cap from my head, and I placed it at her feet.

'I can't do anything about how the world sees you, Diyana. I know you can prove them wrong, but right now, I can tell you that you're never, ever going to be second to *anything* for me.' I felt my chest heave, the tears burning my eyes, right there on the stage as a hush fell over the audience. 'I want you to chase your dreams, I want you to find your happiness behind that wheel, and damn it, I want to make the sacrifices so you don't have to. Rain or shine, Revello or Jolt, I don't care where you are as long as I can be there for you. *Cariño*, you're that top step of the podium for me. You're my Championship. Screw the trophies. I'm begging you. I'm not letting the blessing this world's given me for a second time slip away again.'

Diyana's hands were pressed to her mouth as her shoulders shook, tears pouring down her cheeks. She squeezed her eyes shut, and I waited down there, praying she'd give me some kind of sign, that she'd give this a chance, that she'd let me be in her paddock the way she'd been in mine.

She opened her eyes, and she nodded. Once, twice.

'Screwing the trophies sounds . . . like a good idea,' she managed with a laugh tangled up in a sob, jogging down the steps towards me.

'Oh, come here.' I reached out to her, and I wrapped her up in my arms, pulling her close to me by her hips, champagne all over her suit and mine. I took her face in my hands, and I kissed her, and she kissed me. I could taste the saltiness of her tears and the fizz of the alcohol. And this was so different, the desperation and the relief that I felt in this touch, the way that there were a million hopes and thanks folded into the feeling of her lips against mine.

The screaming crowd, the tens of thousands of fans watching our story unfold before them, was background noise as she pulled away, and she breathed the words I'd wanted to say to her all this time, 'I love you, Mig, I love you so, so much.'

I couldn't hide my smile, even as both of us cried everything we had wanted to cry for the last ten years. 'I love you too, Diyana,' I whispered, my lips by her ear so she wouldn't miss a word, so she knew exactly how much she meant to me. 'You're everything, *cariño*, everything.'

My Championship. My Diyana.

December of 2023 Season

'Deciding to keep racing against Diana Zahrani is one
of the best and worst decisions I've ever made.'

Miguel Ángel de la Fuente
#88, Heidelberg Hybridge Formula 1 Team

Epilogue

Diana

I hummed an old Egyptian lullaby as I pulled a fresh pot of *ghormeh sabzi* off the stove. Dinners had tasted extra-delicious after the World Championship a week ago, I had to admit that much. The *ghormeh sabzi*, my favourite Persian dish, had been delayed long enough. It was time to eat so well that I would go to bed feeling like I'd eaten for an army of thirty men.

I checked my phone with a sigh. Still no word. This idiot was late. He had no excuses tonight. I'd told him Persian food was a delicate art. Seven p.m. on the dot. I thought I had made it very clear, but it still must not have been enough for him. I wondered if he'd been caught by the media or a clutch of fans, neither of which he could ever resist.

'It's not easy putting up with your de la Fuente fame!' I'd prodded him when we got back home after the chaos of the weekend.

Miguel poked my shoulder teasingly. 'Well, it was no different from your Zahrani fame last year.'

I beamed at that. He had to admit we were quite the dream team. Our World Championship trophies, though sitting with their respective teams – mine in Jolt's headquarters, his newly awarded 2023 title with Heidelberg Hybridge – would be tied together in history. Sure, I'd been perturbed by his shiny black car zooming past mine and taking the title for the year, but I, like Miguel, couldn't stay upset for too long. We were at the point where we shared wins and losses, and while we made many of our decisions for the sport first and foremost, we would never put it above one another.

Nevertheless, he owed me the bare minimum. It had been a rough couple of days, of course, considering the crazy fans who had shown up at our door, flash photography included, the paparazzi never far behind once they figured out where we were. We'd moved to my parents' after that, just to lie low for a week or so, but that didn't last, either; we had a bunch of them turn up at our house with their fan gear, and both of us felt so bad that we went out in flip-flops and sweats to sign it all. We returned, exasperated and tired, to our house just outside Dubai – after three days of my poor parents enduring the press – and, me at least, in need of a good five helpings of *sabzi*.

So when a loud rumbling so forceful that it made my dinner plate shake began to thunder outside the garage, I didn't bat an eyelid. Probably sports cars. These Formula 1 fans got gaudier and gaudier every year. I felt bad, but I was starving. I was not about to go and take photos right now. I served myself a great helping of *sabzi* instead.

Yet the car, or whatever it was, just continued growling. Then it revved. Once, twice, three times, more insistent than a small child having a tantrum.

I groaned, grabbing my plate and plodding up the stairs to our room. That was it. I was going to eat this meal no matter *where* I had to eat it.

I was about two spoonfuls in when something smacked against my window.

A particularly nasty curse escaped my lips as I dropped my spoon, standing up from the bed with a start. One more tap against the window.

Oh. So this was *exactly* who I thought it was.

I dragged myself over to the window, yanked it open, and—

Sitting on the road in front of our driveway was the Revello Formula 1 car.

It was resplendent in its shiny, Italian-flag-themed livery. It was unmissable. I couldn't have mistaken it for a mock-up. It was the actual car and, lest I be in any doubt, emblazoned across the front was the enormous red number *44*.

My car.

Which, I now noticed, had a man lounging across its chassis.

'WHAT ON EARTH, MIG!' I shouted as I leaned out the window. Seven p.m., I had told him. But here was Miguel de la Fuente, royally late, causing a ruckus in front of our house.

He just shrugged. And then the idiot held up a poster board.

OKAY.

He flipped it over.

HEAR ME OUT.

I crossed my arms and called, 'NO.'

He just grabbed another poster board.

GET DOWN HERE.

I tugged my cardigan tighter around myself and stomped down the stairs I had literally just used, then out through the front door in my house slippers, rushing down the steps towards the car, where the bane of my existence sat, his infuriatingly pretty hair ruffling about in the bare breeze as he tossed his helmet in the air and caught it with a grin, giving it a little shake.

I planted my hands on my hips before him. 'Explain. Car. You missed my dinner.'

'Well, listen, *cariño*.' He grinned impishly, his deep brown eyes crinkling at the corners. He swung his legs over the side of the car and stood up, so he was closer, much closer, to me. My heart thudded in my rib cage. It had been almost two years, and he still had this effect on me. I could never stay mad at him. 'It took me a hot minute to get all this together.'

I sighed with all the drama I could muster, draping my arms across his shoulders. 'Well, how about *now* you come inside and apologize for your lateness by eating dinner before it gets cold.'

'I can apologize for my lateness . . .' Miguel lowered his lips to mine, 'in much better ways.'

'Mmm-hmm,' I murmured with a smile, letting my eyes flutter closed.

Then Miguel did the *second* criminal thing and tilted his head away. I groaned. 'Oh, my god, tell me this charade will be over soon, Mig!'

'Yeah.' He reached into the cockpit of the car a bit too flamboyantly, squinting in concentration. 'I just needed . . . to grab something I left in here real quick.'

I rolled my eyes. 'Miguel, please hurry up, the *sabzi* is—'
My mouth fell open when I saw him.
He was on one knee before me, holding a little blue velvet

box, inside which sat the most stunning ring of Dubai gold, glowing yellower than Emirati sunrises, set with diamonds in a slight V, a wishbone ring. Like the wings of a falcon.

I could feel my heart booming against my sternum. Maybe this was just a fanciful hallucination on my part, but the way that ring was shimmering, I couldn't deny how real it was. This *was* real.

'You've been by my side for *basically* the last decade. You've been here even when you weren't here. I love you more than life. I don't even know what I'd do if I didn't have you in the paddock. Diyana Heba Firouzeh Zahrani, you are the only person I need in the garage, ever, even if that means we screw the tyres on wrong because our mechanics aren't there. I'll drive on messed-up tyres for the rest of the season if it means I've still got you with me,' Miguel whispered. 'So Diyana, will—'

'Yes!' I blurted before he could so much as finish. 'Yes, yes, a million times, Miguel, yes, I will.'

He laughed as I threw my arms around him and I kissed him, as he slipped the ring onto my finger when I pulled away. Miguel, my fiancé.

All my life, as my career had consumed me and I had been told there were no options but to allow it to, I had tried to cover myself in my driving and forget that I could *feel*. It was impossible to hide now. That child who had been afraid of never fitting into her place in racing, of never quite being good enough, of giving too little and receiving too much, I realized I did not need her any more.

Because after years of being told I had chosen a path of solitude, I had finally found the man who would make sure I would never, ever drive alone.

Author's Note

I open with my usual spiel. I am not affiliated in any way with Formula 1 or the FIA, do not have any claims on real teams or drivers, nor do I reference any factual teams in this novel. While drivers in *Offtrack* may be inspired by the current grid, they are not meant to resemble or represent any persons other than the characters themselves. All viewpoints represented here are my own, and yes, I would like to use this space to unpack a few of them for you readers.

This is my third season as a Formula 1 fan, and frankly, with the advent of F1 Academy, all that's been on my mind since is what happens next – or, more specifically, what could happen next.

I suppose that makes *Offtrack* the product of a bunch of 'what-ifs'. What if F1 Academy worked? What if there were to be a woman in F1, along the road?

The world is nowhere near perfect, and as we are all quite human, things wouldn't be ideal. But in the writing of *Offtrack*, I have researched and read and decided that maybe, it is not women in motorsport who are unprepared for Formula 1. Formula 1 and its culture are unprepared for women.

Diyana Heba Firouzeh Zahrani is essentially an amalgamation of all things good and patient. She is raised humbly, with love, to love in turn, and it may seem like the sport is too much of a burden for her at first, but I want us to ask whether she should have to change to fit a sport where the nineteen other competitors are men. I want us to ask what that need to change does to her, what that need to change says about real-world opportunities. In the words of Diyana, 'You know why women don't get into this sport? It's because no one wants to sponsor us. And I fight *myself* every minute of every day.' IRL, Toni Cowan-Brown, F1 pundit, has said to the Jezebel website, ditto to Diyana, 'Why are we not keeping them [women in motorsport]? Because they're treating them like shit once they're here' (Leibert).

Further, Amna al Qubaisi, Emirati racing driver now in the F1 Academy (she and her sister are my favourites), who happens to be my prime inspiration behind Diyana's character, also spoke to Jezebel about the sponsorship aspect. It is pitifully difficult. She addressed the industry as a person of colour, where she has struggled with being used for minuscule advertising stints that do not provide her with any gain in terms of racing sponsors. The brands, she said, will decide that they 'are not interested in investing'. As with Diyana, Amna's struggle was exacerbated by the stereotypical belief that she must be wealthy and require little to no money to break into motorsport, just because she is from the UAE (Leibert). Internalized barriers like these make it even more difficult to gain the support necessary to thrive in the Formula world.

On top of that, you've got the personalities in control – team principals – and their attitudes. Red Bull F1 team principal Christian Horner was called out last season for suggesting that female fans of the sport are hooked by the good-looking male drivers, in reference to the Netflix series *Formula One: Drive to Survive* (Jaiswal). One wonders how people in power with this kind of mindset would welcome a woman driving F1 with open arms.

Then, naturally, there's the psychological component. The imposter syndrome that Diyana speaks of. Being repetitively gaslit into believing that you are missing *something*, something that the men have. Is it brake pedal reach? Neck strength? Or is it just your skill? The environment that has been cultivated in these series is a breeding ground for such thoughts. From what I have seen, it is a façade that hides the reality. Even with series like F1 Academy dedicated to opening up opportunities at higher levels of the sport, mentality is everything: women are still being set up for failure.

Most famously, the words have been uttered by Sergio Pérez, current Formula 1 driver for Red Bull Racing, though later stated to be a joke, when asked about having a woman as a teammate, that she would be better off in the kitchen. 'Imagine being beaten by a woman.'

Imagine if Diyana Zahrani had heard *that*.

References

Jaiswal, Samriddhi. '"It's Bringing in a Lot of Young Girls Because of All These Great-Looking Young Drivers" – Twitter Thrashes Christian Horner for His Sexist Comments.' *The SportsRush*, 3 March 2022, thesportsrush.com/f1-news-its-bringing-in-a-lot-of-young-girls-because-of-all-these-great-looking-young-drivers-twitter-thrashes-christian-horner-for-his-sexist-comments/?amp.

Leibert, Emily. 'Women Are Not Barred from Racing in F1. So Why Can't Any Crack the Grid?' *Jezebel*, 17 November 2022, jezebel.com/f1-women-drivers-gender-motorsports-1849793355.

Acknowledgements

This book was my 24 Hours of Le Mans, and without so many of these wonderful people, it wouldn't have been possible.

Thank you to my Merc fan mom for her help in drafting up this novel as per usual. And to my dad, who got me on my first episode of *Drive to Survive*. My brother and sister, love you both more than words for every second of every minute I've been blessed to know you both, and to all my lovely grandparents.

To the circle at university that made IC feel like a warm hug: Ria, Ilaria, and Isabelle, I love you all, and you will always get to know the hot tea first. To Chandana, and Jahanvi, sweetest neighbors ever, to Emma, Miguel de la Fuente's OG fan. To Addy, who zoomed through forty chapters in less than a week. Hiruni, Formula 1 fan via early *Offtrack*. Karaoke gang: Ana, Sophia, Maria, rays of sunshine. My support team, my girls at home, Lina, Aditi, Pujal.

To the team at Avon UK for taking a chance with this dream,

these characters I hold dear. Amy, for all the emails I've sent you, the Teams calls, my plentiful questions and the support whenever I needed it. Thank you for your faith in this story and in me.

My bookish community, I have endless love for you. Bridget, who was one of the first fellow F1 authors I met and is now my dearest author friend, I adore you, your work and your happiness, your unfaltering positivity. Teigan, for the beautiful art and the priceless friendship. Ams, for your kind heart and the notebook that houses all my ideas. Apoorva, for all your support every step, working with me in early stages of this deal. Thank you to Chloe, Caylynn, Grace, and Salma, and, of course, my Pit Wall. Desi girls: N.M., Ava, Bal, and Ruby – who sent me her *paneer recipe*, for crying out loud – thank you for welcoming me into this new space with open arms. Special thanks to Soraya for being the force that put *Offtrack* into Amy's hands.

For all my original readers and my new readers, for anyone who's picked up this book. You've done the greatest thing anyone can do for a human being, and that is to believe in me and my dreams. Thank you a million.